An Ounce of Practice

Leo Zeilig

hope**road** : London

HopeRoad Publishing Ltd
PO Box 55544
Exhibition Road
SW7 2DB
www.hoperoadpublishing.com

First published in Great Britain by HopeRoad 2017
Copyright © 2017 Leo Zeilig

A CIP catalogue record for this book is available from the British Library.

Supported using public funding by
ARTS COUNCIL
ENGLAND

ISBN 978-1-908446-58-9

eISBN 978-1-908446-64-0

Printed and bound by TJ International Ltd, Padstow, Cornwall, UK

For Tafadzwa Choto

Praise for *Eddie the Kid*

'Eddie's fraught family life, overhung by his brutal, charismatic father, is at the heart of this honest and powerful novel ... a passionate, sad and well-told book offers a compelling portrait of a flawed young radical.' James Start, *The Guardian*

'Leo Zeilig has written an intense and troubling account of three generations of activists. That he encourages the reader to never quite give up on a character as flawed and damaged as Eddie is a testimony to his command of style and narrative. Zeilig's interweaving of personal trauma dovetail perfectly with his story of the countdown towards the huge February 2003 anti-war march in London.' Paul Simon, *Morning Star*

'Unlike Ian McEwan's tedious *Saturday*, which sneers at the marchers from outside, Zeilig (best known for his work on Africa) knows the movement from inside. But this is no Socialist Realist presentation of heroic revolutionaries ... A very funny novel, satirising the foibles of the left, though always from a position of deep commitment to that same left. It is also a profoundly sad book which constantly reminds us that capitalism and its institutions, above all the family, can only be resisted and ultimately destroyed by those who are its victims, and that the victims are not only oppressed materially, but also warped and corrupted from within.' Ian Birchall, *Socialist Review*

'This book did something unexpected. It described anger. The kind of anger that you inherit and that runs through your blood and somehow ends up controlling your fists and making them hit what or whom you hold most dear ... You will see yourself and people you know in this book. You will become attached to them, and I daresay you will miss them, too.' Diana Méndez, *Socialist Worker* (US)

'This book is the most novel novel I've read this year. It is political but not -making, it is a love story with a totally new kind of love, and an elephant in the room the size of Africa. A marvellous and original book.' Maureen Lipman, *actor and author, Jewish Post and News*

'Ultimately this is a book about how messed up the most well-intentioned humans can be - how someone committed to the revolutionary emancipation of humanity can then beat his partner and children mercilessly. It's a book that explores those contradictions without ever making either of them the defining point in the character's being. The humanity of the oppressor and the (oppressor as) victim are maintained and understood, but not celebrated. I loved this book.' Dan Sharber, *RedWedge*

'I don't know how Leo Zeilig did it. He created a wavering revolutionary, beset with juvenile tendencies and petty bourgeois emotion, and turned him into a wildly, implausibly, universal character. Eddie's struggles with his conscience, the law, his family and his libido, are hilarious and moving. He's an Adrian Mole for the age of Occupy.' Raj Patel, author of *The Value of Nothing*

To educate man to be actional, preserving in all his relations his respect for the basic human values that constitute a human

world, is the prime task of him who, having taken thought,
prepares to act.

Frantz Fanon

An ounce of practice is worth a ton of theory.

Friedrich Engels

Prologue

Viktor looked vague and ponderous. His high forehead and dark, thinning hair and round glasses confirmed that he was always brooding on possibilities, options, the world's ceaseless, never-ending negations. His creased eyes fooled you that he laughed, but really they spoke of his worry, his dilemmas and indecisions. To his secret shame, his eyes were blue and pierced the world with light, with exclamation. If Viktor's face, his thin shoulders and tall, hooked frame said one thing it was *maybe*. The doubt, always present in his overwrought, tortured decisions, spread over his entire build; now his body was the shape of these misgivings. In his curved torso, his head hanging bent on his neck and shoulders, his legs loose and apart, Viktor looked as though he was about to disappear, break up – as if he was going to dissolve back into non-existence.

He sat on a towpath bench just outside London, his bag wedged behind his back. He stared at the wide, blue, improbable sky that pressed down on the buildings and fell between the detached houses along the towpath. Today the sky was the indisputable arbiter, marking out the planes, the tiles on the roofs, the still, sealed water's edge. In the steady blue of the omnipotent sky and the reflective green of the water, Viktor thought he could make the decision to leave Nina and Rosa.

He rehearsed the arguments but, like the last rehearsal and the one before that, it left him more indecisive. The confidence he had felt in the morning, scribbling in his notebook, drinking his coffee, had evaporated in the spring sun. Perhaps this a.m. drug was the only way he could make decisions, rising and crashing on the waves of hope that the morning fix of caffeine gave him, the rush of blood to his head that made him feel for ten minutes as though he could conquer his predicaments, take a step into the world free of the pain and panic of transition.

'Get into your comfy clothes, sweetie,' Viktor had called to Nina as he left Rosa after her second story the previous evening. She had put her small head on his shoulders, her clammy hand resting against his chest under his shirt, her already unusually long black hair pulled forward over her chest and T-shirt. He inhaled her childish, sweet smell. When he stood after the story was finished, having skipped pages and rushed to the end, she had reached up for him. Viktor bent further over her in their night-time routine, and with her sweaty hand she gently removed his glasses, held them aloft, and, with her other hand on his cheek, they touched their noses very lightly and stared into each other's eyes. Viktor looked with amazement at Rosa's wide, black, round eyes as she stared back into his blue ones. Then after a second, as they did every night, at the same time, she emitted a single order: 'Kiss.' She would kiss him on his lips and stay there, mouth against mouth, for a few seconds. The kiss would leave them both comforted, ready to confront the night.

Their nights – the one that he faced today, in a few hours – made him long for Rosa's embrace when he returned, for her thin, ardent arms around his neck. From here he saw the whole evening: not a series of dramatic rows but Nina, standing so straight, her square shoulders and ivory neck, the cardigan zipped over her naked chest and arms. Always her cardigans, worn, Viktor thought, like sacred gowns. Even in bed the cardigan would come off only at the end of the late reading, hoisted over her shoulders, the quick, expert movements under the cover, until the garment was discarded and thrown on the floor as though it had not meant anything to her. It felt like a lie, that this zipped-up sweater was meaningless, when in fact it was everything: her adjustable shield against the world, proof of her agency in life, cloth evidence of being, somehow, in control.

Viktor smiled at this thought, moved his weight on the bench, the boards pressing into him. He recalled the feel of her skin, that first touch in bed after she had finally relinquished all protection, the slow, assured movement of their naked bodies against each other, to find a position to sleep together or the decision, unspoken, to make love.

This spiral of thoughts had started just when he needed confidence in his decision to leave her. He knew he wanted a break. *I must concentrate on the rows. The rows. How they make me feel. What they turn us into. What Rosa sees. The rows.* It was too late already. His mind forced him back to the bed, to Nina, his body curled against her, his hand draped over her, holding onto her breast. The meals together, delicately prepared, presented to Viktor and Rosa. Somehow it had ended up like this, despite their efforts; Nina cooked, proclaiming loudly on pans and plates while Viktor, when he was available, took Rosa through her evening ablutions. Viktor stacked the plates in the kitchen cupboard, adjusted the towels on the radiator in the bathroom and arranged into a semblance of order the arc of toys on Rosa's floor. Nina was the director of the family's domesticity, their tragic financial affairs, the meticulously budgeted shopping, Rosa's entire edifice of clothes, schooling, lunches and the supply of reliable and consistent love. Despite everything, this is what they had become. The couple had only managed to dislodge themselves momentarily from the gendered routine of household labour for them to fall again, almost imperceptibly, into the habitual groove of life.

Expectant and hungry, with their knives and forks held up, erect, Viktor egging Rosa on, the two of them lightly hammering the table, Rosa leading the chant: 'Where's our food? Where's our food?' Rosa clamoured with excitement, her eyes ablaze, nothing else around her except the pleasure of this dinner table anarchy, sanctified by her father, amusing her mother. Nothing else, for these minutes. Rosa's mispronunciation slurred the words into a rhythmic, tuneful spell.

Viktor's black shirt stuck to his arms; he felt a trickle of sweat. He tried once more to reorientate his thinking from these images of domestic joy, to find his way back to what he knew, to what he wanted. *It was that kiss*, he thought, Rosa's kiss, that caught him, tripped him up, hurled him from the decision that he thought he could finally make on the towpath. *That kiss.*

Viktor undid two buttons on his shirt and bellowed the warm air across his body. A young man in a polo shirt sat on the bench next to him. He was thin, gaunt, his legs bowed. Viktor glanced quickly at his profile; the man's nose grew from his forehead into a steep, sharp, dramatic beak. All Viktor could see was the man's oversized nose – his face was entirely obliterated by his ridiculous proboscis. Viktor turned back quickly as though he had just seen the man's penis protruding, unbound, from his unbuttoned trousers. *My god, that poor man*, he thought. *His life has been entirely determined by his jutting, absurd knife of a nose. Overdetermined.* Viktor wanted to cross the two feet separating them to console him, put his arm around him and tell him that everything would be okay, from one nose to another. What was this emotion? Pity? Hooter solidarity?

Viktor mopped his moist head with his hand, moving it in big strokes across his face, then wiped his hand on his cotton trousers. He shook his head free once more of distractions and tried to corral his thoughts again towards the dilemma. If he left Nina, he knew that he would be leaving not their ugly, weekly rows, but their glorious laughter, the sex, her love for him, his for her.

The man next to him on the bench shifted slightly against the wooden slats. From this angle Viktor could see his full face, the nose no longer a separate appendage. Instead the nose was nicely, evenly balanced by bright, large eyes, his lashes dark and long. He had a full mouth and dimpled chin. Together they made his face look palatial and interesting. He wondered if it was a family nose, passed on through generations of migration, haphazard fucking, domestic joy.

Viktor stared at his companion unblinking and the man smiled back. *I could easily kiss him*, Viktor thought.

On this excursion into the sunshine, to the one place in this city not blighted by traffic, where Viktor was sure he could make a decision, he had fallen in love with a stranger's nose. The contradictory, complex parts of the world assembled into one impossible and beautiful whole.

*

Comrade!

I have just read the article you just published on *Mutations*. It is one of the best for weeks and months, and written with real revolutionary principle and passion – no surprise that it was written by a Botswanan, and not by the English, Western chicken-shit professors, heads and second managers who often seem to write for your site. What a refreshing breath of pure oxygen! The Botswanan is a REAL red fighter. No qualms, hesitations or vacillations or left lurches of the English mediocre type. Marvellous. I am pleased you took me up on the suggestion and contacted him.

And of course, 'the centrality of the working class' is the focus of the article. And what a working class! I remember researching the awful decades of shit these workers have been subjected to by their Western-imposed and, still, armed and backed rulers – fantastic. The power to change the world, smash capital and liberate all.

There is a deep personal thrill reading this article, as it is partly my handiwork. I recruited the comrade years ago in Harare. What a legacy, my friend.

Anyway, keep up the good work and keep looking south.

Tendai

*

Biko, Biko, Biko – you could no more say his name once than you had to speak it three times, make it a chant, shout it. *Biko* was a declaration. A siren. It needed to be shouted in meetings, in the crowded lecture theatres, in the city, uttered when others were speaking. Biko! The man, thirty-three – a biblical fact that escaped no one – finishing his second degree, raging, declaring, always speaking, always against the world.

Biko stood against *this* world, these dusty streets, the townships, the broken-down, ridiculous university, the whole towering, collapsing edifice, the streets and paths, the lines of life that connected the country and city he had inherited. The brutality and dictatorship, each part of it, every path that led to every shack, every paved, swept road that led to a new breeze-block palace, each imported, polished window on each new building in Harare, every fresh crack, each fissure of decay, every broken life, lost job, desiccated hope – on every street corner, in the idle loitering of the young and old, in the agony of loss (the only word that could confront Biko's own will, that could suck the air from the great expanse of his name, the effortless spread of his generosity and will and vision) – in all of these places, Biko was there.

Either he was actually there – and he often was *actually there* – or he was metaphorically present, using these upended, broken pavements to preach and teach. To read. To appeal for action. In between courses he taught for absent lecturers and professors, in between the endless in-betweens when the university was shut because there was no power or water or there was a strike, Biko could be found on street corners. This was Biko. He had as much freedom of movement as running water, gushing in torrents along the gutter, out of broken pipes, away from the channels, the paths of order. He was freestyle, wild, open-ended and unordered. On these corners – these idle corners in Zimbabwe's modern crisis – he organised, fought, read, taught. But most of all, as in all things in his life, he extolled and prophesied, the political prophecies of a rational man with an excess of love and hope. Each of these prophecies would have seemed, in another decade or age, like a simple demand for dignity for a normal people, for their elementary rights. Yet Biko had been cast into this role, into his constant, ceaseless ebullience, his never-ending hope, his optimism, by the demands and constraints of his time – of our time.

*

Some months before Rosa was conceived, Viktor and Nina booked their first romantic city break. The package included the train tickets and a two-star hotel for two nights.

Halfway through a duty-bound visit to a museum, the freezing drizzle pelting their faces, standing in the queue with a crowd of tourists breathing into their hands and stamping blood back into their feet, Nina had a meltdown.

'You've got to know this about me. I have got to learn this about myself. I don't cope well with these kinds of trips. I need a toilet.'

Viktor indicated a dedicated oblong concrete block twenty metres from the queue. 'Do you have change?' he asked. She swivelled on the balls of her feet and moved towards the toilet.

When Nina returned, Viktor opened his arms to hold her. 'I can't do this. I can't queue. I thought I could, but I can't. I'm sorry. Let's go,' she said.

'We'll go back to the hotel,' Viktor said, pleased to leave the bitter winter.

'I can't do this. I need to know my limitations,' she repeated. They started to walk away from the museum.

'I think you are being hard on yourself,' he said.

'Don't speak to me. Don't. I am already hating myself for doing this. You're just making it worse.'

Viktor sucked the cold air in deeply. His lungs hurt. 'Listen, darling, it's cold. You have your period. The toilets are filthy in

Paris. I can't think of anything better than lounging in the hotel room.'

'Thanks, but can't you see it's too late for that?'

Despite himself, Viktor muttered, 'Just ignore them. Look as though you know where you're heading.'

'I've no idea where I'm heading.'

'Just don't give them any eye contact.'

Paris looked threadbare against the hard gaze of commuters barging past them. Europe had changed; the carefree city break now involved a tortuous reminder of the continent's decline. Nina's neck was wrapped in a black scarf. Her glasses hung on a gold metal chain against her coat and together they elbowed through the waiting lines of hawkers pushing phonecards, tours, taxis and cigarettes in husky, accented English. Heated pavement grates blowing out hot air were turned into beds, doorways crowded with cardboard and sleeping bags; a mother and two children sat on blankets in a telephone booth.

'This is what their bloody austerity looks like,' Viktor said, hauling the suitcase over the uneven kerb. 'It's hard to be here as a tourist.' He snapped a photo with his phone surreptitiously, careful to keep the faces out of the frame, focusing on the whole.

Viktor's rage at the world was real but impotent. He had been the child politician, under the influence of his beloved Uncle Jack, reading the newspaper at the kitchen table as a boy — slamming Thatcher and Kinnock with equal wrath, trying to enunciate, to find the meaning, to explain and condemn.

'Not if you're positive, Vik.' Nina believed that there was no edge in life which could not be smoothed by taking the right approach, so she unbuttoned her jacket, unravelled her scarf and pulled her jumper away from her skin, drawing the air over her body.

'Positivity is not a remedy if you're living in a telephone box.'

'Maybe, but neither is despair. Your despair is only a performance when you are looking in from outside.'

'Why do you have to personalise it?' he said absently, staring at the map on his phone.

'Let's just try to enjoy ourselves, shall we?' Nina replied. 'We're only here for two days.'

They continued to walk together in silence, their suitcases tapping in unison against the pavement.

Nina saw the Hotel Americain in the distance, the blue-lit sign running up the side of the hotel. Two stars blazed brightly over the doorway.

'We're here, sweetie,' Nina reached for Viktor's hand.

'Hotel Two Stars,' Viktor said. He noticed a man sitting by the door, protected with earmuffs and a fur collar drawn across his neck; he had telephone and lottery cards pinned along the length of both lapels. Viktor took a photo.

'Jesus, Viktor,' Nina snapped.

She's right, Viktor thought. *Why can I only see the hotel's two stars? Why can I only see this man and his phonecards?*

He tried to shake his head clear, refocus away from the man's shame; he wanted to find a path to Nina's world, her automated edit of human suffering. Nina had an ability to see the heated, welcoming reception, the complimentary chocolates on their pillows, the crisp, folded towels, while he saw the stained corridor carpet and that man, that hopeless, eternally present human being, sitting outside their hotel in the night, as he embraced Nina and bathed away the February freeze. Viktor knew that the whole of life, the erratic, fleeting joy of their weekend together, would be reduced in his memory to that man, that unknown, undesiring recipient of his pity. He tweeted the photo.

@ViktorIsaacs #EuropeanCrisis in evidence on the streets of #Paris. #neoliberalism #austerity pic.twitter.co ...

Viktor had thawed his frozen extremities in the short hotel bath, his legs bent and exposed. Nina read. He counted the hours, subtracted the time they would be asleep and comforted himself that soon this city break, this enforced hell, would be over.

*

I should have left her then, he said to himself now, should have got out when it was just a romance, before the memories and the doubts could set in, before he couldn't imagine life without her, before Rosa. Before he had learnt never to travel with Nina, never to leave the city or plan a day trip without taking food for when she started to complain, to fuel her furnaces before it was too late.

Viktor always acted too late.

He saw the whole sequence of his life with Rosa, the weeks after her birth, the visits to the park, the unendurable tedium, the Chinese restaurant round the corner where they ate too often. He saw how, when she was almost three, she would stand on the plastic seat and stare at the goldfish and turn to him and say, 'I am this tall', and 'Do they eat fish?' and 'Does the cooker say die, die, die to the fish and then cook them?' The bright restaurant had embossed dragons breathing fire on the wall. Was this where Rosa had learnt her English starved of prepositions? 'Rosa good. Eat Chinese food. Know how use chopsticks.'

It was here, among those dragons and fish and the wonton noodles that he had watched his daughter grow up, amid the bickering hell of life with Nina and the constant indecision about leaving.

But what he didn't count on was how those memories of Rosa would always drag him back to the restaurant, the school, the playground. If he crossed the street where he had pushed her years before, or cast a fleeting, masochistic glance to the still swings and empty, childless pavilion on his way to work, he would see her not even as she had been: a blur of movement, the hurried, impatient rush to the next moment and his exhaustion. No. She would stand in front of him, frozen in a single frame of life, the colour of her cheeks, the patchwork cardigan with the pink arms sewn together in her mother's clumsy stitches. Radiant, Rosa would stare at him, her head turned up to him from the pram, just to check that he was still there and that they were together. 'All I need is you. All you need is me.'

But it would be too late. She would already be gone.

This was the danger.

At every corner he glimpsed his daughter in the dark braids of a child skipping along holding her mother's hand, the noisy crowd of children pouring out of a local school across his path. *Why wasn't I warned?* he asked himself. *Why did someone not tell me that I would be forever held down by my past with her?* Rosa's presence now loomed over everything he did. *If only I had known what it meant.*

When he was not with her, Rosa was the only person in Viktor's world and it was killing him.

Part One:

Love and Death

Chapter One

Viktor felt a hand slap his back. He jolted forward, looked up to see Tendai and pulled the headphones from his ears.

'So are you coming, Viktor? The protest starts in thirty minutes. You can write about it if you like.'

Tendai folded his tall frame into the chair next to Viktor. His fluorescent jacket was emblazoned with the initials of the company he worked for, Balford and Collins Workplace (BCW); over the letters Tendai had pinned a badge: *Fair Pay, Justice for Cleaners*, with the words circled in red.

'No, I can't. I have a deadline. I'm finishing an article.' Viktor indicated his notebook, his hand holding his place under the black and red cover. 'You know I am writing a piece on the campaign.'

'Good, but we need your presence. Support from academic staff is important.'

'I'm more student than staff. I don't have a contract – zero hours. Worse than you, Tendai.'

Tendai laughed derisively, stretched back in the chair, opened his arms and looked around the café at the muddled groups of students leaning over books, executives, men and women in suits, the canteen staff, three women like him from Zimbabwe – Rejoice, Patience, Sylvia. He dropped his head closer to Viktor's and spoke in a loud whisper. 'Fucking crap, Viktor, man. You are like the bosses, drinking your café lattes, listening to that ... that *noise*, and writing. While we, us' – he indicated the women at the counter with a sweep of his arm – 'the poor, the poor of the poor, we protest.' Breaking his whisper, he laughed loudly again, so that people turned.

'You have it all wrong, Tendai,' Viktor answered calmly. 'Being an academic today means poverty, insecurity – we're proletarianised too. No contracts, no stable jobs, no benefits, no overtime. *Déraciné*, unrooted, forgotten, members of the poors.'

'The poors!' Tendai repeated, mocking.

Viktor had a rule that functioned across British society. The worse the job, the more degrading and humiliating, the more cruel and bullying the bosses, the more respect he bestowed on the worker. In this formulation, exploitation and poverty were answered by politesse and gratitude. Yet in the face of Tendai's goading he was unable to be entirely consistent with this rule.

'You know,' Viktor added, pushing his chair away from Tendai, 'I *am* with you. I support the campaign.'

'Mr Poors, we don't need your seated support, your pity – we need your *presence*.' Tendai could do this: get to the heart of the matter, stick the knife in and laugh so it stung with accuracy, yet the pain of the attack almost instantly dispersed. To press the point, Tendai shuffled his chair closer to Viktor's, recovering the lost distance. 'Some facts: one hundred and fifty new members of the union in six months, in your union branch. All in cleaning and security, all outsourced workers. A campaign – the biggest of any college at the University of London. The demands clear.' He held his hand out, fingers spread, the skin between them fine and clear. 'One, the London living wage. Two, sick pay. Three, pensions. And four, leave. Each demand is about simple parity with University of London workers, man. When we have won these, Viktor – and we will – we will then fight to get cleaning and security back in-house. The final blow against BCW.'

Tendai wondered why he bothered. Viktor was hopeless, always immersed in his computer, his brow knitted as if he was Zimbabwean, as if he didn't have papers, as if *he* was illegal – but this strange man, with his questions, his curiosity and worries and misplaced urgency, somehow softened Tendai.

Tendai rose slowly, prising himself from the chair, leaning and pushing on the table. Finally Viktor answered, 'If I finish this piece I will come.'

'Make sure you do or I will fucking crush you, brother.' Tendai motioned with his hands, a substance – Viktor, paper, capitalism – being crushed, then turned and left.

Viktor watched him turn the collar of his jacket up, hoisting the hood over his head, bracing himself for the cold – tightening the drawstring so only his nose and upper lip were visible.

Tendai's exposed fingers grew numb in his fingerless gloves as he pushed the dustcart around the university, his books open, held down on the cart with elastic bands – fooling himself that he could read and study as he swept and cleaned. His pockets bulged with union forms and campaign material. In the winter he looked like a tramp and could be heard talking to himself, reading aloud. *Oh, poor crippled Zimbabwean beggar, his weeping was all in vain, 'Cos that rich man was never gonna feed him again.* The winter lasted six months on this infernal, ugly island, worse than Cape Town. Here the sun belonged to another, distant galaxy; the UK was a remote planet where real life could not exist.

5

Tendai was not Tendai. He was Soneko Dotwana, and he was not Zimbabwean, he was South African – though what did it matter, these lines that divided Southern Africa, paralysing communities and imprisoning the people. Where there had always been movement, now there were only borders, death, lethargy. Tendai's five-year stay in the UK was part of the historical movement of Africans, he reasoned. It was his right to disperse, roam, *flee as we have always done*, part of the peopling of the planet from Africa, filling Europe, the dark continent, with black faces. *If the first human beings were African, then we, they, were also the first immigrants. We never travelled with papers. Why would we start now?*

When in the early twenty-first century Zimbabweans had headed south to Johannesburg, Cape Town and Durban and north to London, Tendai had bucked the continental trend and fled to Zimbabwe from South Africa. He fled to Mugabe's proud Africa, to the project of resistance and anti-imperialism, and taken a Zimbabwean struggle name. The dream of socialism and freedom north of the Limpopo had dissolved into the air before it could even form. The only remnant of it that Tendai kept was his name. In a bar on his first night in Harare a drunken ZANU comrade called Tendai had listened to his story, slapped his shoulder and said, 'Now you are Zimbabwean. You are our brother, this country is your home and we are your family. As a Zimbabwean, you can farm, take a wife, make a business.' The ZANU comrade then asked him if he had chosen a Zimbabwean name for himself and Tendai responded with elation, 'Yes, I want to name myself Tendai' – a choice that had delighted the man.

In London, then, he was Tendai.

When Viktor had asked Tendai about Mugabe months ago, Tendai's tongue had split, divided in two, his eyes narrowed.

Yet when he spoke of Mandela – the Crowned Prince of Peace and Reconciliation, the poster boy of liberals and conservatives alike, the grey-haired old man in coloured shirts – Tendai spat. He rose on his feet. It seemed to Viktor that he actually floated, hovered over the ground, lifted by his words, his anger and bile still fresh with betrayal.

'When the regime, the racists, the apartheid dogs, wanted to negotiate, they fingered Mandela – not because he was the best of the ANC, but because the clever bastards knew he would talk, bend, compromise on everything. Each clause and principle he would sell. And Mandela, in turn, with his cheap rhetoric, he reined in the movement, turned us on and off, man. Viktor, I didn't even know Mandela's name when I was in Crossroads in 1980. Mandela was the low point of our struggle, our failure, not the symbol of our hopes but the end of them. He was the counter-revolution.'

To listen to Tendai was to be shaken by a gale. The rush of sentences left Viktor winded, his face pelted and sodden. For him Mandela, the man he'd watched being released from prison in 1990, was at worst a benign symbol of the transition, determined and uninteresting. But Tendai's story tumbled and crashed noisily to the floor, upsetting his balance.

'Okay, listen, man,' Tendai said, trying to maintain his patience. It was late in the summer; Viktor stood across from him, on the other side of the dustcart. Tendai was in his T-shirt, the veins raised on his arms, his pale brown face moving as he shaped the story. 'I was arrested in 1985 for murdering a black policeman and I was found not guilty, but in 1992, two years after your Mandela was released from prison, a prison like a hotel – with swimming pool, roof garden – your Mandela—'

'He's not *my Mandela*.'

7

'Of course he is, you whites, you liberals love him. He's yours.'

'No, Tendai.'

'Let me finish, man. In 1992 I am picked up again. I am living in Khayelitsha. Do know you it?'

'Yes.'

'Let me finish. It means *new home*. That's where we were forcibly moved in 1986. South Africa's third-largest slum: shacks, dirt, open sewers hidden on a fucking beach, behind the sand dunes.'

'I've heard.'

'Stop interrupting, man. This time they say they have new evidence, this time they say they have got some township girl, an ANC member, to lie and claim that I had killed the policeman and that I was a township criminal, a *totsi*. I was a troublemaker, a fighter, no *totsi*. Anyway, Vladimir—'

'It's Viktor.'

'Okay, okay, man. On the eve of your elections in late 1993 I am given sixteen years in prison. I serve thirteen years, two months and twelve days.'

'What?' Viktor screwed up his eyes. 'Why weren't you released in 1994?'

'You see, there you go again, man – you whites are all the same, you look the same and you think the same.' Tendai opened his mouth wide, bared his teeth, turned his head to the sky and laughed. 'Botha and de Klerk arrested hundreds of us, maybe thousands, for fighting the real struggle in the eighties. We were thrown in prison for so-called criminal acts and held until the new century. We died in prison for the new South Africa.'

'But, but—' Viktor stuttered.

'*Listen to me, man*. The apartheid government arrested us and the ANC, the Communists, the exiles brought the townships to

8

heel, under their control – that was the deal.' Tendai waved his arms, spoke faster. 'When the deals were made, the so-called legitimate prisoners were released. The illegitimate ones, the troublemakers, the comrades from the townships, we were left to rot. But not by mistake. Not some administrative error. It was easier for the ANC to govern South Africa with white power intact and us in prison. It was a systematic attempt, Vlad, to shut the lions up, those who led the struggle in the townships. Our blood did not flow with red, black and green, you know? We were making our own means. Are you keeping up, Vlad, man? The ANC wanted to clear the country of us. Apartheid and the ANC in partnership. Welcome to the new South Africa.'

'Why don't I know about this?' Viktor put his hands on the cart, held himself up like Tendai.

'No one does.' Tendai looked exhausted suddenly. The thick lines on his face sagged.

'What did you think would happen after the elections?' Viktor's voice was weak and quiet.

'That night, the twenty-seventh of April, I thought I was going to be released in the morning. What a fool I was. The humiliation, man, of that night is a hard thing to bear. For weeks after you feel dead, even when you are alive.'

The conversation was confusing in Viktor's memory. As fast as he chased Tendai he couldn't catch him, losing him in Southern Africa, countries that were remote, exotic to him, the people noble and poor.

The sun scattered the speckled clouds and shone on the men. The London sun had its own peculiarities. The city, too, Viktor thought, didn't really belong. London and all its people, the Congolese, the Polish, the Nigerians, the Zimbabweans, tossed about in the mid-Atlantic between the American, African and European coasts. Whatever this city was, it wasn't English.

Viktor dropped his bag and shuffled out of his jacket, letting it fall to the ground. His eyes stayed on Tendai, who continued, 'I got out and the government gave me sixteen thousand rand – work that out, a few hundred rand for every year in prison. Fifty pounds per year. I went back to Khayelitsha. Three of my family dead, my two brothers, a sister lost to HIV. My mother lived in a shack hawking vegetables. She was a beggar feeding fifteen mouths: my two, my brother's four, my sister's three, her brother's family. And this beautiful travesty shimmering on the dunes, the ocean spraying the shacks, sand blowing into our homes. While the whites and the rich blacks lived in the city without even seeing us. Do you know Cape Town, Vlad?'

Viktor didn't answer.

'I travelled into the city and saw that nothing had changed. Nothing. The city is a monstrosity. You stand on the highest mountain and see the harbour, the high-rises, the villas, the swimming pools, yet strain to see the poor. Only a trained eye can see the shanty town. Tin and wood. Two million invisible souls, the lives of the whites and a few blacks untouched like, like ...' He struggled to find the noun, the place. 'California. Like fucking Surrey. Behind their walls and security. You know what I saw, Vlad? I saw the ANC, I saw nothing. They had done nothing. And we were told to heal, to reconcile. How can you heal when you have no bread and you live in a shack?'

Their faces were only inches from each other, Tendai's spittle sprinkling Viktor's face. Viktor's mind was in a London state, Tendai's story ringing in his ears. His ardour made Viktor's head spin, but he found it difficult to understand. He was eager to grasp the meaning of Tendai's story – a significance that could only be revealed in this city, in London, over this dustcart.

'HEAL?' Tendai screamed suddenly, then unleashed a peal of laughter. 'Malls and surfers wearing Guevara T-shirts! Madiba's

10

a fucking fridge magnet, man. Liberation is a fashion statement. All of them were living while we suffered and died.'

Still stunned, straining, Viktor asked, 'Why did you move to Zimbabwe?'

'Naivety, Vlad.'

The two men were the same height: Viktor drawn thin like the neck of a guitar, Tendai broader. Standing up, Tendai put a hand on Viktor's shoulder. He laughed again. 'Naivety,' he repeated. 'I left because when I saw those men and women, those whites, I wanted to kill them, with the necklace. You know about our tyres? "With these matches and tyres we will liberate South Africa".' Tendai shook an imaginary box of matches in the air in front of Viktor's face. 'I wanted them to burn in the middle of the streets, in the daytime, to die, like I'd killed that traitor in 1985. I felt murder every day. I'd walk to the city and have to steady myself.' His grip tightened on Viktor's shoulder. 'I felt like – like the country was still occupied and we were still at war. I felt it here.' With his other hand flat, Tendai pounded his chest. 'I even started walking the city with a knife in my pocket, my fingers wrapped around it.'

Tendai loosened his hand from Viktor's shoulder and raised his head to the sun to let the light and warmth caress his cheeks, his closed eyelids, his neck. He rocked his head from side to side.

Viktor waited, breathless. Slowly, Tendai continued. 'When I heard what was happening in Zimbabwe, with the white farmers chased out of the country and Mugabe raging against the British, the final stage of liberation – the Third *Chimurenga*, for the poor and landless – I had to leave before I killed. Before I started the war again with my own hands and was killed or sent back to prison.' Tendai brought his hands tightly together around an invisible neck and wrung them.

11

'Mugabe's a thug,' Viktor said.

'What do you know, white man?' Tendai scoffed. 'Because he kicked the whites out? Armed his youth to take over the farms? Challenged British interests? Exposed the Americans? The IMF? What do you know?' Tendai spat out the words. His voice boomed, his words angry, disembodied like the voice of an angel, god, Mugabe, Viktor thought. Involuntarily he stood back from the cart.

'I'm better than that, Tendai. I mean Mugabe was insincere.'

'He was.' Tendai's voice softened. 'But I found that out by experience. What's life without experience, Vlad? Just words – from the Global North, from newspapers, the TV. You have to see and feel for yourself. You have to know, try, fail, learn.'

Viktor looked around him at the large, imposing stone towers of the university, the thin windows, the thick walls. Tendai pulled back the elastic on a facemask he stored on the cart, eased the band over his head and let the mask hang round his neck like a giant shell. 'I can't stay talking. I have to go.' Tendai lifted the cart and balanced it on its middle wheels.

Viktor was desperate. He tried to stall Tendai. 'If South Africa was unchanged when you saw it again, then why doesn't the war continue?'

'Good question, Vlad.' Tendai lowered the cart. 'What is your theory, white man?'

'Because you were in prison, right? You went to prison in 1992 and woke up in the 2000s. If you had lived in South Africa, in the townships, you wouldn't have seen it – at least, not as you did. You had what Rolando Toro calls the third eye of perception; you could see the failure, because you had seen nothing at all. You never saw *the* event of liberation.'

'Right and wrong, Vladimir.'

The second problem, Viktor reasoned to himself, was how Tendai had survived. How had he emerged from prison with the same anger, violence, ready to fight again?

'What was normal to my mother was a disgrace to me. You have to learn and keep learning oppression, man. In South Africa you have to be fooled every day. You have to relearn the normal. But you are also wrong, Vlad. My brother and sister fight, the township burns, barricades, tyres, riots – they cannot reconcile, there can be no reconciliation.'

Tendai's voice bounced off the walls in the courtyard, hit the windscreens of the cars, rebounded and came back to them. He raised his voice, almost shouted, almost sang, Viktor thought, like Mario in *Tosca – Tre sbirri, una carrozza …Va Tosca*. Viktor imagined the guns sounding over the Thames, the London chorus singing, everyone in the university staring down at them from the prison windows, from behind their books.

'You see, Vlad, they do not accept,' Tendai repeated.

Why does this man – Tendai, Soneko, whatever he's called, thought Viktor, *think I am Vladimir? Does he need me to have two names, like him – a struggle pseudonym? A split identity, British and Russian?*

Viktor was silent for moment, then he said, 'It's Viktor. With a K. Vi-k-tor. Not Vladimir. I am named after my grandfather.'

'Okay, whatever you say, Vlad.'

Chapter Two

The packet arrived in a padded envelope. Viktor dropped his bag to the floor, the door still open. He knelt in the hall, a rectangle of light marking the balcony, the walkway light stretching into the darkened flat, parting the permanent night that lived in these sealed-off rooms. He pulled from the torn envelope the small cardboard box of sleeping pills sent dutifully by his sister Amy.

Viktor turned the box in his hands, ran his fingers over the Braille, thought about that evening. The anxiety about sleep, for a few nights, already had started to fade.

He and Nina traded drugs, laughed at each other's lay knowledge picked up on the internet. 'Should I take two Paracetamol tonight, sweetie?' Nina sat on her side of the bed, her back to Viktor, hands twisted behind her, unfastening her bra.

'If you're worried about sleeping, rather take two Nytol. It'll knock you out. You're much too familiar with Paracetamol,' Viktor replied.

'What are you taking tonight, darling?' Nina yawned, stretched her shoulders and back — straightened, sucking deeply on the air.

'I've got a lecture in the morning. I don't know. I thought maybe Paracodol – the codeine worked well last week.'

Nina hauled the heavy duvet over her chest, pulling it to her chin.

'Listen to us,' she laughed. 'We sound like dealers.'

Viktor turned the light off, fell onto the bed, felt Nina's warm skin. He moved close to her, put a leg over hers and reached for her hand.

'We're better than we've been. We haven't taken Tramadol for weeks,' he said.

'Ah, Tramadol. Life is better on Tramadol.'

Their fingers linked and knotted together under the cover.

'Only it constipates you,' Viktor commented wistfully.

*

By midday the sun was beating down on Cecil Avenue, which ran parallel along one side of the National University of Science and Technology, where Biko taught and studied for a PhD that appeared impossible to finish. It seemed that the louder, the more aggressive the heat, the more radiant the day, the louder Biko became; in opposition, with resistance, he swelled. He seemed to tower over all things – he was that blooming, swollen, growing star in a crowded room that people gathered around and drew towards without knowing why. Men were attracted to him even more than women; they felt greater and more generous, broader, for having heard his laughter, his arguments – for having been in his presence.

All was straight in Biko's form except his nose. That had been snapped at the bridge years ago at school when he fought a senior who, with the innocent, simple arrogance of entitlement, had pushed his way ahead of Biko in a queue for lunch. Smaller, adamant, ridiculous Biko had pushed back. Then the two uneven, unequal boys – Biko a head smaller than the older boy – had faced each other, Biko's black eyes staring furiously. The momentary stand-off had ended when the boy had grabbed Biko's shoulders and brought his head down on his nose. Stumbling back, still standing, blood pouring from his face, Biko had thrown his fists and charged.

On the streets leading to the university, along with other members of the Society of Liberated Minds, Biko built activists. He developed and cajoled and bullied. To minds hard and stubborn he applied his arguments with brute strength; to those already rubbed up and eager, he encouraged and channelled and shepherded.

In early September 2011 – unilaterally, without consulting the group's loose leadership in Harare – he began planning a demonstration. Biko saw it all, the pieces, the patterns, and he rushed. The point was, he knew, that students' anger was always ripe, their conditions overflowing for action. If Biko could help to lead, touch off the students at NUST, what other groups would follow? Everything was in the following. He had seen the heroics of student politics and knew students needed allies, needed to break their isolation, touch off the poor in the townships, the workers in the city – in Bulawayo, in Harare.

Biko told the students that errors were more important than successes. 'We learn, comrades, from our mistakes. We synthesise from our beatings, the bruises. From death we grow stronger.' Yet despite himself, his wide reading, his endless practice, he was impatient. And this time he moved too quickly.

What did he expect to achieve? Vaguely, he wanted a revolt that would spread from Bulawayo to other cities and towns, first in the south and then, maybe, to the capital. To Harare. From the revolt in Bulawayo he would prove the importance of impatience over Nelson's caution. Nelson, who spent too much time in the fetid air of the north, who, for all his brilliance, moved too slowly: the whole of Harare's Society of Liberated Minds was infected by caution. Biko intended to show these comrades, these caution-mongers, that action begets action. Only with movement and audacity are we alive. Only then is there progress. He would give his life to the movement and grow the Society of Liberated Minds from its puny educationals and modest demonstrations into the force that it was already becoming in Bulawayo – a hurricane of resistance, of conscious fighters who could challenge the dictatorship.

*

Another email arrived from Tendai and with it more contradictions. Why did Tendai write to a man he saw every day, and in a language of socialist deliverance, describing with ecstatic, foolish optimism every struggle and act of global insubordination? What was going on? Why was this man of the African renaissance harsh and hostile in person and emollient and loving in his emails? Tendai was becoming two distinct people in Viktor's life.

Viktor,

You may already know the good news from around Africa, of course.

Senegal – mass demonstrations halt despot's attempt to legislate himself another term, using stones against police repression.

Burkina Faso – wow, now things in Ouaga are really heating up. Presidential Guard joined worker-student demos, after not getting what they expected.

Uganda – food-price riots (a cause of unrest again, as prices rise over 41% higher – this is an IMF figure) have morphed into anti-government/anti-regime demos.

Swaziland – ongoing pro-democracy demos, workers and students.

Botswana – though the brilliant public sector strike remains suspended, the government is reeling.

South Africa – 200,000 struck on Monday. 120,000 metalworkers on indefinite strike for 13% pay rise, 20% night-shift rise. 70,000 oil depot and refinery workers striking for 13% too, and a monthly minimum wage of £185 a month.

So, comrade, do you know what this means? It's no longer just MENA afire – it's the Middle East AND North Africa AND the rest of Africa igniting too! And these days they have such an admirable model in the MENA revolts and revolutions … so far.

More later.

Tendai

*

Viktor had delayed his visit to the doctor, hoping that he would wake cleansed by the night and a full sleep, free of the plunging despair that held him every day that January. He would knock back a black coffee in the morning at home, the hot liquid scalding his tongue and throat, and his head would spin. He took his second coffee at 8.30 a.m. at King's Cross, bought from the same café booth each morning with his loyalty card. He waited in a queue of addicts like himself, all hauling themselves out of bed and into the winter. Each waited in a different state of disarray, their orders shouted back to them by the barista in faltering English as though they were being branded, licensed to enter the city. The bright-eyed Nepali woman, her hair tied back neatly, smiled at him every morning with intimacy. Oh, how he lived for that smile. When he was third in the queue, she looked across the small crowd and lifted her eyebrows at him: 'Extra-hot soya latte, two shots, medium.' Viktor kissed and sucked at the opening on the lid with the usual sinking realisation that this act – infantilised by a multinational, slurping obediently, in line for the 73 bus to take him to work – was his single moment of happiness in the day.

Fondling his phone, his coffee between his legs, the liquid working its way through him, he composed his morning tweet:

@ViktorIsaacs #KingLatte has enslaved a whole city w/ pathetic pleasures & promises. Caffeinated, we work harder for less. #neoliberalism bit.ly/j3sr8f

Skyward Viktor would fly, the second coffee propelling him further along the incline to the precipice. Sure enough, the crash always came late in the morning, however hard he tried to keep himself airborne. The afternoons, even with classes, the tutorials, marking, the entire rumpus of activity, were merciless. Never let it be said that depression is simply the toad of idleness.

The doctor's surgery was in the middle of the estate. The Meccano flats, with bright red, blue and green balconies, looked like Rosa's make-believe Lego Town, with boutique businesses and bistros and underground parking for professional couples and singles who could pretend that they lived inside a post-postmodern utopia – at least until the caffeine wore off or their balconies started to rust. Viktor shuffled through the rotating door to the lobby and was welcomed by a chemical freshness. The reception desk looked like a hotel's, smooth granite with embedded computer screens. A blankly staring, disorientated Viktor registered with the woman sitting behind the desk.

'Name?'

'Viktor Isaacs.'

'Date of birth?'

'October the tenth.'

'Year?'

Viktor leant forward and whispered: '1970.'

'That's too young to worry about your age,' the woman said, her face barely reaching the counter.

The radiant gleam of the room told a lie: that the health service worked, that it looked like this, polished, new and within easy reach – that health and life could be given out like perfectly cooked meals in an expensive restaurant. Sickness could not cling to these fixtures. There was no place for his depression on the fake-leather fitted benches, the varnished wood, the alloyed steel. The room seemed to refuse all infection. Only the public health posters on the notice board indicated that all was not well in the world outside the estate. Viktor read, shifting his weight from foot to foot:

Dementia. Look out for the early signs:
1. Forgetting the names of friends or everyday objects
2. Having problems thinking or reasoning
3. Struggling to remember recent events but easily recalling things that happened in the past.

Viktor read the sign twice. His heart thumped. His jumper suddenly clung uncomfortably to his body.

His father, Isaac, had phoned last week. 'Jack died,' he'd said, without preamble. 'Jack is dead,' Viktor muttered, still staring at the notice.

Jack, their Jack, *his* Jack, his political lodestar – the man who dominated his boyhood existence, navigated him through the world – who looked like Pavarotti and sang like him too, with his large handsome stomach and black cab. He would sing to them when he was drunk, when he was happy for the mindless, simple joy of eating on the rare Shabbat they marked. He'd push away the casserole Viktor's mother Sonia had baked and clear a space in front of him on the table, as though his voice needed the room. Then he would stand up in the middle of the noisy meal, his stomach pushing his trousers down, his heavy-knuckled hand heaving his weight up on the table, the chair scraping against the kitchen floor. Isaac would emit a delighted sigh, pouring more wine into everyone's glasses – even a splash for Viktor and Amy. Then Jack, a hand scratching and kneading his bearded chin, would sing: Rodolfo in *La Bohème*, always the same part, the same aria, Act 1. The family pressed back in their chairs. Jack addressed each of them in turn, his voice strident. With Sonia, though, he lingered, saving the most beautiful lines for her; leaning forward across the table and touching her hand gently, he sang: *Che gelida manina.* Each time this great man, who already filled the kitchen, would cry as he sang.

You can't simply hand over a life like Jack's. Is Jack dead?

I have dementia. I am not depressed, I'm losing my mind. All I can think of has passed.

'Viktor Isaacs?' A young man with black spectacles and short blond hair stood in the lobby, looking at his notes.

Jack is dead, Viktor thought as he followed the man along the darkened corridor. *Jack is dead.*

21

The consulting room was standard issue: a large examination bed with a disposable paper towel spread across its entire length, a wraparound white curtain, large windows with aluminium blinds, the sort that Sonia had ordered years ago, Viktor thought, made to measure from Wilson's Interiors, an incongruous shop on the high street between the launderette and newsagent. Their blinds had hung crooked against the window like broken wings.

Viktor flinched. He wanted to move to the window and straighten the blind on the cord, measuring and adjusting the slats, as his mother had done when he was a child as if she was flying a kite from the kitchen window. These damn blinds made his guts turn, made him want to move in again with his parents, to help Sonia with her cooking, Isaac with the computer. *How long had she saved for those blinds with the money she'd put away in the glass sweet jar behind the baking tins?*

'What seems to be wrong, Mr Isaacs?'

The doctor is too young, Viktor thought. He wore a gold wedding ring, but his face was uncreased. There were no marks of life on his face, no shadow of a beard.

'I'm depressed.'

'Oh, I'm sorry to hear that. Can you tell me something about it? How long?'

Viktor removed his glasses, looked ahead. 'About a month - no, longer, I think. I have been depressed for maybe a year.'

'Have you felt suicidal?'

'No. Yes. I don't know. I go to bed and wish I wouldn't wake up. That's not suicidal, I suppose. Is that normal? I lie trying to sleep and I fantasise about being executed by a guillotine. I dream of my head being cut off, in a painless second. Only after this can I really sleep. I think I have a guillotine complex – is there such a thing? You know, the guillotine was invented

22

to free execution from cruelty and pain. It was meant to be humane. But I think it is the cruellest way to die. To be alive one minute, dead the next, for there to be no transition. They say the brain remains conscious for seconds after it has been severed from the body. Can you imagine anything more terrifying?'

The doctor stared at Viktor. Then, after a pause, he asked, 'What do you do?'

'I'm a doctor,' Viktor lied.

'I see.' Blondie sounded excited. 'You're one of us.'

'Not really. It's public health. All social science. I'm out of touch, I haven't practised for years.' Why had he lied?

'You're still a doctor,' Blondie reassured him. 'How's your sleep?'

'I fall asleep, but wake and then can't get back to sleep. It's then that I start to fall apart, even the guillotine doesn't help. Destructive thoughts.'

'That's normal. I am thinking of a standard selective serotonin reuptake inhibitor. I would normally go for Prozac, but for the sleep we could take a more traditional route, a tricyclic antidepressant. What do you think of amitriptyline? Old-fashioned, I know, but you will sleep.'

'Good choice,' Viktor said, nodding his head knowingly. He thought again about Jack.

'So we'll go the amitriptyline route,' Blondie repeated.

'I can't stop thinking about the past. The dead,' Viktor said vaguely. 'About Jack. I keep thinking about Jack.'

'Who's Jack?'

'Jack Slomin. Jack died last week.'

'I am sorry.'

'Jack shouldn't have died. Our family friends are all dying. Iris, then Ruth, Joe. I can't stop thinking about them. What

23

happens when they're all dead?' Viktor spoke quickly, staring ahead.

'Maybe you should see someone you can talk to about this.' Blondie uncrossed his legs, sat straight in his chair.

Viktor's shoulders hunched forward and he put his head in his hands. His mouth was dry. 'I don't have a sex drive any more. I can't even ... you know, what do you call it ...'

'Masturbate?' Blondie offered.

'Yes, and my, my, my ... you know ... our ...'

'Penis?'

'Yes, my penis isn't working.'

Point 1: Forgetting the names of everyday objects.

'Depression does tend to kill desire. That's not unusual, we're not robots.'

'My problem is that I used to masturbate regularly, compulsively. Now, not at all.'

Blondie shifted in his seat, pulled his glasses off, cleaned them with the hem of his jumper.

'What if I said,' Viktor continued, maintaining his flat, level tone, staring ahead, 'that before this depression I was an obsessive-compulsive masturbator?'

'Well, there is nothing wrong with masturbating. How often, exactly?'

'At least once a day, sometimes twice.'

'Can we settle on these antidepressants? I can also set up some counselling for you.'

'But surely it's better that I'm not masturbating now, as I was?'

'Well, how would you feel if I said that compulsive behaviour like that might get in the way of developing healthy relationships?'

'I would feel criticised, ashamed. Of course I have meaningful relationships. I have a daughter, for example.'

Blondie wheeled his chair under his desk, pulled the keyboard forward and started to type. 'Well,' he said, still moving his fingers, 'what would you say if I told you that compulsive masturbating is not a problem – that perhaps masturbating represented a forward movement?'

At last Viktor's stream of thoughts and words was stilled. He straightened himself in the chair and turned to the doctor. 'Perhaps you're depraved, doctor,' he joked.

'Perhaps,' the doctor replied, smiling.

There was stillness between them, punctuated only by the satisfying, plastic click of the keyboard. The thicket of worry began to fade, Jack, the dead, his chaotic disorder … the early signs of dementia. *Point 4: Have you noticed that your family and friends have started to die? Have you started to think more about the dead than the living? Do you fixate on flaccid, dying, out-of-sight genitals rather than living, erect tissue?*

'I'm prescribing amitriptyline and a course of six therapy sessions – though there's going be a delay with these. CBT.'

The doctor stood and walked to the door. Viktor followed. They shook hands. Blondie commented, 'I will also make sure your records are changed. They have you down as Mr Isaacs.'

Chapter Three

One of Biko's ideas was to get the students to march to the Reserve Bank in the centre of Bulawayo. There was no other place in the southern city so charged, so culpable. Even the old man deferred, in hushed tones, to the Reserve Bank – the ultimate arbiter of all demands for redistribution, the state's crypt of stolen loot. The day's climactic crescendo, its crashing victory, would come when the students – and whoever else they'd managed to pick up on the protest – would hammer on the reinforced doors of the country's vault. And if they could get inside …

Despite Biko's intentions to keep this plan from the Society of Liberated Minds in Harare and in particular Nelson, news had leaked north. Late in the night before the action Nelson fumbled on his phone, feeling the unusual sensation of panic as he texted Biko.

Biko. I want to state that I am not opposed to any protest OUTSIDE the Reserve Bank. But you must be aware that the Reserve Bank employs guards armed with machine guns (i.e. live ammunition). I very strongly urge comrades NOT to try to occupy or storm the bank in any way as there is the real possibility of comrades being killed. Any such action is suicidal and reckless. We do not need our members unnecessarily killed. Please, Biko, see sense.

Biko was curt in his reply.

What is the difference between this action and storming police HQ, which we have done many times?

Calming himself, steadying the phone, Nelson replied laboriously, as though he was providing comments on a student paper.

Biko. The difference is that bank guards are not trained to restrain protesters. They are trained only to shoot with live ammunition, not stun grenades, shields, water cannon, tear gas or rubber bullets. Just live ammunition. They are trained to shoot anyone who is there illegally. THEY ARE TRAINED TO AIM FOR THE CHEST AND HEAD. They will not issue orders or ask questions first. A bank contains money, which is a critical part of the capitalist system. They will kill to defend it. I do not know who has called the action but I can only repeat my urgent plea. Please do NOT try to breach the Reserve Bank.

Nelson knew who had called the demonstration, and he knew that Biko was the only person in the Southern fucking Hemisphere who would suggest attempting to occupy a central bank – even its regional office.

Biko felt the logic of Nelson's words seep insidiously into his decision-making. Yet he resisted, typed hard on the keys of his phone and hit send.

Again, you presume that we would not consider our own safety. The plan is surely to go as far as is safe. Do you really think they're just going to shoot at peacefully protesting students on their doorstep? I think you are overstating your case. I will personally move as far forward as is safe. Again, your negativity is disappointing.

Nelson hesitated, put his phone next to him on the sofa and took a mouthful of cheap wine. The wine didn't calm him and do its normal, reliable work – he was still panicking.

I only want the best way forward in these exciting times, Biko!

*

Viktor felt his life had been taken over by Rosa. The hours spent changing nappies; the loud midnight howl that would wake both of them, sitting up in bed shocked, as though they'd never heard her cry before. The sounds of her night fears seemed louder than her small body should be able to make. Her fear of the night and nothingness. Her Being Towards Death. From her pushchair Rosa saw London faces, hanging jowls and mouths cast that way by the natural downward pull of England on their bodies and emotions.

'She sounds as though she's being killed.' Nina turned on her side and flicked the switch.

'She realises she's alive,' Viktor said.

'What?' Nina asked. Rosa's crying rose and fell as she gasped for air between her tears.

'She wakes up,' Viktor found his slippers, pushed in his feet, 'and remembers in a second what existence is, and then she cries.'

'Rubbish. She just gets scared,' Nina snapped.

'But why?' Viktor unhooked the towelling dressing gown from the door, his father's hand-me-down. The sleeves rode up his arms, the bottom swung untied around his thighs. Standing in it he felt calmer, comforted – his heart slowed, stopped pounding.

'Because she gets scared of the dark,' Nina repeated more calmly.

'Yes, and of life.'

'Only you're scared of life, Viktor.'

'We all are. Maybe she cries because she knows how much people suffer.'

'Would anyone else think such a thing?'

'I'm coming, sweetie,' Viktor cried. 'Daddy's coming.' Rosa's sobbing quieted, gave way to deep, tearful hiccups. The chorus of howls from her throat fell back into her chest.

'So you're saying,' Nina continued, 'that children detect a pitch of sadness in the world. Like dogs.'

'Not children. *Rosa*. Perhaps that's *her* burden.' Viktor swung the door open and left the room, calling in front of himself as he stumbled along the corridor, knocking into the walls. 'I'm coming, darling. I'm here.'

The whole of Rosa's first two years of life contained her unending suffering. Her crinkled, newborn face had been furious, Viktor thought, from the moment she'd first seen him waiting for her in the hospital, his glasses off, staring down at Nina's dilated, bloodied vagina. Then there had been her relentless crying, her mouth open, the toothless, pink gums declaring her disgruntlement, hunger, pain, discomfort. In the first months she would sound her distress and he would sweat, remove his jumper, pace the room. When it was too much Viktor would sit on the toilet, the lid down, his hands holding his face and cry. He communed with Rosa using his own tears.

Later, Rosa would be in his arms, hanging onto him like a sprig of ivy, the sadness passed, the night settled, and they'd fall asleep, folded together, their suffering ended.

Viktor's heart swollen, his breath obstructed, he'd hear Tosca, speak and sing the words, struggling, stumbling in his bad opera Italian, his accent scratching and abusing the words:

Amor che seppe a te vita serbare
ci sarà guida in terra, e in mar nocchiere,
The love that found the way to save your life
shall be our guide on earth, our pilot on the waters.

His daughter purred in his arms, hovering just out of sleep, looking at Viktor, who sat arched like a shepherd's staff, craning over her. A slight smile creased her cheeks; he fancied they sang softly together.

Each time he tried to lay her in the cot she'd wake, her broad, round eyes would spring open and her chest expand, readying her lungs for complaint. Viktor would straighten his back and bring her again into his lap, muttering, 'And in harmonious flight the spirit soars to the ecstasy of love.' Only when she was fully lost to sleep, thirty minutes later, could he lay her down and return to the bedroom, his own sleep emptied from him.

'What do you sing to her?' Nina asked when he came into the bedroom.

'It's not really singing. I normally just speak the song.'

Nina was sitting up in bed, the pillows arranged behind her, a book spread on her lap, her phone in one hand. 'So?'

'The words are from *Tosca*.' Viktor let the dressing gown slide off his shoulders and fall to the floor. 'They come at the end of the opera when Mario Cavaradossi is about to be led away – before he is shot, before Tosca throws herself to her death, they sing together. I think Rosa likes it.' Viktor pulled the cover back.

'Do you think it's appropriate to sing a death aria to our daughter to get her back to sleep?'

'Oh, but it's not—' Viktor turned, excited, to Nina. 'It's about love *and* life. You see, they have planned it, they think Mario won't die. This is their last love song. "And harmonies of song. Triumphant the sound trembles with new hope." They are going to *cheat* death – Mario and Tosca will be together. Do you see?'

'And which one of you is Tosca?'

'I don't know. I sing both parts. It's more the sentiment that Rosa likes, "the spirit soars to the ecstasy of love".' Viktor dropped back into the bed and pulled the cover to his neck, his long, fleshless feet exposed.

'Well, if it works,' Nina said, yawning.

'It does.'

'I want to read you something, darling.' Nina picked up her phone.

'What?'

'Just listen.' Nina's face was lit by her phone. 'An important project that is currently on your plate requires a very dramatic performance by you. You want to prove to everyone that you are worthy of being where you are. You don't want to disappoint anyone. And you don't want to let a dream slip through your fingers. Relax. You have what it takes.'

'Who sent you that?'

'No one. It's your star sign. Libra, right? I get yours and mine, Gemini, on my phone every morning. I've told you, I find them insightful. They come through in the middle of the night, about the time Rosa wakes up.'

'Do you pay for them?' Viktor asked.

31

'Don't you think it's uncanny?' Nina ignored his question.

'What?'

'The reading: "You don't want to disappoint anyone".'

'No. It could apply to anyone.'

'But it doesn't. It's *you*.' Nina dropped her book to the floor, placed the phone on the bedside table, retraced the path to the lamp. The room disappeared. 'You're the only troubled soul in the house – with your opera, your hopeless causes, your desperate attempts to please everyone.'

Instead of reading her book, Nina had listened to Viktor in the next room, coaxing Rosa to sleep. Now she moved to him in the bed, put her head on his chest, her leg over his and felt his tall, skeletal body, unprotected by muscle or fat. 'I think you are a good father.'

'How can any of us be good parents in such a world?'

'Oh, shut up, darling,' Nina chided affectionately.

'I'm too affected by her suffering.'

'She doesn't suffer. She's a baby.'

'Really?'

'Yes,' Nina said adamantly, then softly, 'I love you, Viktor.'

Chapter Four

Anne-Marie was isolated. One method to shut out the clamouring, the demands on her life for conformity and order, was simply to allow very few people in. It was brutal – and it worked. She spoke to her family – her uncle, an aunt, even her mother – on the phone and rarely visited. For four years she had told them half-truths about her life with Nelson: that this was a developing relationship, that he was a good, radical nationalist, that he understood the continent, knew its history. Then she threw them scraps – mostly lies – when they asked her questions about him on the phone. 'Sister,' her friends in Gombe would ask, 'will he travel with you this year, will we meet him?' To friends and family in France and Belgium she said, '*Nous envisageons de voyager ensemble cette année, mais il est occupé. Je l'espère, nous pouvons faire le voyage au Congo.*' She chose her friends carefully. She knew what they would say and that they would understand.

When he was in Zimbabwe her strange confidant was Tendai. For the first months of his visit, washed up like a prophet, almost delirious, on the shores of Harare, with Nelson's address written on a worn, dirty scrap of paper – raging, pummelling the air, working himself up – she had kept her distance. She was used to these refugees stumbling into Nelson's flat, the HQ of the Society – new recruits, with their complex Southern African global traumas, their tottering comprehension – or lack of it – of the world.

Tendai was different, altogether more determined, angrier than anyone she'd met. He forced Nelson to gather up his arguments, putting him constantly on guard, exhausting him. Anne-Marie resisted Tendai, ignored him, pretended he wasn't there. When he stayed and she realised it was impossible to ignore him, she challenged him, took him on – needling, prodding and mocking. This was precisely the dynamic they both needed. Tendai's sinewy, taut presence, the physical impression he left of stretched leather, his apparent disregard for his appearance and Anne-Marie's scornful distance left them free of sexual ambiguity, of any faint, treacherous attraction. Instead, they had something completely unusual and extraordinary: intimacy liberated from sex, and an almost improbable capacity for honesty. They fell into each other with a hunger for connection that neither had ever known before. Tendai's whole ravelled understanding of his imprisonment, his years of captivity, his confusion, could somehow find expression when they huddled in a corner of Nelson's flat after a meeting or sat up into the small hours in her flat, where they spoke late in the week. Tendai was quickly granted rare permission to spend the night.

Anne-Marie had found a person shorn of the layers of silent assumptions and expectation that, in the global epidemic, had infected everyone she knew. She could speak about everything and, strangely, his contradictory, argumentative responses always satisfied her.

Unable to find regular work, after living at Nelson's, with Society members in Chitungwiza and at Anne-Marie's, Tendai had decided to travel to London on a visa and money he had been, incomprehensibly, able to secure. He could not be reasoned with. When Nelson's great marshalling of words and arguments failed to bend his will, Anne-Marie left Tendai with his decision.

Sitting in the early-evening haze of her living room two nights before he left, taking up her sofa, his legs sprawled, possessing the space, his tone was calm: 'Just because I am going, don't think it means we'll give up our sagas.' *Saga* was Tendai's adopted term to describe their conversations. 'I will be away, but we will talk and email. Nightly, if we have to – our sagas take all night. If you need me. Right?'

Anne-Marie had expressed no opinion about his decision to leave, nor had she enquired about his contacts, the visa. She had given him money, which he accepted without bother or thanks. Her attitude was informed by a continent that was in a state of permanent leaving – of migration and death. Given his options, it was a sensible, entirely reasonable decision, but under any circumstances it would not have warranted judgement. She knew that Tendai would always pass periodically from one place, one climate, to another. As the migrating birds travelled south, he moved north.

She had dragged her blanket from her bed over her shoulders and sat on the floor in the corner of the room, the light from the window striping her legs. 'This life you lead, comrade, will leave you permanently alone,' she teased him. 'You'll die and there will be no one at your funeral, you'll be alone in some miserable London cemetery. *And* I won't come. I wouldn't travel to London for a birth or a burial. You'll be alone on that intolerable island. *Alone*, do you hear me, with no one to miss you. Be warned. An unmarked grave waits for you. You'll leave the world unmissed. I know what this means, I know that part of the world.'

Tendai took the gibe, chewed it over, considered its seriousness: 'You see where you are mistaken, sister? I have lived most of my life alone. You think I wore shorts and lived in a communal cell in Cape Town? I had my own brick room, too short for me to stretch out in, with blankets for a bed and a bucket for shitting. Alone, you say? I have been alone. I was in a cell alone for seven years. Shitting alone for seven years.'

Suddenly he leapt up, then squatted in front of the sofa, his elbows out, squeezing, his limbs flailing, and then he laughed loudly and collapsed back on the sofa. He opened his arms and encompassed more of the space. 'I don't live for my funeral,' he said, more calmly. 'If so, I would not move or travel or live. I wouldn't have arguments or speak out. Fuck my mourners. Fuck the living when I am dead. Let them get on with changing the world. Keep the worshipping of the dead to the politicians. I am a dog of the wind, and we all die alone.' Then, lowering his voice almost to a whisper, emotion strangely heavy on his voice, 'Don't waste your time on these questions, sister. If you come anywhere near my grave when I am gone, I will fucking rise up from the dead.'

'If you do anything stupid in the UK they will deport you. Do you know what's happening in Europe? It's the *chute*. The collapse. The catastrophe. The place is full of racists and little fascists. If you leave London, if you escape any of the major cities on that island, you are taking your life in your own hands.' She pulled the blanket more tightly around her shoulders. 'No, Tendai, don't interrupt me. Listen. I am not joking.' Frustrated, trying to find the words, she lapsed into French. '*Ils chassent les immigrés comme les bêtes.* I know what I am talking about. It's not the Promised Land of jobs and plenty. I have read the reports. I have friends, Society members, who have been arrested and deported. They will hunt you if you put a foot wrong, and you will never know where to put your bloody feet.' Then, laughing, checking herself, eliminating the tone of reprimand, 'And your feet are so big, you only know where *not* to put them. I give you a month, *umngani*.'

*

Two days later they sat unusually silent in Anne-Marie's beat-up Golf at the airport, Tendai's arm draped casually over her shoulder, Anne-Marie gripping the steering wheel hard, breathing deeply – refusing everything that rose in her chest, the bile of emotion in her throat, fighting back each enticement to cry.

'I'm not coming into the airport. You can do that alone,' she said with a gulp of air.

Tendai spoke. 'I said we'll speak when I arrive and then whenever we need to. Nightly, if necessary. Do you hear me? Our sagas need to be fed, I need to hear your voice, sister – we need to talk.' Tendai pushed the passenger seat back, his khaki cloth backpack between his legs. 'And speak to Nelson, okay? Tell him what you want and what you don't want. And keep the voices away, *hanzadzi* – far away.' Frustrated that there was no response, he dug further in. 'Remember, romantic relationships are a colonial lie, a Western imposition. Even in the West they are only, what, two hundred and fifty years old? In Africa, barely a few decades – in most places here they don't really exist. You can be single, you can be childless if you want – you can escape these voices, this, this' – Tendai brought his hands up, rubbed them together, tried to find the words, to create the phrase from the static of his palms – 'this historical anomaly, and *you can be happy*.'

Anne-Marie remained still, stiff, her position hostile. She stared ahead towards the terminal. A couple battled with a battered trolley loaded with suitcases, boxes secured with string and tape.

Breathing in deeply, swallowing loudly, Anne-Marie finally relaxed, fell back into the seat and dropped a hand onto Tendai's knee. 'Okay, I hear you. Our sagas. The phone. The resistance. Now get out of the car before the Brits discover who they have travelling to their island fortress and you're deported before you even leave. Get out.' She turned and, for the first time since they'd left, she looked into his face. His eyes were wet and bloodshot. 'Now go. And I will see you in a month. I give you a month. Only a month. Do you hear me?'

On the journey home Anne-Marie cried loudly, the tears clouding the road, blurring the route, and she shouted, holding the steering wheel too tightly. 'You idiot, you idiot,' she repeated over and over again, '*stupide, bête, idiot, imbécile, débile.*' Who was this rage for – herself, Tendai, Nelson? She didn't know why she'd let him leave, how they'd survive without each other or why they needed to.

She realised minutes later that this cleansing fit of sentiment expressed something utterly new to her: the first and only genuine friendship she'd had. Her friendship with Tendai was freer than she thought possible, clear of obligation, doubt, ambiguity, hesitation. Anne-Marie's greatest weakness was her denial of her weaknesses, her refusal to accept legitimate pain, her efforts to push on. But she was clear about Tendai. She realised quickly that her tears were a celebration of their friendship and their freedom to lean on each other or not, to be in touch or not. And to be themselves, completely (*and when are we ever really ourselves*, she thought).

Almost immediately her life of meetings, funding applications, field trips, conferences – the sub-Saharan jamboree of NGO work – intruded, elbowing any further lashes of emotion aside.

Peculiarly, Tendai and Anne-Marie did not communicate on the telephone. Instead they found their rhythm in email. Tendai's missives were political and positive; Anne-Marie's were infrequent, typed on her phone in bed when she remembered, sitting up, propped against the wall by uncovered pillows. She knew Tendai didn't need the affirmation of her replies, the buying-into-the-friendship, so weeks, even months on one occasion, passed without a response from her. Never did Tendai write (and it did not occur to him to do so) that he wanted to hear from her or that he needed to know she'd received his messages.

It seemed that prison had freed Tendai of cravings, needs, insecurity and fear. Instead it gave him – in certain matters of human relations – an infinity of patience, a capacity to wait, to just be. For his friendship with Anne-Marie there were categories of communication. His full-bodied, entirely present communication was reserved for political involvement. He scoffed at émigré politics, the lazy kinship of being African in the UK; his involvement, his yearning for argument, for understanding, had to include his physical presence, his entire soul.

'In this cursed land, on this dark, primitive, northern island,' he explained, a year into his cleaning job at the university, to other cleaners and security guards gathered for their mid-morning tea in the underground staffroom, 'we have a duty of exposition. We need to reveal ourselves to the sea of ignorance around us.' He indicated the floors above, the seething, weighty complacency of the white-collar masses in their offices and boardrooms. 'This is project number one. Nkrumah called it philosophical consciencism.' The more effort his colleagues made not to listen, the louder Tendai became, raising his voice, demanding attention. Staring directly at Kwesi, who was splashing soap and water on his mug in the sink, he continued, 'Nkrumah saw emancipation, unification and the development of Africa and its scattered people, of which there are a few representatives here. I propose widening the project to the entire Global South *and* North.'

All this, the preaching, the conversations – *head-cracking*, he called it – he wrote to Anne-Marie.

It is the tragedy of our epoch that sometimes we must break bones, crack open the skull, in a series of violent and direct blows. I am busy filling these heads with new sagas. I AM A REVOLUTIONARY SURGEON. I will wear the circles of bone around my neck for each head I have conquered, for each step taken to change the world towards our liberation. I will conquer this city. I WILL lead the inhabitants of this prison out of their madness and fever. Do you hear me?

Anne-Marie heard him and laughed. She lay, satisfied, on the sofa, her shoes kicked off, chuckling, holding the email she'd printed at the office, knowing she'd have no signal at home. The pleasure was intense. Early the next day, before anyone arrived at the office, she wrote back, her coffee next to the keyboard and the grubby, creased pages of Tendai's printed email next to her.

Tendai,

You have sinned and I am writing quickly, before work, to tell you where you have gone wrong. I insist on immediate correction. You speak about filling the heads you have broken with new sagas, but you will understand that these are only *our* sagas. Our stories. These other 'sagas' you mention are not sagas as much as political ideas – theories or arguments. In other words, they are other devices entirely. I forgive you, of course, how could I not, though I insist on a printed apology – in the *Herald* – and a promise never again to use our language for this thing you do to people's heads in London. Reading your words, Tendai, I think it is you who needs to be relieved of the pressures of madness (and the procedure, while we are discussing it, is called *trepanation* – I will perform it on you when you return).

You know I have been thinking about you. For all your bluster, your head-cracking expressiveness, you are the least bitter person I have ever known. I used to ask myself why you are not angrier for the years you spent in prison, with no one who had any clout, any pull or power to help you. You have described it to me: the beatings, the torture. How can any human being spend 9,078 days in prison – you see, I remember the number – and not be mentally broken? That is the mystery, Tendai. You emerged with a beautiful knowledge of yourself and an education, even if this is not the way you tell the story. I remember you saying that after 1994, when you knew you wouldn't be released, you spent a year trying to get yourself killed and the injuries you still carry: eight unhealed broken bones, two collapsed discs, blinded in one eye ... do I need to go on? Do I? But you are less a victim to what happened to you than I am to what did not happen to me. I don't know why I am saying all of this – I suppose I want to say that your emails, these electronic sagas, have helped me to see you.

I haven't made the definitive statement to Nelson, or to my family, but they know I am not going home, wherever that is – to the Congo or France. I am staying here. I belong more to Zimbabwe than anywhere else. The saga of children continues. There is a small child who stays with his uncle — you met him, he lives on the same floor as me. I play with him sometimes. Nelson gets me to read the emails you send and complains that you do not answer him. I consider this an act of solidarity, comrade.

I have a story for you, a footnote in our saga: one morning last week, Nelson declared, after a few moments' silence, stretched on the bed, sipping a glass of wine he'd left by the bed the evening before, 'You know, *mudiwa*, I think I want a child. What good is an activist without knowing children? Save us from a revolution led by childless men and women. What can we know of the world without bringing in new life? Without knowing that love? So — children, comrade, what do you say?' Can you picture him, spread out on the bed like a spider? And what did I say, you ask? I got out of bed and stood over him and said, Tendai-like, 'Is that a proposal, comrade? Maybe you can have one under Any Other Business at the end of the next meeting of the Society.' Then I shouted, 'I will move back to France if you mention this again. Having children is not a revolutionary responsibility, an agenda item, an experience. It is something *women* do.' He stared at me, then nodded his head and said, 'You may have a point.'

I do have a fucking point.

Now enough of this. What I wanted to say, my *remarque improvisée*, why I am writing — and before I decide not to say it or read through what I have written and delete everything — Tendai, grant me some sentimentality. There is not enough in our line of life. You have taught me that the only way to get through life is to love someone. Why do we make it so difficult, this simple message? And yes, I hear you, we have to clear the obstacles to love: the poverty, the rich, the divisions, but the message is that simple. YOUR LESSON – MR SURGEON OF HEAD-CRACKING – IS LOVE. I know you won't like this but it's true, you are really a healer, a *n'anga*. The only thing we have between us is love, and that currency is the only thing that stops us from turning bitter. Love stops us from being poisoned by the bitterness of life. What do you say to that, *hanzadzi*? Do you hear me?

Aside from the emails, his communications typed out slowly, precisely on the reappropriated university computer, Tendai occasionally conceded to Anne-Marie's text messages, her tone insistent, demanding his response. Laboriously, painfully, he answered her, his fingers pressing the keys, the plastic of the phone cracking – cursing the words that wouldn't come.

Anne-Marie: *I need your address, Tendai. I want to send you something. ANSWER THIS.*

Tendai: *I will get it for you, com – in an email tomorrow.*

Anne-Marie: *How does someone not know their address? It's where you live. Get out of bed and open your front door and read the street name and the door number.*

Tendai: *Addresses are complicated in London. Tomorrow. Why do you want it?*

Anne-Marie: *Why? Because I want to phone the police to tell them that there is a dangerous African in the city who can't decide where he is from.*

Tendai: *Hold off mailing me, com. I will send the address when I have located a safe house.*

Anne-Marie: *A safe house! Listen to you.*

Anne-Marie laughed aloud at this.

Tendai: *If you can hold off for a fortnight and make sure the envelope is flat so it can be posted through the letterbox.*

Anne-Marie: *Flat? How am I going to send you a pair of socks and a pullover through some slit in a London door?*

Tendai: *Why are you sending me socks?*

Anne-Marie: *Because it's cold and London is unforgiving. I am knitting them.*

Tendai: *You do not know how to make clothes.*

Anne-Marie: *Listen Mr Know-Anne-Marie, I was taught by my grandmother. I come home and knit. I have started to knit again. I listen to the radio, knit and forget.*

Tendai: *Why do I not know this?*

Anne-Marie: *You do now. I am going away for a few days and will send them when I am back.*

Tendai: *Where are you going?*

Anne-Marie: *I am going to Nairobi for a week. It's a retreat with seven other regional NGOs — we have hired a hotel.*

Tendai: *Criminal.*

Anne-Marie: *Basically it's going to be a big* soirée pyjama.

Tendai: *I see. Sharing a hotel with Africa's Lords and Ladies of Poverty. The poor are grateful to you, com.*

Anne-Marie: *I miss you, Tendai — our conversations, our sagas. I have no one to talk to, not really. Nelson is a constant absent-presence. You know, I wish he was either absent or present, not both.*

Tendai: *He is lucky to have you, even if it will only be when you leave him before he understands that. You need to decide what you want from him and then make a decision.*

Anne-Marie: *Yes.*

Tendai: *Can I lecture you? He will always be an in-out presence in your life. There is only one permanence for the comrade. You need to tell him.*

Anne-Marie: *Yes.*

Tendai: *Use your big sell-out workshop in Nairobi to make the break or to start the break. You cannot wean a hungry child with an empty breast.*

Anne-Marie: *What does that mean?*

Tendai: *I have no idea.*

Anne-Marie: *LOL.*

Tendai: *What does THAT mean?*

Anne-Marie: *Laugh Out Loud.*

Tendai: *Anne-Marie, com, are you listening to me? You are trying to do the hardest thing, to turn your back on the jackals, that chorus of disapproval. But you are not alone.*

Anne-Marie: *I feel alone.*

Tendai: *I am here, com.*

Anne-Marie: *You are in London.*

Tendai: *No, I am not.*

Anne-Marie: *Then where the fuck are you?*

Tendai: *I will not leave Africa, nor will I surrender. Only through hardship, militant action and sacrifice can freedom be won. The struggle is my life.*

Anne-Marie: *Since when do you quote Mandela?*

Tendai: *Occasionally the bastard sell-out could weave a decent line or two. I will continue fighting for freedom until the end of my days.*

Anne-Marie: *Ha, ha. They were all just bloody liberals. Freedom, liberation, independence — meaningless slogans without content. No political economy. No analysis. My grandfather was the same.*

Tendai: *Steady on, com. Lumumba was a bit better.*

Anne-Marie: *Maybe.*

Tendai: *Now you're sounding like Nelson and me.*

Anne-Marie: *No, Tendai, I am sounding like me.*

Tendai: *Yes, you are.*

Anne-Marie: *Sorry, Tendai. You have got me in my* heure du crime. *I can get dreadfully negative.*

Tendai: *Analytical I would call it. You don't have to put up a front for me, com.*

Anne-Marie: *I am happy to have you – god that is an understatement.*

Tendai: *I am glad I can be here. You know I'm here – insomniac lunatic who sleeps two hours a night. I really am always around, twenty-two hours a day. Com, you know that, don't you?*

Anne-Marie: *We just need to be here for each other. As distant as we are – you too must just message me if I am out of contact. I am never far away from you.*

Tendai: *Good. That's what we need and I feel your presence. Mr Surgeon of Head-Cracking has now mastered text messaging.*

Anne-Marie: *I am sending you sagas and peace as you drift into your two-hour sleep, com.*

Tendai: *I am sending you the will to turn theory into practice. In Nairobi.*

Anne-Marie: *I just want love, Tendai.*

Tendai: *I am sending that as well.*

Chapter Five

Viktor filled his bag with books, notes, his computer, wiped the table of the spilled coffee. He stood and walked to the counter, the cup and saucer rattling, his shoulder bent with the weight of the bag. Tendai was right. He needed to participate, demonstrate. But the article had to be completed, posted, syndicated, and he needed to update Facebook.

Viktor took the back stairs that led to his second-floor office – a marble, off-white stairwell, the windows and cased radiators covered in oak, the period toilet a whole restoration, from front lobby to back staircase. The toilets on the first floor held his preferred cubicle, with the perfect heavy three-quarter-length oak door, the low window the height of the ledge, deep enough to hold a bag. Everything was perfect in this building.

Viktor was too careful. He could only proceed in life with a set of meticulous calculations and routines. The morning latte, the table nearest the counter in the university canteen, the final espresso that would function at the allotted moment to loosen his bowels, then the walk to the stairs, the climb. On the first floor he would rest, his nose would itch, and he'd sneeze three times. All things must have their place. The cubicle would be his, the bag swung into place on the window ledge before he'd dropped onto the toilet seat, the cold hard plastic pleasing on his buttocks.

Viktor removed his jacket from the door. Under it he saw the sign:

BCW Prides Itself On Absolute Cleanliness.
If There Is Anything That Dissatisfies You Please Contact Our Service Desk.

Viktor felt his stomach turn, his forehead moisten. He thought of Tendai, the women he knew, the Zimbabweans who cleaned the toilets. *Bastards, They Want Our Complicity In Their Exploitation – they want us to shit and complain. Absolute Cleanliness, what does that mean anyway? Such a lazy use of the absolute. No one since Hegel believes in the absolute. Cleanliness is relative, partial, incomplete, an approximation.*

Viktor stood in front of the mirror, water crashing over his hands, wetting his cuffs. He looked into the mirror, saw the reflection of the clock, translated the reversed hands: nine forty-five. Two hours to complete the article. The shared office would be empty for a fortnight while the other PhD students, temporary lecturers and interns were away. Each hour accounted for.

Tendai said the cleaners were asking for the London living wage. 'Only the London living minimum, man. Eight pounds ten pence per hour. Puny, pathetic, and that's all we dare ask for.' Viktor thought about the demonstration, the crowd of students with their drums, the echo they would make in the courtyard, their voices ricocheting on the concrete. Then there would be the ritual pushing against the security guards, our own swollen-faced brothers in their fluorescent yellow vests, arms linked to prevent the protesters from entering the building. Passers-by averting their gaze – and Tendai, his cart parked, waving a pile of leaflets, shouting at them from the back of the crowd, 'When we win the living wage, brothers, you too will benefit. *Shinga Mushandi*, *Shinga!*'

*

Viktor,

I wanted to email you rapidly a series of slogans from the mass camps I was telling you about in Madrid's Plaza Puerta del Sol. I thought you could use them on your website, or read them to your daughter (a young mind is NEVER too young to understand the sheer necessity and urgency of revolution).

Tell her, tell Rosa, that hundreds of thousands of young working-class unemployed men and women AND children have been living together in a public square (this is the new form of organising we have to understand) and they have chalked these slogans onto the pavements and walls. *Democracia! No nos callaran!* – They won't shut us up! And my favourite, my absolute gut-rejoicing choice of revolutionary slogan is: 'We can't even afford chorizo to put on the bread!' When the Spanish write this you realise that the revolution is coming – that the full Phase 3 isn't far behind.

Then, comrade, there is a board on one side of the square, the sort that we have at the university to advertise corporate funding, but with old black and white photos of anti-fascist workers from 1936.

And the best is for last. This European movement, this occupation of one of the continent's great squares by workers, students, school kids and pensioners has been copied by protesters in Burkina Faso. In the centre of Ouagadougou, nicknamed Liberation Square, there is a permanent occupation of thousands which has also SCRATCHED slogans in chalk on the pavement from Madrid ... with one brilliant, magnificent addition. In capitals the workers have written (in French):

'WE ARE THE WHEELS THAT TURN THE WHOLE WORLD' – these are my capitals.

And in this political statement, they are streets ahead of their European brothers and sisters, who still have illusions – opposing good and bad bankers and politicians, for example.

Tell your daughter all of this if you can and also try to put it on your website.

Yours in struggle,

Tendai

*

The row was hardly dry before a fresh coat was applied. They kept tripping over the unsettled earth, making new arguments where a week ago they had walked easily on the trampled, firm ground. Viktor washed up, splashing water on the dishes; Nina moved noisily around the flat, tidying Rosa's toys, dropping them into the box in the lounge. The coloured xylophone rang unpleasantly as it hit the other toys. Nina continued their row with the flat, knocking angrily against the sofa, shaking the dust out of the rug.

Viktor had optimistically prepared the meal they'd eaten in separate rooms, conducting their fight between mouthfuls, not even tasting the food. *What was it about? I can't remember. All there is, now we've stopped shouting, is the headache, the echo. Our words sliding off the walls, clattering to the floor, the sound of the doors just slammed, hanging in the air.* He shook the water off a pot lid.

Sonia had given them the pot, boxed up in a collection of cups, plates and pans for their new life. *But why this one?* Viktor thought this was the family saucepan, with its faded black swivel handle that could be turned to an embossed arrow if the food being boiled or simmered needed ventilation. He recalled Isaac's hopeless mess in the kitchen: a pot rattling on the hob, flour coating the table, the apron that made him look like a drag queen. Viktor held up the lid, spun the handle; it still turned, thirty-five years later.

'Are you going to finish in there and help me move the bloody furniture?' Viktor raised the lid, dripping with water, and kissed it.

They survived so long, got through the rows that came fortnightly, as if prearranged, by watching television. Straining to avoid conflict and conversation, they watched hours of television together every evening with Rosa asleep. Sometimes, hand in hand, they sat mute, their faces relaxed. Nina tucked her feet under Viktor, interrupting their evening for toilet breaks or between courses eaten on the sofa. The TV added years to their relationship, brought them together as the conscious dead – mouths hanging open, eyes dry, unblinking at the flat screen. Life, it seemed, existed only when they were apart; still they longed for their silent TV communion, their anaesthetised union.

Nina spat out the words across the lounge as if her mouth was expelling poison: 'You bring nothing. Nothing. I never know when you're going to get paid. I have had enough of supporting you, all of us, paying for everything. You should get a bloody bar job. You're fucking useless.'

Nina had the gift of sleep; whatever the turmoil in her life, the dissatisfaction of her days, she slept. Viktor clawed desperately at night, fought his way in, fell asleep exhausted only to wake a few hours later and then gradually, inevitably, feel his world collapse. The boyhood fear – that the veil of life would fall from him when everyone else slept and reveal the true, vibrant horror of everything in the darkness – had been replaced with the pedestrian insomnia of life and failure. His nightly sleeplessness spoke of his hate and self-loathing – his writing a failure, his incomplete PhD a travesty, a symbol of his incomplete, flawed character, Nina's anger with him a symptom of his absurdities, even his online world a retreat from the real one. Even his parents' old age and imminent, certain death (never mind that they were both in good health) felt like a confirmation, somehow, of their disappointment with him. For all his midnight ravings, his pitch-black self-hate, there was an aspect to this demotic, relentless self-criticism that was true. The pain of attack at three in the morning was no less severe for being entirely solipsistic.

Nina's life was no less vivid or choked with questioning, but she was the family's labourer, so she slept in the evening from exhaustion *and* responsibility. Her hunger for books and escape, her capacity for knowledge and learning, were more rapacious than Viktor's. Their love had been kindled by books and ideas. Viktor had taken her writing, her fluent, scribbled prose, seriously and they had shared and talked as though they knew that they didn't have long together. Nina wrote stories and poems – then quickly, hungrily, paralysed by doubt, she buried the notebooks and her frustrations in a suitcase under the bed.

She had been a precocious teenager, smart and wise at thirteen – sharper, more knowing of the world, it seemed to her now, than she was at forty. Nina grew out of school, bristled, fidgeted and needed to escape from the childishness of adolescence, from the mediocre school. By thirteen her family had become a charade of incompetence: her parents separated and her father half-heartedly moved in with his lover; her mother took up with a younger man. Her half-sister was born when she was seventeen. With the divorce the family's aspirational life – the riding lessons, the semi-detached house on the outskirts of Oxford – exhaled its last breath; everything bought on Thatcherism's hollow promises and easy credit was sold and the scattered family became trapped by loans that had become debts, affluence that had become servitude. Nina had worked to pay off her father's debts. Eventually her mother moved to Bristol.

She had left school at eighteen and was working full time at nineteen. Nina worked as a clerk in a solicitor's firm, rising to legal secretary at thirty and finally finding a position in the office of a university department, where she outsmarted, outread, and out-thought the professors with their puny interests, narrow research agendas and funding bids. Even Rosa, the daughter she loved, was a disappointment, a non-fulfilment, and she continued to ache and crave in silence – she dreamed of her writing, of books and occasionally of burning down the fucking offices and corridors where she worked. Yet Viktor – this man who she once thought might save her, who understood her, who listened – had become another burden, another disappointment.

'I think that's an exaggeration, Nina. The last months have been difficult, but I am nearly done with the PhD and I have more teaching next term.'

'Rubbish. What about your daughter? She can't wait. Who will pay for her new clothes?'

'*Our* daughter,' Viktor muttered.

'You're so, so … passive-aggressive.'

'If I raised my voice and slammed doors like you, you'd accuse me of being violent.'

'You are!'

Viktor combed his hair with his fingers. *Next week*, he thought, *Nina is travelling to see her mother in Bristol. The tread on the back right tyre has gone. It will rain and she'll drive impulsively, as she always does. The small engine will whine when her foot presses down on the pedal. Then she will brake on that large, sparsely lit motorway for the turning.*

'Maybe we should just do our own thing. Perhaps we spend too much time with each other. What do you think of that?' Nina sat on the edge of the sofa, her eyes burning.

Viktor was silent. *She'll skid, the car won't stop, it will swerve, veer side to side. Nina will turn the steering wheel hard — exactly as you are told not to. The car will turn over and roll, the roof will crumble.*

'Are you going to answer me? We can start tomorrow. This is how you want us, all of the women in your life – devoted and distant. Look at your mum. When did we last see them? You want us to love you, but you remain indifferent. Isolated. Cut off. And *you* do this.'

The car will roll through the side barriers, over the verge, into the fields. Nina will be killed next Saturday on her way to Bristol — killed by her impetuous, nasty anger. Never happy with where she's come from, never happy about where she's going.

'Do your parents even know you?'

Then I'll be left to bring up Rosa alone.

'What efforts has your mother made to get to know me? What has she done? The mother of her grandchild!'

Viktor saw himself next weekend debating how to tell Rosa; he wouldn't be a hypocrite, he'd tell her straight and not resort to the false comfort of an afterlife. *'Dead. Your mother's dead, sweetheart. Like the pigeon we found in the winter, tangled in the green netting that hung across the balcony. Remember, sweetie, how we buried it, unhooked its extended, broken wings, its claws — and you said that pigeons were lucky because they had wings and legs so they could fly and walk. Nina has died, like that pigeon, sweetheart, she got tangled in the green netting and she's not coming back. Now it's only us, you and me.'*

'Will we bury her in the garden with the pigeon?' Rosa would reply.

'No, darling, we can't do that. We will burn her in an oven until she's been turned to dust and then we can throw her off the balcony.'

Rosa would look at her father, her eyes wide, her mouth open; she would be silent for a moment and then smile. 'Then she'll be able to fly as well. Walk and fly like the pigeons. She'll fly off the balcony.'

'She's made no effort,' Nina repeated. 'She just calls to speak to you. And the food parcels, food that we never eat.'

Viktor had come into the room and now played with his glasses, turned them over in his hands. Nina's blurred form looked imprecise and distant on the far sofa.

'Your mother's a bitch.'

Viktor dropped his glasses to the floor and took two steps towards Nina, his heart pounding in his ears. 'What did you say?'

'From passive-aggressive to violent! What are you going to do? Hit me? You know if you ever hit me I'll leave you. I will walk out with Rosa.'

Viktor breathed in, steadied himself.

Viktor relaxed his hands, his face drained of colour. He stayed where he was, in the middle of the room, in front of Nina.

Nina got up, shook her head at Viktor and walked to the bathroom. 'I'm going to take a Tramadol. Do you have anything to say?' Viktor was silent. 'You are as useless as your family.'

'Consider yourself hit,' Viktor said.

'Fuck off.'

*

Biko's line of communication with the comrades of the north, to Nelson, was through Anne-Marie, the one on-off member of the Society who seemed to understand him. The two spoke nightly. Biko explained the plans, how the movement at NUST in Bulawayo was being organised. Anne-Marie – calm, sanguine, unimpressed – queried his assumptions and goaded him from Harare on the bad lines, calling from her work phone to his mobile. They worked well together.

The line was bad tonight. Anne-Marie's voice jumped, broke up. 'How are you, Biko? Do you need me to send money? You need money to live on, right?'

Biko laughed loudly and leant against the wall of the squat he shared in Bulawayo. 'Live? Ha! We don't really live, comrade. We go for three days without taking anything, but your middle-class sensibilities mustn't misunderstand the poor: in this medium-density area, with my interpersonal skills, we can always find food.'

He slapped the concrete wall with a flat hand, his laughter scattering the static.

'There's a woman – a really conscious, political woman – who is called Magdalene; she steals mealie-meal from her father's store and gives it to us.'

Pausing, filling his lungs, raising his voice again: 'And on bad days, Anne-Marie, we chase locusts to eat. But isn't this communism? Seriously, no, listen.'

Anne-Marie was making no objection.

'I do not mean suffering, but Zimbabwe is teaching us something. Life is difficult, right? You should come and try it. How many of us live here, in this place? Fourteen of us at the moment. So if one comrade has something in his pocket, say, fifty dollars, we share it among all of us, without even a question. No hoarding. No silos of wheat for future speculation. And if we have a sympathetic parent and they give us something to eat, we share it.'

He repeated, '*Fourteen* students staying in a house with *three* rooms. *These* are the lessons in communism, not lessons in middle-class society and good behaviour. Not your privatised little talking shops.'

He stopped, rolled his head on his shoulders, pulled his shoulders back. 'Anne-Marie, are you there? Are you listening?'

Anne-Marie burst through the static. She wanted the rhetoric and grandstanding to stop. 'What are you planning, Biko? You know you can't, you shouldn't be making these plans without coordinating with us. With Harare.' Ridiculously she tapped the phone, tried to shake the earpiece free of dust.

Biko was serious, he replied quickly – he wanted to show her, and knew that she would tell Nelson that he had planned well, that he was organised, that he was quick and impetuous but not foolish.

'So we have formed mass action committees. These are specialised structures to help in the mass action. Now this is not just at the university. These are mass action committees based in the high-density suburbs, where you can have a street or particular area represented by an action committee. Each committee is there, in every area of the city. Take Trenance. There is an action committee which in turn has other smaller action committees in the broader area. When it comes to the issue of students, what we have done is use our own committees – branches of the Society of Liberated Minds – to disseminate propaganda in the schools and colleges. We go into institutions and distribute fliers, calling for the students to come out, the issues – at the institution level we are dealing with fees, paying fees with grain, exclusions, ZANU corruption. The dictatorship. The parochial *and* general.'

Biko dried his mouth, breathed in. The night had come. The grey, grainy dusk was now black. He felt a slight breeze lift the bottom of his trousers. 'We are moving tomorrow.'

Anne-Marie felt her pulse race. She tried to calm herself – to find reassurance in Biko's description, in the plans, in his permanent excitable calm, but she couldn't lift the panic from her voice. 'ZANU-PF, X-Party, will crush you. Mugabe is not going to sit and watch. Come on, Biko, I am not even from Zimbabwe and I have seen Mugabe's brutality and ruthlessness – he is feared across the region. The killings in Matabeleland in the eighties, crushing the Ndebele community, seven thousand murdered in cold blood. This is your history, Biko, not mine. So he will not sit and watch.'

Steadying herself, she stopped, put her feet on the table, pushed her chair back, looked around the apartment. 'Biko, I am just saying, exercise extreme caution in terms of how you are going to move.'

Biko was more serious now. 'It depends dialectically on the participation of the populace of Bulawayo. I personally am expecting a high turnout. The situation in the city is difficult; at the university repression has increased to an almost unbearable level. So people are going to react, but the level of state reaction is going to affect us directly. Mugabe is not simply going to watch. I will be extremely cautious, like a good comrade.'

Biko stopped suddenly, then laughed loudly. 'We don't speak enough about faith. Have faith in me, Anne-Marie, it's not the revolution we are starting tomorrow – just the prelude. Just the first shots. Tell Nelson, tell Lenin, that it's in hand – tomorrow Bulawayo takes over from Harare, like Petrograd took over from Moscow in 1917. And that, like all things, life will come from the margins. From the margins of the margins.'

'Biko! Goddamn it, Biko – just take it easy tomorrow.'

Chapter Six

The day after the row followed the usual pattern. Rosa was dropped at school; Viktor left the marking in a pile on the floor next to his threadbare slippers and dressing gown. Nina took the day off and they made up in Wood Green shopping centre and drank coffee, shopped, caught the first matinee at the cinema and came out thirty minutes before they needed to pick up Rosa, who would run out of the school and into their arms. Their rows and the debts that were drowning the family followed each other, what felt like the entire economy of north-east London sustained on shopping trips triggered by their arguments.

'You look gorgeous in that, sweetie,' Viktor said from his slumped position on the floor in the changing room. Nina had squeezed into the cubicle, a bundle of clothes picked out in the deserted shop. Viktor, his head numb from their row and the long, sleepless night, couldn't concentrate on the newspaper. Instead he waited for Nina to try on the outfits they had chosen together.

'These,' he called out across the shop, 'would look wonderful on you.'

'Okay, I'll try. Do you really think so?'

'Yes, perfect. They're very eighties sportswear. Funky. American Apparel.' How the hell did he even know the names for these styles? Did he understand what 'funky' meant? Still, he got it right. Despite his bespectacled erudition and ankle-swingers, Viktor knew what colours, fit, shapes and cuts would work on Nina's short, curved body. The cubicle door swung open and Nina came out. The collarless tight grey T-shirt exposed her cleavage and traced the contours of her breasts, and the pink leggings and black boots clung to her legs.

'Riding chic?' Viktor exclaimed. 'You're breaking out of your pigeonhole! It's such a relief to see you in pink, and that you can at last put away some of your blacks and greys. We've discovered something here, darling.'

'Thanks, sweetie. Are you sure?'

'Completely. If you don't buy them, I will.'

The staff would stare in awe, occasionally join in the pantomime: 'You are so lucky to have a husband who supports you in your shopping. Mine is terrible.' Night drew over the short day, turning the early afternoon into dusk.

The accusations from the previous night faded.

Viktor carried Nina's bag. The pink leggings made her look absurd, like a jockey or a pole dancer, yet he had insisted on buying them. Now he felt sick – certain, after slow mental calculation, that he had spent more than his overdraft. *What can I sell? The bicycle.* The bicycle with the child's seat that he had, to his own surprise, managed to fit – Rosa had cried with joy as they freewheeled downhill, the wind puffing out their coats, their open mouths filling with air. *Or the computer? My phone? That's it, I will sell the computer and use the one in the office.* Stupid, now he thought about it, that he had his own laptop – and that everyone did. *What needless waste.* The thought cheered him; he

61

would sell it for £150, enough to pay for Nina's leggings, the cinema tickets, Rosa's new school shoes.

They walked through the car park, around cars and shopping trolleys. 'We've really achieved something today,' Viktor said, one hand holding the bags and the other around Nina's shoulder. 'Haven't we, darling,' she replied.

*

Worse than his endless pondering, his life procrastination, the ceaseless zigzags, was the dizzying white-knuckle ride Viktor inflicted on others – on Nina, on Rosa. A year before Rosa was born and five years before the final, absolute separation, he had ended the relationship.

The first time they had sex after he returned, Nina said, 'I haven't had orgasms like that for ages.' Sex had been easy. They moved into each other's bodies, laughing and touching as though they hadn't been apart. They had come quickly in one position. Viktor's fingers on her clitoris as she sat on top of him. Even if he had come too soon – the old problem, the ancient sickness – it hadn't mattered. They lay in each other's arms afterwards, the condom hanging off his penis, its extended knob full of semen.

In the sleepless night, on the first day back, the words that she had uttered about her easy, strong climax leapt back to him, sharp and clear as an alarm. He was already awake, but he now started with a jolt. 'I haven't had orgasms like that' – he repeated the words as he remembered them, searched for hidden meaning. *Did this mean*, Viktor asked himself, *that an involuntary truth had sprung out of her? Had she been having sex with other men while they'd been apart? Is that what she had meant?*

Viktor got out of bed and started to pace around the flat.

He listed the reasons why this new nightmare could not be true. She would have had to produce a life of Houdini-like complexity to have covered up fucking someone else. On her first night back she had sat on their balcony with an electric razor, shaving her calves of their long black hair. She had not performed any differently during their sex; Nina was the same lover. Most importantly she had told Viktor earnestly that she wanted to marry him, that she wanted children and that she wanted them to stop using condoms. All of this he kept repeating to himself, like a religious oath.

Viktor came back to bed and saw her lying curled up, her back to him. She turned to him. 'I love you, sweetie,' she muttered, her voice thick with sleep but soft and sweet. 'Come here. Is there anything I need to tell you?' He lay down, surrendering to her arms. 'Do we need to silence those chattering voices?'

He muttered a small 'Yes.'

'Here, let me hold your head.' She raised herself, lifted her hands and pressed her fingers against his forehead. 'There,' she said, 'all gone.' She turned back onto her side, her back to him, and pulled his arm around her, placing his hand on her breast, pushing her thighs and buttocks into his groin.

The last thought Viktor had before he fell asleep was *Does it even matter if she did?* She was here now and had given herself completely to their plans, to him. She had taken him back.

But two days later those words came to him again: 'I haven't had orgasms like that for ages.' The hymn of reassurances was wearing thin – and the simple, likely possibility that she might have been masturbating didn't even occur to him.

How could he believe Nina again if every time he asked her, with mock sincerity, to tell him everything, there was a new revelation? What did he want her to tell him? How often she had fucked and not told him? About that drunken, steamy night in Paris, years ago, when she was propositioned by a young – far too young – man who then introduced her to his friend and they got talking? Though this had happened before they were dating, it felt to him like duplicity; the very existence of her sexual life independent from him was a betrayal. 'It was one of those silly things,' she'd said, 'when you want to tick something off the list. The threesome felt so wrong, like porn,' she said. *You watch pornography?* Viktor thought. Another item from her list. Wasn't this a male fantasy – erotic dreams of girlfriends starring in duplicitous fuckathons?

We reassure ourselves that these fantasies are just the nightmares of our addled, wanton male brains, Viktor thought, *but it is not true. We really are being deceived. They really are fucking.*

What did Viktor even want? Did he want to feel bad? For his guts, his innards, to tremble? Perversely, he would have felt disappointed if he had not visited the underground pool that flowed quickly with the detritus of old memories. He needed to seek out that ancient sabotage and pain. With Nina Viktor felt alive, vital, only when he could reach into those buried waters and feel the jostling current breaking around his body.

He had become so overwhelmed that he concocted a solution to this fantasy infidelity, one that seemed to him both absurd and sure. He would have to fuck his way equal. Initially he thought it would only take one incident, though soon he realised that he would have to take into account the fact that she had probably screwed this man, this lover, continually for a few weeks – good solid fucking for at least two weeks. He would, in turn, have to make his calculation. At night Viktor shifted in bed, put his arm over Nina's sideward body. *Who could I find? Someone for quick, uncomplicated sex, someone like me, determined to get revenge, to equal up the relationship so we can love again with the old stability and parity, both bloated on half-truths.* He imagined the Nepali barista in the coffee booth with the thick, brown birthmark that stretched up her arm. He imagined them fucking on the counter with the shutter half down, takeaway cups and white lids falling to the floor, the ankles and shoes of commuters scurrying past. The thought pleased Viktor and almost cajoled him back to sleep.

*

Loneliness pulsed and throbbed in Biko and yet he – this man of great vision – did not see it. His loneliness was a craving for the past, for his family, for things which could never be recovered – for the time when his father was younger and Biko would stand by him at the end of the day, after they had eaten, and hear him speak about his own childhood, receive his bristled kisses. Or when he was a little older and running errands for his mother around the township. His need to be with his parents, to find himself in their presence, for them to crowd him, left him despising his own weakness. It drove him to work harder, to focus more on the tasks of now.

He had been a peculiar son. For an entire year his mother had won special dispensation from her husband to allow little Stephan to sleep in their room, at the bottom of their bed – it was years later, at university, that Stephan became simply 'Biko' and gave a second life to the murdered South African activist. His father grumbled and agreed. For the first weeks Biko slept, like a cat or dog, curled at their feet, his cover drawn tightly round him, a hand under their blanket holding onto his mother's ankle. Each concession was never enough; somehow he had clawed his way off the floor, into their bed, into their intimacy. And now sleep wasn't possible, for this inadequate seven-year-old, except through communion with his mother's leg.

'This can't go on. It mustn't go on,' Emmerson said one morning at the end of the first week of their threesome. 'He wants something from us that we can't give. He is finding his way between us, until soon he will lie right here,' he patted the spot next to him in the bed, 'and still it won't be enough, he will want more. He wants to climb right back inside both of us. We need to teach him to separate, or he'll start to resent us – he needs you to be firm. We mustn't spoil him, this child of independence, this born-free.'

Emmerson was right. Biko burrowed back *into* his parents, his hand creeping up his mother's leg until they woke one morning, in the second week of his migration to their bedroom, with his head peering over their cover, his lithe, willowy body squirming between them like an eel. His love for his parents was like hunger.

So a new bed was made up on the floor. Biko slept on pillows dragged every night into his parents' room. In her apron Biko's mother would kneel on the floor, panting, pressing the cushions together with a sheet, arranging the bed for their difficult son. The hard labour of the meal was hers, from washing the dishes in the plastic tub with soap and the garden hose to cooking the *sadza*, cutting the cheap, sinewy meat and frying it with onion. Each evening when the meal was finally served, the bubbles of perspiration on her forehead, Biko wondered how he could lessen the burden of his mother's crippling labour.

Now Biko worried that *he* was the source of her hardship, the reason she was constantly bent over the gas hob where she cooked for the family, and now over the bed she made for him every night in her room. His efforts to help were angrily chased away.

Lying on the floor of their room, away from their touch, his intimacy with his parents grew. It seemed to him as though he was being allowed to enter something entirely forbidden to children, some secret world of adult intimacy, the mystery of his parents' conversations and their physical union. He noticed how simple-minded was their trust. Now that he was on the floor and out of sight, they did not think of him and spoke freely, thinking their boy was asleep or, even if he wasn't, that he would not understand them. *Do they think I am like the dog, like our* inja *who sleeps in the dust on the veranda? Do they think I can't understand them?*

Several nights after his bed was made on their floor, he realised that their freedom to speak as though he wasn't present was not their underestimation of children, it was nothing so sophisticated: his parents were just *exhausted*. When he was not an actual presence, in front of them, between them, demanding their contact and love, he was rendered temporarily invisible.

From his floor hideout he discovered something even more devastating: that, despite the seemingly matter-of-fact relationship between his parents, which appeared to him like the arrangement of *amatshe*, the stones in the fields circling the township, what actually held them together was an entirely voluntary arrangement based on love. This revelation terrified Biko. Love? Love seemed to cast the entire edifice of his family life into the realm of terrible vulnerability. What if something happened to his father, who spoke in such soft, gentle tones to his mother, in words that made Biko sit up in his bed the first time he heard him and wonder who had crept into the room to love his mother? *Kulungile thandiwe, khathesi, ngizakulala njengengwenya.*

And his mother's confident teasing, her control of his father: 'You look like a crocodile when you have been asleep.'

'Maybe I am a crocodile – with a great hunger.' Biko heard the bed creak.

67

'And what are you going to do with that great hunger, old man? Do you still have the strength to swim in the water? *Amandla ethu njengengwenya emanzini ayesemphakathini.*'

The bed creaked and Biko felt his concentration sharpen, his pulse quickening. He worried that his parents would hear his heart pounding.

'Come here,' his mother ordered his father.

Biko, only slightly taller than the end of the bed, stood silently and stared at his parents as they made love. Rolling and tumbling on each other, his mother in charge – wielding his father on her, under her, instructing him silently, with Biko watching, breathless, at the end of the bed.

When it was over his father would always speak in Ndebele, not in the Elizabethan English he used when he taught, when he gave orders to Biko: '*Ngiyakuthanda.*' His mother would respond, 'I love you too, my crocodile.'

Biko would fall back into his bed as satisfied as his parents, disturbed by their need for each other, realising for the first time what was at stake in his family and in the world.

Despite the relative wealth of the family, fed for more than two decades on Emmerson's work in Bulawayo High School and for almost ten years by his role as principal, they lived modestly. His father's retreat from politics, measured in reverse proportion to his son's growing political preoccupation, left Biko with only the austerity he had practised as a young man. Austerity became his new creed. And as Biko grew older, his anger at his mother's labour was only tempered by what he now knew of his parents' real relationship.

'Father, why don't we buy a proper stove and a new sofa? Why don't we have a maid to help Mother?'

His father dropped his school bag on the floor, poured himself a mug of cheap red wine and fell onto the veranda sofa, the day ringing in his ears. 'What?'

Biko set up the fan for his father, pulled the cord though the window, turned the dial until the fan head picked up speed. 'Mother needs help. She does everything herself.'

A smile broke on Emmerson's face. 'Such duty as the subject owes the prince, such a woman oweth to her husband.'

Biko felt the blood in his face; he choked, 'You don't mean that. I know you don't. Women owe nothing to men, do they? Do they?'

Taking swigs of the wine, washing down the day, wanting the fog of forgetting to come, Emmerson widened his smile and told Biko to sit next to him. The sun was hazy in its retreat from the sky. On the horizon where it set, over the row of neat brick township houses, light broke through the torn and stretched clouds.

Biko was proud to be invited to sit next to his father, yet he was still angry. His father put his arm around his son's shoulder and said, 'You are a good boy, Stephan, you ask the right questions. Never stop asking, my son.'

Biko's stomach turned. He wanted to say something. Instead he stiffened against his father's arm. 'That's it,' Emmerson said, 'that's it, boy, rage, fight against us. That's the way.'

Chapter Seven

Viktor wasn't sure who Tendai had become in his life. They had barely known each other three years ago but now saw each other at the university every day. Tendai spoke to him with the most intense intimacy – about Viktor's crisis, his own, the situations in Zimbabwe, in England and the world. There was a mystery to his appearance, Viktor believed, that seemed esoteric – as though this tall, strange, brilliant man had arrived in his life to solve the riddle of *Viktor*'s existence. So, entirely typically, Viktor's understanding was both deeply egotistical – Tendai's arrival, his very purpose, was for Viktor's elucidation – and sexist, he would only realise years later. Only a man, like Jack, like his father, like bloody Verdi, could play the role of liberator and hero.

Tendai recognised his own intensity in Viktor. His next move, he decided, was to 'liberate' Viktor from his destructive obsession with his partner and child. A man must be freed. Only action, movement, could trample the long grasses of distraction.

'Therapy? Antidepressants?' Viktor flinched, wishing for a minute that he had not come to find Tendai, reading in the autumn sun, his feet resting on his cart. 'This is the privatisation of your despair, of everyone's. *This* is the thing that is making you sick. It *is* the source of your paralysis. Of your inaction. Even the brutal, soul-crushing poverty in Harare, in Cape Town's shanty towns, provides a rudimentary, imperfect collective cushion for humanity's need for recognition, Viktor. But your life here,' Tendai circled the air in front of him, then looked hard at Viktor, 'is in the pit, the rancid hole where you live.'

Viktor sighed. 'It's not *that* bad, Tendai.'

This was Tendai. One minute harsh, violent even in his analysis, his criticism relentless, and the next minute emollient and loving, ridiculously caring. His emails were like this too – written almost by another person, a sort of apology for anger and honesty. His caring contained practice and his words always spoke of action. Where most people finish a sentence with a full stop, Tendai finished with a solution: a telephone number, an instruction to move, to call, to travel, to act. A fucking *order*.

Recently Tendai had become convinced that his days of speaking to Viktor were over. His advice had not dislodged his friend from his predicament. Someone else had to work on him – tell him how it was, speak the truth of the world and get him moving again. And the only person he knew with a clarity of movement that equalled his own was Anne-Marie. Like him, she was a refugee from the continent's crisis, from fifty years of political failure and the long, slow death of the emancipatory promise of the sham of independence. Tendai believed that she understood, at least as clearly as he did, what life required.

'Speak to her, goddamn it, she will tell you about things,' Tendai had said finally, exasperated. His feet were now on the floor – ready to stand his ground against Viktor's objections.

'But why?'

'Because she is my friend. She is clearer about life than anyone I know – you'll never find a better comrade of humanity.'

Viktor leant hard on the railing, letting the ledge of the wall take his weight. 'So I should speak to her like a therapist, like these quacks you hate?'

'Goddamn it, just speak to her, man – about your bloody website, whatever it's called, *Refutations*. Interview her for *Refutations* if you like. She lives in Africa. She can be another one of your Third World Exhibits, your Honourable Blacks. Learn something.'

'It's called *Mutations*, Tendai. The website is *Mutations*.'

Tendai was silent. He regretted speaking so harshly. Automatically he started to compose the email he would send later to Viktor.

*

Rosa was asleep in the back of the car they had hired for the weekend. An article on *Mutations*, one of Viktor's own, 'Jouissance as Political Agent', had gone viral after Slavoj Žižek had responded to it. Žižek had hated it, but the advertisements on Viktor's blog – an unfortunate necessity – paid per impression. It was a windfall.

He floated home, above the pavement, half-expecting to be recognised in the street. Picking Rosa up from the nursery, he swung her in his arms, left her pushchair empty and folded in the hall and carried her with her face pressed against his, giggling and chatting as they walked home. He told Nina and received a kiss, planted wet and warm, firmly on his lips.

He took them away that weekend to a place he'd hired in Norfolk, a guest house. He and Nina made love in the long, narrow room, which held a kitchenette, bed and cot, fridge, microwave and a single book: *Literary History of East Anglia*. Rosa babbled in her cot at the end of their bed, laughing with them as they came.

'I suppose that's called a *ménage à trois*,' Viktor said.

'Viktor, that's terrible,' Nina teased.

In the morning they chased the retreating tide on the long beach, their feet sinking into the sand, the sun flashing on and off through the clouds. Rosa was drunk on the space, the great expanse, the undulating blond dunes spread out like a reclining naked body. They rolled down the sand mountains and forgot the city. Viktor held Nina's hand as Rosa played in the sand.

'We adapt, don't we,' Viktor said.

'What do you mean?' Nina asked as they ambled, zigzagging, along the beach.

'I mean we adapt as a species to beauty *and* horror. We got used to the killings of the First World War; life in the trenches became almost routine to the soldiers after a few weeks.' Viktor swept back his hair.

'Oh, Viktor.'

'No, listen,' Viktor lightened his tone. 'But we also respond quickly to beauty – and this,' he opened his arms, 'the sea, clean air, hope. The possibility that we can live differently.'

Nina took his arm, pulled him to her. 'Yes to beauty. Thank you for bringing us here, Viktor, darling. Maybe we should move out of the city, get away from the trenches and killing and let Rosa run on beaches.'

Rosa slept noisily as Viktor drove. An hour from London Nina turned her phone on, her face lit up by the white glare. They saw the grainy vision of the city in the distance; the tops of high-rise blocks shimmered into focus as they reached the summit of the motorway, then went out of view, lost as the night choked and blurred the horizon. In the darkness

73

the fields on each side of the road fell away, leaving only the motorway.

Nina laughed as she read aloud from her phone. 'Listen to what Jo sent me. "Dear Nina, I can't begin to thank you for your wise advice and calm counsel. I miss having you nearby, your positive, loving presence." That's nice, isn't it?'

'Lovely. Isn't it interesting that all your friends and family see you as vivacious, dynamic and wise?'

'What do you mean?'

'That you're a very good friend, wise and positive. Of course, in our intimate relationships we are always so much more.'

When they arrived Rosa thrashed in Nina's arms, resisting her forced removal from the car to the flat and bed: the expression of their collective resistance against the return home.

Viktor folded his clothes, turned back a corner of the duvet and got into bed wearing his saggy pants and vest. He picked up his bedside book.

'She's down.' Nina came into their room, stood at the foot of the bed and removed her clothes, letting them tumble onto the floor. 'Isn't it interesting how you don't see me as wise and vivacious?'

'What?' Viktor looked at Nina over his book, his head spinning with words from his novel.

O Tania, where now is that warm cunt of yours, those fat, heavy garters, those soft, bulging thighs? There is a bone in my prick six inches long. I will ream out every wrinkle in your cunt, Tania, big with seed. I will send you home to your Sylvester with an ache in your belly and your womb turned inside out. Your Sylvester! Yes, he knows how to build a fire, but I know how to inflame a cunt.

'I mean, you said my friends and family see me as wise and dynamic, but you don't.'

Viktor felt his stomach rise, pass his chest through his lungs, squeeze into his throat. He didn't answer, but tried to concentrate on the page.

I shoot hot bolts into you, Tania, I make your ovaries incandescent. Your Sylvester is a little jealous now? He feels something, does he? He feels the remnants of my big prick. I have set the shores a little wider; I have ironed out the wrinkles.

After a minute he filled his lungs and spoke. 'I didn't say that. How can you think I would have said that? I was saying the opposite.' Viktor lifted the book so it covered his face.

'I think you shouldn't be reading that book in the house – it's disgusting.' Nina leant towards him, snatched the book and straightened herself to read aloud. '"After me you can take on stallions, bulls, rams, drakes, St Bernards. You can stuff toads, bats, lizards up your rectum. You can shit arpeggios if you like, or string a zither across your navel. I am fucking you, Tania, so that you'll stay fucked. And if you are afraid of being fucked publicly I will fuck you privately." The book is disgusting and misogynistic!' She threw the book at him. It folded and the spine hit his shoulder.

'It's one of the last century's most important novels.' Viktor breathed in, took the book and found his page.

'You shouldn't leave it around where Rosa could find it.'

'What? Rosa's a baby, how will she read Henry Miller?'

'God knows how it's affecting your thinking.'

'It's literature.'

'Misogyny, not literature.'

'I'm not having this conversation.' Viktor continued to read.

I will tear off a few hairs from your cunt and paste them on Boris' chin. I will bite into your clitoris and spit out two franc pieces ...

Nina came up to him, put her hand on the top of his book, and pulled it down.

'How would you feel if I said: isn't it interesting how all your friends and colleagues think you are so smart but I know that underneath you're not? That I know you're unoriginal and simple.'

'That's a low blow, Nina.'

'Well, how do you think it made me feel? I just want you to understand.'

'Congratulations on making me feel terrible. Is that what you wanted?'

Nina left the room. Viktor heard the water from the shower, the rattle as the curtain slid along the rail. He turned the book over, put his hand on the cover, tried to steady himself. *Cunt*, he muttered, *you are a nasty fucking cunt, Nina.*

Nina let the water slam against her body, stream through her hair, crash and fall over her shoulders, run down her breasts.

Viktor reached for the antidepressants, pressed out the dose, threw the two pills to the back of his throat and took a gulp of water. He waited for the dizzying rush of sleep. *We drug ourselves to survive the relationship*, he thought. *A whole life spent in a single lie — avoiding each other, anaesthetising against the pain of having to be together.*

Viktor thought he could hear Nina crying in the shower. He muttered to himself, powerless, pathetic, Miller on his lap and his throat dry. *Our survival depends on drugs, separation in the week* and TV. Why don't I have the courage to name it, have it out, leave her? Why don't I have the firm, resolute guts of Miller? To fuck and move on? Use my dick to guide me through life, to iron out the creases of existence, to fuck cunt after cunt? I don't take my writing seriously enough, I don't have his confidence, Miller's cocksure certainty in his art — his wilfulness, his anger, his agency to make, create, to delineate a path through all of the cunts.

Nina was talking loud enough for Viktor to hear. 'I have the power to change. I see my patterns and choose to make changes.' Through the sound of the water he heard her repeating the words a counsellor had taught her to relieve the pressure, to focus on herself: 'I see my patterns and choose to make changes.'

It's no good, Viktor thought, tears choking him, his face twisted. The cunt is no solace. He was not Miller: his feelings, his sadness, his sensitivities were visible on his skin. He could not get out. Nina was completely right, about Miller and him and this age-old male pact of misogyny. Through the haze of anger, through his hurt, Viktor could see it; he could see himself. He swung his feet off the bed, put a hand on the wall to steady himself and felt the drug spread and stretch inside him, extend through his body. He made his way to the bathroom.

Chapter Eight

Viktor felt feverish. He dropped his pen, felt his heart race and put his forehead into his hands, resting his elbows on the desk. Sucking in deeply, he could smell the room, the office, the dust, the evening, for the first time. Slowly, he resumed writing.

> Under this dialectic we are crushed by the normal course of events, by daily life. The weight, the pressure of existence, the contradictions and confrontations, mean that we are gradually, inevitably destroyed. Like all living things.

Viktor had five minutes to write before he was due to connect to Anne-Marie. Since the strange email Tendai had sent to them both ordering their connection, they had spoken on the phone briefly. Then, strangely, they had started to text each other and send messages on Facebook. The smokescreen for their connection was collaboration on a series of short articles and interviews for *Mutations*, intended to expose the deceit of Mugabe's left turn, his rural support base and the programme of land reform. Anne-Marie was an insider, a cynical practitioner of microfinance, rural grass-roots development and self-help for women. She worked for Rural Lives, a Southern African NGO funded by USAID – or, as she had said on their first call, 'We call it US-CIA. They are an arm of the US government, but we take their money and try not to follow too many orders – we refuse to carry out open assassinations.' She had laughed loudly.

Viktor read his words again. Should he read them to her? Already he knew that he was thinking about her too much – that the lines had become blurred. Viktor focused, forcing his pen back to the page, to the copy he was writing for the website.

But *Mutations*, this site, our project, does not refer to the personal mutation and dialectic that creates and destroys each of us, from acorn to oak tree to extinction. We mean the radical mutation of political action and movement.

'Fucking hell,' Viktor said suddenly, aloud. 'It's too bloody scholastic. It's not a chapter in my PhD.'

*

Comrade (wrote Tendai),

Apologies for sending you these electronic letters, but things need to be said – today more than ever. And you need to hear them. So I have written a short message on the latest stage, as I see it, of the capitalist offensive and revolution and how capitalist society as Marx wrote cannot 'exist without revolutionising the instruments of production and thereby the relations of production and social relations … and all their train of ancient and venerable prejudices'.

I offer – confidentially, for your eyes only, so don't post it on your website – a flavour of the shifts, changes, refounding landscape of politics around us as real revolutions clarify, open eyes, awaken and alert as yet unknowable numbers of people. The point? This is to help revolutionaries express and organise the coming revolt.

Please take my advice, as my friend, and for now – keep your counsel, watch, listen, read with refounded critical concentration and attention to what is going on. The *cuts* will test us as never before. Immense social forces – capital and the trade union bureaucracy – are moving against our interests. All that was apparently solid is about to melt into air and a whole new period is about to begin – not only here on this miserable island, but across the West and in Africa, despite all non-working-class layers attempts to freeze-preserve, maintain and secure the old status quo.

I understand that things are as unstable at the moment for you as they are for me. When you've got yourself some sort of base/stability, there is a great deal of good news. I may even be able to get you a room where I am staying if you finally decide to leave your wife and daughter. (I can do this with consummate ease as I am the bane of the multinational management here – they have never seen such ferocious, unapologetic blackness in their lives.) But for now, my dear friend, weather your storm and think of the BIG fundamentals.

Remember, you command great respect among so many – your website could be an instrument for reaching and reviving those who have been beaten. But we need to be patient. As Lenin put it, 'Sometimes, there are times when it is good to NOT be in the lead, shaping things, but to be watching, observing, learning. Have the spirit to recognise when something new – a change – must be wrought in reality and in ourselves. Until then, learn, accept that we don't hold sway.' When was that? Early 1917. He was absolutely correct, though he underestimated the progress of the change a bit. So regard this as no originality or presumption on my part – it is Lenin's!

Though, thinking about it again, you have the opposite problem: you tend to sit back and observe too much, so you should discount this lesson from Lenin.

However, in a few weeks, much will have been clarified, and much of it by reality itself.

At university last week you asked how my life is. You said you detect that I am wholly alive, vibrant with activity, contacts – in Africa, which I maintain on an almost daily basis – and that my learning curve is flying off the radar. And in this observation, com, you are correct. Some time ago I abandoned all my other reading, the poetry, the novels and other researches, and from the start of the Tunisian revolution on 17 December last year with my then-lover – who had to return to Botswana – I have been following events obsessively. Sadly, my Botswanan lover left also with her expertise in social media and her ability to record and download the entire cycle of revolutions in our time.

I have spread this information to hundreds of contacts and comrades, in the UK, Europe and in Africa. Real revolution ALWAYS refounds our ideas by a period and process of CRISIS. This is what we are now living through. So yes, as a result, not only have I had the incomparable privilege of forty years as a conscious revolutionary, though for twenty of these years I was under the illusions of Black nationalism – a necessary stage for all conscious revolutionaries from Southern Africa. For ten years I entered a harder school of isolation, and in the last decade I have been active in small groups, but numbers are growing – now my abilities are taking off as never before. I have never known anything like this political vantage point in my mind.

I owe 99% to the work of the Society of Liberated Minds in Zimbabwe, no doubt about it. The Society was my touchstone, bedrock and concrete founding floor. We used to say, 'We are not tall, but we stand on the shoulders of giants.' And still I have so much to learn – and so do you, Viktor. Since coming to this Dark Continent I've continued to read most of Lenin, Trotsky, Marx, but also reread Cabral, Fanon and Biko. If apartheid prison taught me anything, it was how to study. Those six know more of revolutions – the whole process – than anyone else.

I've now spent two solid years – in a sense – rereading EVERYTHING. Hence my verbosity and outpourings to you! It is both timely and apt. This is the most important work of our lives NOW.

I can only say in conclusion – you may not be the only comrade coming to live here – I know we are still cogitating on that, but there are many good options. For yourself – as I have known you as a comrade and friend – I DO think it makes a lot of sense to live around with me, away from your privatised hell, if you can afford it. Your daughter too can come and stay and we can bring her up together. Obviously I'd be delighted if you were to be here. We must never underestimate the revolutionary power of children, to grasp the essential, to fight with ferocity, for the revolution. Our power and impact would be RENEWED.

And from our conversation at university it sounds like you need a break – and, if a com like you, a cadre of importance, does not have a regular place away from domestic misery, you may break. I have seen it happen. So I want you to know that it would not go astray for you to know that, come whatever, you have a solid old friend and comrade here. It's good to know such things and enjoy them when you've taken a knock. You stand by me and I stand by you. Isn't this what we understand by communism?

I have been drugging my sleep almost continually for years, a mixture of sleeping pills, antihistamines, alcohol and sex. I haven't told anyone this, but if I wake in the night I not only can't sleep but I start to despair – which is close to fucking total. And the worst part of the despair? Defeat. I fear that we have been defeated so often that we won't ever be able to win. So this thing I offer you – solidarity – as I have done for a long time now, is not an act of imagination. NEVER. It's just the simple solidarity of SHARING. We share the pain, the torment, the fucking hell of it all.

If you have £530 per month, no further bills, you could come and live here – in this hostel where I stay. You will have what you don't at the moment, with this situation you're in, namely ME.

The battle commences in days, at the latest in weeks and the epicentre in London is our university. Together, Viktor, we can observe and study the fundamentals AND put into practice our plans.

All the best to you, friend, yours in struggle always,

Tendai

*

From the house there was the din of voices, laughter, shouts of argument, one over the other, each trying to be heard. Biko tried to make sense of them. It worried him that his cadre, these brothers and sisters, were making this noise when they needed rest, when they should be planning and sleeping. This was the moment when anxiety flooded him. As usual it made him irritated, and his frustration turned on Anne-Marie for provoking his doubt, for making him question. He knew there would be violence tomorrow, and in some senses this violence would have been triggered by him, *his* decisions and *his* agency. But he also knew that nothing moved in Zimbabwe without violence. With this one fact, the whole of physics had been rewritten to account for the peculiarity of Southern African underdevelopment: from the Limpopo in the South to Kariba in the North, the law now stated that uniform motion tends to remain in that state of motion unless external violence is applied to it by ZANU-PF. Students would be bloodied, even hospitalised.

Biko tried to locate the cricket in the garden of the squat that kept him awake at night. He could hear it now, loud and angry. He moved around the dry, dirty garden with the unwatered tree and dying plants. Words from the house reached him. Eleanor's, the most determined voice: 'Say there is a low turnout, which might be a possibility. I want to sacrifice my blood meaningfully, for a revolution which is going to be a success. Better to die defending an idea that you know will eventually become a success than to continue for an idea that will not succeed at the end of the day.'

At the end of the day, Biko repeated softly, smiling to himself. The chirping became louder when he stood still. The cricket didn't hear him coming. Seeing the small black shape on the ground, under the tree – *so damn small, but what a noise, what capacity* – Biko hesitated, then bent quickly down and scooped it up in a handful of dry earth. He felt the insect twitch in his hand as he walked to the wall at the back of the house and threw the ball of soil hard, over the neighbouring house, into the sky. *Tomorrow is going to be the start of something — a new start.*

Chapter Nine

Even when he was with Rosa he had started to think about Anne-Marie, and with Nina she had become his salvation. She was wherever he went in the routine of their life together: when he cooked, tidied his daughter's room, washed her at night. And in bed with Nina as well. Too exhausted and bored to make love, lying with the covers between them, Viktor thought of Anne-Marie's grainy image on Skype, her wide, open face, her laughter, which held no doubt or hesitation. In the images of Anne-Marie that he had found on Google she was speaking at conferences, in donor seminars, professional, assertive and impossibly, irresistibly foreign. And then there were the photos she'd sent him, weeks ago.

At the end of their first call, Anne-Marie's face barely lit, the connection unusually clear, she had said, 'It seems a pity to leave it here.'

Viktor swallowed hard, rushed to agree. 'Yes, a pity. Maybe we could exchange numbers and set up another interview.' This pretext for another conversation was thin. 'We could work more on the articles and interviews we spoke about.' But why exchange numbers? Why fucking *telephone* numbers? Viktor thought afterwards. It was practically nineteenth-century – yet, oddly, it seemed more appropriate than exchanging emails or following each other on Twitter. It was intimate.

On his way home after the first call Viktor had hurriedly sent Anne-Marie a text, unable to stop himself, his fingers slipping on the phone, composing, deleting, retyping. *Very good to make this connection. Fascinating. Delighted to hear about Zimbabwe's* jambanja. *Soon. V.* Even with the casual veneer of a text, the immediacy of his message was obvious.

For a few moments Viktor had felt guilt-stricken, full of the agony of duplicity, the knowledge of what was going to happen. Then his phone buzzed.

Anne-Marie had texted back immediately. *Likewise, Viktor. Impressed with your knowledge of the struggle. Let's Skype again soon. In the meantime this is for you #BlackWoman.* Then, inexplicably, with no forewarning, she sent a photo of herself – taken in the flat in the seconds after the call. With a pale, naked bulb above her, she stood resolute in a brightly coloured flowered shirt and dark skirt, her hair plaited and twisted on her head.

This was enough to burst Viktor's reticence. Stumbling, he texted her as he found his way out of the university to the tube, his head bowed to the phone that seemed to pull him forward, draw him through life, along the pavements, across roads. In five minutes it all came out. He told her about Nina. His crisis. His daughter. His dilemma. Bemused and excited, Anne-Marie, after a pause, spoke of her own situation – and so in fifteen minutes they revealed everything to each other about their lives. Their connection was a strange, instantaneous twinning of London and Harare: frustrated and unquenched love in the Global North and South.

This had been weeks ago, and now their connection was established. Fixed.

Viktor sat back from his desk, stretched, clicked on his mouse, opened Facebook and hurriedly sent a message to Nina that he was working late with one of his classes. It was already dark, and the lights flickered on automatically in the shared office. He pressed send.

His phone rattled slightly with an incoming message.

Sorry Vik. Can we do the call later, or text, the connection is terrible and it will only FRUSTRATE us? AM x

Viktor hurriedly replied. What did she mean? Frustration because they couldn't consummate the desire to see each other, to see each other's flickering, sepia faces on Skype? Or just the frustration of intermittent disconnection?

The dialectic was playing itself out – Anne-Marie's evening was ripe with change, the possibility of rupture.

At the end of the meeting tonight Anne-Marie was going to tell Nelson that she wanted a break. She wore her black heels and a suit jacket over a long, billowing skirt, her breasts pressed against the shirt buttons. She mouthed the words to herself as she drove with slow, careful purpose from town into the avenues. *I travel too much, Nelson. It's no good how you turn up without warning, expecting sex, and after two days we separate without plans. If I am going to carry on with the Society of Liberated Minds, we need distance.* She could see him already, with a slight smile, his head cocked to the side, listening to her, and then the arguments and charm that he would command into a dreadful stream of persuasion.

Cars and minibuses swerved around potholes, the drivers pressing hard on their horns as if navigation was commanded by sound, not sight. Despite her effort to drive, Anne-Marie heard Nelson's voice, tuneful, eloquent; she saw his hair bundled carelessly in a plastic band, his whole body moving, dancing to his words, declaiming dictatorship, each sentence delivered with a shrug, his hands flat, palms up, reaching into the room, serving his sentences, asking his comrades, the flat, the room, the country, for benediction. He would speak to Anne-Marie in the same musical cadences and tell her that they were meant to be together. As she got out of the car her heel got caught in a pavement grille. She balanced on one foot and bent down, prised out the heel, dusted the shoe free of dirt. *I won't be able to do it. I need him. I fucking need him.*

*

Nina felt pleased with herself. There had been progress. They had been text-messaging while Viktor was at the office and they had somehow managed to communicate – free from having to stand in front of each other, the barriers of frequency, the contempt of household familiarity. Rosa was occupied on the floor of the lounge, her pens and paper out, bent over in concentration, her tongue sticking out of the side of her mouth.

Nina went into the kitchen, calling to Rosa that she had ten minutes before she had to change into her pyjamas. Only then would she be allowed to eat with Daddy when he came home late from work. Concentrating intently on her stick-figure drawings of her friends and the family, the radiant, hallucinogenic sky, the arch of an impossibly beautiful rainbow, Rosa didn't answer.

For now, Nina felt cleansed. Happy, even. She leant over the oven, opened the door a crack. Hot, scented air bellowed up. The meal would be perfect. She would get Rosa ready for bed. Nina would have a shower before bed and brush her teeth, and then they could make love. The thought of holding Viktor in

89

bed for the first time in weeks, his thin, stringy body pressed hard against her, made her stomach jump. She smiled.

'Darling, please pack up and put on your PJs.' There was a flash of something in Nina's head. Déjà vu? She couldn't find the memory. She pulled the plates out of the cupboard above the sink, placed the glasses on the work surface. Nina heard Rosa humming something to herself as she walked past the kitchen to her bedroom.

Suddenly the memory came to her clearly. She saw herself leaning over her homework at the kitchen table, thirty years ago. Her mother had come in and there was lightness in her movements. Her father was cooking, his back to the door – he was wearing the kitchen apron. Nina didn't want to disturb them, so she kept her head down, focused on her project, and pretended to be invisible. Her mother went silently up to her husband and curled her arms around his waist, stood on her tiptoes and kissed him on the back of the neck. Nina was embarrassed and pleased. She lowered her head even further to the page.

In the kitchen tonight she could smell her father's cooking. How was that possible? Had she really cooked exactly the same meal – the apple crumble, the boiled potatoes, the lamb chops? And the love? The love was the same as well. The way she felt for Viktor, remembering her parents. Why had she been in such a rush for Rosa to clear up? She should have left her. Nina called into the corridor, 'Darling, Rosa, when you've changed you can continue drawing if you like – until Viktor's back from work.'

*

The demonstration was a stunt. Students, cleaners, security guards and union members had occupied the university lobby.

Some wore costumes: top hats, badly fitting suits, overalls and dungarees. The revolving door spun, depositing people into the performance. The entire hall, in all its marble, polished brass and varnished wood, throbbed to the beat of drums as the players took their places for this parody of the university. Fat-cat executives, VCs, deans and professors – a detail that appealed to Viktor – in pinstriped suits ordered the cleaners, who knelt on all fours, to scrub the floor. The drum, beating slowly, conducted the action.

Viktor recognised the cast: the cleaners, Rejoice, Moreblessing, Patience, bent over like dogs. The fat cats and professors were played by the graduate students Gary and Wayne. The lift opened, emptying more students and sympathisers into the reception hall. Others stood clapping at the side, taking photos or filming the scene on their phones.

Tendai stood unchanged by the reception desk in his BCW uniform, his lapels ablaze with badges and stickers, a megaphone to his lips. 'What you can see before you is a typical day at the university. The cleaners, those on the floor, ordered, bossed, bullied by the men in the hats, to clean, wash, scrub, so your university, this centre of learning and civilisation' – Tendai spat the words out – 'is in perfect, absolute cleanliness, but they do it on poverty wages.'

Viktor skirted the performance. The impromptu audience, two lines thick, watched confused. The security guards stood stiffly, speaking softly into their collar radios and waiting for their orders. Viktor made his way to Wayne, who was handing out leaflets: CAMPAIGN FOR THE LONDON LIVING WAGE. EQUALITY FOR ALL MEMBERS OF STAFF. Then the same words written in Polish and Spanish and, for effect, Shona. *Campaña por un salario digno. Kampania na rzecz płacy. Mushandirapamwe nokuti muLondon mhenyu mubayiro. Kuenzana*

91

nokuti nhengo dzose netsvimbo. Wayne divided the leaflets and handed a bundle to Viktor.

'Now take the man wearing the suit,' Tendai continued quickly, changing tack. 'He is the vice chancellor. His name is Rory Reynolds and he earns £160,000 a year. He has private health insurance and subsidised accommodation. He works a three-day week.' This information was all true.

The crowd pushed their way forward, jostled to reach the stalls. Those further back craned, stood on their toes, peered at the stage from the circle, the upper circle, the balcony.

Viktor saw the lift open and shut. Suddenly Terry, the union secretary, was standing in the foyer: Viktor could make out his squat, broad body, his red face, the upturned nose, the exposed, flaring nostrils. Terry shook his head to the beat of the drum.

'This man, this fat cat, the VC, prides himself on outsourcing the cleaners to BCW. The dirty work is carried out by fat cat number two.' Tendai pointed with his free hand at a performer, who spun round, showing the audience a figure two printed on an enormous raffle ticket pinned to his back. People laughed.

Terry continued to shake his head, standing motionless in the lobby.

'This man is Peter Green, another pig,' Tendai said, pointing to Number Two. The audience laughed again. 'He is friends with Rory. They went to the same school. Peter is the chief executive in charge of BCW. He earns more than £300,000 per year, plus benefits. It would take Patience thirty years to earn this, but she will be dead long before that. So have you got it? Rory contracts Peter to exploit Patience. Okay, man, now you're getting it. So when you shit, it is Patience who cleans the bowl. Do you now see how the circle is completed? Rory, Peter, Patience and *you* complete the circle. Seal the pact. All of you are human beings; only Patience is a slave, and Peter and

Rory are masters. Just like you – some masters, some slaves. Only you know who you are.' Tendai paused. There was nervous laughter. 'And for those of you who do not know, or who have yet to find your rank, you need to decide whose side you're on.'

Terry's face shone red and swollen. His ears twitched. He walked around the inner circle of the production, along the stage. As he approached Tendai, Viktor could see that his body, his shoulders, his entire self, his ontology, vibrated with disagreement. Terry reached towards Tendai and put his hand out for the megaphone.

Viktor felt a surge of satisfaction. He'd been so close to missing the protest. If he had, he'd never have grasped the relations of oppression, the connections between Patience, Moreblessing, Peter, Rory; between the union, the university and his own work, the PhD; the hegemonic structure of meaning, power, oppression and this, this circus protest, this vaudeville act. Everything was linked, everything came together, the disjointed activities of his life united. Viktor opened his notebook, blood pounding in his ears, and scribbled.

*

The peculiarity of this call, on this night, was that Viktor managed to conduct two conversations, two utterly distinct communications, with two different women, demonstrating a capacity to separate himself that bordered on pathological. And he succeeded. Though he did not mark this night as a turning point, that early autumn evening in the quiet of his university office, that simultaneous, frenzied conversation with two women, was the start of the rupture that followed. The adjacent conversations were held with Anne-Marie, in her messy, bleak apartment in downtown Harare, and with Nina,

93

as she prepared their meal in the flat that they rented with their daughter.

Viktor was really good at this remote fucking – it had the tidy intimacy, the mannerisms and control that spoke to his deepest habits. He could be whatever he wanted, generous and poised, perfectly in control, without the danger of feeling too much or being too implicated in actual human interaction. He was a purveyor of laconic imagery, of the perfect text message. He may not have invented social media, but he was its most adept user.

So his SMS texts to Anne-Marie, his declarations of desire and want, were effortlessly compressed in a few suggestive, brilliant understatements. What an incredible lover he was, in this game of virtual existence.

Sex had been almost entirely driven out of his relationship with Nina; he still desired her, but he didn't want to be disrupted by sex. So he masturbated in the bathroom, over the toilet, kicking Rosa's stool aside, to memories of their lovemaking. And now to fantasies of Anne-Marie, brought to life through her texts, by their sexting.

But in his effort to bring all the force of his incomprehension to his fists, he was now hammering repeatedly at his relationship with Nina. He could feel the force of the blows, the vibration from his own beatings, shuddering through him.

In the middle of a steamy text exchange with Anne-Marie, Nina responded to him on Facebook Messenger – his laptop was open, the message flashed up. *Darling, take your time. I am playing with Rosa and I have your favourite pudding in the oven. Don't work too hard. N xxx*

Viktor's stomach twisted; he felt sick. He put the phone down, leant forward to the keyboard and typed: *I am working.*

Please don't put pressure on me to return. Can you put Rosa to bed for a change?

There was a delay of a few minutes. His concentration was total. He tapped furiously to Anne-Marie, *I kneel down and unzip your skirt.*

Nina responded: *I don't understand. I was telling you to take your time.*

Viktor responded quickly: *Please, leave me to teach.*

Nina's response came quickly: *Leave you? You don't realise how that hurts me. You are everything Viktor, do you understand? EVERYTHING.*

The room was dark, his movements slight — holding the phone in his hands to communicate with Anne-Marie, leaning slightly forward to answer Nina on the computer.

His phone buzzed. Anne-Marie had replied: *I tilt my head back and inhale deeply.*

Viktor typed quickly, without hesitating or searching for words: *I slowly pull down your skirt and run my hands over your panties.*

He reached for the keyboard of the computer. *I hear what you say but feel the latent threat in it and it makes me worried ...*

My god Viktor, where is the threat? Nina typed.

Viktor replied, *You question our relationship.*

A moment later Nina's reply came. *You are everything Viktor, I am being honest. I'm not just saying nice things, this is serious. Can you handle those feelings? Rosa is asking for you.*

His fingers stumbling on the keyboard, Viktor wrote: *I can handle them if I know they are not being dangled or pulled away. You do upset me.*

I can't help it.

We can always help it. You pull away or make the love and commitment conditional. I'll do the same to you, you'll see.

Why do you want to stay angry with me? Nina responded.

Anne-Marie was lying on her bed, her bare legs crossed, the window in her bedroom open, letting the echo of car doors slamming, children shouting, the smell of cooking spiral slowly into her flat. She typed calmly, amused: *I run my hands through your hair. I trace your face with my fingers.*

I am not angry, Viktor answered Nina.

What must I do? Please. Nina asked.

I am not angry.

I'm worry that you pull away.

We are not doing so great at communicating these days, he wrote.

What do you mean?

Viktor didn't respond. Leaning back on his chair, deftly, effortlessly, he tapped on his phone: *I slowly pull down your panties.*

Nina messaged again. *You have my H.*

Thanks, and you mine — for what it's worth.

Mine beats only for you and Rosa. You don't have a V though and you have that as well.

Anne-Marie answered. *I push myself towards you, you kiss me and touch me. You use your tongue.*

What's a V?

Come on, sweetie. Surely it's not only my heart that you have.

Sitting back again in the chair, Viktor stretched his arms out. The light in the room came on. He texted Anne-Marie: *Gently I run my hands up your naked back. I reach your breasts.*

Then he reached for the keyboard and typed. *Vitriol? Your Victimhood? Viagra?*

Closer.

Valium?

It's not Valium. Are you that far away from my Vagina?

96

Anne-Marie swallowed, dried one of her hands on the cover, and replied. *I want to see you. I tell you to stand and we kiss. I take you to the bed.*

Keeping up the pace, understanding the game, Viktor tapped quickly to Anne-Marie on the phone keys: *I want to be inside you. I want to feel you on me.*

Nina typed back. *You haven't seen it much lately. Maybe you can get reacquainted with it later in the week? Tonight?*

Viktor was silent again. He rubbed his hands on his trousers, picked up his phone and focused. The excitement gripped them both. Anne-Marie ran her free hand across her breasts, along her stomach and slowly down. Then she slipped two fingers back inside the soft cotton of her underwear and rocked her hips forward.

Why no answer to my suggestion?

I know how you like to plan your V action, so maybe we could schedule something for the end of next week if you have a slot available.

Don't worry … if it's too much hassle for you …

Anne-Marie had answered, *I am wet and ready for you. I want you now.*

It's true, I have been feeling unsexy, sweetie, Viktor typed rapidly on the computer.

Nina responded, *I feel sexual when I'm around you, we create an energy between us that feeds my libido.*

Viktor answered, feeling an ache in his back, *I have no libido at the moment. No libido, as in none.*

His mouth was dry with desire. He dropped a hand into his lap and stroked his erection through the thin cotton of his trousers. With his other hand he wrote quickly, *I pull you onto the bed and move slowly onto you.*

When are you coming home?

I am trying to teach but I keep getting messages, god knows what my students must think. He typed this slowly, with his right hand.

Let them go. Come home.

Viktor was silent.

Nina messaged again. *Sweetie, are you okay? When are you leaving? I love you so, so much.*

Not long now. I will leave in ten minutes.

Then I am sending all my love and signing off. There can be a sweet absence of words for once, until I see you.

Viktor pushed the laptop away, tilted on his chair, and started to compose his next message to Anne-Marie.

Chapter Ten

The torn clouds spread across the week and separated the outbursts, turning their peace into a no-man's-land. Nina and Viktor dug into separate trenches until the clouds broke, but soon enough the downpour muddied the fields again. Viktor became convinced that there was no more hope that the fields could recover, that he could lay down a bed of grass, give them, at least, a place to plant their feet. Instead they disturbed the ground, kept the earth ploughed and sodden by their fights.

'The moon has a message for me.' Nina looked up at the almost full yellow globe in the clear, starless sky.

'A message for all of us, surely,' Viktor answered.

Still gazing at the moon, Nina was quiet. 'No, I think it has a meaning for me. I need to understand what it is trying to say.'

Viktor walked ahead to the stairwell and started to climb. 'Maybe the whole universe is trying to tell you something. Perhaps we are all here to help your spiritual journey.'

Nina didn't reply. On the landing of the first floor he looked down at her from the closed window. She was standing in the same spot, her face beatific. The moon too was radiant. Viktor almost believed that they really were communing – the moon and Nina. Maybe she was right and the moon, full and expectant, shone for her benediction and enlightenment. *This sickness isn't even narcissism,* he thought, *it's a deeper affliction that she sees in everything she reads, every random constellation of trees, clouds, animals, a hidden meaning trying to reveal itself to her. Why can't she be a proper spiritualist in a church,* Viktor thought, *where at least some of the teaching requires a selfless commitment to others?*

'Viktor, do you think I am psychic?' Nina shouted from the kitchen.

Rosa was in bed. Nina brought in bowls of pasta, tomatoes and bacon and wedged herself into the foam embrace of the sofa's arm. Viktor sat in the other corner, his legs bent under him. The TV was broken, so they watched DVDs on Nina's computer, placed on an upturned cardboard box.

'Can we speak first? I feel as though we haven't spoken for days.' Viktor had wanted the words to come out sympathetically; instead he sounded angry.

Nina leant forward and folded the computer closed.

Viktor spoke nervously. 'How was your day? I wanted to see how you were feeling about the interview tomorrow.'

'You remembered.'

'Of course I did.' Viktor was annoyed.

'I feel tired. Like I want to eat.' She indicated the bowl in her hand. 'I want to watch an episode and then sleep early so I am ready for tomorrow.'

'Are you prepared? Do you want a mock interview? Christ, I really want you to get it.' The interview for the promotion would also make Nina's job permanent.

'Well, we both need proper jobs, Viktor.' Nina reached forward for her food.

'Just the thought of more doubt and worry about the rent, or having to move again. It's destabilising. Hard to write. The job would change that.'

'Thanks for the support.' Nina spoke with irony heavy in her voice. She cradled the bowl.

'Anything else?' Viktor asked.

'No. Nothing. You?'

'I think I made a breakthrough with the thesis. I moved chapter nine to chapter five and removed chapter four. The argument with Foucault, his analysis of 1968 from Tunis, I can turn that into an article.' Viktor was eager to say that he had taken an important step towards completing the PhD – from becoming to being. From finishing to finished. He wanted to explain to Nina what he meant.

Nina coiled the pasta round her fork and forced herself to continue. 'So I spoke to my sister. She had just got back from seeing a psychic. She's made an appointment for me.'

'You're going to see a psychic?' Viktor felt offended.

'Yes. I have seen psychics before. This one is recommended.'

'But you don't know anyone who is dead.'

Nina ignored him, filled her mouth with spaghetti, bit off the strands, let them fall into the bowl.

'I've seen a medium on many occasions. Four times, I think. The last time she taught me how to tap.'

'Tap?'

Nina sighed loudly. 'I've told you, there are pressure points. It's called the Emotional Freedom Technique. Tapping with the fingertips to input kinetic energy on the head and chest while I think about a specific problem, and as I tap I make a series of positive affirmations about my life.' With the fork resting upright in the bowl, Nina demonstrated and tapped two fingers on her wrist.

Viktor's laugh was cruel. 'You can't be serious.'

Nina breathed in deeply, put the bowl down and looked at Viktor for the first time. 'Open your mind.'

Viktor bristled. 'My mind is open, too bloody open.'

Nina sighed again.

'It sounds like bullshit.' Viktor put his feet down, adjusted his position and turned to Nina. He didn't know where his anger had come from.

'And you sound like someone who doesn't understand what you're talking about.' Nina spoke calmly.

Viktor's chest heaved, his mouth dried. 'You are so uncritical. Is there nothing that you doubt or question? You sound like a hippy airhead. Psychics and the Emotional Tapping Technique. Does anything go?'

'I don't need this, Viktor.'

'What is it with your family?'

'Viktor, stop.'

'Anything goes, I suppose. Wizards, witches, psychics, tarot, unicorns – it's ridiculous.'

'And your family?' Nina screamed, finally breaking. 'Isaac, Sonia, Amy? The most egocentric, small-minded idiots I have ever met!'

'At least we know about death.'

'*You* don't know about anything Viktor, except yourself. No, you don't even know yourself. Standing quietly in the corner of life, content that you are breathing and thinking.'

Viktor dug his phone out of his pocket and began scrolling angrily through his timeline, ignoring her.

Nina got up. The bowl crashed to the floor and broke. Her eyes were wet. 'Fuck off, Viktor.'

Viktor kept scrolling, his head down. Nina's friend Jo had posted a photo on her timeline. A naked woman, her arms out, head upturned, long purple hair blowing in the wind, around her the coils of a dragon's tail: *May you flow in beauty tomorrow, Nina, and what is right for you come about. Sending you love and calm strength tonight, so you can rest and communicate with fluidity and your warrior spirit and soul can flower in your interview.*

Viktor dropped the phone into his lap, brought his hands to his face. When he came into the bedroom, Nina was on the floor sobbing, half hidden by the bed. 'Sorry, Nina. I was an asshole. I had an awful day. I took it out on you.'

'Fuck off. You are a bastard. Leave me alone.'

'No, I won't leave you alone, because then you'll blame me for leaving you alone.' Viktor walked round the bed and saw Nina, her dressing gown open, her breasts exposed, her leggings pulled down below her knees. Lying on the floor next to her was the carving knife from the kitchen.

Viktor shouted, 'Shit, no, Nina!'

Later they lay next to each other in bed, both impatient to make even a false peace so they could sleep.

*

Viktor thought how astonishing it was that we are expected, in a single life, an average one like his, like Nina's, to accomplish so much. He could feel Nina next to him, their legs touching, her body already trembling gently in sleep. Had he really achieved nothing at all? Maybe the only lives that came to a decent conclusion were always going to from the beginning. Viktor thought about his mother and father and their busy, normal lives, unwavering from the beginning, while the others, the rest, would remain lost, despite the futile efforts to change the course of events, to change themselves.

How easy it is for us to make mistakes, yet so difficult to correct them, Viktor thought. *How many years to change, to right an error? Five, ten? Ten years to leave a damaged relationship. Twenty to recover.* Viktor thought of all his past mistakes, all the times he had hurt Nina, the things he'd said, the indecision, his cowardly inability to act, to be. To correct these mistakes, how long would he need? Thirty years? More? Two lifetimes? He pulled the cover over his chest, exposing his feet. *We need some sort of machine of rolling correction, a Department of Private Memories and Mistakes, to draw out the lessons from our short, flawed lives.* As Viktor slipped into sleep he felt certain that he could not be clear any more about anything.

*

In the morning, with Biko speaking and instructing almost in his sleep, the students took their positions at the university. Some were posted to nearby schools, others in townships further out of the city. But only the students at the university came out. Four thousand students attempted to access the approach road from the campus that would have taken them to the city. Instead they were viciously beaten. The students, running for cover, were chased across the campus into their halls. The corridors in one residence – nicknamed Baghdad – were covered in blood. One window of a ground-floor room overlooking the courtyard was broken, only the jagged glass left. Students running from the military police hid in rooms and corridors; the police fired tear gas canisters into the rooms. In one room, the canister ignited the mattress, adding flames to the toxic fumes. Riot police in the corridor stopped two students, comrades who had been recruited by Biko to the Society of Liberated Minds, from leaving. Struggling to breathe, one student broke the glass in a window; his head now partly exposed, he was repeatedly hit by police wielding batons in the courtyard. As he was beaten, caught in the broken window, unbelievably – a story that heartened and impressed Biko – he had shouted again and again, 'Ahoy, comrade!' and '*Qina Msebenzi Qina!*' He did not die. By the end of the day, within four hours of the student rising, forty-five students had been admitted to hospital. The full calamity – the utter fucking catastrophe – of the day was clear.

Eleanor's understanding of events was the most devastating. Beside the students in hospital, there were no arrests – the one student the police had genuinely sought, whose name they had sung as they swung their batons through corridors, across heads, was called Biko. Now Biko was on the run. Bruised, pacing the room with its cheap foam mattresses lining the walls, Eleanor sucked the pain through her teeth. The others, some with their heads in their hands, their shoulders slumped, lay curled on the floor.

Biko stood as normal by the door, holding it closed with his shoulder: 'Carry on, comrade, you were saying?'

Eleanor stopped pacing, swallowed, breathed in. 'Open the window. I am dying in here,' she said, bringing her arm to her forehead to mop her brow.

Biko moved to the window, unlatched it and pushed hard on the frame. The darkness helped them all, hid them in their failure and pain. Biko was grateful, to each of them, to Eleanor.

'I have told you, we couldn't get away from the soldiers and police,' Eleanor said. 'They shut down the access from the library. We couldn't get round them. In the end we walked into them, we had to and we knew what was coming – there were ten of us, five women. They ordered us to get down and lie on our stomachs and then they started beating us.' She sucked the pain again through her teeth, filtering it, making it bearable.

Biko spat out, 'Bastards.' A few comrades shook their heads.

Eleanor continued, 'And inside, just beside that junction at the bus stop——' She looked around the room. They nodded, encouraged her to continue. 'There were others who were singing as they were being assaulted by a group of police. After we were beaten we were told to run and join the others. They were also forced to line up and the beatings continued.' She paused. 'Then sexism intervened.' Eleanor laughed. They all looked at each other. 'The chief security officer of the university, you know, that man Benson, came and asked for permission to get the women. So I was saved, comrades, by my gender.'

The room lightened, the mood improved – there was laughter. Bludgeoned and defeated they were, but not dead. On the Zimbabwe scale of repression – on the international rating of bone-cracking and state murder – the day had been slight and the defeat minor. No one dead, no one in a coma, no one utterly, irretrievably lost. There was a victory in this not lost on anyone in the room.

'That's not sexism, Eleanor,' Jethro said. 'Benson was a saviour, a hero.'

Ignoring the interruption, she continued. 'So it was granted, and he took the women to the security control room and then he later telephoned the staff at the clinic, for those who needed to go.' Then, forgetting a part of her story, a link in the narrative, she said, turning to address Biko directly, 'And, comrade, as we were walking away they were also saying that *ndozvamatunwa naBiko,* that's what you have been sent by Biko to do. Go and tell him *kuti hapana zvaano tiita isusu,* that there is nothing he can do to us; we are the strongest army in Africa, and no one can do anything.'

They laughed, let the day's beating wash over them, cleanse them with relief. For once Biko's voice couldn't be heard. He was assessing, calculating, working out what had gone wrong – what he had failed to do, what they needed to do next time. He knelt, leant against the wall, the others speaking quickly, kneading their bruises. Biko heard nothing.

He had spent days before the action thinking of strategies for the best way to leave campus and get into town for the proposed marches, the other feeder demonstrations from the city and townships. What came out of his planning was that he would address a general meeting outside the administration building on campus, which the students had code-named Hunger Palace. From there the students would march through the southern entrance of the university, then along Gwanda Road and into town. When Monday came he had mobilised with other Society comrades on campus and they moved towards Hunger Palace. From there students had started to march towards the exit point, just as he'd planned.

The noise in the room was reaching its familiar pitch. Biko – without realising it – had started to speak his thoughts aloud. 'I was a bit overtaken by events, comrades. By the time I got to the exit point there were about four thousand students, singing and chanting slogans.' Slowly the others turned to him, smiling affectionately at him, at another eccentricity. 'Apparently there was a line of some riot police who were firing tear gas canisters. But they met quite stiff resistance from those gathered there by virtue of the numbers of us, the ratio of students to riot police. We need to get the equations right in future. We can beat them with numbers, comrades.' The others hooted and called out.

Biko patted the air for silence and then continued. 'They eventually ran out of tear gas. They probably called for some reinforcements, so about five minutes after their tear gas had run out, we suddenly saw a helicopter coming in very low and people started dispersing, running in various directions

– but you know the rest, comrades. In no time the college was bombarded with military police, the riot police as well as soldiers – those boys in uniform who don't know who they are, just stupid, dangerous kids with guns mounted on army trucks. There were water cannon, riot police riding in pick-up trucks, others in conventional pick-ups. Mayhem, comrades. It was a state parade, *armed and motorised bodies of men*. We managed to get the entire state to mobilise.'

There were nods of agreement. Biko looked from face to face and smiled. Apart from the fanfare, the declarations, the group needed to understand what had gone wrong. They had the answer before the events had unravelled, before the catastrophe of the day. If the hard work and organising was not done, if all the building in the townships and high-density areas was not undertaken, if the comrades in the Society did not sweat their fucking guts out on planning and undertaking, *like a thousand little Lenins*, as Biko said, then they would go to hell and deserve the damnation. Yet they were so drunk on their youth, their anger and invulnerability that they had not planned or built.

Yet for Eleanor there was more to it even than their failure to organise and their heady rush to action – there was something deeper at stake.

Eleanor had resumed pacing the room, irritated with the interruption, with Biko's assumptions, his arrogant, pushy maleness. *Why doesn't he just listen, we don't need a narrative of a day we organised, a story* – only real once it had been sanctified by him – *that we lived*. She felt the defeat throbbing and pulsing over her body. Damn him.

Biko went on. There were tired nods. Eleanor had moved to the door, her back half turned on Biko – she had heard this before. 'So we see, comrades, the privatisation of the state that had continued through Mugabe's so-called anti-imperialism. Most of us are locked out of the Zimbabwe that our fathers, our grandfathers fought for! We are not recognised. We are not citizens, not human beings, we are treated like trash. But the people will rise up, with the right organisation, with the correct timing and planning ...'

There was silent agreement. They were exhausted, and refused to debate any more. For once, Biko was unconvincing – where was his striving, his commitment? They knew the formula, repeated it to themselves in meetings, to opposition: *In Zimbabwe, whenever there is a movement, it is the students that act first, they act as that spark to the powder keg. It is the role of students to act first, to act as torchbearers, to instigate action.* But what if they remained just a spark, a single fucking flash that could never catch or light the popular will – so sodden and damp, so broken by exhaustion, hunger and defeat? What then would become of them and their precious agency? These militants, with their spotless analysis, were unable to instigate anything.

In their own way they each felt these doubts. The first thing that was taught to them in meetings of the Society was their role in the mass movement; hammering out their confidence in their own abilities, their own scholarly capacities, linking them to the workers, the poor. Biko had been the peculiar teacher of their poverty of agency; the necessity, as vital as oxygen, to touch off the poor. *Without this, friends, we are nothing – useless elites.*

But what were they if they could not trigger the movement?

And what of the poor, those who had left them today and not marched, joined their numbers to theirs, who had left them alone to be bludgeoned by the state?

Eleanor now squared herself up to Biko, her anger calmed, her determination redoubled. She took a couple of steps towards him. 'I should have listened to my neighbours, to my mother's friends. Without any political education, they knew it was child's play. No one was coming out; that's what they said, and I refused to listen. They are hungry, too hungry to march to another promise – for what?' She paused. Biko stared hard at her.

She continued more fluently, feeling the silent support of the others. 'They say we live on a dollar a day. Comrades,' she swivelled in a half-circle to the men sitting and lying on the floor, 'a dollar a day would make us rich. My mother makes a dollar last three. Three days. She is up at five, selling juice-cards and vegetables in town. And how do we live on campus? You know, Zero-Zero-Buns. Rotten vegetables in the townships and a single bun at university.' She gulped, squeezed her eyes hard with her forefinger and thumb. 'What do we say to *this*?' She avoided Biko's unblinking stare. 'The people will rise up with the right organisation?'

Biko spoke into her pause, slowly. 'And they will, Eleanor, but not to our poor, hasty demonstrations and heroics. You are speaking at the end of a day of violence. We will rise.'

'No!' Eleanor screamed, both from the pain that rippled hard and sharp in her body and the agony of his words. 'What I am saying is, they *won't* rise. My mother won't fight – with what, anyway? Her rotting vegetables? People in rags don't make the revolution, comrade.'

By the end of the week Mugabe had publicly expressed 'regret' at having to teach these 'youths', these 'hotheads', a lesson.

Chapter Eleven

Viktor couldn't help himself: he remembered. When Nina arrived home, he and Rosa were sitting cross-legged in the middle of the floor around their CDs, sleeve notes open. Rosa flapped the pages of an open libretto in time to the loud music that deadened the noise of Nina's entrance, the door slamming, her rattling keys and remonstrations. Viktor, his back to the door, sliced and cut the air, conducting *Aida*, shouting instructions and explanations, both of them in the middle of a lake, around them open pages, a dozen paper butterflies. Rosa had given up trying to hear Viktor's explanations. Still he shouted: 'When *Aida* premiered, sweetheart, in Egypt, the audience was full of politicians and businessmen, not ordinary Egyptians. When Verdi heard about this, he raged, he was furious. He wanted the music to be heard by everyone.' Around them sounded the cymbals, the voices of the choir. Radamès and Aida declaring their illegal love, Aida's voice shrill, stirring up the music. Then the familiar refrain, repeated by Aida, by son and daughter, the words joining in a great crescendo: '*La fatal pietra sovra me si chiuse.*'

Nina, her hands on her hips like Amneris, the spurned lover, tried vainly to shout above the din. 'I want the music off. Clear up this room. Rosa, it's bedtime.'

The room was disturbed, the drama cast. Viktor and Rosa, their forearms swinging, arcing with the notes, dipping low, soaring high. Rosa's eyes and smiling mouth turned up towards Nina, wanting desperately to spin their spell on her, take her to Verdi's Egypt. She had to come, to follow them and listen to the crashing waves – not the words, maybe not even the singing, just the sound. To the flutes, the violins, the harp, the cellos, then to Radamès.

'For god's sake, Viktor, you said you would put Rosa to bed. I asked you to do one thing.'

The music was turned off, the notes crashed to earth, the butterflies folded their wings back into the plastic CD cases. Aida and Radamès sped forward quickly to their preordained fate, the tomb, singing stupidly, using up oxygen on a last declaration of love.

'It was so lovely, Mum.' Rosa rushed to Nina, holding her round the waist, looking up and pleading as she cleared the floor. Viktor ran Rosa's bath while Nina noisily tidied the kitchen. In bed, Rosa, her arms around his neck, pulled him in for a final embrace. She whispered, 'Tell Mum to come and say goodnight. We'll play her the music tomorrow.'

'Yes, sweetie.'

'Why didn't they run away?'

'Who?'

'Aida and that man … Radamès.'

'Because it wasn't possible. Both of them were trapped, between love for each other and duty to their families and country.'

'That's funny. I think they should have escaped. I would have.'

*

112

Nina turned the tap, ran cold water over her hands, slowed the pressure, filled the glass. She brushed the capsules into her hand, brought it quickly to her mouth, threw them to the back of her throat and washed them down with the water. *Twice a week isn't an addiction*, she reasoned, supporting herself on a work surface. *Only a minor, innocent prop to get me through the winter until spring. I will kick the Tramadol in the spring. In two months*. She felt better already, pleased with her practical good sense, the decision to relegate questioning until the spring, when the days would be longer and she could emerge from the winter cage.

When she returned, Viktor was tapping away at his phone again.

'Would you put the phone down? If you're going to flirt with other women online, then maybe we should reconsider how we do these things,' Nina snarled, cutting the air with her words.

How did Nina know that he flirted with women online? *Does she know about Anne-Marie?* Without even admitting the treachery to himself, he decided that he must take this affair into a more private venue.

Vitkor realised then, at that moment, that his parents would die soon, stumble over the kerb, struggle to keep up with their interminable bills, grow more decrepit and he wouldn't notice because he'd been arguing with Nina. Ten years would pass and they'd be five years dead.

'I don't have any female friends. And I am scared to contact my friends,' Viktor lied.

'Scared?'

'Yes, scared. Scared that you'll complain.'

'You're a fucking coward.'

'And you're being unreasonable.'

'I need to lie down,' she said to Viktor when he came towards her, her hand up, showing him her palm. In an hour calm would

113

spread across her and she would feel reconciled and generous, ready to deal with the night, with Viktor.

Viktor hurled Rosa's toys, the coloured pages of the scrapbook, the tube of glue, the oversized card game, into a disordered pile in the corner of the lounge. His body ached. He felt wronged. He plugged in his headphones and turned up the volume, and music lurched out of the speakers and thundered through the flat. He pushed in the jack and diverted the sound, his head filled with the opera.

'Viktor!' Nina screamed, then slammed the bedroom door.

He shut his eyes and slumped on the sofa. After five minutes he sat up, yanked the headphones off his head and dropped them to the floor. The distant opera continued to play; the crackle of sound followed him to the kitchen door. He fumbled in the cupboard above the sink, found the pills hidden behind jars of jam and peanut butter, Rosa's clumsy fingerprints traced around the lids. He fingered the capsule's perfect oval then pulled it apart, emptying the powder on the counter. Carefully, he brushed the white powder into a spoon and filled a glass of water. He paused, steadied himself, lifted the spoon, knocked the powder to the back of his mouth and washed it down with water. The bitter, harsh taste filled his mouth. Viktor grimaced, washed the spoon under the tap and dug it deep into Rosa's jam. He took the two ends of the capsule, put them together to make a whole again, and placed them back into the cupboard.

This ritual had continued for more than two years. His absurd alchemy, Viktor thought, eliminated the harmful effect of the gelatine in the capsules. Somehow, by leaving these bastard, voided tablets, he had not really taken it, which meant he was not really a minor addict. Nothing mattered to either of them on Tramadol. The flat disappeared, the night opened to them without threat and the desire that they both secretly held that they wouldn't make it to the morning faded. Both knew about the other's habit, but they took their private transformation separately: Nina in her room, Viktor on the sofa, waiting for the rush of chemical love. Viktor collapsed on the sofa, picked up the headphones, closed his eyes and tried to forget the day, the marking, his contract that ended in a fortnight, and obey the music.

For once Viktor wanted to empty his head of the blog posts, status updates and emails he had to write to keep himself alive, for the invisible crowd of friends who waited for his insights and questions. He imagined a giant hand reaching into the flat, battering down the door, pushing its muscled forearm into the room, gripping his head, squeezing it and draining it in a single violent hold of everything he did, his whole self-serving, narcissistic universe. He was alive only when he was in front of his computer, the grotesque carnival of his public, online life a curse on his daughter. He had even prostituted Rosa to the internet with his observations on childhood, her weekly photo, each artefact of lived experience thrown at Facebook. Every feeling shared, each banality told – what right did he have to do this to Rosa?

If only he could focus on the music. He breathed through his nose and concentrated on his breath. He listened to the libretto, tried to catch the Italian words he knew. He chased away the thought that he should write a series of posts on *Aida*, explain what the opera meant, each lesson in short, pithy phrases, pose each of the opera's dilemmas in the form of a question. He had to get back to the music, concentrate on Rosa. He felt the first waves of Tramadol shudder over him, the warm wind wrap around his heart, circle his head. The last thought before he was completely lost inside the drug was of his daughter, little, impossible, vulnerable Rosa and her automated, terrible wish

115

to be like him, her perfect imitation of him, her awkward, tall frame, her distractions already like his. He feared that she too would never be satisfied, following his soft, absorbent heart, his ever-ready, hopeless compassion. Nina was right.

*

When the split finally took place it came with all the terrible, excruciating agony of loss and regret *and* text-messaging. An ordinary argument became their fork in the road, the justification for separation which was debated and weighed up on their phones – Rosa in bed, Nina crouched on the floor of their flat, huddled over her phone like she was praying, and Viktor stretched out on the bed in his parents' spare room.

Nina wrote message after message.

I am on the floor of the lounge. I have cancelled the meal with my friend. This is what you wanted, to sabotage my only dinner and weekend without childcare, like you will do to anything I put my energy and interest into.

You set me up to seem like a bitch. The alternative is to be a complete pushover, to never do or say anything that might upset you so you can't blame me constantly for your unhappiness.

I let plenty of crappy, childish comments of yours slide. But if I say one thing you react and then leave. You say you love me but I don't feel it.

Viktor responded.

If you think all these things – as I think them of you – we need to split. You don't want me and I don't want you. Simple.

You never take responsibility for your behaviour, it is easier to shift the blame. You do it on all things, Nina.

Nina's messages paused for a while. Then:

I've just cut myself by mistake really badly. I am bleeding and think need stitches. Please come and get me. Must I phone my mum? I can't leave Rosa.

Viktor: *You self-harmed. I will pick you up.*

Nina: *No, my friend's coming. I called her.*

Viktor: *Whatever.*

Nina: *Exactly, you couldn't care less, I know. I wish you could have loved me.*

Viktor: *I wish you had a modicum of self-understanding.*

Nina: *Please come home this eve. Please don't stay away.*

Viktor: *I will leave the car and stay elsewhere, until there is some calm.*

Nina: *Please don't, Viktor. Please. I'm begging you. I wish I could rewind to this afternoon and do differently.*

Viktor: *Nina, I am going to spend the night out to clear my head and calm down a bit.*

Nina: *Where are you staying? Can I come over? I know you need to clear your head but I need to see you.*

A few hours later they took up the fight all over again – sweeping their fists back and forth, catching everything in their path. When this was done, exhausted, Viktor turned his phone to silent and tried to sleep. In the morning he saw the messages Nina had sent in the night.

Please answer.

When you leave like this I have only my own thoughts and they are very scary.

I feel punished and rejected.

I just want to be loved and supported. I feel so alone. I have been alone for months with you, longer and now again. I just want to be loved.

Do I not deserve that? Am I not good enough? Maybe you have found someone else. Is that why you are always late from university?

I hate myself. I wish I was dead.

I don't blame you for abandoning me.

I deserve it.

I wish I was dead.

Viktor cracked the curtains, letting the grey morning fall on him and cast a line of light on the bed. He sat up in bed and picked up his phone to break the hours of silence.

I never wanted to hurt you but I do think our connection is hurtful to both of us. I want that to end. I think we are at the end of the road — as much as I love you.

There were a few moments of silence. Viktor could hear his parents stirring, his father's feet shuffling on the bedroom floor, foraging for his slippers, and his mother's morning words, 'Isaac, dear, are you going to make the tea?'

The phone buzzed again. Nina.

I feel angry and hurt. You wasted years of my life. I wish you had just let me go so I could give you up and let go. I am angry you kept me close and we had Rosa. You kept me close and never committed and now you say it's over. I am angry for staying true to our plans and to Rosa. I betrayed myself.

Viktor responded: *It's over. Go.*

Then he did something unusual. He pressed hard on the phone's off button, holding his finger in place until the screen shut down. There was a flash of light and then nothing.

Viktor had turned off his phone. It was the first time this had ever happened.

Part Two:

Strikes and Separation

Chapter Twelve

The last time they made love it was quick, on the bed, the floor strewn with Nina's bags, half their clothes still on. Just a three-minute fuck, both of them coming quickly and breathlessly. No tears, no veil of emotion lifted in a final climax, just a perfunctory fuck to mark the end.

'That was nice. Now I will sleep easily,' Nina had said. Viktor liked that. This was how she always was before an important discussion – hard-nosed and rational. She was difficult, fragmented, when there wasn't a crisis, but when something actually happened she was always stronger than him. It induced in her a necessity to strip life down to what was absolutely necessary: logistics, raw anger and sex.

Afterwards Nina had taken Rosa from her room, still asleep, and curled round her in their double bed. After the endless months of doubt, the years this relationship had lasted, tearing them both apart, to Viktor Nina was saying that she was inseparable from Rosa. The lie of their individual units was exposed finally that night by this simple motherly act; Rosa came from her, was cleaved of her flesh, from her body, and her home would always be with her mother.

Viktor scrambled to get Nina back, pleaded to her in emails, fought her doubts with furious, eloquent reassurances. No more questioning, complete combination of their lives, everything that had been wrong would be, through decisions that were now being made, put right. At the start of this renunciation of his past, his old crimes, his sickness, his incapacity, he had felt cleansed, as though he was being truly honest with himself for the first time. This public flogging felt redemptive. He could start again – if he could only believe, utterly, completely in this latest resolution – clear and cleaned.

Nina had accepted his apology at first and said he could come back, then haggled almost every day, creating new, exhausting conditions: another child, a house with a garden, marriage, double-barrelling their names, joining Jew and Gentile. The list was long: reconciliation, unity, togetherness, an unambiguous and committed universe.

But she didn't want him back.

*

For three months after Viktor and Nina separated he slept in his parents' spare room. There were two shelves above the single bed. The top shelf contained items from his childhood: a soft brown bear, a duck with a yellow beak and a navy-blue waistcoat knitted by his mother, an encyclopedia. The lower shelf in the spare room was allocated to Amy, the relics of her childhood selected by Sonia: a plastic doll with moving eyes, one permanently cast down in a hideous wink; a boxed set of C. S. Lewis's *Chronicles of Narnia*; a chipped mirror ringed by a pink frame of forget-me-nots.

'Mum, why do you still have those silly things in the spare room? They look eerie, as though you're waiting for the urns with our ashes, to finish the commemoration once we're dead,' Viktor said.

'Don't talk like that. You're not going to die.'

To avoid the sadness when he entered the room, the reminder of the many deaths he and his sister had inflicted on their parents, on themselves and each other, the phases of lost childhood, adolescence, adulthood, Viktor covered the two shelves with a large towel.

Nothing seemed to please and distress his parents more than having Viktor under their care for a few months. He stretched out on the spare bed, his feet hanging over the end, his hands behind his head, and heard Isaac shuffle into the bathroom in his slippers. He didn't want to listen, to hear the routine – always a routine with his father – the muted song from *Rigoletto* or *La Traviata* as he sat on the toilet for his evening bowel movement, straining and singing. He raised his voice, the tune high and loud, as he squeezed and pushed, then abruptly lowered into a baritone with a moan as he reached satisfaction. Viktor frowned. The sound of his father was eternal, the same movements, only slower now. Viktor remembered sitting at his father's feet, staring up at him as he shaved.

Twice Viktor had been woken by the sound of his parents making love. Shocked, he had thought at first that he was still asleep. He had turned on the bedside light, but the arc of pale light over the bed only confirmed the darkness and amplified the soft groans of his parents rhythmically fucking along the corridor. On the second occasion he was woken, his parents' tired, hollow bodies reaching perfect harmony, Viktor masturbated himself back to sleep and thought how like death is the sound of love. *How like the noises I made with Nina. Life*, he supposed, *is always made with death – climactic, wordless beginnings and speechless groans at the end.*

He sat up in the bed, wondered if for another night he would have to sleep over the blanket, because the heating, which sapped his father's meagre pension and their sleep, remained at 24 degrees day and night, winter and summer.

*

Anne-Marie wasn't entirely clear what it was she wanted any more.

Anne-Marie didn't want kids, of this she had always been clear, but at a certain age – she could chart it, she'd just turned thirty – the chorus rose, the shouts (sometimes it was actually shouting) had become so loud that she was no longer entirely sure what it was that she wanted.

What right, she would rage, *do they have to tell me what I need and think? And why do they always shout? My family is like the whole of the Congo*, she thought, *terrified that it will be snuffed out so the people have to roar, toujours hurler. Such fear of non-existence, such fear of death, these people.* She received calls at regular intervals from her grandmother – of all people – her mother, her aunts and uncles, until she began to feel that it was her duty, her mission, as a member of the Patrice Lumumba clan, to reproduce.

Her uncle, a remote figure in her life, had made a lucrative living on his father's name. 'The Lumumbas,' he'd said, patiently, forthrightly, 'are the country's, the continent's, most successful family.' How could he say this without irony? 'But, Anne-Marie, our future is *précaire* because our numbers have fallen dramatically. Some believe that the answer is to forget our history, our heritage, our name, in other words to rewrite the rules, to forget, but I don't. You need, we need, children, in our name.' On how exactly this name was to come about, her uncle was not precise. 'And Anne-Marie,' he said after a pause, taking a sip of morning-warmed Primus, 'I am prepared to step in to fund fertility treatment if necessary. I know a clinic in Paris. You need children, *we* do.'

There were many aspects to the calls which horrified Anne-Marie. The concern this sloshed, permanently incoherent uncle had given to their name – what did she care, the surname she had long ditched was to her a burden, evidence of failure, *the continent's most successful family – oh, Uncle, in that case pity the continent, pity our people.* His attachment to the name, the only thing his father had given him, was a sort of salve to his personal failures, collapsed business ventures, money borrowed on the back of the legacy – of the family name – his political organisation (*Mouvement National Congolais – Lumumba, le deuxième*) that thought it could reproduce Patrice's programme, reprint it word for word to reach the promised horizon. Each one of these ventures, each racket, had failed and his latest absurdity was IVF-ing the continent full of Lumumbas.

Beyond her family's efforts were others – comments, casual, almost polite, about her age, *her* needs. Office colleagues would enquire with a wink, a squeeze of her shoulder, about children – always *when*, never *if*. It was a mystery to her that these comments came from people she didn't know, with the presumption that somehow they could ask her about children *and* touch her at the same time. From the woman who sold her breakfast, a single orange, at a pavement stall on Tongogara, it was never a single child but children. The woman put her hands on her hips, swayed, knowing, familiar – pointing her finger in the direction of Anne-Marie's midriff, nodding: 'Where you will sit when you are old shows where you stood in youth.' What did that even mean, exactly?

How was she to escape this pressure without going mad, without doubting what she had never doubted? People she

127

barely knew told her that to be full, complete, to be fulfilled and known, she needed not a single child but a flock, a gaggle, a fucking *herd* of children. Nothing could satisfy the desire for children, for the wheels to turn, for life to be given and then taken, for sense to be made of life; it was an appetite that no reason, no sense, no desire could appease. Congo's gods of the sky, of the earth, of the river would never be satisfied.

And Anne-Marie didn't know what to do. All the things in her life that had felt private – her decisions, her body – became claimed, with a hideous clamour, by everyone else. Was it possible, she wondered, battered (and it was a battering) by the pressure of so many fingers and opinions, to escape society? To reject its demands for conformity and order? Younger, more confident – she was now thirty-eight – she would not even have understood the question. Perhaps this was the secret of youth. Now she knew it wasn't ever entirely possible, and that to try too thoroughly was to risk your own sanity and hold on the world. Anne-Marie realised that in small measures it was possible to survive in the cracks, in the twilight of the rules. She already lived alone in Harare, travelled unaccompanied on the continent, kept her lovers at a distance.

Nelson was going to be different; he was going to break the mould. Yet, exuding rejection of the crippling project of ZANU's dictatorship, the neoliberal nightmare that had destroyed Zimbabwe and capitalism's centuries-old project on the continent, he bumbled in matters of personal relations. To the pressure to settle with Anne-Marie and have children, he seemed to suspend his harsh judgements of the existing social order and agree. Perhaps they *should* have children. Although they never explicitly discussed the subject – like all things in their relationship, it was casually 'present' – he assumed that they would amble into parenthood. Anne-Marie would be the parent and he would continue to speak and organise and turn young comrades into cadre at his knee – or take care of the children on weekends. Only in this respect was he utterly vague and unquestioning.

With Viktor, she hoped, or intended, things to be different – children were not his project; his child seemed to be his predicament. In an abstract way Viktor was already her ally, and she did not press him on the details of his dilemma and the particular commotion of his life because of the complications in her own. There was an unspoken solidarity between them. Viktor understood her and, strangely, even in their deepest moments of intimacy, they did not discuss children or plans, their particular, strange relationship cartography. Viktor knew that in the desperate stakes of life perhaps the most she could expect from society, from her family, was to be left the fuck alone.

*

Comrade Viktor!

Thanks – again – for your (far, FAR too) kind words. And given that you are going thru a personal hell (which I've had to a couple of times) it's only natural for comrades to be at least supportive in communication and in person. If what I write helps inspire too, then so much the better. After all, all such 'hell on earth' is produced by bosses' conscious competitive accumulation – the source of all exploitation, oppression, inequality and suffering. There is no other force 'organising' this – not even wild nature – which we could, long ago, put into a tamed form. But this is not even on the capitalist agenda, far from it. They're wrecking that too.

As I have said before, if a room here would suit you, of course I and my little circle would make you warmly welcome – and I'm sure you'd enjoy all the rich debate/arguments and promise among these marvellous young thinkers, struggling their way through the increasingly tangled coils of the vile UK capitalist reptile.

On the political situation, I think the overall 'literary' type of keynote of our times is: *Tout – ça change* and *de plus en plus ça change!* No force on earth – whatever the West and its remaining despots in Africa do – can eradicate now the fresh refounding of the distinctive fundamental principles of revolutions which so enriched it. In the newly awakening minority epitomised by the struggle at the university, we have found a new spirit to forge the future.

ALL the thousands of honest, genuine, sincere, real socialists who joined organisations, as I did in Zimbabwe, to learn, organise and lead the people to full international armed insurrectionary seizure of all power – must drink deep at the oases, those wonderful, still young, rampaging revolutions of the poor of Africa and Arabia. And this, Viktor, can only come with practice – YOU have to DRINK.

Drink very deep indeed, Viktor – with an alert mind – to check that what you are doing, supporting and 'going along with' is even remotely related to those oases and founts of the actuality of revolution and the sole source of our theory – the actual, sensuous, flesh-and-blood revolutionary practical-critical activity. DRINK, comrade, DRINK.

That wonderful goddess History tantalised me by waiting till I was 60, with years of training, to deliver three revolutions in one northern winter – so far, more to come.

So, all my life HAS been a preparation. The people are awakening. Stay tuned.

Sala kakuhle Viktor!

Tendai

*

Viktor didn't know what to make of Tendai's emails, nor did he fully understand how these messages were so radically different from the conversations they had at university. Cajoling, irritated and provocative, Tendai raged at Viktor, tried to work him up, move him on, get him to break from his congenital impotence. Gnawed, knotted Tendai would stand over his dustcart, a streak of dirt across his face, his bottom lip pouting, turned out, spitting forth his words. 'Get going, man, goddamn it. Break the habit of a lifetime and move. *MOVE.*' Viktor aroused the exasperation of the gods and ancestors, uThixo and uDali, and made Tendai angry. And what was so goddamn likeable about this hopeless man anyway, this splinter of wood?

Forever seeking the kernel, the real core, the point at which transformation comes, some budding contradiction, Tendai recognised in Viktor the necessity to burst the shell and get to the heart. The real thing. 'You, you, you are shut up, enclosed, trapped in this, this capsule, this case, this container, a hull, a husk, a shell, a false vessel.' No word ever seemed to fit. Viktor's eyes widening in horror, all of this for him, these words, this effort, these attempts – to provoke him to break from his inertia and get to his ripe, seething, fraught heart. To the damn truth. Tendai tried everything, in the day when he felt charged, angry and alive, when he had the force – and he felt keenly the memory of his lost years in Pollsmoor, his enforced absence – he hit, kneaded and coaxed Viktor; physically tried to grasp the carapace of Viktor's resistance and wrench it away, remove it to reveal what he knew was beneath.

At night, in the darkness, in the rented three-by-two cell in Wood Green with the shared bathrooms, Tendai applied an entirely different ointment. In his voluntary confinement he became emollient and analytical. At three in the morning, almost repentant, regretting his anger and impatience in the day, he wrote contained, encouraging and loving emails to his comrade.

Hunched over a computer requisitioned from the university, Tendai hammered methodically on the keys, his fingers curled, his elbows out, mouthing the words. Identifiable in form, he was changed inside, his spleen relaxed, his organs flat, wide, free of tension – there was a strange transformation at night. The night and darkness gave him peace, not the horror of the unknown but the comfort of obscurity, the prospect of suspension – for a few hours – of the whirlwinds of the day, when he could think and plan and be with himself. The in-between existence of the night lightened his life.

Yet when he was done composing, Tendai would stand up, stretch, crack his back, open his arms, tighten his muscles, tilt the screen so he could see his words, and almost in a fever he'd read half the email aloud and then, when his hostel neighbours had been woken, he was away again and had fallen back onto the side of his bed, writing once more. Each act of passivity – and writing to Tendai was a passive anathema to life – had to be repelled and countered by its opposite: an act, a stand. So even these emails had to be performed and infused with the raw perfume of existence.

And the hail of emails kept coming, relentless, random, loud – arriving unexpected, without preamble, the sentences starting halfway in. For months Tendai rapped his knuckles pink on Viktor's temples.

*

Viktor leant back in his office chair and felt his back click. He straightened his shoulders and lifted the lid of his laptop. He felt good. The site was getting more hits than before, the campaign was receiving oxygen, there were donations coming in. The air around Viktor this morning was dizzy, thin, excitable – it felt like euphoria, a breakthrough. He wondered whether this was what Tendai has been getting at. Biko was going to connect to Skype at 10 a.m. Zimbabwe time, and the interview would be recorded and posted on *Mutations*. A sensation. A fucking exclusive.

Viktor was deeply, obsessively committed to *Mutations*, of which he was editor-in-chief and publisher. There he wrote, for once, without any modesty. He believed that the website was the leading voice of the European left, offering radical perspectives on politics, economics, science and culture to an online audience of 50,000 a month. 'The appearance of *Mutations* has been a bright light in dark times,' declared the blurb on the site's About page. 'Each post brings penetrating, lively debate and analyses of matters of real significance from a militant left perspective that is refreshing and all too rare. *Mutations* is a vital and really impressive contribution to sanity and hope against the madness of the quotidian.'

The site was not the leading voice of the European left, nor was it even a minor voice of the British left – rather, the website had mutated into a noticeboard for Viktor's own musings, with occasional contributions from invited writers. Then, following the contours of the editor-in-chief's depression, there would

133

be weeks, even months of fanatical activity, with daily posts, analysis and updates, syndicated to Twitter and Facebook, and for a time *Mutations* would genuinely swell to fit the hyperbole of its About page. Its list of contributions and articles would make the most hardened e-activists break out in a sweat, wondering at the team of writers, the alchemists of content it must have writing about The Truth On Chavez, A New Strategy, To Fight Another Day and Sartre's Last Will and Testament.

So *Mutations* was constantly being taken out of retirement. Recently it had been resurrected as the online platform for the struggles taking place at the university. If the battles within the university were led by Tendai's unsteady genius, then Viktor would wage the war for publicity and solidarity online. The strategy was simple. The direct and immediate focus was the campaign itself, so Viktor would post updates from the front lines, but he would also try to do something that he believed to be entirely original. He would burrow into the backstories. If the cleaning staff – his comrades – were from Zimbabwe, South Africa and South America, then his efforts would be to raise readers' consciousness about these countries.

On his first blog post in the series on Zimbabwe, he made the intentions of *Mutations* clear: 'We must set ourselves the task of understanding. *Mutations* intends to collect and analyse data from Zimbabwe, to get to the root of the crisis in Southern Africa – to work out who benefits and who pays. We seek to understand the pain and struggles in the lives of those in Zimbabwe. We realise that these are not individual problems, and they cannot be solved individually. In *Mutations* we will be asking how we can take action.'

Viktor's assignment for *Mutations* this week was an interview with Biko Mutawurwa. The path to Biko had been fairly direct. Tendai had introduced him to Anne-Marie – an attempt,

Tendai believed, to draw Viktor out of himself, to connect him to the *real*. Though Anne-Marie had jolted him south, to see beyond Europe, it had not succeeded in ridding Viktor of his old bile and distractions. Tendai's curious diagnosis of Viktor's predicament, of his active inaction, was typical of his flawed overstatements, requiring an understanding of political history to appreciate psychological upset: 'You see, Viktor, com, those who make a revolution halfway only dig their own graves. You need to orientate south, beyond Gibraltar and your Dark Continent, this City of Darkness, this great primitive citadel.' Through Anne-Marie *and* Tendai, then, in a further attempt to draw him out, Viktor was introduced online to Biko.

From Biko came today's interview. From London to Harare; from nation-state to global activism.

Viktor logged on early to do research for the interview, to find out what else Biko had written, whom he followed, what he read. He stared at dates, circled and underlined words, names of places and people he had read about before. He opened a website for an American NGO in Zimbabwe and saw images of bent, bloodied bodies, bruised and faceless. These victims of Zimbabwe's modern *chimurenga* looked posed, pornographic. Viktor felt the optimism leave him in a flood of misery. He felt sick. His hand stumbled across the desk; he found the paper cup and knocked back the last lukewarm mouthful of coffee.

What could we do with this degree of overdetermination? Poisoned and condemned by history, how could they – Biko, Anne-Marie, Tendai – move? What hope was there for action? Oppressed by this history, from Rhodes to occupation, empire and colonialism and then defeat, to a failed, violent independence in 1980, Viktor couldn't see movement and possibility – only the curse of circumstances.

There was the familiar, strangely comforting sound of an incoming Skype call; Viktor looked up at the screen, saw the pulsing, throbbing image of Biko waiting to be answered. The fleeting despair dissipated.

'Biko!' he said loudly.

'Comrade,' Biko answered.

The screen flickered and cleared, the square, coloured pixels configured and Biko's face could be seen, around him a bank of computers with people working and making calls of their own. There was a familiarity to the scene that Viktor recognised. He relaxed.

'I am going to record this interview, if that's okay,' Viktor said, smiling.

Biko smiled back. 'Fire comrade, fire. I have thirty minutes. Anne-Marie told me you are a serious comrade. We like serious. So fire.'

Viktor had a habit that he found difficult to shake; he had to justify himself, speak of the great fury of the internet. So to the willing, beaming face that shone out of his laptop – the image of Biko failing and breaking every few minutes into a thousand miniature cubes – Viktor rattled out his justifications. 'Thanks, Biko, for this opportunity. Just quickly, I want to tell you about the site, *Mutations*—'

'I love the title,' Biko shot in. 'Mutations, yeah. Radical mutations, revolution, rupture. Beautiful, comrade.'

Viktor felt embarrassed – ridiculous and exposed. He adjusted himself in the chair, looked down at his notes and spoke. 'Can I ask you some basic questions? What position do you hold in the movement and what is your full name?'

Biko leant forward and stared directly at the camera eye at the centre of the screen. 'My full formal name is Stephan Mutawurwa, but I started using the name Biko for fear of victimisation, and now the name has stuck. I am the Research and Education Secretary for the Society of Liberated Minds and the President of the Bulawayo Student Union.' He paused, sat back, then remembering something, came forward to the screen again. 'And I forgot, I am also a PhD candidate in engineering.' Biko felt comfortable, entirely at ease – he was in the mood for speaking and relished this chance to extol, to give vent. The words lifted in his stomach. They wanted to get out and show themselves.

Viktor continued, his head still bowed into his notes. 'Can you explain something about your political evolution?'

There was no hesitation in Biko's response; he had answered these questions before, for other interviews – for American and Australian left-wing papers and websites – but there was nothing stale in his response. 'I started off as a rebel without a cause in high school. I remember it was when the Chidyausiku commission was set up by the government and run by Godfrey Chidyausiku – for a new constitution in Zimbabwe. They came to Goromonzi High School, where I was a student, as part of their outreach.'

Biko paused, thought quickly and resumed more slowly. 'Now, you must understand that the struggle over a new or redrafted constitution is not the dry process it might sound like in the UK. It is a popular process of democratic control across Africa, and in Zimbabwe the commission was seized by democratic forces. So we had a writers' club that I organised as a sort of a study circle, with our own, confused political views, which were mixed, muddled – and when they asked us to make a presentation to the commission, I was nominated. It became my first public political statement.' Biko stopped again, then laughed loudly, so loud, in fact, that the sound distorted and Viktor looked up from his pad and quickly adjusted the volume on the computer. He checked if the interview was still being recorded.

'When I look back at it, I can see it was a ridiculous little exercise in constitutionalism, the procedures of a shame democracy. Pathetic and audacious. Times were different then. I said that we demanded that in the new constitution there be a two-term limit on the office of the president. The next day in the *Daily News* the headline was, 'Schoolboys Harass Chidyausiku'. It was also the quote of the week in the *Financial Gazette*! After that, the little group I ran met Comrade Nelson, who had just started at the University of Zimbabwe as a law lecturer. He was Chair of the Society of Liberated Minds – he was in Bulawayo as part of the campaign against the constitution – and he found us. He hammered on the door of my family home clutching the rolled-up newspaper, his locks hanging even longer than they do now.' Biko remembered the scene. His mother had answered the door and stood, her arms on her hips, assessing Nelson with naked bravado. 'We sat speaking for four hours in the backyard, then he invited me to Harare and we spoke.' Biko laughed again, 'Rather, *he* spoke, for what felt like days without stopping. He managed to silence me! I attribute my political clarification to the Society and the programmes we carry out on the ground.'

Viktor started to relax. He enjoyed the musical dance of Biko's words. 'Can I ask you about your family background?'

Biko didn't hesitate. 'There are more interesting questions, but if you want, comrade. I am the first-born son and the only son, and I have a sister after me. My father was the principal of Bulawayo High School. He was involved in the armed struggle. My mother is late, she was self-employed and occasionally worked as a trader, going to commercial farms to sell jerseys she had knitted.'

138

Viktor was confused. 'When you say late, just to clarify, do you mean deceased?'

Biko was perfectly still. He was not smiling; he looked at the camera intently. Viktor met his eyes. 'What else could I mean? Late. Deceased. Dead,' Biko repeated.

Viktor flushed, coughed and pulled his notes up. 'What were your political motivations, your ideas and thoughts at the time – can you tell *Mutations* about your political evolution?'

Biko was leaning back, smiling again. The screen was clear and his eyes were wide, alert. 'We have been trained by leftists, by Nelson and others. We have been trained. The issues were around class analysis, to start off with. We are very much dialectical materialists, and we saw an obscene accumulation of wealth by the political elite under the guise of people empowerment.' Biko found his groove. This was where he wanted to be.

'The degeneration that occurred in the institutions, the degeneration that occurred within the fabric of the academic offering at the university, is something that we viewed with scepticism. We saw it as a conspiracy by the neo-political elite, but there was also a frustration which Mugabe now uses as his own. We saw what we call the un-rattled Rhodesians' establishment. So, you know, you had this obscene accumulation by the black political elite, but you also had this totally undisturbed, unperturbed privilege of the former elite and what seemed to be an organic or strategic alliance between the two elites. The emergent black elite and what we often referred to as the conspiracy of silence, they were beneficiaries.' Biko stared intently at the camera, at Viktor, wanting his comprehension.

'Government ministers suddenly owned commercial farms. They had been given them by their white counterparts and worked hand in hand with the white commercial farming sector. You had an incestuous relationship between the former oppressors and what we viewed then as the new oppressors. So we were motivated, I mean, we were ideologically clear. This was in the late nineties. At school and university we identified the administration and the police force as the pillars of strength for the establishment. So we attacked. We still do, you know, since we went all out to try and make them dysfunctional, to expose their true nature and show themselves.'

There were too many words in Viktor's life, and now he could feel them caressing him, falling on him, showering him – he was distracted by their sound, their clatter, and fought hard to find their meaning. He felt Biko's sentences sensually, his punchy, insistent phrases gathering under his arms and in his throat and ears. There was something more to the meaning, a greater significance, than this interview – something in his tone, in Biko's movement, in the dance he was making of the interview.

Viktor's palms were wet. He held on tightly to his notes and read the question: 'How had the nature of student protest changed? What was going on in Zimbabwe's societal relations in the nineties that was different from before? Can you describe for our readers and listeners the mutation of social classes?'

Biko's laugh was long and hard, but not mocking – he spoke affectionately. 'So, the alienation of labour, of the working class, from a possibility of a settlement or accommodation with the regime around any sort of social contract from ninety-six, ninety-seven, and the rapidity with which higher education was privatised – both of these processes were coming from IMF and World Bank structural adjustment and were willingly, even enthusiastically introduced by the regime, by the jackals. So essentially this meant that we no longer had student discontent but outright student rebellion on our hands.' The screen broke

up, tried to re-form – Biko shouted suddenly, 'A REBELLION!'
The picture formed. Biko was leaning forward. Viktor thought
of Tendai – he had the same habit of expressing himself in
capitals, to give to his words more than their flimsy life and
simple meaning. If life depended on so little, then these words
must be wielded, breathed into, made to tell, to march and to
fight.

Biko was still talking. 'So you had the most violent
demonstrations, and then a third thing that happened during
that period: the prices for almost everything were liberalised,
the fuel price increased, everything shot up. And in the
government the largest number of redundancies was created
there; now you had students supporting their parents on their
stipends which were not enough because their parents had
been laid off work. So ...' Biko opened his hands, then brought
them together in a sweeping movement and held them together
under his chin – he looked around, almost wanting the others,
the workers, parents and students working at the rows of
computers in the cyber-café to pay attention and listen. 'So, in
a sense, as poverty increased, you had a convergence of these
forces. And the critique started off really being around issues
of social economic justice. The right to a living wage – the
students started couching their demands around the right to
a livelihood.'

Viktor was excited; he forgot himself. 'Ah, so you mean the
student became, in a sense, a worker?'

'No,' Biko answered, then, pausing, he screamed: '*No!*'

Biko was not angry; his exclamations were simply that,
exclamations – the desire for things to be clear, for his listener
and for himself. Words were an inadequate gauge in themselves,
so, as Viktor had picked up, he sought to hurl them, make
them into more than they were. In some ways this was Biko's

understanding of revolutionary action – into the vacuum and darkness of life we had to shout, and if there was no answer, if nothing came back, we had to shout louder. The shouting was dictated by the void, and into it he had to throw fresh salvos of words, each with instructions to struggle and fight. Viktor, occasionally astute to human passions, saw this; he understood that Biko had an appetite for life which could not easily be satisfied.

'No, comrade,' Biko was calming down, 'students were not workers, for the simple reason that there were no jobs. The two thousands was the epoch of retrenchments. They were, in a way, parent and student, declassed.' Then, stopping, he adjusted his back, felt the satisfying click of his vertebrae, licked his lips. 'Think of the state of the Russian working class after the civil war in 1922. What did Lenin say? "Dislodged from its class groove, the Russian working class has ceased to exist as a proletariat." I am exaggerating, comrade, but not much.'

The interview ended a few minutes later, with warmth. If Biko could have reached into the computer screen – and on the video Viktor posted on *Mutations* a few hours later, it looked as though he was trying to – he would have grabbed his interlocutor by the shoulders and shaken him in humour and goodwill. Viktor expressed his desire for the men to meet again, like this, across the cybersphere. 'This is not meeting, comrade, nothing like it. If you want to meet, we need to do it in the flesh, and then you will see what I have been saying. Do you hear me? Then all of this, this' – he spoke almost dismissively – 'analysis will be clear to you and it will make sense. So if you want to see and feel for yourself, you must come.'

There was something peculiar to Biko that Viktor couldn't quite work out. He seemed old – not tired so much, but wise beyond his age, which was thirty-three. Viktor wanted to write about this, to find the tools and a framework for understanding. As he packed up his computer and the shared office slowly started to fill with postgraduate students and sessional lecturers, Viktor tried to work out the paradox. Biko's vision seemed so great – there was a euphoria of expression. How easily he spoke of liberation and revolution. Viktor thought of his own political experiences, the generation of activists he knew. *Our horizons are fixed on parochial concerns. We have never been stretched by such demands, by a dictatorship*. Again Viktor felt he was on to something. 'Goddamn it,' he said aloud, so the students he passed in the corridor looked up at him, 'we need a struggle against dictatorship or we'll never grow as a people.'

Chapter Thirteen

What was it about his daughter he didn't understand? He got her wide, black eyes, the shy twist of her face away from the Skype camera (to avoid her own stamp-sized image in the corner of the screen) on those long, painful calls. This much he understood. What he could not see was the adult in her, how the memory of everything they did together was imprinted with such precision in her mind, and then covered up, so convincingly, in her dance steps, in her child's games. She recalled everything but never stated the recollection as an adult might: 'When I saw my father in September he brought me a small bottle of lavender essence, and each night we would inhale its sweet smell and say that it would allow us to dream together. To share the same dream.' Instead she remembered surreptitiously, secretly, with such silent pain, like a child. The memory delicate, like the smell of lavender in the air.

On their weekend together he announced, 'I brought this, sweetie,' pulling the small vial out of his pocket. 'Stand up.'

Rosa jumped out of bed and reached for the bottle. 'What is it?'

'Wait, Rosa.' Viktor stood next to her bed. Levelling their heads, they stared at each other. 'It's lavender, but crushed into oil.' He held the bottle forward so she could see. 'The oil contains the smell. Now every night we need to do something with the oil.' Rosa was jumping on the mattress. 'But it only works if you are still.'

Viktor unscrewed the lid, tipped up the small, brown bottle into his palm, then put the vial carefully down and rubbed his hands together quickly to create a spark, to set fire to the oil. Rosa was perfectly still, moving her eyes between his face and hands. 'Once you have done this you cup your hands, sweetie, round your nose and breathe.' He then sucked in deeply, his face masked by his cradled hands.

'Now me, now me,' she shouted and, methodically following the instructions, copied her father.

'Only a drop on your hand,' he warned. 'That's it, rub them together quickly.' When she was done, she inhaled her fill. Rosa dropped her hands and stared at him, her eyes glowing.

'That's not all,' Viktor added quickly. 'Before you finish, you have to unruffle your sleep-wings so we can fly to each other in our dreams.'

'Really?' Rosa asked, her five years battling with her younger self, wanting to believe.

'Absolutely. Like this—' and Viktor raised his arms, moved his hands, stretched his wings.

Rosa was transfixed; again, when he was done, she followed his instructions.

When their separation was established and only phone calls and video streaming connected them, Rosa never mentioned the lavender, her sleep-wings, or the absurd night-time ritual on the bed, her eyes locked onto his with determined intent. *If we both dream tonight, we can be together.*

Yet two days ago on the phone, she had said, 'Should I read you my Christmas list?'

'Okay, darling.'

'Well, I want a kitten, a doll's house, a pram and lavender essence. That's all I want.'

*

Viktor picked Rosa up from Bristol. The thing that got him was the house. Even though Nina had someone who came round to tidy and to pick Rosa up from school three days a week, there was still an air of shabby neglect. It felt like this family – of mother and child – were only temporary sojourners in their own home. The furniture was carelessly bought and badly assembled, Rosa's room painted a rough white, her colourful toys organised neatly on the chipboard shelves. There was nothing on the walls, though, no real effort, no alphabet chart, no cute kitten, just two tatty postcards from distant cousins. The house felt to Viktor like a holiday rental. Each room carried a faint whiff of what it should be. Their home was devoid of the rough and tumble of life.

Viktor had done this. He had drained those rented bricks of family – so he thought. Nina's now lined, permanently tired face sat on his conscience. He had done this to her as well.

Only after Viktor had left Nina could he recall clearly all the moments that had led up to it, to each point, the last meal, the last night, their final conversation. Now he recalled them each and thought, *At that point I could still have reversed the decision*. Even afterwards, when they were apart and she was in Bristol and he in the bedsit in London, if he had stepped in then, he could still have reversed the decision to leave her.

In their days together Rosa lost her first tooth, caught it in her hand as she was quietly sipping her hot chocolate. She had been wobbling this precious, small piece of ivory for days, refusing food, alerting strangers that it was loose. Yet when it actually tumbled to earth she took it to her father, who made a fuss and kissed her, announcing to the café that Rosa had lost her first tooth. 'Please, Viktor, it's only a tooth,' she said firmly. They rolled up a piece of tissue paper and she soberly and methodically dabbed the bloodied gum. They then folded the tooth in the tissue and placed it inside a round silver box, decorated with plastic coloured jewels and tiny triangles of mirror. Rosa then spoke about how everyone she knew would be excited at her new smile, 'Viktor, don't tell Lara. She'll say, "Rosa, you look different somehow." And Mummy, Mummy will be amazed.'

Viktor was now certain that he had failed the elemental lesson of life – yet another lesson – to bear witness, to be with the people you loved, to share with them as they experienced and rejoiced, hold on when life tried to break them, as they were broken, before they left. Then Viktor realised that this was the problem, the point: that life can never be saved until after the loss. Only the irrevocable makes us decisive and determined. Clawing back afterwards is always impossible.

Nina's love was like her outbursts: she made an enormous amount of noise, but behind it the wounds were never very deep. On the first weekend, when she stayed with her mother after the split, she discovered that she was strong and could see no way for the two of them to be together. How could love turn on two days' conversations and wine with her mother? How could he be forgotten so easily?

That weekend Viktor lay on his parents' floor howling so loudly he was worried he would disturb the neighbours, with the memories of her coming into their flat, crossing the brown wool Persian rug with its geometric shapes, calling from the bathroom and toilet, her staccato presence frozen in each room.

Now his head became choked with her. On the first week apart he couldn't see a way through to clear the air.

What a long arc of life – the frustrations, desires, joys, all for her. He recalled his obsession with her body, the flattery of her form, her young, hard, insistent body, the firm rise of her breasts when between her legs he reached up and held them, played with her nipples, savoured her pleasure, her taste. How long did it take to find the way to that position? To that angle and precision, his head wedged between her thighs, resting on one leg, his tongue free, his hands touching her. How long had it taken to find this hold? A year? Yes, it was a year, he now remembered. That second trip to the bed-and-breakfast in Kent, how she said after she'd come, 'We've found a new position that works well for us.' He had laughed and waved her comment away.

How long had it taken them to find a way through the rows, the absurd misunderstandings, the screaming? Three years? *That's it. It was three years.* Those last three months, curse them, when the code had finally been cracked. How they had planned for the wedding they never had on that glorious, sweet, absurd day marching along the clifftop, planning with stones and a stick on the sand how the celebration would be organised and where the guests would sit. *Remember how we laughed. How that made us feel, as though we were dancing inside.* How long?

All that time, and love turns on a weekend.

Each moment in his life dragged up a memory. The train together into town, that trip, before Rosa was born, to Stonebridge, the casual forgotten walk from the station now summoned. Each place polluted, each occupied. Viktor had thought she was too beautiful for this to last. He summoned the sight of her again, in her underwear, her breasts pulled together tightly in her bra. How long was he trapped by her beauty, befuddled, lost? Two years?

Through weeks he struggled, unable to divert himself with anything. His usual tricks to cast off melancholy only left his chest heaving in pain. He longed to get out of the country for a week, to move for a moment to a place free of her, but he could see no beyond, he could will forward no future free of her. Nina's occupation of everything had settled hard on his life. *Goddamn this virus*, he shouted one night, still sobbing.

Did I live those times, that life, alone? Were those memories my invention? What does it mean that I am broken, that she cannot see a future, however hard she tries, for us in London or Bristol? He didn't mind so much that she had already consigned this life to her past, but her refusal to be paralysed by loss astonished him.

'Let her move on, man,' Tendai told him. 'Let her have another lover.'

How does she not feel the regret of lost life? Why doesn't that stop her, like me, prevent her from breathing, like me?

'You don't know, it is not like that, comrade,' Tendai told him, slapping him on the back. 'But you need to get up. She hasn't extinguished your force. You just need to turn off the light, see things anew. The dawn has come, Vik. The dawn. The fucking dawn.'

*

Recolonisation started slowly. Sheer time did this, in part: pacing up and down his parents' street, rolling around in the sheets in the spare bed, the smell of her eradicated slowly from his skin. The memory of the sofa where they watched TV no longer so redolent of her movement around the flat. Then one night, when his parents were out, he ran the bath and lit candles. They threw uneven, nervous, twitching light into the dark room, with the sound of the radio and the tumbling, hopeful water filling the bath. In this din he managed to throw out the shadows and find relaxation as the warm water lapped over his body, immersed his thoughts, drowned his missing.

*

Before the protest, Gary had listed the Order of Service: 'We start with Tendai on the mic. Then everyone comes in, the cast, the mock cleaners, the top hats. Wayne and me will be shouting orders and snapping the air with our riding crops. Then Tendai hands the megaphone to Moreblessing and while she speaks, we graffiti the wall. Moreblessing finishes, turns, we distribute the union leaflet about the campaign. Got it? Another run-through?'

Tendai raised the loud-hailer above his head; Terry stretched, tiptoed, reached up. 'Give me the fucking megaphone, Tendai,' he growled.

Keeping up his banter, Tendai handed the square plastic microphone to Moreblessing, who had come to his side. She put the microphone to her mouth, pressed the black trigger and spoke.

Moreblessing did not flap in the wind. She stood unruffled by the storms of crisis, arrest, family death, defeat and failure. She was no heroine of London, of Harare North, as much as Viktor tried to see her as the repository of his exotic, romantic imaginings, a symbol of the UK's underground workforce, clandestine, visa-less and noble – a sort of ambulating, collapsing nation in her single force. Instead she stood her ground with a certain dryness, an economy of emotion. Her caution came from the burdens she carried, the need for slow, steady steps so she wouldn't stumble.

Cautious in London, mouthy in Harare, only Moreblessing's refusal to concede to unfairness remained unshaken. Despite Tendai's appeal to the epic, the big story that drew everything together, she refused any political association. The external conditions of her life stripped her of humour, forced her to shed anything that was surplus to survival. 'We're Africans, Tendai. We've seen enough revolutions, enough tunnel vision, projects and transformation. Why haven't you men learnt? With your ideas for another world that looks like Mugabe's revolution – his *chimurenga*, only with new men in charge.'

Moreblessing was a nurse, a midwife and a geographer with a master's degree from the University of Zimbabwe. She was a mother of two children of her own and a wife to Jonathan, who had moved to Johannesburg and disappeared, and mother also to the three children of her dead sister in Gweru. She had arrived in London on a temporary visa and stayed, lived in a shared house in Stratford with school friends from Harare and worked without a visa cleaning the university from seven in the morning to two in the afternoon, then for the agency Caring Hands, on the night shift from six to six, looking after Derek, who had multiple sclerosis. In Moreblessing, Caring Hands secured a nurse and a carer for far below the minimum wage.

Moreblessing pushed past Tendai and Terry and spoke without pause or hesitation in her perfect university English. 'You may not be aware, but the majority of outsourced workers – me, Tendai, Patience and a hundred and fifty others who work for BCW – receive no statutory sick pay and the legal minimum of holidays and pension provision. When we are sick, because we don't get paid we still come into work. So if you come away from the university sick, it may be because we've been forced to come into work unwell.'

Terry continued to hiss, trying to distract her. Moreblessing held out her arm to keep him at a distance. Gary, with his lean, sinewy body, leapt onto the reception desk, reached for Wayne's hand and pulled him onto the wooden counter. No one noticed them chalking on the far wall, behind the reception desk, EQUAL RIGHTS FOR CLEANERS.

'We cannot visit our families. We have to cut holidays short so they fit with university closing times.' Moreblessing hadn't been home for five years – since she arrived. If she left the United Kingdom, she couldn't return. The money she earned was worth more than her presence to her family, the great, draining, distant extended network of dependants who required her efforts for their survival. The Zimbabwe dozens with their clamouring needs – when one died another was born, or another child was orphaned. Her youngest, Dora, now twelve, wasn't sleeping. Moreblessing soothed her deep sobs for her mother on the phone, a hand smothering her own tears, consuming the international phonecard in a single ten-minute call.

'When we grow old we have to continue working, as we don't have pensions. For the last year we have run a campaign for equal rights.' Suddenly she turned to the wall behind her and paused her commanding, unembellished speech. The audience, which had grown and crowded the lobby four lines deep, turned with her and faced the chalk graffiti. She repeated, 'EQUAL RIGHTS FOR CLEANERS.' Everyone stared at the wall. The effect, the timing, the sudden appearance of Moreblessing's words emblazoned on the wall made the crowd sigh together, then clap.

Tendai, standing tall and wiry, the MC for this protest circus, bent down, put his mouth to the microphone and repeated,

'EQUAL RIGHTS FOR CLEANERS!' Then, forgetting himself, he shouted, 'Viva socialism! Viva the cleaners!' and punched the air.

'For a year we have held demonstrations and stunts and received thousands of emails in support. Dozens of organisations, MPs, party leaders, have supported the campaign. The university, this great centre of learning, is now regarded as hypocritical, a bedfellow to exploitation, not learning.'

Defeated, with his thick arms folded high on his chest, Terry glared at Moreblessing. Everyone else turned to face the far wall, hoping that this small black magician would conjure more words, project another slogan onto the wall.

'And the university refuses to consult with us. They say they are talking to BCW but these talks are meaningless if they do not involve us, the workers.' The security guards paced nervously. Their radios crackled, popped, emitted faraway voices; the noise filled the silence between Moreblessing's sentences.

Despite everything – the defeats, the early starts, the hours of cleaning, the numbing buzz of static that rang all day in her head as she walked, enveloped in her ankle-length coat, to her second shift – Moreblessing believed that words, speeches, the simple act of description could persuade the system to concede to the logic of her explanation. The manifold proof presented to the university in leaflets, stunts, theatre, peaceful demonstrations, would eventually yield justice. Fair, proportionate protest would unravel unfair practice. She had an exaggerated confidence in *the people*. These people, watching her now, hanging on her words, if shown the right path, could not be deceived. When they held their protests, when she spoke, Tendai shepherding the crowd as Gary and Wayne appealed, *the people* would follow. Understand. Moreblessing forgot that she could not be everywhere at the same time and that there was no miracle of explanation or description.

'Our campaign is not going away,' she continued. 'In the summer we have more action planned. In the autumn there will be mass protests and occupations with students. We are discussing strike action with our union.'

Terry grimaced and muttered to himself, 'Like hell, like fucking hell there'll be a strike.' His lips lifted above his teeth in a snarl. 'No, we're fucking not.' The distant voices on the radios became more frenetic.

Moreblessing believed she could draw in her foes, persuade the BCW workers who refused to join the union, even those who refused to talk to her. It was always white workers, she noticed; it was the British security guards who told her to be cautious, that this was not how it was done, who presented the management's case, the argument that 'in this day and age of cost-cutting and competition, the workers had to take a hit'. Sometimes their intransigence broke her and she became certain that these obedient whites were biologically predisposed to shun unions and strikes, accept orders, obey their superiors.

Moreblessing concluded, 'But this action is necessary. We are proud to work at the university and don't want its reputation damaged. We say: work with us to bring back equality and fairness to the workplace, and hope to this once-great university.'

Moreblessing smiled, satisfied that the audience had stayed until she finished. Wayne, with a T-shirt that clung to his torso, started to clap. The crowd joined him and a few people whistled and cheered – as if they had been watching a theatrical production.

The crowd of sixty stayed immobile. The security guards who were called to contain the rebellion vacillated as the team handed out the propaganda. The mood was jovial.

154

Viktor saw the police first. They barged into the lobby, their charge heavy, their movements crowded by equipment: the thickly padded vests, the belts weighted with truncheons, torches, pepper spray, the heavy, inflexible boots. Viktor reached for his phone and started to film.

*

Tendai put himself between the police and his comrade, and a security guard tried to push him away, his hand flat against Tendai's chest. Not thinking, Moreblessing tried to intervene. The arresting officer took her hand, attempted to twist it behind her back and led her away.

In the mayhem Terry started to speak. 'We disassociate ourselves from any strike action – the situation has not reached that point, nor do we expect it to. We are engaged in constructive discussions and negotiations in the Partnership Forum.'

Moreblessing pulled her arm away from the officer and shouted at the two officers now holding Wayne and Gary. 'Why are you being so aggressive?'

'Because he is under arrest,' one of the officers answered. Other policemen came into the lobby. Some of the spectators stepped back, wondering if this was more agitprop. Moreblessing held on to Wayne. Copying her, Patience put her arm around Gary. The guards slowly prised them, limb by limb, from their comrades. A security guard continued to hold Tendai back.

Terry spoke. 'These arrests are unnecessary, but the action was unprovoked. It was not sanctioned by the union branch.' Tendai knocked the security guard's hand out of his path. He recognised the guard, who had once told him that he didn't speak to Africans like him. 'Blacks should sort out their own countries before telling the UK how to run its affairs.'

His path cleared, Tendai rushed to Terry. 'You bastard. You are our bloody regional organiser, you're meant to be on our side, man!' With each word Tendai prodded Terry hard in the chest.

Moreblessing screamed to the crowd. 'A gang of men are assaulting your colleagues. Why are you standing there? This isn't about fighting terrorism. Why don't you fucking help?' As soon as the word came out Moreblessing was silent. It was the first time she'd used a swear word, and it felt good. 'Fucking get up and do something!'

The foyer started to empty after the men were dragged away. Two security guards closed and locked the tall double doors. Wayne and Gary were carried away unhindered. Moreblessing walked up to Terry, her face flushed, her nostrils flared. She raised her hand and smacked him hard across the face. 'Shame on you, Terry.'

Chapter Fourteen

Initially it didn't bother Anne-Marie that Viktor and his life seemed in disarray. For a period before his separation from Nina she couldn't just call or text him, the necessity of secrecy forcing all the power into his hands, but she liked this sense of fantasy, of make-believe, that this gave their friendship. But when Viktor disappeared for weeks on end into his own life, his own problems, although she didn't react, she was confused – and it bothered her that it bothered her. She reassured herself with the absurdity of their connection, even questioned her own sanity – laughing to herself at her feelings for a man she'd never met.

Viktor dreamed of Anne-Marie, and when he woke the memory of the dream clung to him, hung on him all day and became his new obsession. Before long every activity in his life was in some way motivated by her – the hours until their next call, the text messages punctuating his day, all things a countdown to her.

'She's fucking seduced me,' Viktor said to himself in the morning, more worn and stiff than when he had fallen into bed. There was no dopey escape, no temporary reprieve as he woke; the night had been dense with dreams of her. A prison where they were locked up, forced every afternoon to come together and dance. Every day at the prison dance he would see her and she would smile innocently, nonchalantly, at him – and then dance, pressed tightly against someone else. The man she danced with was large and tall, his erection visible inside his trousers. These dreams were crude, worthy of no analysis. *She seduced me.* He knew also that it would not be enough to simply send messages. The obsession needed actualisation; he needed to reach beyond the screen and their calls to see her.

*

The offices were cleared and the staff ordered out. Tendai insisted they hide, camping out in Viktor's office. The corridor was quiet, the carpeted thud of running, pounding feet gone. In the office Tendai stretched out on Viktor's chair, sitting perfectly still. Viktor stood by the door, not moving, his hand to his lip, his head turned to his guests. Moreblessing and Patience both huddled under the desk, their heads resting on their bent knees. Only Viktor, with less to lose, was serious, his face tight with reprimand, ordering silence to the room of fugitives, who had seen worse. Viktor saw the wide, insolent smile on Tendai's face, his arms folded behind his head, his legs out, and felt his pulse hammer. His back was wet with perspiration. He looked at Tendai, this humble, courageous, modest man, this African Gramsci, Sartre, Guevara – Viktor checked himself. No, this African-African, not a dead white man.

Afterwards Viktor was oblivious to the voices, the planning, Tendai's arms flapping. Patience standing with a marker, writing on the whiteboard on the wall over the desks, Tendai working up their outrage with the police, the university, Terry, the union, the whole damn bureaucracy. Viktor plugged his phone into the computer and uploaded the video: almost twenty minutes of the stunt, then the arrests.

Moreblessing repeated, shaking her head, 'Three months in the union and still nothing.'

When the women were gone, Tendai turned to Viktor and put a hand on his shoulder. 'Well, Vlad, what do you think of Patience and Moreblessing?'

'It's Viktor.'

'Take Moreblessing.'

'I don't know them,' Viktor spoke. 'Brave, I suppose. Very brave. Two jobs, without papers. How does she survive?'

Tendai answered, 'Like we all do, because we have no choice. She was one of the first in the union and she says what she thinks. A strong worker. What do you think about her?'

Viktor had watched her closely during the re-enactment, her head wrapped in a colourful strip of cloth, her soft nose, prominent cheekbones and pert, upturned lips. When they ran along the corridor Viktor had shouted directions from behind her – 'Left, straight on, right, two floors up' – and he'd noticed her long black skirt, how strangely out of place it was. She held it up on both sides so she could run, as though she was practising a curtsy. Viktor had seen her strong calves, the thin bones of her ankles, the material of her skirt drawn tight on her waist, around her buttocks, her breasts, which kept their shape, hardly moving as she ran. Was this what Tendai meant?

'Come on, Vlad, don't be shy with me, man. I could see how you were trying to impress her.' Tendai looked up at Viktor and winked. 'I've noticed the extra attention you give when there are pretty women around.' Viktor moved away from the door. He felt exposed. 'Listen,' Tendai continued, 'if you like her, I can speak to her. We could do it here.' He spread his arms out, indicating the room.

Viktor was confused. 'Speak to her?'

'Yes. I know her.'

'No, I don't want you to speak to her,' Viktor stuttered, his face red. The perspiration started again.

'There's a thing she'll do. Don't pretend you're not interested. You've separated from your wife, right? The mother of your daughter.'

Viktor was irritated with Tendai's intrusion. He sat on the corner of the desk, lifted a pile of papers to his lap and pretended to sort through them.

'Don't play the coy smart man. The two of us and Moreblessing. The three of us with our clothes off.'

'What are you saying?' Viktor exclaimed. Was this a test? Maybe Tendai was trying to rattle him, to get him to show that he was like all white men, repressed, racist, terrified to be naked in front of a black man, to have sex with a Zimbabwean woman. Viktor decided he'd better play this carefully. 'I don't think this is appropriate.'

Tendai had already occupied the room with his socks and their odour, his feet resting on the desk in front of him, the books he'd absent-mindedly fingered and left open. 'Okay, let me be clearer,' he said. 'We could use one of these desks. You lie on it, maybe we will need two desks, she's on top and works on me. See?

'Listen,' Tendai continued, 'you're a cerebral, sensitive man. If you go for another one of your difficult women, it'll kill you. If you like Moreblessing, I can fix it up for you. I don't even need to be there.'

Viktor remained silent. He was disappointed with Tendai, with this conversation, with himself. What was happening to him? He reflected on his recent dreams about Anne-Marie. The drugs had chased sex into his unconscious.

Suddenly Tendai announced, 'I've been evicted. I have nowhere to stay, man.' Viktor tried to think of reasons why he couldn't put him up: his small, impossible bedsit, Rosa's visits, Tendai's penis – there simply wouldn't be room for all of these things in his single room. 'I'll stay here, Vik,' Tendai said suddenly. 'I can put the desks together and sleep under them so I don't trip the lights. There are showers on the first floor, right? I'll be fine.'

'It's not my office,' Viktor said.

'What time do the others come in in the morning?'

'It's free for two weeks. You can stay for two weeks.'

Tendai leant against the wall, a book open in his hands. 'You know, Patience said to me yesterday, "Let's make love like pigs, on the floor."'

'TENDAI!' Viktor shouted, raising his hands from the computer. Tendai smiled, then winked at him.

*

Comrade!

No need to apologise. On the contrary – I'm sorry I'd failed to grasp the hell you're going through. Certainly don't worry about 'having to' reply. No pressure – none at all. Rather comradely sympathy and solidarity with your domestic inferno.

And we're not alone, my friend. Everyone I know is going through some new degree of hell from the enemy class, some of it structured into the 'cuts'. A best friend/comrade is suddenly a full-time carer as well as a parent and worker, after complications with his partner after a minor fall. Students, as well as workers, are cracking up with financial pressure and bullying. The now two years of wage freeze is savaging millions of families/workers. Pubs emptying. Imagine that, the English public house, the sodden, stinking, beer-stained shit-holes (we have similar places in Zimbabwe and in South Africa) are now empty. And the English are drunks, so imagine what this is going to do to the class. And the struggle.

So the point is this, comrade: each case can seem 'individual' or personal – but it's not. It's UNIVERSAL. Stress is pandemic now. Conditions are obviously different in Africa, but the enemy is the same.

As you'll know, this is no coincidence/accident! The ruling class is on an all-out offensive right across Europe AND Africa. And the crisis is also the messy birthplace of Revolution too! Tunisia, Egypt, Libya, Yemen, Bahrain AND Burkina Faso, Uganda, Nigeria and more. It's no wonder that Egypt just came to Spain. Africa is coming to Europe.

And in being so palpably 'from below', an unled mass, it is the reflection of our crisis, with all that is now corrupted on our side, the trade union bureaucracy, the very left itself a corrupt, rotten, fetid, out-of-touch leadership that urges full reliance upon the most corrupt, most incorporated trade union bureaucracy in the world. Trotsky once called them 'the most counter-revolutionary force in Britain'.

Anyway, I am losing my way. I wanted to write that you, com, with the skills at your disposal, with your computers and in your crisis, you need to throw yourself into generalising the struggle against the deepest, most protracted crisis of capitalism for a generation. This struggle is taking place at the university – in our union, in our fights. Start at the university.

Comrade, can you hear me?

Tendai

*

Viktor and Nina's communication was restricted to curt emails stripped of superfluous information, simple instructions almost barked. *Tell me what time and confirm. Rosa is used to your unpredictability. Tell your mother to stop feeding Rosa sweets. Tell me, tell me, tell me …*

Still his whole body would shake, his heart race, and he would clench his jaw and tighten his muscles to hold still. No sooner had the weekend with Rosa begun than the end signalled its presence. Rosa waited with her case on the bottom step, staring impatiently for her father's large head to appear in frosted glass and the garden gate to sound his arrival. Viktor folded himself down, received Rosa's embrace and then made an effort, stood, his legs apart, one arm holding her, the other searching blindly for the case. Along the path towards the train he dropped down slowly to the ground, lowered Rosa onto the pavement and pushed his nose into her hair, kissed her and told her to walk as her clammy, excited hand found his. She fell back, unable to keep up with his long strides, then skipped back to his side, her pleasure turning their first walk together, after four months apart, into a dance.

Rosa's feet in her new black boots, playing hopscotch on the pavement, marked out her feelings, telling him and anyone who cared to look at them that the tears, the separation, the nights of missing, the long, secret wishes and prayers they had both made to themselves, the dreams, had dissolved and were no more. All that mattered was that simple stretch of pavement, the short distance to their train, the cold sky, the sun beating down on the clouds, its glare almost too bright for them to see each other. Their bony, identical fingers were linked in a union that made Viktor fear their separation again in three days, the moment of parting which would throb for weeks afterwards. Rosa's love-saturated heart would be broken once more. How many times can a child's heart be broken? How many times would *he* break it? When would his own capacity for killing his daughter finally give out?

Viktor pulled Rosa into his arms again, her legs clasped around his waist. They boarded the train, found a seat, Rosa dragging her bag behind her. *If our species has a limitless capacity for savagery*, Viktor thought, *then we also have an infinite ability to love again and again.*

Knitted deep into the separation was the thought that his missing for her would fade, lose the bright, radiant sorrow. The relentless movement of life would drain even their love. Maybe, he thought, if they stayed on this train, both of them in the same stubborn, decisive grip, time would career past, ruffle their hair, try, but fail, to prise apart their heavily planted hands and let them move on. The slipstream of time would drag at their bodies, then fall away and leave them on the platform and their parting would be cheated.

They dropped the small case in Viktor's second-floor bedsit in Archway. He lived in a single miniature square room with a fold-down sofa, a small, shared shower cubicle in the corridor and a sink and two hotplates resting on a fridge in the corner of the room.

'Can we make the bed, please? So that we won't need to do it tonight. I want to see where we're sleeping,' Rosa asked, in her adamant, organised way.

They folded out the sofa. Viktor emptied the wicker basket of the duvet and pillows.

'A sheet, Dad, we need a sheet.'

'I don't have one. I normally use a large towel.'

'In that case,' Rosa said, 'we will buy one today. We can't sleep without a sheet.' She organised the cover, set the pillows under it and took out her clothes, removing the long white socks she wore to stop her boots from chafing her shins, two dresses, a book, a hairbrush and toiletries. She arranged each item in a corner of the room, lined up along the wall.

'Daddy,' she asked, looking at the room, 'are we poor?'

Chapter Fifteen

It cost his mother a month's wage and took her a year of saving to buy Biko the tweed jacket with the wide, plunging pockets, large enough to hold a book, two books, one on each side. He looked like a schoolteacher, her seventeen-year-old son, already with his matriculation certificate and owlish glasses and long, long words, lapsing into English in the middle of sentences. When he first put the jacket on, her head swelled, her face flushed and she squinted hard in the light to see him. Her large, bossy boy always led the children in their games but was attentive to her, unlike his sister.

Each week she spent more time in bed, the curtains drawn late into the morning.

The shame rose up again, drying Biko's mouth. Gertrude was older than him. He walked back from school next to her, in his new jacket. Her eyes narrowed with her smile when she saw him waiting for her. 'Mr America, you look like a white man. An American.' She put her arm around his waist and let his hand rest on her lower back. The ripple of muscles, the rise of her buttocks chased away his breath. Her pale blue school shirt was buttoned tight against her breasts. Her breasts, that he had noticed, when she lay in the sun with her friends between classes chiding, teasing the boys. But instead of teasing him now she allowed him to walk her home, taking the long, circuitous route through the township, past the small brick government homes evenly spaced and painted white so that on the road they looked like the dots on a domino. On the paved road Biko pretended that Gertrude was his and that their confident, meandering steps were taking them to his city house next to the National University of Science and Technology, or to his home in Harare or Johannesburg.

When they reached the gate to her house Biko dropped his hand from her back and put both of his hands into the deep pockets on either side of his jacket. In one pocket he felt the loose pages of his book. That morning he'd got in late to school — he'd been reading as he walked, the brittle, tanned pages disintegrating in his snatching, overeager fingers, his feet stumbling unguided on the road to school. The book was telling him something and he read hungrily, trying to grasp the meaning before the pages disintegrated entirely. Now, with Gertrude, the pages felt like a collection of autumn leaves. He struggled to rehearse the passages he'd committed to memory:

We are forever pursued by our actions. Their ordering, their circumstances and their motivation, may perfectly well come to be profoundly modified *a posteriori*. This is merely one of the snares that history and its various influences has on us. But can we escape becoming dizzy? And who can affirm that which does not haunt the whole of existence?

'You can come in if you want, my mum will still be at the market,' Gertrude said.

Biko heard her words, yet the meaning only came to him seconds later. He nodded his head and his entire body shook. He battled to coordinate his legs, to stop them from buckling and get them to propel him along the short path across the broken paving stones to the door. Gertrude reached the house, it seemed, in a single bound and pushed hard on the door. In the shadowed interior her face was half-lit. His hand perspired over the pages. Who would believe him? Gertrude seemed to Biko like a full woman pressed absurdly into the school uniform of a child. Her tall, perfect body made her aloof, even with her teachers. How sophisticated and how unlike the adults he knew.

The door opened into the kitchen, which smelt of food cooked on the single-ringed hob suspended over the gas cylinder, the table neat, with a plastic floral tablecloth and four clumsy chairs made from cast-off wood, the kind Biko saw being hawked on the edge of the township. There was a doorless arch that led to the lounge and a pile of mattresses leaning against the far kitchen wall. They were poorer than his family, he calculated quickly. Gertrude probably slept on the scrubbed kitchen floor with her younger brothers and sisters. She led Biko through the kitchen to the lounge and the torn sofa. The fridge rattled noisily, its dented white door held closed by a clumsily knotted piece of wire.

Gertrude let her school bag slide from her shoulder, fell on the sofa and patted the place next to her. Quickly Biko removed his jacket, which seemed incongruous and new in her house. He folded it carefully over the arm of the sofa.

'Let me try it on, go on.' Before Biko could respond Gertrude had jumped up, taken the jacket from the sofa and thrust in her arms. The padded shoulders slopped on her, the cuffs swallowing half of her hands. She strutted up and down the small room, admiring the jacket. Occasionally she raised her eyes coyly to Biko. 'What do you think, *mudiwa*? It looks better on me than you, no?'

Biko was still trying to drain his head of blood, slow his racing heart, the unbearable expectation that emptied him of words, let alone coherent sentences. No one did this to him, nothing silenced him. 'It looks fine,' he said dumbly.

'Only fine?'

The front door swung open and hit the kitchen wall. A small girl wearing a grey school dress, her hair scraped into pigtails, ran into the room. She looked at her sister, then at Biko, and rolled her eyes, her smile exposing her missing teeth. 'Who's that?' she demanded.

Gertrude swivelled on her heels, turned to the girl and shouted, '*Akungitshiye!* Play in the garden, I tell you!'

The girl sucked her teeth and laughed at the couple. *Even the children today are being rude, behaving strangely*, Biko thought. The girl ran out.

Gertrude turned to her guest, her hands in his jacket pockets. 'What are these?' She pulled out a fistful of yellowed pages and read slowly, 'The couple is no longer shut in upon itself. It no longer finds its end in itself. It is no longer the result of the natural instinct of the per ... pet ... uation of the species, nor the institution ... alised means of satisfying one's sexuality ... The Algerian couple, in becoming a link in the revolutionary organisation, is transformed into a unit of existence ...'

He needed to leave. If he got back before the sunset he'd see his mother. He'd sit by her bed and read to her, even if she was motionless and didn't speak.

Biko heard the front door close, but a moment later it opened again. The girl's small, spongy fingers pushed gently until there was enough room for her to squeeze through, though not enough to make the door yawn and alert the couple.

The girl beckoned to a boy her age to follow, and together they tiptoed on the bare concrete floor and stood to either side of the archway, watching.

It was a cold early winter evening and Gertrude had to work quickly. 'I want the jacket,' she said matter-of-factly, as if they were discussing a trade of fruit in a school packed lunch. She rolled up the sleeves, creasing the arms, the cool, mauve lining that felt like a caress when Biko put it on in the morning; the fabric sliding and licking his bare arms in his regulation short-sleeved school shirt. His mother had sewn the label in carefully, perfectly above the inside pocket, with his name in capitals: STEPHAN MUTAWURWA. When she'd presented the jacket to him, pulled it up his arms, hooked it over his shoulder and dusted imaginary dirt from the lapels, she stood back, came forward, did up the buttons, undid them, sizing her tall son, cocked her head to the side and moved him as if he was a mannequin in an Edgar's shop window in Bulawayo. She looked at him in silence, peeled open the jacket, held the two sides open, felt and admired the lining, indicated with a slight nod of her head the inside pocket and below it a smaller pocket for change. She seemed almost reluctant to let her son go. They savoured the moment, Biko striding around the bedroom gazing into the fragment of broken mirror that his mother held for him.

'I want the jacket. We'll do an exchange.' Gertrude slipped the jacket from her shoulders and let it fall and crumple on the floor. Biko squirmed but didn't move. Gertrude started to unbutton her shirt slowly, the fingers lingering on the strained cloth. 'So what do you say, *mudiwa*?' Her large, dirty white bra was exposed. Biko gazed at her slender, narrow waist. The sky-blue shirt hung to either side of her breasts.

170

'This,' she said, 'for this,' she pointed to the jacket on the floor.

Almost unable to speak, Biko groaned affirmation. The children stared from their hiding place, their breath, like Biko's, stolen, fixing them in place.

Gertrude fell to her knees, parted Biko's legs and began to release his belt, pulling it away from his waist, gripping the leather strap to spring the metal buckle. Biko's trousers opened and Gertrude fingered the zipper, pulling it over his stiff organ.

Biko swallowed loudly but his mouth remained dry. His father would hit him for coming home late and for losing his jacket. There was nothing arbitrary about his father's discipline: it came if there was any infraction to his code. If the children returned late or were insolent, if there was a bad mark at school – even Biko's older sister, Janet, a clerk at a Bulawayo solicitor's firm, was hit and she took it, her eyes bulging, her face flushed. His father was slightly built but strong, his slim arms hard, and he would pull the children into his chest, embrace them, let them feel his stiff, sinewy form.

Gertrude rolled down his boxer shorts. Biko's penis twitched rhythmically as if *it* beat blood around his body, flooding his head, commanding his spirit.

The front door is always locked, but the back door that leads to the hall is normally open, Biko thought. *I can climb over the low fence, put my foot on the handle, lever myself over. I may be able to get in without him seeing.*

Gertrude directed Biko to the sofa and then dribbled saliva into the palm of her right hand. She cradled Biko's penis and started to masturbate him. The children hidden in the kitchen craned, strained to see, their mouths open.

Biko groaned as Gertrude's hand thrashed faster and faster. *If Mother has died, he won't hit me when I come in. He won't even notice that the jacket is missing. Instead he will pull me to him. The house will be full. The cover will be drawn to her neck and the women of the neighbourhood will be chanting and praying loudly. If she's died.*

Biko was losing control. The children inched forward and stood openly in the doorway. Biko saw them, but he was already taken. Something seized his spine; he arched backwards, pressing his shoulders into the sofa, lifting his groin forward, up. Still Gertrude pounded. It was as if he was being possessed, a new being entering his body, forcing him into a different shape, contorting him in an agony of pleasure. The children watched, terrified at what tortured mutation would emerge. They drew even further into the room. Biko's taut body finally broke, and he let out a cry that he didn't recognise. As he came the children stepped backwards. Biko's eyes closed. Jets of come shot out in three great streams, over the sofa, onto the floor, leaving a streak of pearly white beads across his shirt. And Gertrude kept moving her hand hard against his balls and up again, until the last drop pulsed out with a final squeeze of her hand. He was completely drained. He dropped back into his seat. The children sighed, gulped in the air, and noisily turned and ran out of the house.

Biko made his way through the township. It could be cold in the early winter; around July the wind blew through the lanes of tin and brick houses and made the roofs flap and rattle. There was a large population of prostitutes, who came out at dusk. They used the shadowed alleyways between the shebeens or the bush ringing the shanty town. When Biko was smaller he would lead gangs of friends into the bush to follow a prostitute and her client and watch the unstifled fucking. Semen, still visible, sometimes stained the well-trodden path.

*

No sooner had Viktor built Tendai up, turned him into a colossus of the liberation movement, an eccentric genius of the continent's great, tragic history of revolt and plunder, a one-man freedom fighter who joined the Global South with the crisis-ridden North, than Tendai veered off and plunged headlong into the garbage. Why couldn't Tendai just be an honourable goddamn stereotype, a cliché, a figure of unequivocal righteousness – drawn in bold realism with a jutting Lenin jaw, beautiful and serene?

Viktor trudged along the corridor, his feet sinking into the baize carpet, the thick pile slowing his strides. He'd dropped his keys into Tendai's hand and Tendai had practically pushed Viktor into the hall, his hand curled over his shoulder. 'We'll talk more tomorrow. Don't worry, Vik, this place is perfect cover.' What did he want to talk about? The betrayal of the ANC? His prison sentence? The struggle in London for pensions, sick pay and holidays? Or Tendai's sex plans, the office turned into a boudoir, the PhD interrupted again by their love triangle?

Right now Viktor wanted less complication and more predictability. He pressed the button for the lift; a red light illuminated the downward arrow. Viktor turned and pushed hard against the stairwell door. As he started to descend he heard the bell, then the doors to the lift opening.

Tendai, he thought, was absurd, with those dark glasses covering his bloodshot eyes.

The mild breeze caressed Viktor as he walked to the tube. Nina had cancelled the mediation. 'If you can pay for it.' Her email had been so angry she couldn't write his name, or her own; instead she had signed off with a single lowercase *n*. Anger stripped Nina of her grammar, made her put a premium on words, as if it was costing her to write to him. It was two hundred pounds, two hundred more than he could afford. 'It only works, Mr Isaacs, if both parties contribute and pay an equal share. In these circumstances, maybe Ms Thompson is not ready for mediation.'

No mediation, no Rosa. Viktor wondered why everyone was in such a rush in the morning to get to the office and again in the evening. These eager, aching souls, so much noise and chaos, no spiritual peace – just the rush home, the panic, the television, a restless sleep. *No mediation.* The words went round and round in Viktor's head. Last week Tendai had been unyielding: 'You can't play with these bourgeois institutions, marriage, the family, and expect to come out unscathed.'

'I wasn't actually married,' Viktor answered pathetically.

'Whatever, Vik, you wanted children, a family, then after a time you decided you didn't want it any more. It's not a revolving door. You go in, and when you try to get out you find yourself pursued and hated, with lawyers, police, the courts.'

'It wasn't that bad.'

'You have basically lived most of your life like a bohemian, an artisan, and it doesn't go with these other' – Tendai searched for the word – 'structures. You can't get out just like that when you want, man.'

Viktor took the stairs to the tube, pushed past the queue to the lifts; the wind spun around the spiral staircase, catching his hair. *Maybe I should have had the threesome. Perhaps Tendai needs it to escape the years in prison, the past, the UK Border Agency, the disappointment with Mandela, with Mugabe, with me.*

Viktor saw Nina laughing, falling back on the bed, trying to pull on her stockings. Viktor and Rosa stood at the foot of the bed, loving her together. The threesome. Suddenly Viktor's stomach felt swollen with missing, the mistakes, with Tendai's sorrow. He heard Tendai's words once more: 'You see, Vik, the fight we were waging wasn't the fight we were prepared for.'

Viktor had started to medicate again for his insomnia. When the prescription sleeping pills ran out he moved on to Kalms Tablets, a handful at a time. He even took them in the morning, after his second coffee, to compensate for the rising panic the caffeine awoke in him. In the afternoon he took another mouthful before his tutorial groups, and again when he tried to sleep. When the Kalms Tablets didn't work, he took pure, concentrated valerian in 300 mg capsules, six a night. With this complicated alchemy Viktor managed to remain stoned. Tendai – a master at fooling doctors – had secured six months' supply of Tripoline and split the script down the middle, three months each for him and Viktor. Between their university conversations, the emails and the drugs, the men lived and slept the same doped, dreamless life.

For a week, since the office had become Tendai's base, the desks had been pushed together to create a series of underground tunnels between their metal legs, so Tendai could crawl and sleep at night without tripping the light sensors. It was an urban guerrilla's warren right in the heart of the university, the enemy camp. He handed Tendai coffee, cradled like a prayer. Tendai was fully dressed; only his feet were bare. The room was stuffy. A tangle of blankets spilled out from under the labyrinth of desks.

'You see, com, we were great activists. We came up with our own responses, we made our own means. The courts, the street committees, everything. But we never translated it into how we could rethink liberation – our weakness, Vik.' Tendai held the paper cup of coffee in his two hands. Viktor had not slept. He'd waited impatiently for the morning, dopey, exhausted, unable to lie still or get up.

'We never brought,' Tendai paused, 'our practice into contact with theory.'

Viktor followed Tendai, put his coffee down and spoke with the same irritation. 'Yes, this is what I am trying to write about in my dissertation. The mythical belief in the power of the liberator is linked ontologically to the lack of confidence in the people in their own power. So we have to develop a more fully articulated counter-hegemonic ideology. A theory that can provide us with everything.' As he spoke he sprinkled the carpet with coffee and saliva.

Tendai rubbed his foot, cracked the knuckles on his toes, 'Oh, Vik.' He spoke softly. 'What you need is *less* theory. Get it the right way round. You can have your ideas, your theories, the PhD, after liberation. You need to spend some time in a township, not in a bloody school.' Then, raising his voice, 'Practice, experience; the rest is sterile nonsense. If you haven't seen and lived, what good are you?'

Viktor sulked silently.

Nina had screamed down the phone: 'Your mum's a fucking bitch, your dad's bloody useless. Your life is a complete disaster.'

'I hope Rosa's asleep,' he had answered pathetically.

'Well, what do you care? You'll read it in the newspaper if she dies in a road accident.'

'Please don't talk like that.'

It was not the insults to his parents and the hypothetical death of Rosa that kept him up after the call, but the thought that perhaps Nina was right and his life was a disaster. Tendai could see it. Everyone knew that he was bloody useless, a bitch, a disaster.

'I am going to the toilet,' Viktor announced to Tendai and left the room.

He undid his belt, let his trousers fall, patted the pockets of his jacket for his phone, then sat on the toilet and scrolled through the list of operas until he found *The Marriage of Figaro*. He skipped the first tracks to find the song he needed, '*Cosa Sento*', and pushed the headphones deep into his ears, letting the music interrupt the voices of reprimand and correction – the truth in both Tendai's and Nina's words. He tried to concentrate on the lyrics, letting them carry him away from gravity's pull, lift him above the steely London sky to the uninterrupted blue light, following the planet's rotation, always above the clouds, forever in the day, away from the night: *Non so più cosa son.*

*

When Viktor returned to the office, Gary, Wayne and Moreblessing were sitting together, lined up on the swivel chairs. Tendai sat on the table, his empty shoes on the floor like giant upturned shells echoing with the sound of the sea. Moreblessing was speaking.

'I had to argue with Audrey, Emma and Geoffrey not to leave the union. "Three months in the union," they said, "and nothing has changed." Audrey nearly hit the hall warden yesterday when he told her to finish cleaning the room even though she was at the end of her shift. "Three months and nothing," she kept repeating. BCW owe us overtime. At last count sixty of us had not been paid for two months. *Two months*. And when Terry takes this up with them – at the Partnership Forum – they say they're having problems with their payroll department, that the systems are down. We're going to lose members. Three months in the union for most of them and still nothing.' Moreblessing's hair was straight, shoulder-length, with a centre parting. She sat on the edge of her chair. When she stood she reached Viktor's chest, yet she was broad, her shoulders square, her neck ringed with faint lines, her skin dark, with a small but prominent mole under her nose.

'Patience is a vice,' Tendai said.

'Three months, and they already want to leave the union.' Gary was a stalwart organiser and union representative, but in these meetings – the Militant Caucus – he posed as the liberal union man, always seeking the counter-argument, imagining himself in an agony of contortion and metamorphosis. 'We need to defuse the anger – go round and talk to them. I am available. I will lean on Terry to pressure BCW.'

Viktor sat by the door and listened to Wayne's handsome American English, the short, informed sentences always clear. 'You heard Moreblessing, Gary, the system is broken. It's a joke. The forum is a joke. It keeps Terry, senior management, BCW and the vice chancellor happy, but it has delivered nothing. The system is broken; we have to do something *now*.' Wayne was the youngest in the room. He was also the anomaly, a twenty-five-year-old MA student dispatched by his well-connected family from New York, his idiomatic Spanish learnt from the family's Mexican maid and nanny. He was Moreblessing's height, with a stubbled chin, receding, short-clipped hair and red, dry, blotched skin.

People, Viktor thought, *are simple, well-meaning, goodwilled. We want to be treated fairly and if we are, we glow. It takes so little to make any of us feel the community and solidarity of our species.* The thought made him feel proud: that he'd given Tendai his office, that he had, even now with his mute presence, played a part in this worthy battle to demystify oppression and expose the university.

Tendai spoke after Wayne. 'Gary, man, our role is not to defuse the anger of the cleaners. Do you understand that, when we're not paid, we don't eat? That is not a metaphor.' He turned

178

and looked at Viktor. 'When the cleaners and security guards are not paid, how do we send money back for our families? We need to strike, we *have* to.'

Some sentences are meant to hang in the air. Tendai had thrown down the word *strike* as if placing in front of them a complete, fully built crossroads. Wayne and Gary blinked.

Tendai brought them back to life with a deep laugh. 'You Brits, you fools! I mention strike action and it stuns you into silence and paralysis. Don't do a Terry on me – the strike weapon as last resort, we don't want to disrupt the Forum, our good relations with BCW and Human Resources. Bullshit, man. You know, years ago in South Africa I remember wondering why, after more than a hundred years of working-class struggle, the UK had not delivered us from capitalism. We looked to the trade union movement in the UK, but you are completely enslaved!' Tendai's tone was severe and bitter.

'I'm American,' Wayne asserted.

'You'll be denounced,' Gary said. With his pure activism, free of party dogma, he saw the union's only purpose as its members. The hectoring full-time officials were occasionally useful, normally not. If the cleaners, security guards, Tendai and Moreblessing decided to strike, then by virtue of this simple, democratic formula he would support them.

'Denounced by who?' Moreblessing asked. 'The union will support us.'

Though Wayne did not really understand Viktor, he appreciated his passive support, the blog posts he'd written on the campaign and that Wayne had edited – removing the references to philosophy, the long descriptions of slavery, the master, hermeneutics, the call for therapeutic violence – and turned them into leaflets. Wayne also understood practice, shorn of ideology and political obfuscation. To this end he had, more than anyone else, recruited members to the union, spent months with the cleaners, speaking in Spanish, preparing multilingual leaflets and translating union propaganda. His strange hybrid family of wealthy New York liberals had taught him discipline and perseverance. His mother, a brilliant organiser of soup kitchens, charities and campaigns, was always holding on, waiting for Lefty, for a new campaigning leader of the Democrats. Someone more like Roosevelt, like JFK. Wayne was committed to changing lives today and realising small, possible dreams tomorrow – not the tomorrow of theory, the New Era, the Promised Land, but the simple day-after-today. He didn't understand Viktor's abstractions.

'Will the outsourced workers support the strike?' Wayne asked.

'More than that, if we don't strike now, soon, we will lose members, dozens, and then they will strike anyway.' Tendai's goading was never cruel. He stretched and yawned loudly, clicking his back, then flipped his shoes up and pushed his feet in.

'I'll spread the word. The cleaners are meeting at lunch. I will need Wayne to translate for Maria, Juliette and the others. The union will be behind us,' Moreblessing said as she stood. She lifted her hand above her head for a high five and Tendai slapped it.

Viktor stayed by the door, still distracted. 'What do you think, Vik?' Gary asked. Viktor was staring at the group, his eyes stinging. He imagined the men's penises, each sliding in and out like trombones, unaware as they carried on speaking. *Maybe this is what Tendai meant, the cock as a metaphor for the strike, a code for organising, for expansion, for growing the struggle.*

'Viktor?' Gary repeated.

Viktor surfaced. 'I am with you. All of you. I will write a piece, a satirical article attacking the vice chancellor.'

Chapter Sixteen

For all the high-minded attention to theory and his online search for truth, Viktor cajoled himself to sleep with YouTube clips on his phone. With the lights out, his glasses reflected scenes of jungle mayhem: hippos savaging crocodiles in Kruger National Park, American safari tourists commenting in the background: 'Look at the croc, the hippo has him in his mouth; he's holding him with his tusks. That boy has had it.' In another clip, watched five million times, a man was mauled by a bear in a zoo. Each time the effect was the same: Viktor would become profoundly depressed, the adrenaline coursing through his body, keeping him awake, his mouth dry. He was convinced that these wild animals were like him, caught in a necessary, brutal fight for meat, trapped by their own personalities, sex obsessions, unyielding natures and complexes, their low, violent egos like his.

Viktor made the inventory of his own life, the charge sheet read out in judgment of his failures. There was the porn, sometimes three times a night. He searched for videos of amateur couples – like him, he thought, lovemaking he could believe in, a story that revealed life's proper character, where love could be detected as the couple hammered into each other. What sort of father leaves his daughter for pornography? His penis enflamed, masturbating at night when he should be pulling the covers over Rosa, reading her to sleep.

The buildings, the network of roads, the hospitals and services, the friendliness on the tube only disguised what we really were: bodies, thousands, millions of them, muscular, angry, sweating, grunting and fucking. His refusal, he realised, to commit completely to the strike – to his colleagues, his parents, his daughter – could be put down to all this fucking.

'Daddy,' Rosa had asked him the other day, 'are you part of Mummy's family?'

'Not really, sweetie.'

'Well, are you part of mine?'

'Yes, of course. You are my only child. My number one.'

'But I am part of Mummy's family.'

'Perhaps I am, then, sort of.'

'Are you married to Mummy?'

'No.'

'But you made me.'

'Yes, we did.'

'I'm confused by all this family thing.'

*

Biko knew his father would be looking out for him, the evening guests, neighbours, friends gone. He would haul himself over the fence without a noise and let himself in through the back door. The bedroom he now shared with his sister was the first room he would pass. In the morning, he thought, he could wear his old nylon blazer. His father would silently hit him, but if his mother had died he would be spared the punishment. Biko remembered the pages he'd left in the pocket of the traded jacket: 'What is involved here is not the emergence of an ambivalence, but rather a mutation, a radical change of valence, not a back-and-forth movement but a dialectical progression.' The fantastical language of revolution spoke of a world mutated by struggle, a new and re-cerebralised consciousness – an end to poverty and suffering and a promise to turn men and women into equals.

The agents of this revolution would be the lowest of the low, the wretched, lumpen poor, living like he did, in Third World cities and slums. They would cast their fists against the oppressor and give vent at last to their hearts, to their guts, to their pounding heavy chests. There was an answer to his anger, to the township's wrongs, in these pages, the glue binding dry, flaking on the clustered pages, those strands of thread hanging from them. He started to run past a group of children who were kicking a ball of crushed paper and rubbish in their bare feet. The gravel billowed clouds of dust. Perhaps he should go back. She'd already have thrown the pages out, and he would never know how the story ended. But now the pages were lost – his mother too, soon, unless he ran hard against the path, stirred up the road. He could forget, if he could run faster.

Biko's thoughts returned to Gertrude. He was sprinting. When he should have been at home, he had been with Gertrude. *Never again*. His foot stumbled on a rock and he slowed down. *More direction in the future, towards a goal. Study, understand, focus, organise.Work up the slum, the country, against the grain. Rid it of thugs and murderers. Remember who they are. Remember the* Gukunranda. *Commit the names of the dead to memory.* He felt his calves give out, throbbing. His back was wet; his loose shirt clung to his body.

Biko held the door to stop it clattering against the wall, easing it open with his hand, but still there was the sharp scratching of its hinges. He could hear his father – he knew it was him even though he had not heard that sound before. There was something in the low, deep pitch of his howling that could only be his father. When Biko entered the kitchen, his father was squatting on the floor, his arms holding his head. Biko's sister stood motionless at the table staring at her father's crouched, folded form, the strongman brought low. Emmerson stood, his red, bloodshot eyes fixed on Biko. He moved round the table and held his son in his arms.

*

After four weeks the strike won. It seemed to Viktor as though everyone in the world had, in their own way, participated in the victory. At the core of the strike were the cleaners from Zimbabwe, Poland and Peru. Even the others, those who could be classified in the symbols of our time as white, English, were in reality hybrid islanders. Gary was from Jersey, where, he claimed, he had acquired his thick skin, his weathered, salt-splashed face and alcohol problem.

The strike had been coming for months. The long-predicted wave crashed hours after BCW gave out monthly payslips to its staff and not a single hour of that month's overtime had been calculated or paid. Whether it was incompetence or provocation, the cleaners decided that the arrogance, the petty, constant bullying, the long hours and the diabolical pay were now too much. Though a noticeable shudder went through the staff when the envelopes were torn open, it took some kind of vanguard to start the strike – a spontaneity that is always the start of organisation.

Four Zimbabwean cleaners left their posts, abandoned their carts and walked through the university corridors side by side, calling to other cleaners to down their mops, to the security guards to turn off the infernal radios pinned to their lapels, to all of their colleagues, their *camaradas*, their *towarzysze*, to straighten their backs and join them for a meeting. Later the women would recall the feeling; how they were overtaken by an anger greater than themselves, controlling the university, feeling as though they had finally come to life, the students and lecturers parting in wordless awe before their bustling, focused fury.

When the meeting resolved to strike illegally – though the matter of the law was not discussed – two of their number, Moreblessing and Wayne, volunteered to prepare a statement and a list of demands. As the word spread, others walked out. Some of the cleaners broke their mops and turned over their carts, leaving the toilets and lobbies strewn with buckets and cleaning fluids. Their subjugation and humiliation, which had for so long seemed permanent, was obliterated in the first hours of the strike.

The porters who delivered tea and coffee to the deans for meetings removed the trays of white cups and saucers from their trolleys and dropped them on the ground. The loud shattering of china made them laugh. They broke the cheap tin tea urns, the flood of tea on the carpets and tiles threatening to drown the university. Others locked away their equipment in cupboards to which only they had access. In this way a large percentage of the university's tea and coffee utensils were removed entirely from the game. This simple genius meant that in a few minutes, every department, senior management meeting, seminar and conference at the university was immediately affected by the strike. Strikers carried along by the quickening, ripening atmosphere recognised that, to deans, professors, doctors and chief executives, not having morning tea is a fate worse than

185

death. If the strike had succeeded in nothing else, starving the university of tea, coffee and biscuits had hit at the entire superstructure of London higher education.

So great was that initial momentum that even those who habitually doubted became staunch and unlikely defenders of the action. The whole rich square mile of Bloomsbury was caught up in the strike, wealth and complacency rubbed out as buckets commandeered for the purpose were rattled on every street corner, passed around each neighbouring university and workplace. In three days every university in Bloomsbury had sent donations for the strike fund and delegates to the picket lines, to stand stamping the life back into their sore, cold feet and their doubting souls.

Gary, in his calm, sedate manner, was overjoyed. 'We are going to win this dispute! We'll push out Terry and the union bureaucrats from our branch and give back dignity to the outsourced workers. No' – he suddenly proclaimed, correcting himself – 'the *workers* will win that dignity for themselves.' The union full-timers hurried to the large, impromptu picket line to tell the cleaners, pickets and security guards that this was not how you run a strike. The strike could not be supported. Indeed, the union would have to denounce the strike or the government would sequester and seize its funds. If the workers wanted to strike, then there were procedures, legal methods that must be followed.

The day was bright. Fallen leaves sprinkled the car park where the workers stood, the winter sun stone-white – as if, Viktor fancied, the entire sorrowful solar system, the far galaxies and universe, watched the distant fight and heard the drums now beating on the picket line. Viktor decided that the picket-line drumbeat was a celestial message. *This* was the message Nina had been looking for when she stared at the moon: it wasn't just for her but for all of us.

'Viktor, come back! Ground control to Major Tom!' Gary snapped his fingers in front of Viktor's face and shook his arm. 'I need you to find Wayne. We need him to translate for Terry.'

On the morning of the third day Terry had blustered into the crowd shouting, using his bulk to shoulder through the strike, muttering profanities, speaking and reprimanding members he recognised. 'Bloody hell, do you know how long it's taken us to sit down and negotiate? Tawanda, you should have known better. Fucking hell, where are Gary and Wayne?'

When Wayne was eventually found, Terry was fully worked up, bristling and erect, the hair on the back of his neck raised. He stood in front of the crowd, waved his hands, flapping them, trying to lift himself above the ground, to defy gravity. But Terry had misjudged their mood. He thought that he could hector them with his normal bombast, his customary appeal to good sense and to his high office. What he did not count on was that these familiar members, some of whom he had recruited himself, were no longer the same. The strikers were rowdy, still giddy on their audacity, their bloody-minded action, the shock that they were no longer the same work-tired, humbled creatures who huddled around radiators in the basement and thawed out their fingers on chipped mugs of coffee before their morning shifts. Their moorings had snapped. They were not sure who they'd become.

'Can you shut them up?' Terry's face blushed red and white. His throat was dry. Next to him were Wayne and Tendai, the milk crate dragged into place as a podium. Wayne spoke in Spanish: 'This buffoon, *este idiota*, from the union office wants to speak.'

For the performance, the theatre of it, Tendai also addressed the crowd in Shona, although there wasn't a Zimbabwean in the crowd who didn't understand Terry's English. 'Terry *ibenzi*.

Pane mhando mbiri dzemapenzi, mhando yekutanga ndeye mapenzi anoziva zvaanoita asi ronyarara zvaro. Kozouya mapenzi anonatsoita wupenzi hwawo. Terry *ndozibenzi rokupedzisira.'* ('Terry is a fool. There are two types of fools: those who know they are fools and keep quiet, and those fools who practise their foolishness. Terry is the last type.') The crowd laughed.

Terry continued: 'You have spoken well today, friends, and your message has been heard. Now we need to go back to our posts. Let us' – he opened his arms to suggest Wayne, Tendai and himself – 'speak on your behalf and negotiate with BCW at the Workplace Forum we've set up.' He paused; Wayne translated. 'Terry says that the Workplace Forum speaks for you and we have to go back inside. I say that he has done nothing for us, nothing, and that we ignore his advice and send him back to the office to waste someone else's time.'

Terry blustered again. 'Management have told me if we don't clear the car park and move away from the main entrance they will be forced to call the police, who may make arrests. I don't know your individual circumstances, but they will check papers. As you are on an illegal strike, your union can't support you.'

A woman screamed from the back: 'Bastard. Go back to Mummy or we'll spank you!'

Terry turned to Tendai, his eyes wide, his lips puckered and tensed. Tendai raised his arms in a slow, dramatic shrug. There was a cheer. Tendai's locks flowed over his shoulders; his coat was too small, the sleeves above his wrists; a silver chain was visible on his open neck; his taut body, stripped of fat, stood tall. When the cheering subsided the same woman jeered affectionately and called out, 'It's Jesus. It's the black messiah!'

Tendai's insolent, drawn face was serious. He shook his head and spoke in English: 'This man says we must return to our jobs, to the insults. He says if we don't, the police will come and arrest us and send some of us home. The union won't fight for us.' Tendai paused, then spoke more loudly. 'I say that *we* are the union, and if we fight then the union is with us!' There was another cheer. Tendai's voice carried over the heads of the strikers to the offices and departments above the car park. 'There are no foreigners here except the bosses.'

That was the end of it. Terry was jostled from his place and the crowd rejoiced as though they had already won. They embraced each other, linked arms, kissed. Then they marched around the university singing in Spanish, Polish and Shona – exclaiming, encumbering the streets, the road filled with their bodies. Two London buses were forced to stop. The passengers stared down from the top deck, smiling despite themselves. The last of autumn's leaves rained on the marchers, who danced and skipped like children.

*

Viktor always counted on the clean getaway. By this he meant that he could let Rosa down gently, according to a formula that he had worked out. Two days before their separation he would announce, at regular intervals, the exact time of their separation, explaining to Rosa that they would see each other again soon. Although he might be a large, floppy elephant of a father, always losing his wallet, unaware that his shoelaces were undone or that his daughter was hanging on his arm, tugging him for attention, repeating in her old, patient way that it was bad for his eyes to focus for too long on his phone, he would remember – and he always did – to call her the day after they'd parted and talk like they did when they were together. So when they reached their last day together, Viktor, following his tested

189

technique, declared that Rosa was the most important person in his life, that he loved her and that it was only his relationship with Nina which had broken down.

'Imagine a really good friend, Rosa, and that you play together every day at school, but suddenly, and over and over again, you start to fight and bicker ...'

'What's bicker, Dad?' she asked.

'It means to argue over silly things. So after a while you decide it's better not to meet up in the playground or go round to each other's houses after school or have sleepovers.'

'Is that why you're not staying with us any more, Daddy? Because of the bicker and sleepovers?' Rosa asked.

'Well it is, I suppose, sort of.'

'But Daddy, I don't make babies with my friends.'

Viktor was silent for a moment. 'Yes, that's true. You don't. Maybe that's where the comparison breaks down.'

He would always say that he had not stopped loving Rosa. In fact, though he never said this, he loved her more fiercely with each month. When their final day together came with a heavy thud, Viktor believed they should have expunged their emotions; rid, freed themselves of the horror, this odd couple facing imminent rupture and loss.

The dreadful climax of separation was never lessened by their waiting or by Viktor's preparation.

On the last visit, the night before the end, Rosa had sat on him, folded herself into his lap, and refused to permit any bodily severance. Even during the day she had skipped to his oversized strides, following him even to the toilet, insisting on crouching on the floor until he had finished. Nesting her head under his neck, kissing him there, with the words, murmured and intense, that she too loved him, that he was Number One, a place he shared jointly with Nina.

When she read the first page of the story on the fold-down futon they shared, Viktor commented, 'Your reading, Rosa, is much better than mine was at your age.'

She said, as though she knew he was going to say this, her answer ready, 'But Dad, that was the old days, when everything was dumb.'

Always an answer, this daughter of his, to assuage his guilt, tell him it was going to be okay. How did he draw out the nurse even in his six-year-old child?

Viktor and Rosa arrived late, huddled together on the train, then the bus, longing somehow to stretch the tunnels and tracks and create infinite distance between the grimy stations. They sat away from the doors, two rows behind the driver, to avoid the blast of cold air, as the bus stumbled and jolted towards their separation. Rosa's eyes were dry. Through the whole ordeal she even forgot the purpose of their journey, animated by the familiarity of the area and the anticipation of her grandfather's embrace.

Rosa started to explain the area's topography: 'There was a charity shop just here, where Granny bought me this cardigan, but it's closed now.'

'A charity shop closing? That's unusual in this cursed country.'

'Yes, Daddy, but it's not the only place. Over there by those houses, behind the boards where I would play, Granny says there'll be a McDonald's, though we will never eat there.'

The sorry eyes of Nina's mother greeted them. Viktor had always liked the woman. She enveloped Rosa and exchanged pleasantries with baggy, hopeless Viktor, and still Rosa did not cry. When Viktor knelt to give his valedictory speech – perhaps his fifth that weekend – she put her thin fingers over his lips, the infant flesh already gone from her body, sealing them closed, and pulled from her open raincoat a folded piece of pink paper. She told him to read it when he was alone.

They waved, each of them, the awkward grandmother, Viktor and Rosa, all the arms, a whole chorus of farewells raised skyward.

Around the corner, already proud of himself, composing the sentences he would speak to his parents, he opened the folded paper and read:

> Dear Viktor, I will always love you with all my heart. The love-hearts I gave you can help you when you miss me. Give this letter a hug or a kiss and I will receive it. I can also send you hugs and kisses. Lots of never-ending love, from Rosa.

Next to these words she'd drawn a heart, framed in a pink box, circled by smaller hearts. He bent over, suddenly winded, unable to breathe, his head splitting. One hand covering his face, he sobbed and sobbed, as men do, in shame.

In the days that followed, trying to patch himself up with faint assurances, Viktor tended – in a system of thought every bit as rigorous as his formula for separation – to stir up a hurricane of regret that gathered and swelled into a storm that sucked in each person in his life. He thought of Nina's mother, her patient, tolerant welcome of him into her life and their Thursday ritual of phone calls. This generous, unsuspecting woman had accepted Viktor only for him to betray her hospitality. Her visibly drooping limbs and atrophied muscles were evidence of the path to extinction onto which he had casually thrown her.

In the storm Viktor's mind went next to Nina; in the week after his weekend with Rosa, he longed for her and questioned each hesitant step he had taken away from her. That path too had been cast by his hand, and it had led Nina into the arms of an even more volatile lover. Nicholas, Viktor had heard, was

Nina's college friend and was unable to leave his wife but was granting Nina, to Viktor's strange consternation, casual sex. Such a ripple of misery, arcing continuously away from the one fatal mistake he'd made – to leave, to hesitate, to tear himself from Rosa and Nina.

Worse still than the damning of his parents, his ex-mother-in-law, Nina and even his daughter, was Viktor's inability to be with Rosa without an eye on his watch – keeping a mental note of the passing days until he would be free to answer the urgent queries from his website, on his Facebook page, to press on forever with his PhD. He was sure she saw the distracted flicker in his eyes when she stared up at him and searched his face with hers.

'You know, Daddy,' Rosa said in one of those eye-to-eye appeals, 'when I am with you I miss Mummy, and when you go I miss you.'

Viktor curled his arms around her and did not answer. What could he say? That it was better like this? That unlike other children, who saw each parent every day, at least their time together was unusual, each moment savoured? *You see, Rosa, we have made of our relationship a turning point, so each occasion we're together we turn away from the ordinary and move in a direction that no one else has taken. We represent a break from the crowd. Life, sweetie, is not worth living unless it is made into a turning point, a new path. Do you see, Rosa, how special we are?* What else did he have, apart from his theorising? Yet Viktor knew that she really needed something else entirely: to have her father as part of the crowd. Present. Rosa needed dense, predictable, ordinary everyday life.

Viktor realised that his mind was not at rest. Nothing was right because there was no *act*. Yet still his thoughts ran into him, crowded him, and he realised that all his words, his blogging, his thinking, was for nothing. Not for the first time, he understood that he had to make these things in him die – for his incessant doing was without life, and without *the act* we are nothing.

Chapter Seventeen

Tendai paced the room in a pair of Viktor's old tracksuit bottoms and an off-white T-shirt, moving on his large, creased feet. In one hand was an open book of Cabral's writings. He needed to speak – he had a whole sleepless night of thoughts and plans to discuss. He wanted to read this essay, the one about revolutionary suicide, the nation and commitment. Tendai waved Viktor down and commanded him to sit in his desk chair by the wall, next to the door.

'It's no good, Viktor, these things you have made,' he said, pointing to the pile of cards stapled to thin strips of wood. 'They are too artistic, too much writing. We need slogans, simple, a few words. You need help. We'll set up a Strike Publicity Committee. Your posters are beautiful, but what are these? There—' Tendai held a single poster in front of Viktor, the words cramped like a newspaper, with emblems at the bottom: a bird, a square box with a capital F. 'These ... what are these?' Tendai spoke curtly, so that the words seemed to come out as accusations.

'Those symbols tell people that we have a Facebook page and a Twitter account. They are there to direct our supporters to the online campaign.' Viktor spoke slowly, calmly, to Tendai's agitation and excitement. He always slowed down to irritation, spoke lethargically, attempted to redress the balance and bring the atmosphere level again.

'That's not right. We don't want that. We don't want art, articles, an online campaign. We need something to stir the *rage*. To keep the fire alive.'

It was true: Viktor, who had a talent for drawing and had once seen himself as an artist, had sketched pickets, black figures marching and fat BCW bosses, their stomachs bulging out of their waistcoats, their pockets stuffed with money. Over these elaborate drawings he had printed the strike's demands: Equal Pensions, Equal Pay, Equal Sick Pay. Beneath each was a paragraph.

The drawing had been for Rosa, perhaps even more than for the strike.

When he had Rosa at the weekend during the strike, they had stayed up late in his bedsit, the coloured thick-nibbed pens strewn over the floor, the two of them on their knees, planning and discussing. On one placard Viktor had drawn an entire scene: children holding their parents' hands, the same child in a marching crowd, identified in the different scenes by the red scarf tied round her neck. Rosa loved it. That night, before they had to surrender the posters to the strike committee and before he had to surrender Rosa to Nina's mother, she slept with them next to her. She surveyed the posters from different distances, from the back of the room, held out in her stalks of arms and then inches from her face. When she was asleep he worked on other posters, drew a frame of ivy around the website address, added the slogan *We are no longer scared*. On one poster he drew the strikers with Rosa at the front, marching closer and closer in each frame. Carefully, so as not to wake her, he slid the new placard over the old so she would wake to the new scene, her small, scarfed body growing larger and larger, until in the last frame the girl on the poster was alone. Viktor's own pleasure matched Rosa's. She said nothing in the morning, only stared at the card, running her hand over it. This was how they spent the weekend, in a fever of creation, each drawing, breaking for lunch, until the girl was still and there was a pile of twenty posters.

With her finger on each frame Rosa followed herself approaching, growing and then retreating back into the crowd until the girl was hand in hand with a man she knew was her father. Father and daughter became the emblem of the strike, the space for text overrun by their battle for two-dimensional presence; the strike, its reasons and arguments, had become their context. When they arrived at Bristol she clung to the cards, the bundle Viktor had tied together with string and that she had asked to carry, and then she clung to him.

He wanted to take Rosa to the picket line, make her his protest, his affirmation of life, and show Tendai, Moreblessing, Gary and Wayne that this was what he was fighting for – that if the strike won, if they started to win, all of them, against the company, the university, the unquestioned routines of daily life, then victory would look like Rosa: the black hair across her face thrown upward as she ran, her arms out, fingers apart, her dark eyes challenging the world to be as generous as she was in her forward, limitless rush into his arms at the station.

Viktor stood his ground and brushed aside Tendai's criticism. 'No, we will use these posters and I will make some more with your slogans.' That was it. Tendai did not pursue the matter and no Strike Publicity Committee, beyond the ad hoc, informal one of Viktor and Rosa, was formed.

*

Day after day, Viktor saw Moreblessing leaving the office where Tendai was camped. Early in the morning when he arrived, he saw her hitching up her tights, adjusting her shoes, pulling the BCW waistcoat over her dress. Viktor battled with himself, uttered in a low voice some basic principles: that Tendai's business was his own, that what he did, what *they* did, in the office was the concern of no one except the two consenting adults. No potentate, king, politician, friend, comrade, man had a right to comment. Tendai's sex life, his longings, his need to quench his loneliness each night on the floor of this office, was his alone. But when he saw not just Moreblessing coming and going but other women he didn't know or recognise, and the faces of union members he vaguely recognised, he did not approve.

'Tendai, I want to speak to you about something.'

'Fire, man.'

'I am uncomfortable with the way I always see women leaving the office. First, I said that you could stay here, but it's risky. Second, it concerns me that you may be having all of this, this ... *intercourse*.'

Tendai threw his head back and roared with laughter, exposing his long, sinewy neck, his Adam's apple pointing into the room. 'Intercourse!' he repeated. 'Brother, I don't have intercourse. I *fuck*. I express myself. I explode into the world. I shine my blackness down, down, down like a radiant black star. I combust, like the Big Bang. Intercourse, hah, not me, man.' Tendai's voice was raised when he finished. He held his crotch and gyrated to the echo of his own singsong polemic.

'Oh, I see. Well, how do the women feel about your Big Bang? Do they know how many of them there are?'

Tendai stood with his feet apart, his arms on his hips. All the life-generating joy and humour fell from his voice. 'Does the force of a black man's sex upset you, Viktor? Do you disapprove of fucking and loving? Is your idea of life all this, this ... art' — he waved one of his hands over the pile of Viktor's posters — 'and handshakes? Ask the women if I haven't lifted them to the heights. If I haven't taken away the misery of your city for a few hours, helped them escape in these arms, with my force, the toilets, the shit, *your* shit, that they clean day after day, man. Ask them, white boy. *Intercourse.* That's what the dead do. The racists.' Tendai stared at Viktor, daring him to speak.

Viktor boiled slowly. He weighed and calculated. 'You confuse my sentiments. I am only asking about the women. Do they feel the same way about your force? Is the experience really as escapist as you say?'

Tendai felt the pulse hammering in his temples. The blood pounded and pulsated in his wrists, in his groin, his breath grew short, he started to sweat. When he tried to answer this boy's insolence, the words swelled and choked him, blocked his throat. He breathed in deeply and walked closer to Viktor, so that he was standing a metre from him. He pulled down the front of the tracksuit with one hand and with the other pulled out his penis. The veined penis was pale, as pale as Viktor, the circumcised oval crown like the head of a garden snake. Involuntarily Viktor pushed himself back in the chair, less from the shock of exposure than the sudden revelation that this man, his friend, was showing his modest, perfectly normal penis, unremarkable, like his — smaller, even. Tendai released the elastic so the trousers snapped closed, sending his penis flying upward until it disappeared again into the tracksuit.

'I see,' Viktor said. 'But I don't think that changes my argument.'

Tendai laughed. The anger Viktor had raised quickly abated; he felt exhausted and staggered back to the ring of desks. Viktor soldiered on. 'We have a duty to be decent, to our lovers as well as being' – he struggled to find the words – '*principled* in the union. One cannot be traded for the other, no matter how confident we feel about our sexual needs.'

Tendai reached for a T-shirt and wiped his brow. 'Okay, Viktor, I hear you. But remember, when your country invaded and settled in our lands, you tried to control our entire beings, our sex. You made a sin out of loving and joy. Brother, be careful with your words.'

Unflustered, laborious, Viktor replied, 'That's another error. I did not take away anything. My family was living in a Jewish shanty town in Romania during the Conference of Berlin in 1884, and on my mother's side they were refugees from pogroms in Russia. What was done to you, Tendai, was also done to us. Your nation-versus-nation argument breaks down and can't be joined even by that thing in your tracksuit.' Viktor smiled and the men laughed.

'But don't take my last pleasure, my release, my escape, comrade. Leave me something. Let at least my body remain free and unoccupied by your Jewish, Zionist morality.'

'Wrong again. I am not a Zionist! All I am saying is be careful. Sex has consequences, and power.'

'ENOUGH!' Tendai shouted, throwing the T-shirt to the floor. 'Now the strike! Let's speak about how we're going to tear the fucking heart out of BCW and the university.'

*

Tendai didn't understand Viktor's crisis, nor could he ever have – the bundle of confused emotions, the choices, the dilemmas that this ungainly man shed like petals, his permanently knotted brow, the time wasted on his worries, his fingers falling heavily on his keyboard, on some absurd formula or incomprehensible formulation. Tendai knew the importance of book work, the need to study and read – all those years in prison had taught him that. But this was different. Viktor was lost. Life, for Viktor, it seemed to Tendai, was a series of questions that led only to entirely contradictory new questions. Despite Tendai's refusal to become involved in personal issues, in the garbage of people's lives, Viktor had ensnared him – and, if he was honest, he harboured a desire to unknot Viktor's brow, to bring him some perspective.

'On the one hand,' Viktor said, the two men standing across Tendai's dustcart, 'I think it might be better for Rosa if I wasn't in her life. She is affected by the rows between Nina and me. But on the other hand, without me around she'll be lost. She'd be less able to find balance in her life.'

The strike was only five weeks over, yet the men cast furtive, nervous looks around them as the conversation unfolded. Over the whole car park, the distant, low winter horizon and the cars, the skip, the uneven paving stones, they kept watch. 'The problem, Tendai, is that Nina and I should have stayed together, for Rosa and for ourselves. We were suited – the north London Jew and the working-class girl who did well for herself. But she became frustrated with me, present but always distracted. I never learnt anything.' Viktor paused, stared blankly in front of him. 'Still, it was the right decision to separate. It is better like this.'

Viktor rambled, looked into Tendai's decorated dustcart, its stickers proclaiming *Justice for Cleaners and Security Guards. End Low Pay. Support the Strike.* Tendai decided that pointing out Viktor's inconsistency didn't work. Neither did laughing and stamping his feet to mark the place when the sentence broke down under the weight of another oxymoron. Nothing worked.

Viktor would still be left where he had started — tottering on the edge of the cliff, always about to fall. Still Tendai tried to show him the necessity of resolution in all matters in life — to seize hold of what you wanted today.

*

Viktor and Anne-Marie continued to communicate by text, and the occasional email. The tone veered from fevered, intense, sexual messaging and conversations to questions about their lives and who they were — how they had been made and what life meant to them. That night, for the second time on Skype, Anne-Marie answered Viktor's questions about her birth, flattered by his interest, his obsessive curiosity.

'I was born in the Congo. The centre of the continent, of what you call "the heart of darkness".'

'Of course I know the Congo,' Viktor replied eagerly, quickly. 'I don't call it that.'

'I spent eight years in Kinshasa and then we moved to France. Do you know the Congo's history?'

'Yes, some.'

'Well, I have a famous grandfather.'

'Who?'

'Guess.'

'Mobutu?'

'No. My family would chase you out of the house for even suggesting that.'

'Well, I give up. Who?'

'Five guesses, Mr London.'

'Viktor.'

'Okay, Mr Viktor, five guesses.'

'Is he still alive?'

'No.'

'When did he die?'

'Yes-or-no questions only.'

'I give up.'

'You can't. Four more questions.'

'Was he very famous?'

'Yes.'

'Was he killed?'

'Yes.'

'Now you're going to tell me that your grandfather was Lumumba.'

'Yes.'

'I don't believe you,' Viktor said.

'Patrice Lumumba was my grandfather.'

'You mean figuratively, yes? The grandfather to every child of the Congo.'

'No, my grandfather. My flesh and blood, *mon pépé*.'

'Prove it,' Viktor said, his disbelief beginning to break.

'"We have seen our lands seized in the name of allegedly legal laws which in fact recognised only that might is right. The Republic of the Congo has been proclaimed, and our country is now in the hands of its own children." Or, if you want it in French, "*La République du Congo a été proclamée et notre cher pays est maintenant entre les mains de ses propres enfants.*"'

'So tell me more, comrade Lumumba,' he said.

'When Mobutu declared that my grandfather was a national hero, my grandmother and mother returned home. She refused most of the official engagements, except the ones the family had to attend. And we lived in his home – we still do – on Boulevard du 30 Juin and went to the local school. Then all his children came back from Egypt, Hungary, France, each of them back to the country his murderer had made.'

'You make it sound as if they didn't want to return.'

'No. But they were obeying their father's orders. Their dead father and his insistence that everything would change in the Congo. "To my children whom I leave and whom perhaps I will see no more, I wish that they be told that the future of the Congo is beautiful and that it expects from them, *comme il attend de chaque Congolais, d'accomplir la tâche sacrée de la reconstruction de notre indépendance et de notre souveraineté*, for without dignity there is no liberty, without justice there is no dignity, and without independence there are no free men.'

'You can quote all his speeches?'

'That was a *letter* to my grandmother, not a speech. It is the minimum you'd expect from a Lumumba, wouldn't you say?'

'Yes. Yes, I suppose so.'

Sitting in her darkened flat Anne-Marie laughed loudly, freely. 'He thought the Congo would write its own history. We all lived in the old house, a gift from Mobutu, with my grandmother and my mother brought up on Patrice's naivety, thinking she had to live out his wish. So literal. My grandfather's curse – my mother, my aunts, my uncles.'

'Curse?' Viktor was breathless, impatient, he had begun to sweat.

'He was wrong. Lumumba lost. We lost, but his children felt obliged to return to the Congo.'

'Christ!' Viktor stood suddenly in his office. He paced the room; he straightened his shoulders. 'Your grandfather was Lumumba. Lumumba. Do you realise how incredible that is? I had his speech pinned to my door when I was a student.' Viktor moved back to his computer, stared into the camera, his forehead creased. 'Yes, now I can see it. The resemblance. You look like him.'

'No, I don't!' Anne-Marie exclaimed. She was used to surprise, white colleagues who would ask her to dispel the rumour, then proclaim their admiration for her grandfather's stand against the Americans and the Belgians, those who now paid their salaries. But this performance, this man's need to declare himself standing, this release of excitement with his entire body, his flailing, octopus arms, was different.

'Listen, Mr London, my grandfather was wrong. He was an absolutist when he needed to compromise. He didn't understand that a deal had to be made. Some sort of compromise needed to be made; death and sacrifice is never an answer.'

'You're wrong,' Viktor declared. 'The Belgians didn't want to concede anything, nor did the Americans or the British. They wanted him gone. Eliminated. Instead your cautious, moderate grandfather simply stood up to them – the whole cabal of the West. For him, independence had to be independence.'

'And for that he was murdered and we got Mobutu, the Congolese American, for more than thirty years.' Anne-Marie leant back in her chair, enjoying Viktor's performance.

'No, no, he took a stand and didn't budge and then took action to defend his position. *Action*. For that we will always be in his debt.' Viktor's mouth was dry; his heart beat heavily.

'What good was he dead?'

'He knew that he might have to die; that to defend the Congo it might be necessary to die. The necessity of death to achieve freedom,' Viktor responded quickly.

'Rubbish. It was hopeless, he was hopeless – you know, before he was arrested and transferred to Mobutu's force, he tried to persuade the troops to release him. My mother used to tell us the story. Bedtime stories in the Lumumba household: this is how your grandfather was killed, children.'

Anne-Marie's family – each of them – came into focus: her grandmother Pauline, more formidable and unyielding even than her husband, barefoot in the kitchen stirring the stew, her petticoat stained, the apron she never removed, that made her look like the household maid until she opened her mouth and a gush of Batetela came out, refusing until the end to speak even in Swahili or Lingala. *Every decision a principle*, Anne-Marie thought, *my grandmother like my grandfather, their determination painted on the immense canvas of African politics and in each step of their lives, great and small*. Pauline had disregarded everything the colonialists had brought: their language; the paved, useless city of Leopoldville; the poverty in her village of Onalua, in Kasai province, which had meant *her* parents had been forced to harvest rubber every year or starve.

Absent-mindedly, speaking quietly into the microphone, Anne-Marie said, 'I adored my grandmother. She had an enormous amount of courage and an extraordinary zest for life. She was always so positive. She loved drinking and smoking but hid the cigarettes, because it had been illegal in her day. But she was also quite a stubborn woman. "Those who don't work don't eat," she'd say, "but once the work is done we will party."'

Before they left again for France in the eighties she had sat at her grandmother's lined, sun-dried feet, looking at the thick rhino skin on her heels that meant she could walk across the city, on the rough gravel in the street, without looking down. Pauline told her granddaughter that she had argued with Patrice on the day of independence. She had refused to attend the ceremony with the Belgian king; furious with her husband, she threw his suit and shoes from the balcony of this house. Patrice had run outside in his underwear, gathering his clothes, dusting them down. All this on the most important day of their history.

Pauline joked that she was the only person who could silence Lumumba. Pauline and the Belgians.

Finally Viktor sat down, afraid that he would miss something.

'He was a romantic,' Anne-Marie continued. 'He thought the world could be changed by speech. By a torrent of words.'

'An idealist,' Viktor said.

'Like Nelson. Probably like you.'

'I've never been compared to Lumumba.' Viktor smiled.

'I wasn't paying you a compliment.'

Anne-Marie was amused by Viktor: his certainty, his conviction about something he knew nothing about. 'In France no one had even heard of Lumumba, except our Congolese friends. I was a little black girl growing up in the *banlieue* in the eighties, missing my grandmother. My mother taught me pragmatism, getting what you can and not dying. I was about twelve and we were studying geography. The teacher – a tall man, maybe your height, Monsieur Couper – he was always trying to be our friend, and when he failed he was offended like a child and became cruel, *brutale*. In the winter some of us had to wear our coats in the *salle de classe*, because it was *vraiment froid*.'

The quicker Anne-Marie spoke, the more she stumbled on her English, chewed up the words, spat them out, replaced them with French. '*En face d'une carte de l'Afrique – il est là et mon cœur battait fort et je pense que tout le monde pouvait m'entendre. Déjà, à douze ans, j'ai compris le racisme en France. Cet idiot et sa carte de l'Afrique. Avec la règle dans une main, il a mis son autre sur la carte de l'Afrique et dit: Ici, mes élèves, est le Kenya, ici, c'était le principe colonie de Grande Bretagne en Afrique. Nous étions tous de l'Afrique dans la classe, d'une manière ou d'une autre, et cet idiot montait Afrique de l'Ouest.*'

'Do you realise, Anne-Marie, that you're speaking in French?' Viktor queried.

Anne-Marie continued without hearing him: 'So this idiot teacher covers up half of West Africa and says it's Kenya. Then he points to the Congo, he's learnt something at least, and says, "Here is the heart of Africa – where people still live in grass huts and worship the elements."'

She picked up a book and read, mocking her teacher's voice, "'Africa, south of the Sahara Desert, is inhabited almost entirely by peoples with very black skins. The opening up of the interior of Africa commenced with the expeditions of English-speaking explorers such as Livingstone and Stanley. But many groups of negroid peoples are now making rapid progress." Then he says, I remember every word, *il a demandé s'il y avait des étudiants du Congo dans la classe.* "Is there anyone here from the Congo?" He's just told us that we're primitives and now he wants me to put my hand up, *levez la main*.' Anne-Marie raised her hand.

'So what happened?'

'*Rien*.'

'What?'

'Nothing.' Anne-Marie's voice tailed off. '*Rien du tout*. Everyone is silent. There were four of us from the Congo and none of us put our hand up.'

'I'm not surprised.'

Speaking in French about Paris, Anne-Marie's accent changed, thick with her memories of the *lycée*. 'When I left school a few hours later I had my hood up over my head and I cried all the way home. I have never felt closer to my grandfather than that day, the betrayal of everything he stood for, his stand against the racists. "We have known ironies, insults, blows that we endured morning, noon and evening, because we are Negroes. Who will forget that to a black one said *tu*, certainly not as to a friend, but because the more honourable *vous* was reserved for whites alone?" His own grandchild didn't defend her parents, her grandfather, to this, this, him, this … *tas de merde. Idiot!*' Anne-Marie's eyes glistened. She let the tears fall, roll over her cheekbones, along the side of her nose, into her mouth, wetting her lips. Viktor wanted to lean forward and kiss her, to taste the salty, clear water.

'I understand the sense of betrayals,' Viktor said.

'Ha. You're not going to make me feel better. I don't want your sorrow.'

'I don't want to sound trite. I think you let down the Congo – I think *you* let down your family.'

Anne-Marie was pleased with Viktor's response. She continued, 'I didn't ever tell my mother. I told her I had fallen and hurt myself.'

Chapter Eighteen

'I knew a professor like you in South Africa,' Tendai started.

'You knew a professor?' Viktor repeated, looking at Tendai for the first time, his tone mocking.

'Yes. He used to visit me when I was in prison.'

Viktor smiled.

'Why are you smiling?'

'Because I don't believe you knew a professor.'

'Because I'm African?'

'No, because you've told me that no one visited you in prison,' Viktor continued pedantically. 'I mean, from the description of your life in South Africa, I don't see any professors.'

'Eissh, man, you're stubborn.'

'Okay, what about the professor?' Viktor felt the chill of the day grip his legs and arms. He unbuttoned his coat, tucked his jumper into his trousers. He was pleased by the distraction, to be with Tendai.

'The professor was like you, stubborn.'

'Is this another one of your apocryphal stories?'

'Just listen, goddamn it, man.' Tendai stretched to his full height and put his rough hands and fingers together, holding them below his chest as he did when he spoke to a crowd – as though he was about to release a bird. 'It was December 1995 and he was diagnosed with leukaemia. They sent him to Europe for treatment.'

'Who is *they*?'

'His friends. The university. Goddamn it, man, I don't know. He returned and was better for a time. Then he got sick again. Worse this time. He was working on a book. A book,' Tendai repeated.

Between the parked cars a woman walked towards them holding the hand of a small child. They were dressed alike: black, padded winter coats, tight like skin, the coils of their matching scarves wrapped around their necks. Viktor watched them approach; he lost the thread of Tendai's story.

'A book. Always distracted by a book. He knew that he didn't have long and he had to finish the book. A book that was going to change the world, inoculate the people to lies, reveal the filth, show them how to fight. How the planet could be changed. But he had only months to finish the book.'

The couple were only a few of cars away from Viktor and Tendai. Viktor turned to face them. Tendai continued, 'The only place that could save him or keep him alive a little longer was a clinic in America. But he refused to leave. For him America was still a place of lynch mobs and racists, so he stayed in South Africa and finished his book.'

As the woman and child moved nearer to the two men and the dustcart, the small boy trailed behind his mother, fell back and jumped forward again.

Tendai continued, 'The only thing that mattered before this man died was his book. The sicker he got, the more he drove himself into writing. Waved away his wife, his son.'

211

When the boy was alongside the two men he looked up and smiled. His whole face tightened and creased, his eyes narrowed, his cheeks bulged. His mouth opened into a gummy, spaced smile, revealing different-sized teeth. His forehead stretched, the eyebrows widened and spread. The boy's face shone, breaking open to the stranger's stare. Viktor felt his heart suddenly pound. Quickly he remembered to return the boy's smile.

Viktor held the smile on his face as they passed until his face ached. The boy's head twisted, craning back. Then suddenly the boy raised his flat hand and blew a kiss. Viktor was startled. A smile was one thing, but a kiss blown across the few metres that separated them was something else entirely. *What does it mean?* Viktor wondered, his smile giving way to concern. *Is it a sign? Does the boy know me?*

'A month before the man died, his wife — Vlad, are you listening, man? This man's wife brought him news that his book had been published, and the first reviews had been excellent. Then do you know what happened? After he had used up his last months writing, he was now almost dead. Vlad! Vlad? Goddamn it, man, listen!'

Viktor was still looking at the mother and son walking away. *What would it be like*, he thought, *if each of us smiled and blew kisses at strangers? Is this the way? Would this make us feel better?*

'So she came into his hospital room with the news that his masterpiece was successful and he was done. He could die now in peace. And you know what he did?'

Viktor uttered vaguely, 'What?'

'Did he rejoice with his son? No. He pushed them away again. Was he delighted to have completed the book that his entire essence had reached for and craved? No. Only then did he realise that he had days to live, and he writhed in horror

212

at his end.' Tendai gesticulated wildly, saw that Viktor wasn't looking and screamed, 'LISTEN, MAN!'

The boy was still in sight. Viktor willed him to turn again and wave, send another kiss from his palm so he could cast his own back to the boy, tumbling, turning in the air – which would be his way of telling the child that he must continue giving kisses to strangers.

'Did his book matter to him? Did it? Like hell. All that mattered to the man – listen, Vlad, Vik, this is the point – all that mattered was another day of life, a few more moments of existence. Do you hear me? That's all that ever matters. All there ever is. No last book, but *life*, only *life*. A book weighs little against life. A particle, an ounce of life, is worth a dozen successful books.'

Tendai waved his hands. 'Do you hear me? Do you hear me?' And in case Viktor hadn't heard, Tendai screamed again, '*EXISTENCE!* There is nothing else. Seize it, Vlad. Goddamn it, man, *are you listening?*'

Tendai spat out the last sentence, spraying spit over the dustcart and across his interlocutor: 'He only understood life when it was over. Only the book. The book was all that mattered. If he was going to die, then at least he'd leave the book. This great manifesto to change the world.'

After a moment, calmer, Tendai asked, 'And have you heard of the book?'

'I don't even know who the professor is.'

'*Exactly.*'

Viktor saw the small boy and his mother turn away from the university and disappear.

Tendai didn't speak; he extolled, his arms and hands shovelling the air, fanning the atmosphere.

A colleague Viktor had spoken to a few times pushed through the far doors and started to weave between the cars. He swept back his thinning hair, exposing a bony forehead and pulsing temples. He was younger than Viktor, but his professional senior; he always seemed breezy, laughing easily in the corridor. During the strike – the great marker for the strikers – he had used the side door, avoiding the picket line, the drums and the petitions.

Tendai concluded, flipping his final words in his hands, pushing them towards Viktor. 'For these reasons you must go. You have to leave.'

'Leave?' Viktor queried. 'Go where?'

'To Zimbabwe.'

'Why?'

Tendai sighed, then laughed, throwing back his head and shoulders.

The man greeted Viktor with a thin smile and said hello. Viktor was surprised and wondered with genuine astonishment how the man knew who he was. Somehow Viktor thought that the impression he made on the world rendered him invisible – that his face was a faint smear drawn on a dirty window.

Growing irritated with Viktor's refusal to listen, Tendai spoke loudly. 'Wasn't that your colleague who didn't support the strike? The scab.' In the distance the man heard. His head twitched slightly.

'But why Zimbabwe?' Viktor asked, trying to draw Tendai away from shouting an insult.

Spent, Tendai put his hands on the dustcart, straightened his arms, hunched his shoulders. His head sank on his neck and he recovered his breath. 'Zimbabwe. *Zimbabwe*,' he repeated, distracted.

'Why do I need to go to Zimbabwe?'

'Because you need to get out of here, away from your people. *Away*. You are choking. Paralysed. Stuck. You need to dislodge your life from its groove. Derail yourself. Because you are bloody lost, man. Viktor, you are dying. Maybe you are already dead.'

'But why Zimbabwe?'

'Why not? I went to Zimbabwe from South Africa when I was lost, when I wanted to kill every *umlungu* in Cape Town. I became bloody Zimbabwean. I called myself Tendai.'

'The last thing Zimbabwe needs is another white man.'

'For god's sake, man, *I* am the black nationalist, not you. Go to France, then. Poland, Russia. Just *go* somewhere.'

'What about my daughter?'

'Take her. Go without her. I don't know. What good are you to her like this, anyway? You need the fire. You need to *burn*. If the strike – our bloody strike *and* victory – hasn't clarified the world, then you need a sharper, harder plunge. You need capitalism without any clothes. Go and come back angry, with some rage, some action, some bloody *practice*, Viktor. With *life*, man.'

He couldn't tell Tendai, but Viktor had been hatching the same plan – Zimbabwe was where he had decided to go to consummate his plans, to learn, to act – and to see Anne-Marie. Though how could he avoid the distractions and actually leave?

If Viktor left now, quickly, ran through the car park, he could maybe catch up with the boy, speak to the mother, bend down on one knee, stroke the child's cheek, reassure him. Tell him that he had received the message, he had heard, seen, understood. If only he could find the boy and his mother, then everything would be solved. He could explain to Tendai later why he had to leave. He should tell the boy about the strike. About Moreblessing. If the boy met Moreblessing, he would understand everything. Her compact arms, so strong from cleaning, and how during the strike she would just open her mouth and let her life spring forth, the compressed pain, loss, anger, exhaustion frothing out of her lungs and heart. Moreblessing wasn't scared of anyone. Viktor would tell the boy all of this; he needed to know, to see. The icy drizzle would spray the boy's head, wet his face, his eyelashes catching the rain, turning the drops of water into tiny watery globes, each reflecting Viktor back to himself. Each sphere a witness to the truth of Moreblessing, of the strike, of Tendai and of his trip to Zimbabwe.

Chapter Nineteen

Tendai had first given Viktor the idea of visiting Zimbabwe, but it was Rajeev Nasaden who employed him to work on the Zimbabwe Independent Media Centre, managed entirely online – which would allow him also to post on his own website, *Mutations*. Rajeev lived on the crashing wave of the twenty-first century, a beautiful, frenetic Londoner whose Indian parents owned two hundred local shops. 'We're a bloody racist cliché! My parents live in the same semi we moved into in 1972 when they arrived from Gujarat, but they have corner shops in every major town and city in the country. My brother is a banker in LA. I don't talk to him.'

Rajeev had round eyes drawn from perfect circles and eyelashes that scraped his glasses. He was known by every self-respecting London activist. They seemed to assemble around his life force. Yet he remained impervious to the men and women who fell in love with him, his concerns intensely focused on the last thing he wrote, on the land-grab by multinationals in Mozambique or the travesty of GM crops in South America. Nothing escaped his activist reach and, though he was obsessed with his ego, his ego was obsessed with activism.

Viktor admired how Rajeev refused the distracting ephemera of love affairs. Rajeev respected Viktor's contemplative approach to life, his political commitment and his blog – but Rajeev urged him to focus and fulfil himself by finally stepping in. Speaking on video chat two weeks before Viktor left, in gapless sentences, Rajeev's voice rose to a high pitch, louder than Viktor's objections. 'You've spent life testing the water, nervously moving around the water's edge, then running away when the bottom of your trousers catches the surf. Get in, Viktor. People will put you up. You can write at last for a movement, a people struggling against dictatorship and neo-liberalism.'

Rajeev spoke without taking a breath, so that there could be no place for doubt. Viktor wondered if a person could really be freed from self-questioning by the simple effort of speed and compression. Rajeev refused the anxiety that Viktor generated. In their diametrical, asymmetrical ways and their matching obsession with electronic communication, they understood each other perfectly. Viktor left on a mission to write for the ZIMC.

*

Viktor wore a silver bangle. In his first year with Nina, on a day trip to Whitstable, she had insisted on an elaborate present for his birthday. They had waited patiently for the bracelet to be slowly stretched, a four-hour procedure, until it could be prised over his hand and onto his wrist. Either his hand had grown or the silver had contracted, so the sign of Nina and the banal happiness of that day had held its place for eight years, refusing to yield even to soap.

'It doesn't come off,' Viktor explained to the man processing his hand luggage, belt and computer through the curtained X-ray box. The man nodded. 'And it always sets off the alarm.'

'Then it's probably better to take off your shoes, or you'll only be sent back.'

Dutifully, holding the side of the table, he bent and pulled off his black trainers. He felt a strange intimacy walking in front of strangers in Europe's largest airport with no shoes, his trousers beltless, slack, treading on the gummy carpet.

A tall black woman on the other side of the security arch beckoned to him. 'Move through, move through, please, sir, with your arms raised.' The machine buzzed. Viktor held his hands above his head and stood, smiling. 'You'll have to wait for my colleague,' she said.

'I'm happy for you to search me,' Viktor responded.

'I'm not allowed.'

'Oh, that's interesting.' Viktor's arms were still raised in surrender.

When his turn came, Viktor was ready, as usual, with an explanation. 'It's been almost eight years and I haven't been able to remove the bracelet. A present from my ex. Each time it's the same, a hold-up.'

'Sir, I will have to run my fingers inside the top of your trousers.'

'That's fine. Help yourself.' Viktor felt the man's breath on him, his fingers expertly touching him, running his cupped hands down his legs, grazing his crotch. The touch was comforting and it made Viktor want to cry, confide to the man, seek his solidarity. 'We're separated now but I can't take the bracelet off, it doesn't want to be removed. We have a daughter. It was such a nice day.'

The man smiled, nodded knowingly, and reached for a small baton with a wide paddle-head. He began to pass it over Viktor's chest, his crucified arms, reaching deftly behind him, bringing himself forward so the men stood body to body.

'How old is she?' the man asked.

'She'll be seven soon. Rosa. She's called Rosa.' Viktor spoke in a torrent. 'I separated from her mother, though we tried to make it work. I don't know what it was, the pressure, work, money. Do you have children? I'm leaving for a few weeks and then I'll be back. Zimbabwe. Did you hear about the strike against BCW in London? Almost three weeks. Unofficial. They were forced to recognise the union, pay overtime. Are you unionised?' Then, fingering his bracelet, his hands still over his head, Viktor concluded with, 'The funny thing is that it was such a nice day in Whitstable. We were happy.'

'You can drop your hands now.' The man turned the bracelet around Viktor's wrist, examining it. 'It's nice.'

'What?' Viktor asked.

'The bracelet is nice.'

The man's smile was soft and knowing. Viktor didn't want to move. He wanted the search to continue, for everything to be found, his thoughts and secrets, all of his mistakes examined in this airy open confessional.

'You can go now.'

'Okay.' Viktor found his bag, shoes and belt holding up the trays. For a moment he did not feel too bad about capitalism.

What did it all mean? What did it mean that he was travelling to Zimbabwe, that his mother and Isaac were in London and his daughter somewhere else? What did any of it mean? He felt dizzy as he stepped onto the moving walkway. His head spun; his temples pounded. He was blocked, unable to escape. Images, smells, colours suffocated him. Viktor put a hand on each side of the moving rubber belt and tried to steady himself.

He sat at the back of the departure gate. The bustle of activity around the fixed plastic chairs grated on him: the evident happiness of families, the children playing between the rows of seats, parents chatting together, oblivious, carefree. A small queue of passengers was already forming. Viktor silently mouthed his mantra: 'I can still decide not to leave. I don't have to go.'

Viktor looked hopefully at a woman sitting opposite him. She had neat shoulder-length hair and a tidy blouse. Her face was pointed at the book on her lap; she was, perhaps, his age. She lifted her head to greet Viktor's gaze and her book slipped from her folded legs and fell on the floor, the pages fanning out loudly. The woman seized the book and brought it back to her lap again, her fingers and knuckles straining to hold it. Viktor smiled sympathetically at her and she briefly, nervously returned his smile. *Maybe this woman, this nascent romance*, Viktor thought, *will bring me the decisiveness I need. Help me to board the plane, build up my life again with the help of her love.* He felt his heart flutter.

A Tannoyed voice, lost in the steel and concrete rafters, sounded. People looked up, confused. The announcement sounded again. Viktor could feel his stomach turn; he looked around for the toilet. Their messages were so fevered, unreal, the calls so disembodied – full of fleeting lust and dreams – that Anne-Marie had not entirely believed Viktor three days ago when he had sent a text about his mission to report on Zimbabwe's crisis for *Mutations* and to say he had booked a ticket and would arrive in a few days in Harare, and that she must inform the Society and Biko. Could Viktor really materialise? How does virtual become real, how does inaction become action in a life of remote connections and hypothetical existence? The only answer Viktor had received from concrete, actual, real and specific Zimbabwe was, 'Really. Are you coming?'

And now he asked himself the same question. 'Really, really. Am I going?'

Soon the hall was empty. The Tannoy sounded again. 'Viktor Isaacs please proceed quickly to Gate 21.' Viktor saw the flight attendant standing at the counter, mouthing the words into the microphone. He was the only figure left on the plastic chairs. *They know it's me.* He slipped further down the chair. Finally the solitary man came out from behind the desk and walked quickly towards Viktor. Viktor rummaged in his pocket for his phone and pulled it out violently. He thrust it quickly to his ear, pressing it hard against his head. The man moved deftly between the benches, weaving his way towards Viktor – the man who was holding up three hundred passengers and their families, the airport, the whole of Harare and Southern Africa. Could a solitary act of indecision from Heathrow halt the entire world?

Viktor straightened himself in the chair, then leaning forward, resting his elbows on his thighs, he mumbled loudly into the phone. The man approached him. Viktor's voice rose: 'An operation? What should I do? No, goddamn it! I am at the airport, about to get on a flight. Should I come?' The flight attendant, clipboard in hand, stood in front of him. 'Sir, sir,' he said urgently, 'are you Mr Isaacs?'

'Listen, I have to go now. Okay. Now. I'll phone.' Viktor dropped the phone from his ear, cut the imaginary call with exaggerated performance. 'Yes,' he said to the man's question.

'You are holding up the plane, sir. We have to go now. Can I have your boarding card and your passport?'

Viktor held them out. The man snatched them from him, then raised a radio and spoke to his colleague.

'Quickly,' he snapped, enjoying the urgency, the break in the tedium of boarding. Another man had joined them, wearing a suit with airline insignia on the shoulders. Flanking Viktor, they passed the desk and moved into the tunnel stretching to the plane.

'Christ!' Viktor shouted as he moved along the passageway with his companions. 'I don't know what to do. My mother is in hospital.'

'I am sorry, sir, but you have to decide.'

The men were now at the gaping mouth of the plane, a slice of its interior exposed, passengers in Business Class visible in profile, settling into their seats with drinks. Two female flight attendants stood inside the plane by the door, another man outside the aircraft in a green vest.

'Sir, sir!' was now being shouted at him, the charade of politeness stripped away.

'Tell me, please, should I come to the hospital?' Viktor shouted into the phone.

'Right, we have to close the door. Step aside now.' The flight attendant stepped back quickly into the plane, the heavy hinged door was heaved out for closure. 'Step away, sir, now.' Viktor was given another shove by the vested man. Sweat dripping off his phone, down his ear, onto his shoulder. The lethargic, stiff airplane door swung slowly into place. The staff on the plane stared at Viktor's diminishing form.

It was not clear to him afterwards what made him drop his hand from his ear and throw himself, diving through the narrowing gap in the closing door, landing fully in the midriff of the flight attendant, winding him, sending him back onto the floor. For the sake of pure perversity Viktor threw himself – further into complexity, into crisis, onto the plane.

On Viktor's impact the flight attendant tried to steady himself on the narrow sides of the galley kitchen, reeling, losing his footing. The man fell. The plane was thrown into confusion:

passengers, who had heard the raised voices and agitation outside the plane, now saw a man lunging, throwing himself at the aircraft. From the cabin there was a loud collective sigh, then a series of exclamations and low screams.

Eventually Viktor stood and patted his trouser pockets for his phone. Flustered, he adjusted his jacket, stood in the entrance of the cabin and spoke to the Business Class passengers. 'Everything is okay,' he said, panting, his heart thrashing in his ears. 'It is a family emergency. My mother has just been admitted to hospital in London. A heart problem.' Then to the disbelieving faces, 'It may be the end.'

The winded, injured flight attendant pulled him into the galley kitchen. 'Sir, you have jeopardised the safety of the plane and the airport. You will sit in your seat now, sir, and for the rest of the flight not move. Sir, you could easily be fined for your behaviour.'

Viktor was escorted to his seat by two flight attendants, passengers bobbing up and down, hungry for gossip, as he moved row by row through the plane. Only now did he realise that his phone had flown in the opposite direction to his hurtling body and landed, not in front of him inside the aircraft, but behind him in the UK.

He sat on the plane, gasping not from the battle with the flight attendants but from the absurdity of his choice. The plane pitched and jerked as it ascended, the porthole shutters down and the fluorescent light of the miniature video screen lighting up his vertigo. Viktor imagined that he was aboard a spacecraft plunging through the earth's atmosphere. Normally a nervous passenger, he was now surprisingly calm. The plastic lockers over the passengers creaked like old wood. Viktor marvelled at the thought that the plane might plummet to earth, break up and splinter over Central Africa, and he could be shaken free of life without having to do anything.

*

'So why the hell are you coming to Harare?' asked a red-faced man with a grin, strain showing on his taut, sun-bleached face as they shunted along the plane to the door and the portable stairwell.

'Oh, work,' Viktor said, trying to sound vague.

'Work? In this fucking hellhole? What sort of work?'

Before he reached the exit the man had already begun to sweat. His accent was a low, lazy Southern African drawl. Viktor felt lost.

'I'm a writer,' Viktor said, edging along the narrow plastic corridor. He wanted to impress the man, then shut him up.

'What sort of writer? A journalist? You have come to bring down our dictator? Well, one thing you have to understand is that this country is run by barbarians. They have just come out of the bush. They are stupid, uneducated bush monkeys.'

Viktor let out an involuntary exclamation: '*What?*'

'Bush monkeys!' the man shouted.

No one in the orderly, slow-moving line seemed to notice. Viktor had known racism, had heard people mutter abuse under their breath, but not with this confidence. The man's statement was not made out of anger – just some sort of belligerent avowal.

'Maybe talking about grown men and women as bush monkeys isn't appropriate,' Viktor answered.

'They are fucking monkeys!' the man repeated in a flat, factual tone. 'You will see it soon enough.'

225

When Viktor emerged finally from the ordeal of customs at Harare International Airport, clutching his bags, the fat racist was waiting for him. 'My name is Louis Kappas. I live in Harare. I'll give you a lift.' He didn't wait for Viktor's response but grabbed the two suitcases in an agile swoop and then passed them to a black man in worn jeans and a tracksuit top, who walked through the sliding doors with the bundle. 'Where are you going?' he asked.

Viktor had been meticulously planning the trip, studying maps and lists. *If I go*, he reasoned, *I will have at least learnt the way to the guest house: up Sam Nujuma Street, then left to Herbert Chitepo Avenue and right to Mazowe Street*. But he let Louis lead him to his car.

Rusting flagpoles lined the road from the airport. The traffic moved under a large concrete bridge emblazoned with the words *Welcome to Zimbabwe*. The short stretch of motorway to the city was scattered with slow-moving cars, and in the distance Viktor could see the skyline of the city, a large blue tower that shimmered in the morning heat. On the side of the road were smartly dressed people walking towards the city. Viktor bounced on the hard seat as Louis, his sleeves rolled up, his brow wet, jerked the car around the potholes, muttering curses between his infinite racist narrative.

Of all broken cities, why had he travelled to Harare? This hybrid metropolis, with its leafy suburbs, detached houses set back from the airport road with long front lawns and wide, generous porches, was now so disgruntled, the roads potholed and the manicured grass, the marvel of White Rhodesia, overgrown, the entire inland conurbation overtaken by crisis and failure.

'Most of us left years ago,' Louis explained. 'This country was beautiful, it had everything, grew everything. Then this regime of fucking monkeys ruined it.' He glanced towards Viktor. 'We are going the way of the rest of the continent, every country north of here. The same incompetence, the same fucking monkeys. I used to live in Zambia, and it happened there. You don't know anything, but you'll see. It's what happens when you allow blacks to take power. You see, they only have a tribal mentality, fucking monkeys.'

Louis slammed on the brakes. Ahead of them cars were banked up. A few vehicles were parked on the grassy verge beside the motorway. Already just visible between the cars, a small minibus lay on its side. Louis put his hand on the horn as his pick-up screeched to a stop, then reached for the window behind him, opened it, and shouted, 'Godfrey, go and see what's happened.' Quiet, obedient Godfrey climbed out of the open boot and walked between the cars until the two men in the cab couldn't see him any more.

When he returned, Godfrey spoke quickly. 'Boss, there's been an accident. Some people are dead. The ambulance can't get through.'

'Fucking hell,' Louis said. 'Come on.' He beckoned to Viktor. 'You'll get your first lesson in the Dark Continent.'

They weaved their way through the traffic, the sun already hot on their backs, the open, blue sky filtering through the broad, sparsely leaved trees lining the road. Viktor looked around him. It felt strange, beautiful even.

As they moved closer to the accident, Viktor's pace slowed as his gaze fixed on the bent, abnormal metal, the glass, the bloodstains. Louis trotted quickly towards it, Godfrey at his heels. There were small groups of people gathered in circles; apart from a single woman wailing, the place was silent. Viktor's first thought was that they were praying. The bus was sprawled across the green embankment, its windows broken. Fanning out further over the verge, around the upturned vehicle, were bodies, completely still. Children, adults, thrown from the minibus, lying inert; detached fingers severed from a hand. Groups of people stood beside them.

Viktor stared. His stomach turned – a child lay on her stomach, her head turned to the sky.

Viktor heard Louis shouting, 'Get out of the fucking way, someone help me!'

Viktor stopped walking and watched Louis, who scrambled between the bodies shouting, though his words were unclear. He saw Godfrey and Louis hurriedly moving the sprawled figures onto their sides. Louis dropped to the ground, crouching over one large, bloodied body and jerked the head back, opened the mouth, lowered his mouth for the kiss and breathed. The motion was slow, intimate, raising his head to catch his breath, then down again to breathe into the mouth. His movements were careful, the precision almost pedantic – his hand cupping the man's face, adjusting the neck to ensure the flow of breath into the punctured, crushed chest. When this action seemed to fail he hammered the man's chest, knowing already that it was futile; angry that this bastard black man, this fucking monkey, had refused his order to live.

After repeating the action over and over, he finally stood and moved on, this time to a teenage girl.

Viktor felt people brushing past him, moving to the scene. In the distance he heard the whine of sirens and over the cars the lights of an ambulance. Louis waved his arms at Viktor. 'Grab the kid's legs. Quick. I need to get back to the twin-cab before we get jammed in.'

The girl's shirt had ripped, exposing her dirty white bra. One side of her face was disfigured by swelling and blood. One arm was bent, twisted hideously, as though reinvented with new, absurdist joints. Viktor took her legs under his arm. Godfrey changed places with Louis, freeing him to run ahead of them to the twin-cab.

When they reached the vehicle Louis had already reversed over the central reservations. The window down, his large arm hanging out of the cab, he hit the door as he spoke: 'Put her in the back with Godfrey. We can get her to a clinic in the Avenues. They will only kill her at Parirenyatwa.'

Viktor and Godfrey edged the girl to the back of the pick-up. One eyelid flickered open. 'Into the back, quick!' Louis screamed.

The child was delivered to the hospital. Louis disappeared into the building with Godfrey, shouting at Viktor to sit in the café he indicated.

Strangely calm, Viktor sat down at a table outside under the large hanging trees. The avenues were wide, perfect, and the sun shone through the trees, dotting the pavement and the tables with uneven, flinching circles of light. *Here*, he thought, *nothing happened, no death, no accident, no Zimbabwe.*

There were two pretty white children, twins with short blond hair that was dishevelled and thin. They wore ill-fitting shirts bunched over their matching trousers. One child sat on his mother's lap coughing, looking blankly at the adults in the café. The other child wandered around the garden, then crawled around the feet of the mother's chair, clutching a small, dirty toy elephant that rang with an internal bell. After a moment the mother stood, stretched and dropped a few notes on the table with languid indifference. The children started to bicker and moan with the same aimless disinterest as their mother.

Thirty minutes later Louis emerged from the hospital. Viktor swigged back the last mouthful of coffee, placed five dollars in single bills under the saucer and joined Louis by the car.

Exhausted, Louis looked up at Viktor and leant on the back of the twin-cab. Godfrey stood behind him, his head bowed. Louis's eyes were wet.

'Look!' he shouted finally, pointing into the boot. 'Clean it up when we get back, Godfrey. I don't want any of her kaffir blood in the cab.'

Part Three:

Harare

Chapter Twenty

The house was ringed by high terracotta walls decorated with razor wire, their gates controlled by a remote in the car. The tripwire and sensors screamed and shuddered in alarm if anyone black – who had not been invited in to clean, cook or garden – tried to enter the compound, to expropriate Louis's expropriated wealth. Viktor spent his first days enjoying the simple absurdity of his situation, waking up in the morning on the oversized bed in the guest wing of Louis's mock-Tudor house, full of endless corridors decorated with collages of family holidays: Kariba Dam, 2001, in the Drakensberg; 2008, *en famille* in Zanzibar, every member of the family on jet-skis, dining at large hotels, staring out of topless jeeps at animals, running into the water.

Why does this family holiday in Africa, Viktor thought as he made his way to breakfast on the first morning, *if they hate Africans so much? Why do they even live in Africa? Why hasn't Mugabe repatriated this family of Greek-Rhodesian Zimbabweans back to Athens? I must ask Louis,* he muttered to himself.

One element of Louis's empire stretched into the Congo, transporting unprocessed copper from Katanga through

Zambia, from Lubumbashi to Zimbabwe and South Africa to Durban through his transport business, TransGlobal – a name which was neither catchy nor geographically correct.

'We used to go through Mozambique to Beira, but the route was fucked and it's quicker to get to Durban,' Louis lectured Viktor on the morning of the third day, delivering a jug of coffee to his table as he spoke on the basics of Southern African political economy.

'It sounds to me like colonial exploitation – unprocessed raw material exported for processing in the North,' Viktor commented, his tone matter-of-fact, conceding nothing to his host.

'If you mean China, you're right. The ships head straight to China.' Louis displayed no offence at Viktor's comment. He saw the statement as a fact.

'Don't you think that your business is a parasite on the continent's inability to process its own resources and develop itself? Aren't you selling off the continent?' Viktor said, his voice flat and unanimated.

'These monkeys couldn't develop a community of grass huts, let alone a continent. I run businesses that give some of them work.' Louis was stout, heavily built. His arms and shoulders moved quickly, as if he mined the unprocessed copper in Katanga himself. He paced the kitchen, his steps hard and deliberate, his sure, confident footing breaking open the earth, claiming the continent. He hoisted himself onto one of the granite work surfaces opposite the table where Viktor cradled his coffee.

'They are not monkeys, and I find it offensive that you use that word,' Viktor said.

'Kaffirs, then.'

'No, not kaffirs. Fellow human beings.'

'Primitives,' Louis said, crossing his legs. 'Are you happy with primitives?'

'Your attitude is primitive.' *The man – this primitive – relishes contradiction*, Viktor thought.

'You'll see.'

'Yes, I do see. A racist businessman making money exploiting people, communities and countries he labels primitive. If you keep calling human beings animals, you will probably be shot like one.' Viktor put his coffee cup down and stood.

Louis laughed, jumped down from the counter and shook Viktor's shoulder vigorously. 'I like you. I like you. Very funny! Shot like an animal. Great.' The more Viktor disagreed with this man, this white tsunami of Southern Africa, the closer Louis seemed to be drawn in.

Louis's other business interest, the Zimbabwe branch of his empire, was a café, Kappas Coffee, in central Harare. 'The best coffee in Southern Africa, Viktor. Come by and I'll feed you. Coffee beans grown on my own estate near Mutare, in the Eastern Highlands, where they are also processed. Processed, dried, crushed, bagged, exported. Do you hear that, Viktor? *Processed*!'

*

After more procrastination, finally Anne-Marie had resolved to tell Nelson that she wanted a break. Coming from work, she wore her black heels and a suit with a pencil skirt to the meeting. As she entered the block of flats, almost surprised she recalled that tonight Viktor was going to be at the meeting. And what then? What had their friendship, their connection, actually meant to her? How real was it? Was it possible that Viktor believed that their virtual romance – the heated, absurd things they had said to each other in text messages, on Facebook – represented a real relationship?

Anne-Marie stood still. She held onto the handrail that led to the stairwell and let her thoughts go so that she could hear the meeting upstairs, the secret, implausible gathering of grown men and women who took on false names, so incomplete in their disguise, and gathered for noisy weekly discussions. After a moment she corralled her thoughts again, chased away the distractions, found the way back to herself. *He is so lost in his virtual world, so utterly absorbed in it, that he actually thinks we are having a relationship, and now he has come to Zimbabwe to see me. A black fantasy, an African adventure.* Anne-Marie tried to stop herself from thinking harder on the point, because she knew where it would lead. Involuntarily she felt her chest heave with shame at the thought of the messages, the photos *she'd* sent, the cravings *she'd* had for him. Had she driven all of her loneliness, Nelson's neglect of her, the fucking heartache of Zimbabwe onto safe, remote Viktor? She wondered if her need for him was really hunger for Nelson – the man she wanted but couldn't have.

'Damn it,' she said aloud, her hand gripping the rail hard, 'I'm doing that thing again, that bloody overthinking. It doesn't get me anywhere, only takes me round and round.'

Would he even turn up? They had communicated a week ago. Viktor had said that he was arriving on Thursday, that he had been in touch with Nelson and would be at the weekly meeting of the Harare Central branch of the Society of Liberated Minds. He had told Nelson and Biko that he was coming. *Tendai tells me I have to see for myself and that my learning counts for nothing. I NEED TO SEE* (his emphasis). *So I am coming to Zimbabwe to report on the crisis for* Mutations.

After Viktor's first text, Anne-Marie had not responded. She wanted her silence to tell him not to expect anything; if action

236

was what he needed, then he had to know that it was governed by laws separate to the unreal digital jurisdiction they'd briefly inhabited. She wanted to say that all those intense, meaningful exchanges — the snatched calls, the messages, the sexting, the make-believe fucking — they'd done in the ether, had meant nothing in the stakes of real life. But she couldn't say this, because it *had* meant something to her — she too had needed the feelings, the desire, the mystery.

On the same day, two hours after his last text, Viktor had sent a final message: *And I am coming to see you as well,* mudiwa.

Before she climbed the stairs, to ground herself and find her beautiful insignificance, Anne-Marie looked up at the open and generous night sky, almost always clear in Harare — strange how a city sky can be so wide, how it can show the stars so clearly amid the sound of the country's poverty and traffic. She fancied she could see the entire universe. A warm breeze wrapped itself around her, but still she felt her skin prickle. Tonight she wasn't satisfied even by the universe. Next to the bed in her flat lay the book, *The Physics of Nothing*, spread-eagled on the floor, a gift from a friend in South Africa. Anne-Marie started to climb the stairs, reluctant to reach the top before she could answer her own question. *And what of dark matter? We know only 5 per cent of the total energy density of the universe, but what of the 95 per cent we do not understand? What of the all-encompassing darkness?*

'Damn it,' she said aloud as she reached the top step. The truth was that she hadn't really understood what she'd been reading the night before, and now she had the meeting. Insignificant *and* ignorant. 'And what about Viktor?' she asked herself again.

*

Viktor unfolded the address, held it under the dim yellow light inside the car and read it to the driver. 'You can walk. It's only five minutes through Harare Gardens and straight up.'

'I don't want to walk. Can you take me?'

'I haven't got any fuel.' The driver coughed into his hand, catching the phlegm in his hand and wiping himself clean on his trousers. He was old and his face was creased like tissue paper.

'Can you get some?'

Louis had offered Viktor his car and a driver, if he was determined to contact these people and work on this ridiculous website. 'If these fucking blacks want to kill themselves, let them. Mugabe won't hesitate. He's a tough, mean bastard. Stay here. Stay with us.'

'Give me some cash and I'll fill up.'

Without looking at his passenger, the driver – his eyes fixed ahead on the cracked windscreen – fought with the gears, grinding the stick into place. The car shook and lurched into the road.

Viktor pushed the seat back, his legs still bent against the dashboard. The bag he had carried onto the plane rested on his lap. Books, pamphlets, the educational materials he had been instructed to bring. The email lay printed and unfolded on his bag, listing exactly what to buy, in what quantities and where to find the group. The bag was open on Viktor's lap. It couldn't close, the thousand jagged teeth of the zip splayed into a cloth smile. It had never worked. Isaac had given it to him when he was a boy; Isaac had used the bag when *he* was a boy. Viktor rubbed the bag with his hand. The faded red material felt strong, firm like a confirmation of life. At the end of life the only thing left in the universe would be Isaac's old school bag. Viktor gripped it tightly.

He felt the flood of doubt course through his body again. He tried to imagine the meeting, but he couldn't. When he thought about Anne-Marie, drew up images of her, the laconic texts, the heated messages, he felt his pulse thud heavily in his neck. He needed this rush, the certainty of her that he felt in his chest, in his coiled gut. Even the clarity of his feelings for Anne-Marie was fraught with uncertainty. Viktor felt the springs of the worn car seat pressing, nagging under him, and he adjusted his position. He told himself that he was here for Zimbabwe, not Anne-Marie; he was following Tendai's advice and seeing life for himself.

Finally the car slowed, jerked out of gear, hit the high kerb and stalled. Viktor said nothing, handed the driver a ten-dollar note and hauled his bag out of the car.

*

The low-rise blocks of red-brick flats were on the corner of Fourth Street and Josiah Tongogara, with a high perimeter fence ringed with barbed wire. The gate was operated by a security guard who covered the day shift from a wooden footstool under a golf umbrella. When a car turned off the road he would stand, grip the rolling gate and drag it open along its iron track. As the car drove through he would tip his cap, revealing a mass of black and white hair. In the evening the night watchman arrived and pulled on the uniform he shared with his colleague, both men changing in the dying light behind the umbrella by the gate. When the nights were cold the night watchman would huddle, his legs and arms pulled tight against him, catching interrupted sleep between gate duties.

Flat Four, Calder Gardens, was on the first floor, behind the walkway that ran the entire length of each floor, linking the flats to each other and to the stairwells and communal balconies. The swept and polished concrete, the car park full of twin-

239

cabs, jeeps and family cars, belied the crisis. The block, like the neighbourhood, was part of what was known and still spoken of with hushed awe, as the Avenues – a middle-class, inner-city community of large blocks of well-built flats, lavish housing complexes that snaked north from the city centre. From Calder Gardens it was a ten-minute walk downtown. There were swimming pools and intercoms. The small open-air shopping malls boasted expensive, fully stocked supermarkets, even a delicatessen with imported hummus, anchovies, olives and salami. Until recently there had been a theatre and bookshop, but deep into the crisis these had dared to sell books critical of the regime and stage plays that savaged the dictatorship with flimsy metaphors. The tree-lined Avenues had a strip of private clinics, dentists and a small hospital.

Yet even this area, with its boutique hotels and constantly budding array of flowers, jacaranda trees, bougainvillea, gumtrees, palms in continual bloom, was bursting apart. The roadway was cracked, the pavement strewn with vegetables and fruits lined up in rows on sheets of flattened boxes, the sun scorching and ripening the produce. One large open-air mall, once a haven of liberal, independent Zimbabwe and the decade-long flush of optimism after 1980, was circled day and night by groups of unemployed men, students and township youth who begged, stole and threatened the shoppers, who drove with the windows up and the doors locked.

The flat was the temporary headquarters of the Society for Liberated Minds, where the organisation's printing press, reams of paper, books, library and pamphlets were stored. Once a week the front room, behind the kitchen, was lined with plastic chairs, a table placed in front of the window, the banners and posters of the movement stuck to the surrounding walls, and the room would fill with students from the university, unemployed workers and the township poor. These were activists, each in their own group: the Zimbabwe National Student Union, the Patient Action Campaign, or trade unionists, sacked printers and clothing workers still active in their hollowed-out organisations.

Nelson lay on the uncovered foam mattress, aware that he would soon have to clear the room of his books and the bed and prepare for the meeting. The students, his students from the law department, had recently shut down the university, arguing and bullying other faculties to come out. The Society for Liberated Minds had members in the Zimbabwe National Student Union, a body that was not what it had been. Nelson – when every other lecturer had turned politician – was hated with a certain respect by the regime. His battered Toyota Corolla, the blue metallic paint chipped and scratched, was always full of students, riding low, the wheel arches almost scuffing the tyres, on his slow journey up Fourth Street to Mount Pleasant and the university for morning classes and again in the evening, when he stopped at the teeming bus stops, leant across the passenger seat and shouted, '*Ndiri kuenda kuma* Avenues, *pane anoda kuenda here.*' ('I'm going to the Avenues.')

Students, men and women, elbowed and rushed to get in. The fitful tape deck played the same tape, struggle songs from the seventies. Nelson kept rewinding the same song:

Nora Nora kani Nora Vakomana
Mhururu kuenda nekudzoka vakomana
Nora Vakomana.

His eyes would fill with water and he would tighten his grip on the steering wheel. He drove slowly so he could proselytise, elaborate on an argument to his captive audience, win them to

241

a proper meeting, not this ambulating, cramped discussion: the raised voices of his hitchhikers, his own loud, tuneful oration competing with 'Nora', the distorted, loud, slurring words of Elliot Manyika.

'No, no, listen comrades, these bourgeois nationalist fuckers are on the move. What's your view on this, comrades?' Before anyone could answer he'd continue, 'For me it raises the bells of Mugabe in 1997 to 2002, but in the context of Egypt, Tunisia, the Occupy movement, Greece, Brazil, Turkey. See what's happening in South Africa – these are Mugabe's real regional and continental disciples and heirs, but they may go further than Mugabe and potentially unite, radicalising sections of the rural and urban poor ... Comrades, don't you see, don't you? Comrades, our side has to move!

'Our hard and painful experiences here in Zimbabwe show the absolutely critical need of a sizable pole of the revolutionary left – but one concretely rooted in the key centres of the emerging struggles, one equally rooted in an internationalist perspective.'

Then straining, slowing the car, pounding the steering wheel to the music, to the sound of his own words, 'That's what we are trying to do in the Society of Liberated Minds. Egypt shows that the world has entered into an unprecedented period of revolutionary upheavals which will dwarf any that have occurred in human history. I mean, I mean' – Nelson lost his breath – 'I mean, seventeen million people on the streets of Egypt! Comrades, we must be ready.'

*

Nelson gave the impression of assembling his talks as he delivered them, handling a bundle of newspaper clippings, a pile of books open at a certain page. Long pauses just as the small, intimate audience crowded into his flat, expecting to feel the satisfaction of an argument consummated, a dramatic, damning denunciation reaching its climax. Instead Nelson tantalised the audience, stopped mid-flow when he thought the room had been comforted by his analysis, intentionally stuttered over a word and with a series of apologies, continued. 'Sorry, comrades, I can't find the quote I am looking for,' as he spread the papers across the table, his fingers outstretched, covering the tabletop with print as if sealing the gaps. Nelson fought against satisfaction and catharsis; instead he urged complexity in the battle for organisational and ideological lucidity.

Viktor stumbled across the car park to the stairway, pulled forward by the weight of the bag. Slowly he dragged himself up the flight of stairs to the first floor. He found the flat and knocked timidly, then eased the door open. Nelson was speaking when he entered, holding his glasses in his hand, stabbing the air with the other. Anne-Marie turned her head quickly to the door without a flicker of her previous questioning. She smiled and patted the space on the bench next to her as if they had seen each other in the morning and this was natural – as if they knew each other.

'The problem is that there are some people who are more equal than others in that movement. There are others who are now sitting at the head of the table and deciding how much the others should eat, in particular those who formed the party. So it's not just a question that involves everyone, it's a question of whose interests are now being championed by the movement. And our problem was that the interests that were now being championed were not the interests of working people. And mind you, comrades, Y-Party was not formed as a broad movement for everyone. Y-Party was formed after the hosting of what was called a Working People's Convention in 1999. So I want you to be very clear about this.'

Anne-Marie's tiny braids, tipped by white, yellow and red beads, hung on her shoulders. She smelt of perfume heated by the day's perspiration. When Viktor sat down she moved closer to him, so her leg pressed against his. Leaning towards him, she whispered, 'Good to see you, comrade, what took you?'

Nelson continued: 'Right from its base, Y-Party was marked with the stamp of workers, the unemployed, the poor and the peasants. And then intellectuals like ourselves in the Society for Liberated Minds, who sympathise and fight for the cause of these people, were also part and parcel. The rich, the white farmers, the business community, only came in after February 2000, and a whole lot of other people moved in ...'

Anne-Marie was irritated with Nelson, his self-conscious tricks and studied pondering, his flirtation with the women *and* men in the room.

'So, comrades, *sei tisina kuramba tichiita mamovement kusvika tabudirira mazviri*? But very soon, we believe that the conditions will be right again for the emergence of a real movement that will take on the Mugabe government and the dictatorship. And we will also take on the bosses and the capitalists of this country and region.'

'Tell me if you want anything translated.' Anne-Marie held her hair away from her face and turned to Viktor, speaking softly into his ear.

'Remember that these businessmen and women came in to hijack this programme. So we remained in the party until 2002, when we were expelled precisely because we wanted to fight them from within. But it is clear to us that after 2002 the party leadership had then been hijacked. And indeed, we have been vindicated up to this day. The elections have again been rigged, and Y-Party still insists on going into that parliament and taking on this thing. If Y-Party had been ready to mobilise its membership and the working people, the urban people, by now Mugabe would be history.' Nelson paused, staring at the audience.

Anne-Marie leant towards Viktor again. 'Y-Party refers to the Movement for Democratic Change, the opposition.' Viktor's ear tickled. The skin on his neck, his arm, the side of his body vibrated with her presence, as though the words were crawling on their own thin, lettered legs.

Viktor longed the meeting on, willed Nelson and his prevarications, his sub-clauses and deviations, to continue to prolong this sensation, the pressure of her thigh against his.

It was this simple, distracted first contact that meant everything to them – because in its strangeness, in the almost-familiarity of it, they both realised something completely astonishing. Their fantasy of contact – on the phone, in text messages, in emails and on Facebook – had been *important*. It was a fantasy, but beneath the fantasy was a real need for each other – a longing, an ache for the old to finally die and give way. The power of what they now felt was at the utter appropriateness of their first actual meeting *and* the immediate peculiarity of it.

Nelson seemed to be goading the crowd, who called back to his words, agreed with his thumping anger. Nelson wanted the audience's detachment rather than their seduction, yet this outcome was, he knew, anything but original.

An old woman, her large waist and buttocks covered in a coiled red and green cloth, stood up and shouted, '*Jambanja, jambanja* now! *Ndikamubata chete MUGABE!*'

Everyone laughed, took a breath and then went on laughing. Anne-Marie whispered, 'She says if she ever sees Mugabe in the street, she'll sit on him.'

Nelson replied, '*Shinga Mushandi Shinga! Qina Msebenzi Qina!* But, sister, we have to sit on the whole of X-Party and Y-Party and then take over State House, the land and the country for ourselves.'

Anne-Marie added, '"*Shinga Mushandi Shinga*" means "As workers you must be courageous".'

Nelson paused, put his glasses on and looked around the room. He looked at the couple sitting huddled together at the back of the room, and heads turned towards them.

Viktor sat up, feeling guilty, convinced they'd been caught, that he'd broken a basic rule and that this crowd of twenty souls could see right through him, with a vision and intuition he imagined was common in Zimbabwe. The audience, Viktor fancied, could penetrate his translucent body and see all his faults and failings: *My relationship with my parents, my daughter, my habits, my money problems, my prejudices, my writing, my height, my hair.* Despite their large, open smiles and welcoming, lifted eyebrows, they could see that he was a fake, that he did not bear the stamp of a worker, that he was not unemployed or poor.

He felt himself filling up with misunderstandings. Could Anne-Marie also see everything, peering as she was into his ear, into his brutal, raw, ridiculous soul?

Nelson addressed the room, staring over his glasses, his hands moving over his notes as though transmitting the text to his brain from his fingertips. 'We have a comrade from the UK who has joined us to help us make our way through the next few months.'

Anne-Marie elbowed Viktor.

Then, staring at Viktor, Nelson spoke loudly in Shona.

Anne-Marie translated, 'He is welcoming you. Saying that you've come from the UK to participate in the next phase of struggle in Southern Africa. He says you're going to speak to the meeting.'

'When?' Viktor asked, alarmed.

'Now,' she said.

*

After Viktor had introduced himself awkwardly, stuttered, thanked the room for allowing him to come and then, apologising, sat down quickly, Nelson dropped his glasses on the table, cleared his throat. 'It is normal that we finish our meetings by singing "The Internationale", first in English and then Shona.'

Chairs scratched against the concrete floor as people stood. Anne-Marie folded her legs, clicked her tongue and didn't move. She leant over to Viktor, resting a hand on his knee, and hissed loudly, 'You don't have to sing. I think it's ridiculous. You know ZANU-PF have the same ritual in their meetings? Only not "The Internationale" any more, but recordings of comrade Elliot Manyika singing struggle songs from the guerrilla war.'

A few heads turned to the couple. Nelson led the choir, almost shouting, 'Oh ye prisoners of want ...' Viktor sat nervously, worried that he was offending his hosts to keep this woman company.

Nelson was right; the movement had been stolen, their party hijacked by the NGOs and the middle class. Away from the city centre, Harare's roads and alleyways flowed with sewage; the people dressed in old, dirty, torn clothes; yet this, Viktor was told, was new. Twenty years old or less. There had always been poverty in Zimbabwe – hunger, droughts, early and plentiful death, short lives snuffed away by simple sickness – but this urban decay, this despair across every township from Highfield

247

to Chitungwiza, these living corpses in rags and bare feet, was new. For a brief moment there had been hope, Nelson had said: jobs in agriculture, schooling and work in the city's factories or in government offices. Now the country was hollowed, its bones emptied of marrow, the skeleton frame ready to crumble. Nelson had seen the streets crack and rupture like a ploughed field. NGOs had set up in commandeered compounds, in suburban houses abandoned by their white owners in the suburbs. Fleets of Land Rovers travelled to islands of stocked shops, delicatessens, video stores, florists – goddamn flower shops to service the community of expats, the wealthy elite. All making their way comfortably on the racket, the collapse. And the opposition, like the regime, had grown – as Nelson had said – 'fat and thick' on their MP salaries and handouts, while the poor had been abandoned just when they had started to take charge.

All this Nelson had said.

The small crowd filled a room barely large enough, Viktor thought, for a bed. Between those standing he could make out the words to 'The Internationale' written in a thick marker in Shona, taped to the wall. Nelson moved his arms, facing the group like a conductor, taking them through the text.

They were better in Shona, singing loud, dangerously imprudent, their backs heaving up and down, trying to push the walls back, to make more room with the force of their singing. And Viktor thought, *What great gusto. How large their ambition, how just the cause, but how few our number, always so few*. He felt sadness, pity. *What can this room with its hungry and sick souls hope to achieve?* Clinging onto the wreckage of a movement, to a single, short moment, as the furious, angry storm broke them one by one, ripped them away, pulled them under before their time.

The last line of the song was repeated even louder than before, in case Mugabe hadn't heard this final declaration, this challenge, the attempt to reclaim the song for the Zimbabwean poor. Viktor sat amazed, almost believing, as the crowd raised their fists and sang:

But if the ravens, the vultures
One morning disappeared
The sun would shine still.

'Romantic nonsense!' Anne-Marie exclaimed. 'Dangerous, too.' She stood and placed a hand on Viktor's shoulder. 'So, finally we meet.'

'I enjoyed the singing. I come from a family of tone-deaf opera singers.'

'But I doubt you sing the songs of the Zimbabwean dictatorship.'

The meeting was over. Nelson spoke loudly to a group around the table, shuffling his papers into a pile, his glasses perched low on his nose.

'I suppose you want to see the General,' Anne-Marie said.

'The General?'

'Oh, he hasn't told you? It's our nickname for him. He loves it.'

Viktor stood, almost skimming the ceiling with his head. He could never blend in. Instead he was obliged to separate himself, peel away from his family, stand aloof from the world, gesticulate from his airless summit.

'So we are out of the virtual and into the real. From theory to practice, Viktor.' Anne-Marie got up and turned her body towards Viktor. She was strong, broad, full, beautiful – *properly made*, Viktor thought. She radiated a physical, confident presence. There were no excuses or hesitations in the way she looked; all parts of her a statement that was complete. Her pleasing roundness; her full, absolute breasts; her adamant, unequivocal legs and arms; her buttocks strong and insistent. There was something delightfully arrogant about her appearance. For once Viktor did not need to work anything up in himself; for once, he could just feel.

The sense of concreteness coming from her physical presence said to Viktor, *You're really here, you're really here in front of me*. Though he was giddy from her actually being there, the proximity of her body, it was not even really about her body. It was about the feelings that flowed over him – and this was something Viktor was not accustomed to.

Viktor answered her. 'I already have several interviews set up, and trips to Bulawayo and Mutare. It feels good to be here.'

Anne-Marie's feet felt good; she stood flat and firm on the floor. Lucidity and desire did this to her, gave her fluency. If it was her clarity and resolution that drew Viktor in, Anne-Marie decided, it was his utter, unusual looseness, his near refusal to be like any man she'd met, that attracted her. Much of this was bullshit, of course, and she knew it – Viktor *was* like other men. He flinched when challenged, needed to speak and be heard as though his very fucking life depended on it and wore his insecurity in the raw, painful open. He chafed, stumbled, doubted, undermined, like all men she knew. But he was also different. He listened intensely and strangely – craned forward, lowering himself to her, thought about what she said, paused, chewed on her words. When Anne-Marie spoke and he agreed, when he thought she'd found something, he would nod so furiously that his head would blur, his features streaking in the slipstream of agreement. Anne-Marie found this sensation strange. His focus and attention on her worked up between them like static electricity; the invisible jolt of connection made him irresistible to her. And Viktor was oblivious, of course. Utterly fucking ignorant.

Yet she'd been irritated by Nelson's melodrama, his beliefs. With Nelson life was always about to be fulfilled. There were constant ridiculous promises, another dawn because the last one had been destroyed. Revolutionary maximalism, absolute absurdism – no better, she thought, than a preacher offering salvation in a church. *Life after death, freedom after we've won. I know what I am. I know what I want. I know how to dream today.* Nelson, the prophet of becoming. The striving to arrive, the perfect moment, the fucking Promised Land. *Not for me*, Anne-Marie thought. *I have always been present. I am. I do. I give.*

Anne-Marie saw herself as a child: the back door of their house in Kinshasa, the concrete garden, the plastic umbrellas that magnified the naked, ferocious sun, suffocating her when she played under them. She felt the humidity running off her skin, her tongue sticking to the inside of her mouth, tasting the salt in her sweat. *Even then, in the Congo, I was practical. My whole childhood, lived for years in that high-walled outdoors, was led sensibly – time had to be used for practical, small projects. Small dawns.*

She rested her hands on her hips and turned back to Viktor, who was standing astride his bag, looking around the room. She felt her pulse slow.

'Welcome!' Nelson gripped Viktor's hand and kept hold of it. 'We're pleased you made it.'

Nelson looked to Anne-Marie and smiled.

'You shouldn't sing in this building,' she said. 'Why don't you just put the megaphone outside the flat and send an invitation to X-Party?'

'You see what we have to put up with in our ranks?' Nelson's voice was deep and soothing.

'I enjoyed the meeting,' Viktor said.

'Good. We can do meetings. You will have to do one for us. Where are you living? We need to talk, plan.'

Anne-Marie felt the ground slip, her feet sink into the concrete. *Don't let him get to you. A movement of becomers – that's what he is.* In Nelson's future they would finally be free, all of them: in South Africa, in Zimbabwe, in the region, even in the Congo, in this mixed-up, complex, impossible world. *Nelson only arrives when we have sex. Only then does he become.* Two weeks ago they had fucked – his plans with her as real as the crimson, out-of-reach Promised Land he conjured in these meetings. *No more*, she had said to herself, *no more sex.* Always the same thrusts, the same position, the same characterless sex – practical only in his fucking. The political sweet nothings he whispered to her after he came. '*Mudiwa*, darling,' he said, 'I want to talk to you about our position in next year's elections.' *And he wouldn't even notice if I stopped seeing him, if I took Viktor in.*

Anne-Marie spoke. 'The General is the most dream-prone comrade in the movement. And his songs are the most ridiculous.'

'Come, come, comrade, don't demoralise us. We need to show our overseas visitor our best side.'

'Don't patronise me,' Anne-Marie snarled.

'We need dreams, great big dreams,' Viktor said calmly.

Anne-Marie laughed loudly from the back of her throat. 'In that case, you'll be in good company here.'

Nelson tucked his hair behind his ears and looked at Anne-Marie without irritation, a slight smile turning up his mouth. 'We're not in the business of dreams – they won't get us anywhere, unless the working class can move beyond X- and Y-Party. Y-Party is what we call the MDC,' Nelson added for Viktor's benefit.

'Yes, I know, and X-Party is ZANU-PF,' Viktor replied.

'Exactly!' Nelson's easy, broad smile relaxed over Viktor. 'A few years ago we had to take struggle names and code our language, so we could talk openly without exposing comrades. I'm sometimes known as Oscar, the General. Anne-Marie as Hopewell.'

'That sounds quite romantic. Quite Bolshevik,' Viktor said, trying to mimic Nelson's confident, generous explanations.

'Nothing romantic about it, comrade. In the nineties our organisations depended on it. We had no choice.'

'But he's right,' Anne-Marie interjected. 'You are a romantic. All the communist insignia, the old bearded white men, "The Internationale".'

The room was decorated, almost wallpapered with posters, a life-size print of Lenin staring stocky and rosy-cheeked into the fields. A chipped plaster bust of Marx sat on the table, his white features soiled by handling. On another wall was an enlarged photograph of a short-haired man speaking, one forefinger extended, pointing into the camera and the room. Nelson saw Viktor looking.

'That's Oscar, the real Oscar. He set up the Society of Liberated Minds. The HIV tsunami has dealt the group a heavy blow. We need to plan, comrade. I liked the articles you wrote on your first impressions.' Nelson quoted, '"Zimbabwe is a monument, a ruin to a failed project" – excellent.' He moved back to his desk, pulled a sheet from the pile of papers and read: '"I feel as though I have arrived in a country of the living dead, a dictatorship which doesn't seem to be visible on the streets, only in the faces of the poor." Good, but wrong. You see, Viktor, every dictatorship has to build up its social base – in this sense, X-Party is a social movement. It was the war veterans, the old liberation fighters, who we almost won to our side in the late nineties – but now they're with Mugabe. His Praetorian Guard. Behind them the Youth, the Green Bombers, who were trained at National Youth Training Centres in the rural areas. Both of the old man's social bases are visible … you'll see.'

Nelson, Anne-Marie thought, dropping into the chair again, kicking away her shoes, *runs his own Counterblast News Agency to explain the true nature of things, the unnatural order. Even when he comes down from the podium he makes speeches. Everything he says is a desperate attempt to clarify, to push his understanding against the great cacophony of society's deafening norms. He truly believes he is indispensable to the movement and can't be replaced – the weight of bloody history upon him.*

'We can make good use of the website,' Nelson continued. 'None of us, apart from a couple of students, have had much time to work on the internet, but we need it. You will be useful for us.'

Viktor's mouth was dry. He rested against the wall. 'Of course I want to be helpful, though I have to cover all bases. Hear what everyone is saying.'

Nelson threw back his head and laughed deep and slow, his long locks of hair swaying heavily. 'A true liberal. A true English liberal. Of course, of course. There'll be no problem on that front. My comrade here' – he nodded his head to the side, indicating Anne-Marie – 'thinks I'm too soft on X-Party, that I should be harder, and some think I'm ultra-left with Y-Party. So don't worry, comrade, you'll get the whole story and *we will* use you.' He laughed again.

Nelson's generous, free confidence was deeper, more compelling than his stage show. Viktor liked him, and didn't know how he'd be able to refuse the dizzy gusts and headwinds of his charm.

'Soon you will need to see the students. Our best students and militants are in Bulawayo, but that can wait. You need to understand Harare first. You must meet Guthrie Madhuku – he writes for the government paper, the *Herald*. He's a friend, an X-Party intellectual. He thinks we've got it wrong and that land redistribution, the development of a black propertied class and delinking from the West are real advances. He's impressive, very smart.'

'But he's ZANU,' Viktor said limply, perplexed.

'That doesn't make him a fool,' Nelson answered quickly.

'But it does make him complicit! The rag he writes for backs up everything the government does. He's a fucking bully,' Anne-Marie snapped.

Nelson paused, then persisted with his plan. 'Then you need to meet Arthur Biti, Y-Party financial and legal adviser. He was one of ours, we trained him. He was at the University of Zimbabwe with me more than twenty-five years ago. He was a good socialist. Now he is hopelessly out of touch. He travels to the US, the UK, fundraising – goes everywhere Business Class. We drink together sometimes.'

'I've got to go.' Anne-Marie stood, holding her shoes in one hand. Her eyes were ringed with exhaustion. Her large silver earrings flashed, her heavy lipstick still showing up bright red. 'Where are you staying, com?' She addressed the question matter-of-factly to Viktor.

'I was planning to stay in a guest house ten minutes from here.' Viktor longed to say something serious, to show Nelson and Anne-Marie that he understood and that they could rely on him.

'That's no good, probably not safe. Those Avenue guest houses are crawling with the CIO. The Central Intelligence Organisation, comrade. Stay with me, here. You can have that mattress.' Nelson indicated with his head the folded, stained rectangle of foam in the corner.

'You'll drive him out of Zimbabwe in a week,' Anne-Marie said. 'I have a lounge and a sofa. You can have that – of course you're staying with me.' She reached for Viktor's arm and squeezed.

Viktor tried to object. 'No, I'm fine, probably best to stay where I am.'

'Rubbish,' Anne-Marie said firmly. 'We'll get your stuff now. I have running water, a proper kitchen, security. You won't know you're not in London. You can even pretend that I'm white, if you like.'

'London? That's not what I meant—' Viktor spluttered.

Nelson polished his glasses on his shirt, put them on again, pushed the frame up his nose and stared at Anne-Marie. 'I will fix an appointment with people this week, or next week. You'll have to be careful with Anne-Marie. She thinks we can change the world one microloan at a time.'

'I'm not interested in changing the world, only Zimbabwe. And today, not sometime when the people have risen up against your X- , Y- and Z-parties, the old man, capitalism, the church.'

'You see, Viktor, you'll have to watch her.' Nelson was laughing again.

Chapter Twenty-One

Viktor was pleased to be leaving the flat, following Anne-Marie's bare feet peeling against the concrete floors, showing him the way to the stairwell. How strange it felt to be suddenly presented with a new life, with friends, comrades, meetings, a bed. And Anne-Marie, who he felt as though he'd known for years and years, with her anti-politics and her good sense. *What does it all mean?* Viktor thought.

Before they left the flat Viktor had introduced himself, his head bowing slightly, to each member of the Society. The students, the workers, the groups, the organisers, each of them had names he recognised, that he asked them to repeat: Trotsky, Stalin, Lenin – there were two Lenins – Sankara, Lumumba, Cabral. Each name presented without irony, without even the prospect of humour.

'Bad activists copy, good activists steal,' Anne-Marie explained later, shaking her head. There was even a Rosa.

'Like my daughter,' Viktor said automatically, excited.

'Yes, of course, your daughter.' Anne-Marie drove, speaking fluent, accented English.

Anne-Marie thought about her offer to Viktor; she warmed to him, to his odd assumption about them. Nelson's unfocused, faraway eyes had looked through her when she invited Viktor to stay with her. The offer had come out suddenly and surprised her. Had she wanted to deprive Nelson of a plan, of his ordering of everyone's lives?

She was unaware that Viktor had been speaking, a whole outpouring about his daughter, his ex. 'I mean, I didn't tell you much when I was in London. We would have killed each other. We only survived the first years of Rosa's life with drugs, and only enjoyed Rosa when we were alone, away from each other.'

'Who took drugs?' Anne-Marie asked, her interest mildly stimulated.

'We did. Nina and me. I was on antidepressants and for her it was painkillers – Valium, Tramadol, anything she could get hold of. We were either at war with each other or stoned. That's why I left.'

'Because of the drugs.'

'No. Yes. Because of the war – the extremes. Lurching constantly from insults to blowing our minds. You know the poem, "half the time sloppy stern, half the time at each other's throats"?'

Anne-Marie didn't understand. It was late and she needed to sleep, so she could get up early and drive to Gweru. 'I am beginning to get this, Viktor; you came to Harare to escape.'

For a moment Viktor didn't answer. Then he spoke in a rush: 'I suffer from depression. I'm introspective. Not the defensive guilt of a paranoid person, rather a conscious, ego-syntonic sense of culpability.'

Anne-Marie laughed. 'Do you always speak like this in the flesh?'

'Like what?'

258

'Like a book? Like a doctor?'

'When I'm accused of something I haven't done I feel guilty.' Viktor stared ahead. 'These are classic traits, you see. The sadness a characteristic of anaclitic depression. Oppression and injustice drive me crazy and I can't act. I don't have the anger to act. The anger of the paranoid, the moralisation of the obsessive, the anxiety of the hysterical. They all act. Move. Rage. Not me, I am just sorrowful. Sorrow.'

'Sorrow?' Anne-Marie repeated, and laughed again.

'My real action and commitment are my tears, I suppose. Paralysing bloody pity.'

'Well, Zimbabwe doesn't need your pity.'

'I know.'

'And, I suspect, neither does your daughter.'

'Rosa.'

'Does Rosa need your pity?'

Viktor felt suddenly exposed and ridiculous. Perhaps he would ruin Harare as well, pollute it with his guilt, his depressive anaclitic disorder, his battle for balance on the tightrope of existence. They arrived at Anne-Marie's flat.

As Viktor washed off the day in the bathroom, tipping cold water over his shoulders, Anne-Marie moved furtively around the flat, closing the curtains – on the windows that had them – and turning off the lights. *Does he even find me attractive?* She saw his awkwardness at the meeting, his hesitation when she offered him accommodation, as evidence that he was disappointed in her body, in her real-life curves and imperfections. As she moved around the flat, trying to tidy up, she grew irritated with him, with the situation that had thrust him on her. He hadn't even asked if he could come. He had given her no notice, no time to have tried to lose ten pounds before his arrival. She stared towards the bathroom door and muttered, irritated with herself *and* her guest, something a Facebook friend had said to her once: *Lord, give me the confidence of a mediocre white man.*

In the preamble of doubt and nervousness, stilted, stiff, they moved around Anne-Marie's flat as she prepared their night, arranging the bed, the sheets, the pillows. Viktor kept himself apart, constantly moving his bag to different places in the flat – beside the sofa, to the corridor, the hall by the front door.

Eventually, tired, wondering how she was going to do this, Anne-Marie stood in the hall, her hands on her hips. Viktor stood by the entrance to the kitchen, his T-shirt crooked on his shoulders, feet splayed on the floor like flippers, holding his bag by its torn handles.

'Come here, Viktor,' Anne-Marie ordered softly.

Viktor moved slowly towards her.

'Can you just drop the bag, please? You're staying, right?'

Viktor stopped a foot away from Anne-Marie, bent, dropped the bag between them.

'Come here, I said.'

Stiffly Viktor shuffled forward a few more inches.

Anne-Marie reached up, put her hands on each side of his face and smiled. Viktor could smell her skin, the dying perfume, the day, the film of sweat on her hands – he wanted more, to feel her damp warmth over him, to taste her. Still he didn't move. He avoided her eyes. He stared at the floor.

'Here,' Anne-Marie said again, pulling his face towards her, forcing him to bend. He lifted his eyes to her.

Viktor felt an overwhelming flood, a rush of everything. Images came for him, surrounded him – of his life, his people, their exhausting, intolerable love, their claims on him, his on them. Before his lips reached Anne-Marie he saw his daughter – her arms around his neck, her long, combed, black hair, the want on her face that he'd never understood – he saw Nina,

260

too, a terrible questioning around her eyes as she stared at him. He felt his chest hollow, lurch up and a deep feeling of desire and regret.

Yet the kiss and embrace was as passionate as he had ever known. Their tongues quickly found each other and moved together. His kiss told her that at last she had his full attention; they were both desperately in need of someone to give them life and hope.

Anne-Marie put her hand under his stretched, faded T-shirt and laid her fingers on the base of his neck. Viktor copied her, pulled away her blouse and slowly moved his hand up her chest, resting his hot palm between her breasts. She groaned.

Anne-Marie took his hand and led him into her room. Viktor immediately reached for the light switch and turned it off. 'Turn it back on,' Anne-Marie said. She lay on the bed, strewn with clothes and unmade, swirling sheets. Slowly she started to unbutton her blouse, instructing Viktor to lie next to her. Propped up on her pillows, she peeled the blouse open and wriggled further up the bed. 'Take my bra off. Reach round my back and unclip it.' Viktor leant in, his breathing short, uneven, and coiled his hands behind her, fumbled, undid the bra. She breathed heavily on his neck.

Her nipples were hard. Viktor kissed them, taking each one in his mouth and lightly running his tongue around them. Holding his head, Anne-Marie moved it in the way she wanted his tongue to move.

Briefly Viktor felt his thoughts drift, his concentration dip. He wondered if *this* was the problem – that our modern consciousness could only be satisfied by the thrill and ecstasies of sex, that there was no human experience to rival its climax and destruction. Quickly he was brought back by her fingers running lightly along his spine, and the thought scattered before it could take further root.

Their breathing had become deep, synchronised. Anne-Marie's skin puckered with moisture. She moaned each time he moved his hands and sighed in a different note for each part of her back, her legs, her neck. Viktor ran his hands, dragging his fingertips along her skin, and he fancied that she sang.

'Help me with this, Viktor.' Gently she pushed his head away from her. She unzipped the tight skirt and Viktor pulled her panties down with it – lace, he noted, as though she'd planned for him to see them. Her pubic hair was thick and dense.

Viktor stood awkwardly beside the bed, fumbling as he undid his trousers and levered his shoes off. He knelt again on the bed and ran his hands along the inside of Anne-Marie's thighs. She sighed and let her head fall back. Quickly he sank his face between her legs and breathed in to get her whole scent. He sucked in her smell, filled himself with her.

Her thighs were dark even against her dark complexion. Timidly Viktor kissed them, working his way up, listening to her breathing. When he took a first tentative lick she gasped and writhed, placed her hands across her breasts, breathed in deeply.

Viktor felt the pulse in his head beat heavily, his erection pressing into the bed. Instinctively he tried to think, to reason, to find an analysis, and began to raise himself on his elbows, but Anne-Marie interrupted. 'Come back here.' She held out her hand and drew him closer, positioning him again between her legs.

He moved the tip of his tongue inside her, around her, exploring, and she trembled. *Such subtlety and care*, Anne-Marie thought, *he is painting me with his tongue*. Still, thoughts crowded in: Nelson's face, his ironic smile, the meeting, his Lenin pose, one hand on his hip, another pointing into the room – his million-strong movement of thirty people. Then her mother's face, stern, disapproving, telling her to come back to Kinshasa, work with her, live in the family house. Viktor craned his head, looked up and tried to find her face. He reached for her hand, knotting his fingers into hers.

After a few minutes she said, 'Stop.' Viktor raised himself again and looked into her eyes. 'This is like breathing to me,' Anne-Marie said. 'Do you understand?'

Unwilling to break his silence, to ruin the moment with his words, Viktor nodded.

'Lie down next to me.' Anne-Marie patted the space beside her.

Viktor moved to her side and pressed himself to her. He felt himself falling. Only the bed existed, nothing but the bed, raised on its tall legs, thrusting them into the night, into the dark sky, the noise and clutter a faint, invisible chatter beneath them. Above them, the moon. He felt the smooth skin of her back against his chest, her buttocks pressing into his groin. He wrapped an arm around her, held her breasts, kissed her neck. They were lost. Between them there was an anarchy of passion, an uncontrolled ache of desire that flowed quickly in their veins.

Afterwards, unable to stop kissing and touching each other, they gradually fell into a deep, temporary sleep in each other's arms. Even when they woke, the rawness, the daily fatigue, the cynicism that had been inside both of them was gone. They felt nothing but the momentary, pure echo of their lovemaking.

In the conversation that followed their nap, as they talked long into the night, Anne-Marie thought about Nelson. Viktor was able to talk to her about his dilemmas and even his failings with an intimacy and vulnerability she had not experienced. Strangely, she thought, it made her feel as though she was forgiven for her own faults and failings. Somehow she had always put up a front of femininity and, with Nelson, a pretence of being an Iron Lenin. An Iron Lumumba. Nelson wanted a faultless woman *and* a militant revolutionary. Already, with Viktor, she experienced a sense of solidarity with a lover – something she had never known.

Without exactly knowing what she was doing, she found herself questioning him, testing him. Was there a place in his life for her, and in her own for him? Was there a future for this? For Anne-Marie there was the instinctive, innocent question: *Could we be together?* This was followed by the learnt one – self-protection and political formulation – *Should I even care if we can? Would that stop me from feeling what I feel and doing what we are doing?* Yet she knew that for her to break through the doubt and questioning, the ingrained cynicism, she would have to disown these ideas – to clear herself down to zero. Somehow these elaborate processes of thought had to be unlearnt in her as well.

The *line* always had to have its place. Political rules, formulations, theory had taught her to close herself up and, in her own way, to keep life at bay. But in the innocence of their connection Anne-Marie felt unprepared by her training, hampered by all of her experience and learning. She may have appeared to Viktor as wonderfully liberated and sexual, but for all her bombast and confidence, she realised, she too needed to bubble out of herself. To become unprepared, untutored. Both of them were too practised at life, too imbued with ideas, they didn't really know how to live.

They were faintly aware, as they lay awake, propped up on their pillows, the sweat of their love sealing their backs to the sheets – their minds emptying, unable to entirely refill and clutter – that this first intense, meaningful, playful night together had started something.

Viktor felt his mind attempt to turn on its familiar axis, casting about for a reference, a book, a guide – did Hegel have anything to say about this? Was there a companion for these sensations in Žižek? In Baudrillard, maybe; something about the simulacra and simulation? He felt a faint nagging – surely he needed to find *the* text for this experience?

He caught himself. With different degrees of severity, these encumbrances of thought were killing them. Tonight it seemed that, for the first time in years, they were really living.

*

Comrade!

I know you have arrived by now and are immersed already in the sea of action and life that is Zimbabwe. I am writing in a rush to tell you that everything is changing: all long-stagnating rustiness, flabbiness, habit-based, outdated political priorities, emphases, tactics and old 'formulae learnt by rote so mindlessly repeated by those regrettable old comrades in the North' – as Nelson recently put it in an email to me, is falling away. But in the newly awakening minority epitomised by the struggle at the university we have found a new spirit to forge the future.

Now everyone can see the forces active in this ongoing red-hot molten lava of the African-Arab Revolutions, where the locomotive driving force of the working poor is plainly evident to anyone who can watch a YouTube video (yes, comrade, on your urging I am finally watching YouTube).

And certainly MOST – I would say ALL – activists I've read have FAILED the acid test of the reality of revolution. I have read your posts on *Mutations*, *Refutations*, whatever you call that bloody thing, and I saw the article you republished from the Society of Liberated Minds (the organisation that made me what I am today). But I am worried - they seem to have inserted a paragraph into a young Tunisian socialist's account of his involvement in the revolution, stating that 'the trade union federation started and led the Tunisian revolution'.

As Nelson often repeats, 'Facts are stubborn things'. My Botswanan partner, who has come back to me, and has now moved into my small room, has watched innumerable phone videos from the Tunisian workers who uploaded them AS THEY MADE THE REVOLUTION: first in Sidi-Bouzid, then Sulyam, then Kazzarin, the first big industrial town, where the State tried to kill it dead with a massacre (48 shot dead in the head), then to the south, the west, and then north, taking in every town – to Tunis. And it's damn obvious from the videos, that it is groups of young, sometimes older workers running to the next town to spread it – phoning ahead, getting gatherings together. This process went on all through December, unifying FOURTEEN towns and cities, *before* the union federation called a 'token Symbolic Strike of two hours'. This can in no way be characterised as either 'STARTING' or 'LEADING' anything, let alone 'the Tunisian Revolution'. TELL NELSON THIS.

Sala kakuhle Viktor!

Tendai

Chapter Twenty-Two

Harare was perched with uncertainty on the red earth, its sprawling bungalow belt and high-density slums ringing the distinctive, shimmering skyscrapers in the downtown streets and avenues. The economic meltdown, the plunge, had thrown this thinly rooted city to the ground. In the middle of roads and on pavements, like a thousand mouths speaking, potholes opened and craters appeared. It seemed that the ground was absorbing this brick and concrete metropolis, this interloper, pulling up the shallow foundations of the city. The red earth broke through the tarmac, upturned paving stones, ploughing the city into a field. Moving around Harare now required ingenuity, daring and a hard heart. The city was being expunged in a slow, tragic urban earthquake, all human plans and designs swallowed up, the borrowed and desecrated land retaken. Harare showed Zimbabwe the way.

Yet it was not the city's demise but its opulence that puzzled Viktor. As a child he had counted the miniature figures surrounding a half-built pyramid in a picture book and wondered how this society could have survived so long, building tombs to a family tyranny for a millennium. Now he asked, with the same innocence, how the city's wealth had not been expropriated, its high rises not occupied or levelled to the ground. How had the poor let this go on for so long?

If the urban space had been prised open, the skyscrapers reclaimed by the earth, then the human sojourners were also brought low. 'People in rags don't make revolutions,' Primo Levi said. So why did his comrades point to the undone, the life-drained rabble moving around the city, as the force to unseat Mugabe and refigure Zimbabwe? Harare's human mass had been dispersed. Where once there had been unions recruiting and organising in the city's celebrated industrial areas of Southerton and Workington, now the factories, bottling plants, clothing depots, industrial outlets, were hollowed-out hangars squatted by human jetsam. Where was the class ready to shake off its chains and fight? Instead the residents were left desolate and alone. There was a silence to the city as people waited for free lifts on pavement corners, hung limp hands into the road, queued speechless for combis and walked in single file over miles and miles along roads and highways to townships – Highfield, Zuwadzana – the colour and will washed from their faces.

'We are in a city of the living dead,' Nelson remarked, laughing coldly.

Through the full range of biblical catastrophe – flood, plague, poverty, dictatorship – the Society of Liberated Minds never failed to organise its weekly meetings. A week after Viktor's first meeting, there was another.

When the speech had finished there was the routine of arm-raising: fists out, some raised, unclenched hands, others waiting until the last chant to punch the air. Viktor was no longer unknown or considered only with curiosity. This was the closest Viktor got to being accepted, to being more than a white man, a *murungu* and foreigner: he looked like them, like

Stalin and Lenin, like a Zimbabwean socialist, with his single pair of grey trainers, size thirteen, with the hole for his big toe on his right foot, the bare long toe protruding, the holes in his jeans, the elbows gone from his sweatshirt.

Nelson beckoned to Viktor from the windowsill. The window was open and the hazy, speckled dusk danced on the parked cars one floor down. The men smoked, drawing hard on their cigarettes, blowing the smoke in the direction of the window. 'You need to listen to this, Viktor,' Nelson said, and laid his arm across Viktor's back.

Stalin was speaking. 'Mandela. Mandela. Gone are the days when we have to worship him. You have to remember, comrades,' he looked at his small audience, cigarette in cupped hand, 'we thought the release of Mandela was going to add to the bloodshed and revolution and that liberation was going to come. But, man, he was so peaceful that he calmed us down, told us to put our spears down, to settle in peace and liberate peacefully, that's what Mandela taught us.'

Lenin was nodding his head furiously. 'Even us, here in Zim, thought Mugabe was right, but he told us that fighting with guns and explosives would fail.'

Stalin interrupted. 'Yeah, that the buildings would come apart and then we'd only have to rebuild them! But we all thought that when Mandela was released – and we fought for his release – that he was going to make a difference. Look at South Africa today, look at white people.'

'Come on, you guys, don't just give me the standard black nationalist bullshit,' Nelson said, his arm still draped across Viktor's back. He squeezed Viktor's shoulder and turned towards him. 'We've got to make our white guest feel welcome.'

Viktor bristled. 'Don't moderate on my behalf.' He felt Nelson's breath on his neck, the smell of his smoky, moist mouth.

'Esssh, man,' Stalin said, his wrinkled, scarred face raised in a smile. 'But I still feel those white individuals are separating the nation.'

Lenin struggled to return the conversation to its previous theme. 'In South Africa and Zimbabwe we were fooled. In South Africa Mandela told you to hang up your spear, that he was going to liberate you with this settlement thing, all that rubbish, reconciliation, peace, the TRC.'

Nelson added, for Viktor's benefit, 'The Truth and Reconciliation Commission, led by Desmond Tutu, to bring healing and amnesty for apartheid killers.'

'I know, I know,' Viktor said, irritated, wanting Lenin to continue.

'So all that healing nonsense, the TRC, was a puppet structure,' Lenin resumed. 'In 1980 in Zimbabwe, Mugabe did the same thing. "Love your enemy, put away your guns, end the revolution".'

Nelson nudged Viktor and muttered, 'Listen, listen.'

'I *am* listening,' Viktor said, annoyed.

'So,' Stalin said, taking up the story again, 'we feel oppressed and our hearts are bleeding inside. My people find themselves in a very confusing situation. There are these barriers, Mandela's barriers, and we are trying to find a way through.'

'Yeah!' Lenin exclaimed.

'Exactly,' Nelson said. He played with his cigarette, brought the rolled tobacco to his lips and drew in deeply.

Almost to himself, leaning against the window pane, Stalin spoke in a hushed voice. 'The fight came to an end and our people had died. A lot of comrades were killed. The day I had to vote in 1994, I never slept. I thought I would get my freedom. Move into a proper house.'

Nelson interrupted. 'Tell Viktor, com, about what happened to your mum.'

Stalin got excited. He took the cigarette packet, rattled a single cigarette free, brought it to his mouth then repeated the action, offering the exposed cigarettes to Viktor, Nelson and Lenin.

'Okay, comrade,' Stalin continued. 'We were the fighting units inside South Africa, in the townships and squatter camps. We brought apartheid to its knees. We took over the bush with our shacks and these areas became no-go areas. We built our shacks by force every time. But when the ANC was unbanned, the comrades from outside, from exile, came back – and then there was trouble. The regional office of the ANC in Johannesburg came to stop us. They told us to disarm but we hated it. We were told to give up our ammunition. The one thing that we hated was for a person to come and disarm us when he didn't arm us in the first place.'

The grey dusk had turned black; the room was empty except for the four men standing by the window. The city had felt airless, closed off, all day, the sun shining between storms, the road and pavement steaming. There was a loud crack of thunder and rain started to fall again, heavily, hammering the ground, the cars, the roofs, ricocheting loudly off the gravel.

'Fuck, look at it,' Stalin said, flicking his cigarette butt out of the window.

'A monkey's wedding,' Lenin commented, staring at the window.

'Carry on,' Nelson urged.

'They wanted the troublemakers gone,' Stalin said. 'The ANC wanted us silenced. We were a, a block to their settlement. We were the troublemakers and we didn't accept them, so they targeted us.'

'What? The ANC? You mean they wanted to remove you?' Viktor asked.

271

'No, they wanted to kill us, com,' Stalin explained, speaking directly to Viktor. 'They took the decision to target me. I had to be killed. I felt drowsy that day. I was with my mother in her shack, lying down. And outside I heard, "Stalin, Buhle, you are going to eat shit today!" and they started to fire. I shouted to my mother, "Lie down and don't move." So they fired. My mother was thinking it was some silly boys that were playing. So she stood up and got hit in her stomach.' Stalin stopped suddenly. 'She died.'

All the men were quiet. Viktor struggled to understand. He wanted to ask Stalin to repeat the story so he could write it down. His hand patted his jacket pocket, feeling for his notebook.

Lenin put a hand on Stalin's shoulder.

'You know what the guy said outside?' Stalin continued. 'He said, "We finished them." Jesus, comrades, I feel like I'm going to cry.'

Nelson, shaking his head, spoke first. 'Those nationalist bastards. Those fuckers.'

After a moment Lenin said, 'Here it was the massacres of terrorists in the eighties. Twenty thousand dead. Mugabe and ZANU spiked our guns. Stole our revolution. But we still thought it would be better with a black man at the table. We were wrong here and there, we were so fucking wrong. *Sei tisina kuramba tichiita mamovement kusvika tabudirira mazviri?*'

Chapter Twenty-Three

Viktor heard his mother's voice in his own.

To the untidy kitchen in the flat he shared with Anne-Marie, he muttered aloud to himself, 'We just need to tidy the surfaces, organise the cupboards and then we'll be able to think clearly.' These long, lamenting complaints about cleanliness he had learnt from his mother's desire to organise the world, sweep it into order, arrange it into lines.

On their fifth day together, Viktor, the lover-lodger, had reordered the flat. He hooked up improvised curtains, wiped away the layer of dirt lining the skirting boards, dusted the lampshades, removed the black dust ringing every frame: the photos, the glass-covered, clip-framed map, the picture of the rosy-cheeked cherubs flying over a bowl of bloated fruit. The essence of each object in Anne-Marie's flat was the mark of dirt: proof of her liberation from domesticity, her refusal to clean the flat or, more significantly in Southern Africa, to get anyone to do it for her. Her escape from the master-slave dialectic.

Anne-Marie swung open the door to the wardrobe. Viktor was already in bed. 'What have you done?' She pointed to her folded panties, the ironed trousers, the shirts hanging neatly on new hangers.

'What?' Viktor answered.

'You have tidied my clothes. You had no right. I don't like my clothes folded or the flat so clean. It's ridiculous.'

'There was a dirty black layer of dirt over everything.'

'Dirty black, did you say?'

'Yes.'

'Then wash your mouth out with soap. *Mon Dieu*, do not use the words black and dirty together.'

'Well, it wasn't a white layer of dirt.'

'What is dirt, anyway? Material in the wrong place – it is colour-blind.'

'I won't use the word black.' Viktor felt offended. He had wanted to surprise her, to show her the small joys of swept floors, dusted lampshades; the order of twinned socks, folded skirts, pressed trousers – to thank her with cleaning.

'So not black, okay, just dirt. Just dirt, Viktor, no colour. Let's get this right – not blackmail, black economy, black sheep or in the black, as you say. Or Black Africa.' Anne-Marie spoke with a faint, teasing smile.

'Okay,' Viktor said, pulling the sheet to his chin.

'And don't clean my flat or my clothes.'

'But two years of dust is black,' Viktor protested.

'Neither black nor white,' Anne-Marie retorted.

It had taken Rosa months to learn how to wield her hands, submit her body to her sovereignty: lifting them with effort, dropping them on an object, coiling her fingers, then lifting them again. Viktor felt as though his mother had entered him, in his words and acts, her hands, aching and stumbling, the skin discoloured and thin, commanding his.

The fight to empty the flat of dirt, to cleanse the system of mistakes and find the route home – back to where Viktor started, to identify the spot on the map where it went wrong, when he had been carried away from the people he loved. So many mistakes, so little time to correct them. Nothing helped. *I will scrub Anne-Marie's pots and pans tomorrow, the cupboards above the sink. I will finish cleaning the flat, wipe down the surfaces, mop the floor.*

*

There is that surge, a *da, da, hmm, hmm,* and then the charge, the thrusting violins like a dance, all tiptoes, across the whole floor, until the cellos, a whole roomful, exclaim and the steps are loud, full, hearty and declaratory and the room is no more. Instead it is an entire life, immense, every particle, each living thing proclaimed. Then the wooden floor, creaking to each step, gives way, bursts, sending shards of wood flying. The orchestra, the audience, with each new mounting, rippling note, breaks into the clear blue sunlight. The mist covering the land, hovering over the ground, uncertain what to do, is now forced by the music to disperse and leave the world to song. With tears in their eyes, children sing: '*Cinque ... dieci.... venti ... trenta ... trentasei ... quarantatre.*'

Viktor sat in the moulded red chair, headphones hugging his ears. The gym where he worked in the morning was full of dirty furniture; behind him was a row of computers. The flatscreen televisions were tuned to sport – rugby, tennis and cricket – the men watching them large, unnatural, genetically modified, with South African dentistry. Viktor ran his tongue over his teeth and found the hole, the spongy gum, the loss.

Around him, it seemed, were the same cast of white men and women from the TV, built like the modern continent, human flesh carved in perfect angles, their legs falling straight, the feet arched correctly, the square, accurate shoulders and faces, noses, mouths, ears formed with no allowance for humanity or individuality. It was the cast of settler, etched with the same rigour and inhumanity as the lines that were drawn across towns, villages and life when their ancestors had divided Africa.

But what was this capacity to remain stupid after four generations? Viktor asked himself.

'It is the mentality of the settler,' Nelson had said, his words still ringing in Viktor's ears. 'You have to understand the type – have you read Fanon?' Nelson spun around in his chair, his hair held down by a black beret, the locks hanging over his shoulders. He read the titles, making his way through the volumes until, 'Here, here. Listen, listen, Viktor.' He flicked quickly back a few pages and read: '"In the colonies, in normal times, that is, in the absence of the war of liberation, there is something of the cowboy and the pioneer even in the intellectual. In a period of crisis, the cowboy pulls out his revolver and his instruments of torture."'

'Cowboys, adventurers, racists,' Viktor muttered.

He studied a man in his sixties, his face wrinkled by the sun, his silver watch setting off his brown all-year, all-over tan, a towel thrown over his shoulder, the newspaper open in his hand and his feet set apart. There was nothing crossed, folded, uncertain about him. Each of his thoughts placed firmly on the certainties of the ground, of his land, his order – he was man as statement and exclamation of colonial settlement.

Viktor looked down again to his notebook and let the music occupy him again, fill his head, run down his spine until he was taken over by it:

If you would dance, my little Count,
I'll play the tune on my pretty guitar.
If you will come to my dancing school
I'll gladly teach you ...
Sharpening my skill, and using it,
playing with this one, playing with that one,
all of your games I'll turn inside out.
If you would dance.

The gym had arrived in great crates and was assembled by a team
sent from Johannesburg. The steel frame, the partition walls, the
tiling, the red and white paint, the coffee machine serving soya
and decaffeinated lattes, the chairs that cocooned Viktor, the
banks of computers and screens, the rows of machines, bikes,
treadmills, shoulder, arm and thigh presses, the cupboards to
lock up valuables, to leave your brains, character, hope. Even
the mould of the pool had arrived on the back of a lorry that
spent a week weaving its way from Beitbridge to Bulawayo
to Gweru to Harare. The *Herald* had run a feature on the day
the gym was due to open: 'The Virgin Active state-of-the-
art gymnasium is proof of the positive business environment
created by the government, uniting the ruling party's twin
ideologies of Marxism and entrepreneurship.'

Viktor's head fell again to his page and he read the last
sentences he'd written:

Zimbabwe, like the rest of the continent, is still trying
to escape the country's colonial legacy. Mugabe's anti-
Western polemics indicate a hesitant attempt to build
a black bourgeoisie. Whether ZANU's project of black
empowerment and ownership can be seriously developed,
or if it is even sincere, remains to be seen.

Viktor smiled, pleased with his formulation, the way the website had begun to take shape, the confidence his writing had assumed over the last three posts – he felt a momentary rush of excitement. What did it mean? Would his pieces be picked up by a news agency? Would he become the guerrilla journalist everyone spoke of in London, Washington, Paris, translated into French, Spanish, Mandarin? The exposé of white privilege and wealth still thriving across Southern Africa, the finely wrought, nuanced arguments that spared no one, the sparse, startling prose that took on the totality of African social relations and broke down ZANU's nationalist hegemony, revealed the British government's meddling with the opposition, the role of landed property, their black puppets? Viktor leant back in his chair, stretched out his arms and breathed in, his own hopes flying free like released sparrows, the unruffled stiff feathers pounding the air, the room as great and beautiful as his own shearing ideas.

The orchestra caught up with the voices, harmonised:

Here I am at your feet,
with my heart is on fire.
Look around you,
and remember the betrayer!

The birds flew higher and higher, reached the sky. Viktor's own possibilities lifted: a literary prize, a collection of his writings, recognition, celebration. Final proof that it had all been worth it, the sacrifices, the absences, his disappearances, each of his failures absolved by his writing. At last he'd prove Nina wrong, show her he'd been right to leave, how he had needed to follow his talent, his mission.

He was deaf to the gym with its streams of cooled air sealed away with the opera and his dreams. He straightened himself in the chair, sat up and stretched again. His hand caught the headphone lead, dragging it from his ear – he heard the metal clank of the weights, the scratching of the broom dragged over the floor by a black cleaner. Rudely his flock of birds scattered, hit the wall, fell into the pool and drowned.

The woman cleaning the floor was his mother's age. She wore an ankle-length mauve skirt and dirty black slippers. Between each stroke on the floor she stopped, leant on the handle and tried to recover her strength before going on. No one noticed her. Viktor pushed the earphones back onto his ears, closed the notebook and got up. He reached for his wallet and walked to the wheezing woman. He bent over and handed a ten-dollar note to her, sealed in the palm of his hand so no one saw, a trick he'd already learnt in Zimbabwe. She looked at the folded green note and let the broom fall to the ground. 'Thank you, mister. Thank you, sir,' she said.

Restored, Viktor left the building, his birds perched again inside his hollowed chest, ready to fly.

*

Whether he admitted it or not, there was a competition – and, for now, his daughter had lost. He was with Anne-Marie: in bed with her at night, making coffee for her in the morning, sharing the greatest part of his life with her. He had chosen her over his daughter. *This was the history that will be taught*, Viktor said to himself, *and it will assume the same truth that states that Lenin led to Stalin.* Family proceeds along the path of least resistance. He could have stayed in the UK and not boarded the plane to Harare; he could have resisted Anne-Marie's advances and not reciprocated with his own. He could have surrendered any attempt to see life beyond Rosa. He could have badgered, pestered, used the law. He could even have killed Nina – that at least would have marked the historical record, imprinted on the little girl's consciousness his determination to be with her.

Instead he had thrown himself into the spinning, ceaseless rotation of a different universe. Viktor was now elsewhere, living and breathing in a place permanently caught in the shadow of Rosa's absence.

'Do you know what the one paradox is with Nelson? It's his vanity,' Viktor said one late evening when he returned from another mission on Nelson's orders. 'He knows how he looks – those long dreadlocks and Mandela shirts. And he speaks so carefully, it's all so crafted. I can't figure out where the man is. He seems to be pure politics.'

'It's not true!' Anne-Marie exclaimed. 'Nelson's a bloody entrepreneur. Have you seen his back room? Full to the ceiling with sacks of mealie-meal, sugar, oil. He doesn't park his car in that garage. There's no room – it's full of barrels of petrol. He could blow up that entire block of flats. Viktor, Nelson is a capitalist, or at least a cross-border trader. There's your contradiction,' she said, swinging her feet onto the bed. 'He has excelled in the crisis. Scarcity has made him more than his revolution ever will. How do you think the organisation is paid for? The paper? The travel? Nelson is a dreadlocked capitalist in the heart of Africa. You know how it goes – "Fighting from arrival, fighting for survival". Drop your romantic notions. Look elsewhere, *mudiwa*, if you are searching for purity.'

'It's not romantic,' Viktor protested. 'Even with his trading, I find it hard to see beyond the politics. He is the most entirely political person I have ever met. I feel I know him. Maybe not like you, but as hard as I try to see the person separated from his political interests, I can't. I honestly don't think Nelson *exists* divorced from politics.'

280

Anne-Marie sighed loudly. 'You don't know him, or you don't know Zimbabwe. Every inhalation is political. If you make it through the day, then into another day you've survived. And that's political. Each week is a battle to scrape dollars together, to make a day's *sadza* last three. And then you go to bed dreaming that God will take Mugabe and X-Party will be struck down with a biblical plague. Because the MDC have their – *leur museau dans l'auge*, their snout in the trough – and nothing can be changed through simple endeavour any more. The only resistance left is God's. See, you've got me now.' She kicked at the wall, irritated. 'Just don't cast me into your London drama of heroes and villains from the Third World. All Zimbabweans have done is fail. Not quite as catastrophically as the Congolese, as my family, but they have failed. Failed.' Then, almost shouting, as though the point could only be made in French, '*Échoué!*'

Viktor stretched back on the chair, bending the plastic back and cracking his vertebrae. He felt the night through the open window. It was a strange winter. The cloudless night skies blew a hard wind, but in the day, in town, moving around in taxis and queuing in glum, silent lines for lifts, the sun burnt.

Anne-Marie swept her braids behind her ears, her mouth open. The whites of her eyes shone in the room, the crescents of four moons orbiting her irises. Playful, her speech finished, she leant forward and ran her hands along the insides of Viktor's thighs. 'Did you fall for my eyes or mouth first?'

'Your mouth.'

'Good. I'm pleased it was my mouth.' She laughed and licked her lips. 'Should we go to bed?'

'Bed?'

'Yes. Make love. Don't you like making love with me?'

'Yes,' Viktor answered, looking down, avoiding her eyes.

'Don't be shy. I know you do, *chéri*.'

They both stood. Anne-Marie pressed herself against him. 'Now I give you permission,' she said, 'to be as romantic as you want.'

Anne-Marie, after their first night together, had, with the minimum of romance, started calling Viktor a number of different appellations: darling, *mudiwa*, *molongani na gai*, *chéri*. This was not an act of possession, just a daily acknowledgement that the sex – the most easy, joyful lovemaking Viktor had ever experienced – had changed something between them, bent the normal conventions of friendship.

No matter how much or how little time they spent in bed, Anne-Marie always gave the orders. 'Tonight I want to feel the air on our bodies when we *faire l'amour*,' she'd say, flinging the windows open. Or she'd say, '*Mudiwa*, let's just sleep tonight,' let him drowse with her arms around him, and then use her hands to get him hard, to make him come. 'Good boy,' she'd say, and then fall asleep.

Most of all, though, she loved to cajole him into explicitness, to draw from his lips things he would never have dared speak. Perhaps she needed to hear them to believe them. She was in this mood tonight. 'Tell me what you want, *mudiwa*.'

Viktor deflected. 'You know what I want,' and drew her close. Anne-Marie smiled and shook her head, pulling away.

'No, com. Say it.'

'I … I want,' Viktor fumbled, 'I want to masturbate you.'

She clicked her tongue. 'Masturbate me! So clinical! Are we in a classroom? Tell me what you *want*, Viktor. You can type these things but you cannot say them to me?' She pushed him onto the bed, a little roughly, and straddled him, pinning him with the weight of her body. Her eyes flashed with amusement.

'What you *mean* is that you want to fuck me with your fingers. Isn't that right?'

Viktor nodded.

'Say it.'

He flushed and looked away. 'I want to … to fuck you. With my fingers.' His voice was quiet, earnest, a little shaky.

Anne-Marie laughed. 'Do you, *mudiwa*? No one is listening. Say it like you mean it.' She leant down to kiss him. Viktor felt, at that moment, something change in him. He took her by the waist and twisted them, suddenly, so that he was on top. She landed on her back with a grin. This time he spoke with confidence: 'I want to fuck you with my fingers. To start with.'

'That's it, *chéri*! Now you are here with me.' She reached up and took his hand.

Chapter Twenty-Four

One of Viktor's first missions – part of Nelson's efforts to
hammer Zimbabwe's complexity into the visitor, and to
test a man who had waltzed into town and right into his ex-
partner's bed, something Nelson never mentioned – was a
four-hour interview with X-Party's ex-MP, Guthrie Madhuku.
Guthrie was outspoken, slicing and chopping with his hands
at everything before him: the foolish elites of his own party,
occasionally even the old man. He spared his greatest wrath
for the 'imperialists and the puppets', he said, who had now
organised themselves into the MDC, the opposition funded and
supported by the British, the Americans and the Australians.
He roared his disapproval, the skin drawn tight over his hollow
cheeks.

Viktor journeyed through Harare to the township and the
large brick house Guthrie had built for himself, in the middle
of a constituency that used to be his until a young, stupid MDC
member only just out of university had won the seat from him.
Sitting at the back of the ten-seater taxi that drove, in these hard
times, with twenty passengers, Viktor prised the window open.
His leg was bent high into the seat in front of him, his head half

out of the window. The taxis passed the high-rises, down the large boulevards. In these parts of Harare, if you averted your gaze from the gutters, the city could look almost prosperous.

Viktor liked the warm breeze on his face. He liked feeling free from the need to speak, to try and convince the passengers that he was not like the whites they'd seen in Zimbabwe, in Borrowdale, in the four-by-fours, on TV, who until recently had owned 95 per cent of the land, living like kings and queens and sending their children to private schools in South Africa. He resisted the urge to tell them that he was on their side, whatever side that was, and that his family struggled, that his parents survived in their seventies on a state pension that was so modest it kept them awake at night. He wanted to say that he knew Zimbabweans who lived in London as desperately as they survived here in Harare.

Or, worse still, the desire which had overwhelmed him when he last took the taxi to rip his headphones out of his ears and speak about the music he was listening to. Squeezed between two women, holding bags of bruised and rotten vegetables on their laps, in a cascade of words, Viktor had explained that Verdi supported the revolutions of 1848 and that it had been illegal under Austrian occupation in Northern Italy, where his operas were performed, to play an encore. 'You see, an encore was deemed a political act and outlawed. And Verdi, the greatest composer of all time, perhaps the greatest man of all time, was on the side of the poor, the wretched. Even when he was famous and his music was performed across the world, in Egypt, across Europe, in North America, on this continent, he composed for us, for the poor.'

Continuing, fevered, Viktor spoke quickly. 'When he wrote down what he did, under his name, he didn't write composer, dramatist, director, but farmer. Farmer!' Viktor had shouted in the taxi. 'Do you hear that? He was still the son of a peasant, a smallholder, tilling a plot of land. Like Zimbabweans; he *was* practically Zimbabwean. Verdi was Zimbabwean, like you. Do you see?'

Forced to sit next to a man who had clearly lost his senses, the women had nodded their heads nervously and looked at each other. Viktor had plunged his hand into his bag, removed his iPod and given each woman an earpiece, insisted they insert it as he played the opening piece: 'Do you hear that? The hope of liberation. The sweep of the music – and that last part, where the entire orchestra rises, lifts. There is no harmony for over a minute, until the voices hit that high ... You see the effect? What Verdi wanted was the sense of an entire oppressed nation singing in a single voice ... You hear it, the whole chorus singing of their oppression? This song became an anthem of the poor, farmers, hawkers, like you. Do you hear that whistle, the flute? Verdi put it there as a sign he was against the police, against the Austrians. Against ZANU. Do you hear the flute?'

Over the sound of the opera, the two women, shocked, obedient, listening to the music, Viktor had shouted, with tears in his eyes, '*Do you hear? Can you hear the flute?*'

Viktor phoned Guthrie, a finger plugging one ear, the phone pressed hard against the other, to tell him he'd arrived. He walked through the labyrinth of narrow, muddy alleys between the old brick houses, the shacks, the dried-out front gardens with tufts of dying grass.

As Viktor found his way through the township he turned up his hoodie, pulled down on the string cords, shuffled his hands into his sleeves and tried to vanish, to un-white himself. Instead of a *murungu*, he was a township youth, moving unnoticed through the neighbourhood. The effect was to turn this stringy, oversized white man, with worn jeans and trainers threadbare enough to arouse the pity of even the most distraught Zimbabwean, into the Grim Reaper. Children drew back; mothers and fathers came out of their shacks to stare at this cloaked, bent figure of death, come to remind them again that though they may have just emerged from oblivion, they were soon to return.

Guthrie saw Viktor's head over the gate and he laughed.

The house was absurd, grandiose and incongruous: two storeys, pebbledashed, painted white like a London semi, like Archway. The plastic grass on the front lawn sweated in the heat. Guthrie stood on the stoop. Around him was a crowd of people, sitting in the garden and leaning against the brick walls, beside them checked shopping bags fastened with safety pins, all of them quiet, seemingly unaware of each other or of Guthrie who sat with one arm resting on the open door to the house, sipping a bottle of Zambezi.

They're trying to levitate the house. It's a religious wake, Viktor thought. He raised his hand to greet Guthrie. *Any minute now they're going to start chanting, 'Jesus is number one', and this breeze-block monstrosity is going to take off and lift clear of the township. God will have finally acted in this forsaken country, not to liberate the poor, but to rid Highfield of bad architecture.*

Guthrie did not waste time. He shouted for Viktor to let himself in and then, in Shona, for chairs and beer to be brought out for the guest. The two men sat, the plastic legs of the chairs skidding and splaying under their weight.

'So you're a Nelsonite? Another intellectual from the school of theory and high principle. I respect him, Nelson, he's better than the entire rotten MDC and he believes in his principles, not like those pretenders, Tsvangirai, Chamisa, Mutambara, who know nothing. But he's wrong.'

Viktor tilted the bottle of beer, sipped. 'What do you mean by wrong?'

'As in not right. Wrong. Incorrect. In error. Prune Nelson of his rhetorical superfluities and what is left of our idealist? He says he reads Marx, Engels, Lenin, but he needs to step out of the world of ideas and see the real world of people and choices. He's pampered, swollen by starry-eyed idealism. He has his hopes fixed on uprisings in Nigeria, Burkina Faso, France, the UK. But it's infantile. It is a childish pseudo-Marxism.' Guthrie slurped on his bottle and wiped his mouth aggressively with the back of his sleeve.

'I think that's unfair. Nelson seems sensible to me. He's aware of the real world. He doesn't support the MDC, but argues that an MDC government would at least open democratic space, so that real struggles could take place.' Viktor tried to exorcise the schoolboy debater, to deepen his voice.

'Fools. All of you. Tsvangirai in power? It will never happen. What is he, this ex-general secretary of the trade union movement? Neocolonialism operates in the MDC. What does Nelson think? The Brits, you lot' – Guthrie waved a hand in Viktor's direction – 'are battling to install Tsvangirai to speed up the arrival of the dictatorship of the proletariat, led by Nelson Chitambure. What conceit. What naivety.'

Viktor interrupted. 'That's not Nelson's position. He says the ZANU-PF government is petit bourgeois, that ZANU's anti-imperialism is fake.' As hard as he tried, Viktor still sounded scholarly.

'Rubbish! And that position reveals him for what he is: a romantic fool, not even against capitalism.' Shouting now, Guthrie waved his hands in front of Viktor. 'How dare he take the moral high ground about ZANU's character! The neocolonial pressure we have lived through since 1980, when we made too many compromises, all that nonsense that even Mugabe fell for, preaching "love your neighbour, love the white bosses". But now Nelson must see that for the first time in Zimbabwe since 1980, for the first time on the continent, ZANU is overthrowing the neocolonial past! But your Nelson—'

'He's not *my Nelson*.'

'Your Nelson,' Guthrie repeated, 'and his fake leftism amount to refining and perpetuating neocolonialism!' Guthrie's tone, the excitement in his voice, raised each word almost to a scream. '*How can you miss the revolutionary import accomplished by ZANU-PF in the last ten years?*' Guthrie paused and took in a mouthful of air, restoring his faculties, and continued. 'I mean, the best, truest revolutionary elements of ZANU-PF, not the self-serving time-wasters, but the revolutionary reforms that have been forced through against international and domestic opponents – British, American, the EU, UN, NATO, all the jackals – in the puppet structures of the MDC as well as against opponents, opportunists within ZANU.'

Guthrie turned his head and shouted into the house, shrill and loud, his principal oratorical devices. 'More beer, more beer! do not close off'

'We've learnt from Mao, from the Chinese, the importance of tactical alliances. Unite with the Kuomintang to oust the Japanese. We have localised ownership of land.' Guthrie tore off the bottle-tops with his teeth, handed a bottle to Viktor, spat out the buckled cap and drained half of his bottle into his mouth. He continued: 'ZANU-PF nationalists have domesticated class contradictions over the country's prime means of production. This is the best way, the only way, of moving towards the full and final socialisation of land. We have created a giant wedge between a comprador petit bourgeois politics by creating a real national bourgeoisie. A step forward.

A giant step forward. As a Marxist, how can you not defend that? What are you, anyway?'

'I don't know. More a humanist. A Hegelian, I suppose. Fanonian ...' Viktor mumbled.

Guthrie laughed. 'Nelson has sent me a London Hegelian. I tell you, he is more lost than I thought. Is your recorder still running?'

'Yes.'

'Good. What we've seen recently in the new land disputes is the landless peasantry fighting the new African latifundia class. Open black-on-black class struggle, inconceivable when the white landed aristocracy ruled Zimbabwe. Never before seen. A new class of African bourgeoisie landowners based on really existing property relations, in a continent that has only seen, since 1960, since independence, a caste of middlemen, profiteers, the pseudo-bourgeoisie, overseers of Western capital. Do you not see?' Guthrie reverted to upper case: 'And THIS, NOT abstract, romantic, learnt-by-heart quotes from Lenin and Marx, has taken the African revolution one GIANT step forward!'

Viktor was confused. He wanted to interrupt but didn't know how. Surely this sunken old fighter was correct. Why hadn't he seen it? Why couldn't he see? Nelson, beautiful, vain and irrelevant, running against the grain of history just when, for once, history was moving in the right direction. *Why must we, the left, the thinking ideological poor, me, Nelson, Tendai, always be on the wrong side when it matters, always seek out the lost cause, the losing argument? What DNA do we carry that causes us always, everywhere, to get it wrong?*

Viktor wanted to get up, stretch his legs across the stoop, but he couldn't. All around him was this silent, unmoving crowd, leaning against the house. In front of Viktor, on the floor, around the two men, were dozens of silent, waiting Zimbabweans. *Why did Nelson send me here? Is this another test?* Guthrie's voice resounded around his yard.

Guthrie drained the beer, then cast the bottle by its neck onto the gravel drive. It smashed and pieces of glass flew into the air. Guthrie dropped his arm, felt blindly on the floor, found another bottle and brought it to his mouth. 'Drink up, come on. Drink. DRINK!'

Viktor sipped his beer nervously.

Staring out, in a more reflective tone, Guthrie continued, 'The only nation that has been able to outdrink us is the British. How is London? I spent years in the city on a scholarship in the sixties. A Commonwealth Scholarship. All I wanted to do was read, to be in the country of the Brontës, Marx, Engels. Dickens. Agh, Dickens!' Guthrie straightened in his seat and spread his arms, holding an open bottle in one hand and an unopened bottle in the other. '"I see a beautiful city and a brilliant people rising from this abyss and in their struggles to be truly free, in the triumphs and defeats, I see the evil of this time and of the previous time gradually making expiation for itself".' He turned his head to Viktor and smiled. 'I was studying at King's and applied to stay in Bloomsbury. The university found me a room with a childless couple in Croydon. Fucking Croydon. Have you ever been there? Let me say this, Croydon is not the cradle of English civilisation. The husband was an old army captain who had served in Burma, Manila, Indochina. He sat snorting at me through dinner. But the wife, ah, the wife, she was excited to have an original black man in the house. She thought I was some sort of stallion, brought up in the jungle. On my first night they served me tinned spaghetti on toast. I wanted to leave and get back to Africa that night. Croydon, horrible place. The English suburbs are death.'

'I tend to agree with you. Much of the UK is like Croydon,' Viktor replied.

'Yes, racist and ugly.' Guthrie paused before continuing on the old track. The mood was calmer now, even amicable, the two men having managed to find a place in south-east London, where they could meet. 'You see, Nelson, he is preoccupied by names, figures, characters. And Zimbabwe has them all: Morgan, Robert, Tendai, each of them partial and flawed. He is close to each of them. Zimbabwean society is so small, so he feels personally disgusted by ZANU's betrayal. As a child in the eighties, he grew up adoring ZANU like a son loves his father. Now he's also outraged by MDC's veniality. He is a child in revolt; the Chitambure School is the School of Betrayal. But as a Marxist, a genuine Marxist' – Guthrie threw another bottle onto the lawn and started to pick up speed again – 'what are people to social processes, to the dialectic?'

Viktor finished his beer and held the bottle in his lap. Guthrie asked, 'Have you finished?'

'Yes.'

'Then throw it away.' Viktor delicately placed the empty bottle on the ground.

'No, throw it!' Guthrie ordered.

Dutifully Viktor picked the bottle up, tried to aim for the narrow drive, the modest, plastic lawn, to cast the bottle over the heads of the figures squatting and sitting around the two men. Inexplicably the bottle spun in the air, turned like the sails of a windmill and flew towards the crowd sitting at the far end of the garden. Silently the two men watched the bottle twist and turn in the air. It missed the gate and continued over the garden wall, out of the compound and disappeared. There was a thud, then a scream of pain.

Viktor jumped up. 'Shit, I must have hit someone!'

Guthrie leant forward, grabbed Viktor's arm and pulled him back to his seat. 'Forget it. You have to see the big picture, comrade, not the individual act, the single blunder. The process, not the person. You have to learn to distinguish between social processes and people.'

After another swig of beer, Guthrie continued, 'You see, ZANU is rooted deep in the countryside, it has real support. No local party will be able to unseat it in the coming elections, in any election. What's more, the MDC is weak, corrupt, blundering. However fair and transparent you make the elections, ZANU will not be removed.'

Viktor spoke quickly. 'But when have elections ever really been fair in Zimbabwe?'

'Often. True, we had to muddy a bit, crack some skulls at the start of the century to make sure the MDC was roundly defeated. If we had naively allowed an MDC victory, we would have seen a second Rhodesia. Worse and more violent than the first, more than anything we had done. White-run, white-led, white-aligned, with the usual black puppets. Supported by the imperialists. It would have required a war worse than the last to decolonise us. A nasty, bloody *chimurenga*.' Guthrie was drunk now. He leant forward and began to enunciate his words loudly and with great effort. 'Do you not see? What the French did in Mali. The British and Americans in Iraq and Afghanistan. Does he want to take back Zimbabwe to classical neocolonialism, the blight of the continent since independence? How will the poor be more confident then? His thinking, this Nelson of yours, is the thinking of the true theorist of the petit bourgeoisie. A suicidal Narodnik.'

With this Guthrie fell back in his chair, stretched, then dropped one hand over his face and rubbed his eyes. He sighed. The sun had fallen back from the porch and was retreating quickly across the garden. When Guthrie lowered his hand and looked again at Viktor, he seemed exhausted.

'I moved away from Croydon after two weeks and stayed with Zimbabweans in north London. I felt like a guerrilla fighter, planning, fantasising where I would plant a bomb, Algeria-style. The theatres on the Strand, Harrods, the coffee shops in Covent Garden. For the first months this was how I survived. I would take the war against colonialism to the motherland, to their soil. At the weekends I would dress up and go to the Savoy, the Dorchester on Park Lane, take the lift to the top floor. And in the middle of the empty corridors I would take a shit. Oh yes, I would turn over the chamber pot right in the middle of the carpet to acquaint those Sons of Albion with the colour of my dung. That was a sweet feeling. If I could have got into the palace I would have done the same things right in the middle of Queen Victoria's suite.'

What could Viktor say to that? As much as he tried, he couldn't avoid the image of the youthful, gaunt Guthrie crouching in a London hotel, holding open his bum cheeks, pushing and grunting against a mighty enemy with hopeless, alienated agency. Who would have had to clean up his protest? Before he was a cabbie, Jack had worked shifts in hotels as a lobby boy. Plain, gentle, opera-singing Jack – who as a child Viktor had loved most after his parents, even before his twin sister – would have been forced to clean up the mess of empire. In Viktor's own childhood he had fantasies wishing his own death would come before Isaac's, Sonia's *and* Jack's; now he realised Jack would have been charged with cleaning up Guthrie's dung. Where was the logic in making an enemy of the Jewish UK proletariat? *They are your natural ally, Guthrie, not the Sons of Albion.*

After a short pause, Viktor replied, 'Well, today it is Zimbabwean asylum-seekers who have to empty the chamber pots in London hotels.'

Guthrie nodded at Viktor's comment. It seemed to please him. Then he shouted again for more beer. There was a noise behind them in the house, the faint, just-audible peeling of the seal as the fridge door opened, and the heavy clink of bottles.

'For all the respect I have for your Nelson, he's dangerous and sows illusions. He should know better. An educated man of Nelson's calibre preaching in the language of Marx and oppressed workers is dangerous. You see, Enoch, I take my politics seriously.'

'My name is Viktor.'

'Never again in Zimbabwe will any politician with foreign support win an election. No power in Zimbabwe will be wielded against the disinherited. This is the historical road that we have set this country on. No longer are we simply Zimbabwean for ourselves! We have become a continental symbol of the final struggle against neocolonialism and neoliberalism. You see, Enoch—'

'It's Viktor.'

'Viktor, we are the coming storm. We are the future. Already the youth in South Africa look to us, follow the old man, watch us for inspiration. They wear our T-shirts: *Mugabe is Right, Seize the Land*. The whites, the puppet blacks, they are living on borrowed time.' Guthrie stood, lifted himself onto the centre post of the stoop. When he was standing he shook a little on his legs, waited for the rush of blood around his system to settle. He looked out over his plot of land. Viktor looked with him at the front lawn, the dead souls, the rusted Toyota in the drive, the bonnet open, its insides gutted, the leads, brakes, wheels spread around the carcass. 'Do you know African history?'

'A little,' Viktor answered.

With a sweep of his arm, indicating the horizon, the row of shacks, lean-tos, plastic port-a-loos in the near distance, Guthrie said, 'We are what Ghana was in 1957 to the rest of the continent, still struggling under colonialism. We are a symbol of a black government, a beacon for the future. Except we have learnt from the last fifty years. No compromise with the whites, with the north, no gentlemen's agreement with the imperialists. The history of colonialism, stolen land, pillaged mines and minerals, has been corrected not with slow steps and compensation but total expropriation. No reconciliation. All of this in a single step. The backward nigger history of failure and defeat on the continent has been transformed. We have set it on the right course. The failure, the lies, the theft, the inferiority that we Africans have internalised and passed from generation to generation is going.' Guthrie paused, then continued breathlessly, 'You see, the coastal shelf of our continent is deep with the remains of our dead ancestors – slaves, victims, the bodies of defeated armies. No more, Enoch, no more.' Guthrie fell back once more into his chair, sighed, and said, '"It was the epoch of incredulity; it was the season of light".'

Sometime later, after more beer, Guthrie walked Viktor to the gate. The two men lingered, not wanting to part, to break the spell.

Still confused, his head awash with beer, Viktor struggled to focus in the grey-brown night that had settled on the township. 'Can I ask you, Guthrie, who all these people are?' Viktor indicated the still, silent people lining the house and garden.

Guthrie turned quickly around, his eyes wide; he surveyed the garden, the front of his house, the perimeter wall. He looked again at Viktor with raised eyebrows. 'Oh, them?' he answered casually. 'They're just my family from the rural areas.'

'What are they doing here?'

'They live here.'

As Viktor walked away, trying to find the route back to the main road, he heard Guthrie shout, 'Tell Nelson I say hello!'

Chapter Twenty-Five

Viktor could no longer sit still and chase away the sadness long enough to write. Although he sat in his familiar place, listening to the mechanical grumble of the coffee machine and Louis's salutations, he was unable to find the pleasure of routine, the comfort of his own company, the joy of *Tosca*, which had once given him hope. Instead everything marked time: the song, the arias, the finished page, the coffee drunk, the road paced; each represented a loss, a step away from Rosa and towards his mother's death.

Weeks after arriving in Harare he phoned his parents. He reserved his most acute feelings of guilt for his parents; nothing could command as much fear and self-loathing as they could. He pictured them cowed and bent by his absence, his father more cantankerous and irritable and both of them maintaining their rigid and insistent defence of him, no matter how irrefutable the evidence.

Viktor had sent two cards obtusely referring to 'pressing work' and promising a telephone call. The front of the first card pictured an elephant ambling in dirt-brown scrub, leafless trees in the distance, a field of trampled earth around the animal.

Viktor wondered if the elephant would comfort his mother, show her that he was in good, reliable, ancient company.

Sonia wanted her son next to her. His happiness meant more to her than her own meagre joys – the meals she prepared, the books she read, the games she played with her grandchildren. Though Isaac knew how to elbow pain aside, he too brooded for his son. And Viktor? He was given what he wanted, only he did not recognise it and gave it away again. *Everyone wants what they don't have – except my parents*, Viktor thought.

Walking to the telephone shop, it was for his mother that his heart lurched. His parents lived by separate phones in the same house. Sonia hovered around the kitchen phone that had been fastened for thirty years to the wall and had never needed to be repaired or serviced. She made phone calls laboriously, winding the dial, placing her finger nervously into the numbered holes. She answered the phone with the same caution: 'Ye-e-e-e-ss?' Isaac, upstairs in his study, where he spent the day playing Solitaire on Viktor's twenty-year-old computer or, when he was asked, doing his daughter's accounts or working for his old employers, would seize the phone when it rang and exclaim, 'Yes, who's there?' in sync with his wife's separate, tentative echo.

Viktor picked his time, knowing where they would be midweek, the shopping done. He would only have to speak once to both of them. He sat in the corner cubicle of the vaulted telephone shop. The morning was quiet and cool, the windows to the street open, half the stools empty, with little to distract Viktor from his parents' faint, faraway voices.

'Mum,' Viktor said, 'it's me.'

'Who?' came his father's voice, booming, resounding in the receiver.

'Me, Dad. Viktor.'

'Joseph, is that you?' his mother asked.

'Who's Joseph?' Viktor asked.

'Joseph!' shouted Isaac.

'No, it's me.'

'Viktor!' they said in unison.

'Vik. Vik. Vik,' his father stuttered with emotion.

'Who's Joseph?' Viktor repeated, offended.

'I don't know. Sonia, who's Joseph?'

'Joseph? We don't know any Josephs, unless you mean Joseph who lives off Muswell Hill,' Sonia answered.

'We haven't been in touch with him for years. Why would he be phoning?' Isaac asked.

'Did they leave a message?' Sonia questioned.

'No, Sonia, he hasn't phoned us for years. Anyway, I think he moved to Tel Aviv with his daughter,' Isaac said.

'Did they? I didn't even know he had a daughter. What about his wife?' Sonia asked.

'She died. Remember, he was alone, never remarried,' Isaac said.

'Oh, that's terrible. He must be devastated,' Sonia commented.

'Sonia, it happened years ago.'

Viktor, still holding the phone, stood up, adjusted his position, folded a leg under his buttocks and sat down again. *Do they even know that I'm on the phone? Have they forgotten that I called?* He saw his parents communicating to each other on separate phones like household walkie-talkies, gossiping about a long-dead neighbour, the sound of their voices reverberating through the hallways and stairwell.

Isaac was still working in his mid-seventies, keeping the accounts of the estate agency he had run for forty years but never owned. Viktor knew his father's mood hinged on the single, precarious possibility of a call from his old employer. The obnoxious son of the old owner, whom Isaac had teased, lifted onto his desk, sweeping aside the survey reports, maps, calculator when Martin was a boy. A boy who had grown up cursed with too much attention and money. Martin was the same age as Viktor and he held Isaac's daily happiness in his hand. 'No one does it like you, old man. Can I borrow you for a couple of days to fix our figures?' Speaking with familiarity, unaware how Isaac bristled.

'Mum, Dad,' Viktor said, 'I'm sorry I haven't phoned.'

'Your mother was worried, Vik.'

'We were both worried,' Sonia said, her voice clear.

'But you got the cards, didn't you?'

'Yes we did, son,' Sonia replied.

'Are you okay? We just didn't understand why you had to go like that. Without telling anyone.' Isaac's voice cracked.

Viktor was silent.

'Stop that, Isaac – he's on the phone now, isn't he? Are you safe? How's your health?'

Sonia, dressed in floral blouses and pleated blue and grey skirts that she ironed meticulously on Sundays, the same day she hung out her underwear neatly on the line, seven pairs. Even when he was small Viktor had averted his eyes from the sight of his mother's underclothes and had not joined in Isaac's gentle chiding: 'Do you have different days of the week marked on them, honey? Tuesday's pants, Sunday's pants?' His mother had laughed bashfully behind her hands.

Sonia had slaved until her hands were red and chapped, cooking and serving food in the Lemon Tree café and takeaway. 'My mother is a chef,' Viktor had announced proudly to his school friends. Her spread of plastic and wooden chopping boards was arranged in the kitchen for every eventuality, it seemed, except creativity – yet her food, cooked for her affluent high-street customers, was an inspired fusion. It confused her north London fanbase and stunned her family into dinner table silence. What wondrous tastes, knotted together with mathematical precision and with cleanliness worthy of an operating theatre, not a working-class Archway kitchen. She still cooked there sometimes.

'Well, I'm okay. I had to come here quickly because of the crisis in the country.'

'What is this crisis to do with you, Vik?' his father asked.

'I'm a journalist, you know that.'

'Since when have you been a journalist?' Sonia enquired, speaking quickly, her voice wavering. 'Darling, I thought you were a college lecturer doing a PhD.'

'Yes, I am, but I'm also a journalist.' Viktor felt the conversation slipping from his prearranged script. The large, rusted fans chopped lethargically at the air above the bank of phones and cubicles.

'You mean your thing on the World Wide Web?' Sonia stated.

'Blog. It's called a blog, Mum.'

'Your father reads me what you write,' Sonia said.

'It's not just a blog. I write for other websites, online magazines. I'm working for an online activist newspaper.'

'That sounds dangerous, Vik. Are you being safe? I heard the other day about these scams, these 519 scams,' Isaac said.

'It's 419, they're 419 scams, Dad, and they're from Nigeria. I am in Zimbabwe,' Viktor corrected him, trying to keep his tone flat.

'In Zimbabwe!' his parents exclaimed together.

'Zimbabwe? Why are you there?' Isaac added.

'I explained. I told you I was in Zimbabwe. Where did you think I was?'

'Well, we knew you were in Africa. We thought it was Zambimwe,' Isaac said defensively.

'Zambimwe? There is no Zambimwe. It's Zimbabwe, in Southern Africa,' Viktor explained, irritation creeping into his voice.

They were silent for a moment, then Sonia asked, 'When are you coming home, sweetie?'

'He's doing important work, Sonia. He knows what he's doing, don't you, Vik? He knows, he knows ...' Isaac's voice trailed off.

'Yes, I know,' Sonia interjected, 'but it's not him, it's where he is. I don't understand why he has to be doing this work. I think it's interfering.' The hurt in her voice was clear.

'Sonia, we have taught our kids to interfere and look after their neighbours. The bottom line is, he has a big heart, that one. I am proud of him; maybe he'll bring some sense down there,' Isaac boomed with false momentary confidence.

Viktor agreed with his mother. What was he doing here, interfering in a country, a continent that had already been ravaged by white people for centuries? He looked at the other cubicles, people locked into conversations, watching the counters nervously as they ticked away their change, pricing their conversations with families in South Africa, in the UK, the US, quickly arranging the pick-up from Western Union, hurrying out the family news, conveying somehow a sense of love and missing.

Sonia spoke again. 'Of course I'm proud of you, sweetie, darling. We both are. So's Amy. We were saying that the other day.' His parents continued their intercom conversation, agreeing and conferring with each other.

Viktor was silent.

I have made them suffer again. We are diminished by old age, nothing else. As we are pulled towards death we lose everything — wisdom, hope, perspective and taste. Viktor's most uncomfortable reflection was that his mother's cooking, her great, creative endeavour in life, was suffering because she was losing her power of taste. As his parents spoke to each other, arranged their evening, spoke about Amy's children, Viktor thought, why couldn't his mother's taste buds remain unaffected by ageing? He wanted her to stop ageing.

'Vik, Vik, are you there?' Isaac shouted down the phone.

'Yes, Dad, I'm here.'

'Have you spoken to Rosa? Is that woman letting you speak to your daughter?' Isaac spoke loudly, stridently.

'No, Dad. I haven't phoned. I've been sending her postcards. I don't know if she gets them.'

They were all silent again; the phone hissed and bubbled with static.

'When are you back, Vik? We miss you,' Isaac finally said.

'Soon, Dad, soon, Mum. I promise. Soon. I'm almost finished.'

*

Dearest Comrade – and friend – Viktor!

The short response to the storm in Southern Africa is: YES, YES, YES, at last you are getting involved, Anne-Marie has told me how you are helping! To being involved, in any way, in the struggle of the exploited and oppressed, with the aim of inspiring others to do likewise! You are learning well.

I have even started reading your fantastic writings on *Refutations*.

You write a lot, my friend – but if you will allow me a comment, your writing is still overly scholarly and suffers

303

from the preponderant postmodern stupidities of much of what my poor comrades would describe as bullshit. Comrade, I am saying this because I care!

But the interview you published with Guthrie, that X-Party apologist and dog who I remember arguing with, was perfect. This is the way. What ingenuity and guts you showed, to obtain this rare example of a history and an experience unknown to the ignorant socialists I find in this Dark Continent who know nothing of Africa. I have gained the harsh impression that none of the good activists I have met in Europe have any real idea of what exactly is happening in Africa because there is NO serious contact. Together we are changing this. Your contribution could in practice be colossal, my friend. Long may you continue to make such an invaluable contribution. Bolsheviks as solid and serious as Nelson and Biko are a rarity, and you are now with them in the Southern Hemisphere.

But I still find your ideas and arguments too abstract for the realities of the contemporary struggle. Remember that the most powerful 'ruling idea' remains that THEY are born to rule and WE are born to slave, obey, to be subservient and deferential. The vast majority of workers (and all the oppressed too, of course) live still today with a certain degree of being overawed, overwhelmed and overimpressed – partly because of being overworked, overtired and overstressed.

Early on I was taught that there is in politics, as in nature and maths, nothing less than one, except zero. Individually we remain vulnerable to all the venomous physical, intellectual, ideological and spiritual poison they pay an army of academics, politicians, pundits and other scum to bombard us with daily. This has been going on for 5,000 years. The Greek slave-owners invented the three Fates, who spun the thread of life to tell us we have no control and we must therefore accept our fate. I remember Nelson at the back of a meeting room explaining to a young comrade that Mandela, as the arch-reformist/social-democrat/traitor, was the epitome of 'fatalistic paralysis'. Like a rabbit in the headlights.

Imagine Nelson Mandela as the epitome of fatalism. How the world turns on a lie; our job is to expose these myths, reorientate, dislodge such notions. Dethrone.

You know what the Society taught me? For years in prison I saw comrades, fighters, real agitators, become disillusioned with liberation shortly after the false dawn in 1994. Did we think these revolts and the failed revolution in South Africa could be anything but merely political, without a revolutionary tradition? The Society in Zimbabwe taught me that we had to create the conditions in which we could try to build real, revolutionary movements – for next time. But the key point remains to shatter the self-limiting, immiserising pessimism that our rulers so desperately wish to inculcate in our movements and among our comrades. You, Viktor, if you will allow me, seem to have inculcated much of this defeat and paralysis.

And can the poor win? Can we overcome the pessimism that you represent? For those who have only experienced defeat, pessimism is epidemic. They haven't lived through gigantic struggles where the power of the poor and working class is obvious. Like Marx, Nelson's attitude, Biko's too – have you met him yet? – is the opposite: the only way to enter a fight is to win. To never compromise. Anything less is to limit oneself at the outset. Of course have exit strategies, but the whole approach to the enemy must be to smash them to pieces, to annihilate the rich TOTALLY.

I've become so full of anger that while in conversation last week with Jason and Wayne, I advocated locking all the rich up indefinitely and making them clean toilets and floors for life (the toilets that Moreblessing has to clean, that brilliant, stoic fighter who practically won our strike single-handed). Then I stopped myself and stated publicly that I'd personally volunteer to machine-gun the whole lot of them dead just to make sure none of them came back. No hesitation at all, despite being brought up a 50 per cent African/Christian pacifist, I know how to handle a gun. You see, com, after Sharpeville I realised we must have guns as good as theirs.

Finally, did I tell you that I'm in mid-battle trying to avoid being evicted again? I've made it clear that I'm barricading myself in and have a full set of tools to take at least two or three of the hired thugs with me if they try to use force. If they kill me I'm taking some of them with me – sorry about the melodrama – but you must fight to the death for everything! Have you learnt that yet in Zimbabwe? These cowards, these thugs from the English suburbs sent to evict me, do not realise that this time they have picked on a fighter from the largest, most violent township of filth and dirt in the Global South. *Khayelitsha*. This struggle is somewhat preoccupying me at present.

Please explain these circumstances to Anne-Marie, I haven't had time to email her. Tell her that our sagas are close to my heart and that when I am alone I think of her, but for now I have sent her this strange Englishman (you) for purposes of head-cracking and re-education. She will know what I mean.

What I want to say before it crushes me, too, is that sometimes I am overwhelmed by love for my comrades, for all my brothers and sisters in Zimbabwe, for the whole of

Africa, for you too. If I could I would like to put my arms around all my comrades, in an embrace as great as the feelings in my heart, as large as the world, as beautiful as life can be. Sometimes I fear what is happening to me, these feelings, these fantasies of love.

Yours in struggle and absolute ecstatic excitement at life.

Tendai

Part Four:

Bulawayo

Chapter Twenty-Six

To write the big story, Viktor realised that he had to do more than sit in front of his laptop at Louis's café. *Nelson was right*, he thought, *if I want to know what's going on in Bulawayo, in the south, I have to visit.* Even Louis said, in his usual, gruff way over breakfast that morning at the café, 'You have to go if you're going. There is no fucking substitute, Vik. If you want to see what's happening, you have to go. I have a truck leaving next week, I can get you on it.'

Viktor refused Louis's TransGlobal transport and took the train. Nelson set up interviews, proposed articles, gave him titles, leads, arguments. Rajeev, from afar, did the same: 'Inside the Opposition's City', 'Dictatorship from Bulawayo', 'Twenty-Five Years Since the Massacres'. In addition, Viktor had been told, so close was he now to the Society of Liberated Minds' decision-making body that he was ordered to speak at a Bulawayo Central meeting of the Society.

Lenin, wearing a cream jumper and black jeans, his locks tied tightly back, took him on the cramped minibus taxi to the station, speaking the entire journey, too loudly and confidently even for this working-class transport. Viktor tried to silence him by lifting his hand.

'You know what you have to say, right, comrade? Comrade, do you understand? The comrades are commodified; they are being dragged into all sorts of ridiculous channels by the NGOs. But Biko, Biko — god, Biko, wait until you meet Biko.' Lenin broke off, sucked the air noisily between his teeth. 'Biko is the best.'

'I have spoken with him, before I left the UK. He's impressive,' Viktor said.

Ignoring him, Lenin continued, 'Tapera is reliable but has a family and isn't always around. Tell them about what is going on in the UK, how it's connected to us, to Zimbabwe, to Africa.'

'I don't know what's happening in the UK, or how it's connected,' Viktor objected.

'Yes you do. Don't be crazy. Then move on to Mugabe and ZANU's fake anti-imperialism. They were correct to raise land, impose nationalisation and redistribution, but they are cynical, fakers, opportunists. *Fake anti-imperialism*. Repeat it. Mugabe is using these issues to hold onto power. We argue for real distribution of the country's entire resources. Led by the poor. Understand? Now repeat the main points, explain them to me.'

'I'm not repeating anything.'

When they arrived at the station, the two men pushed their way through the crowds to the platform. Lenin, shouting now to keep up with the mass of people, their luggage bundled together in plastic bags and boxes, said, 'Tell me you get it, comrade: no nationalisation without workers' control, no state capitalism. Zimbabwe's wealth to the people, to the poor. Do you get it?'

'Yes, yes!' Viktor replied loudly, his voice heavy with irony. 'Distribution linked to a revolutionary movement. I get it. I get the formula. I will preach for your doomed project.'

Lenin smiled, shouted something that Viktor couldn't hear and punched his fist in the air. Then, as Viktor was carried through to the platform on the tidal crowd, he disappeared from view.

The journey was cold, the first-class carriage and fold-down beds bare. The sheets and blankets that had recently been issued automatically were no longer available even for a fee. The compartment filled with a silent group of men who showed no curiosity at Viktor's presence, which left him feeling offended, so used to a tourist's notoriety, a white man's fame.

The train shunted its way slowly to Zimbabwe's second city, travelling through the night in a series of great episodic jolts. No sooner had it gained a reasonable mid-twentieth-century speed than a whistle would sound and the carriages would jerk and shudder and the immense mechanical snake would slow, then shriek to a complete stop. Each time, Viktor's companions seemed, in their sleep, to utter a collective, resigned sigh. Lethargic, weary, the train meandered reluctantly along the old tracks, arriving hours after schedule to a city already completely awake.

Bulawayo was a low-rise city with streets of whitewashed shops and tin roofs, wide avenues and parks. The police, present and aggressive in Harare, seemed to be entirely absent. The sun shone, glazing the city with a clear morning lustre, almost turning, Viktor believed, the crisis and the ZANU's fake anti-imperialism into a wholly benign force, an illusion.

'I could spend a few weeks in this city,' Viktor said to Biko in a burst of impromptu goodwill when they met outside the station.

Biko was ten years younger than his guest, with a high forehead. He was a tall, spare, loose-jointed man, tastefully dressed.

'How did you know it was me?' Viktor asked.

He hit Viktor's shoulder. 'Because, com, you are the only whitey on the moon!' Biko bellowed, laughing with his head tipped back.

'Of course, I forgot,' Viktor stuttered.

*

'Listen, my friend, it doesn't look good. The UK is not a friend to Zimbabwe. This is not your colony now. My friend, you are disrespecting us, interviewing this man who we know, in public, in our city. It doesn't look good, my friend.' There were three policemen in the room.

The office was evidently a place of activity, empty cups collected on the corner of a desk in the middle of the room, papers stacked high. Chairs, their backs broken, one with three legs, circled the desk. Like so much in Zimbabwe, this hive of human activity and repression looked abandoned. Poverty makes a relic of any country.

Viktor's legs were crossed. He uncrossed them, sat up, felt the back of the chair hard against his spine. 'I am sorry, Constable.'

'I'm not a constable. Call me *sir*, Mr Englander,' said the tall, thick-built man who had shoved them into the room.

'Yes, *sir*, call us all *sir*, my friend,' said his colleague, who was leading the arrest. He was small, his shoulders narrow. His glasses slipped down his nose. He pushed them up with his palm and rubbed his nose in a single movement. He had a small moustache – like Mugabe, like Hitler – and one eyelid was permanently half-shut.

'Officer, sir, I am a PhD student. A researcher doing historical work on Zimbabwe. The liberation struggle. I am against the British government. I think they must stop meddling in Africa.'

Viktor saw Biko put his head in his hands, his elbows resting on his knees.

Hitler laughed loudly, his mouth open, head back. His colleague sitting on the three-legged chair rocked, tottering on the missing leg. Other policemen came in and paced the room, ignored by the officers conducting the interrogation. They looked at the prisoners, smirked, circled the desk and left.

*

Before long the orders and speech-making began. 'It will be useful for us to have you here. You can show the comrades that not all whites are racists and imperialists – as Mugabe tells us. We've got lots of questions for you.' Like Lenin, Biko spoke loudly, pressing his point by taking Viktor's shoulder, touching his arm, holding his hand. Each sentence, each word, he exclaimed like a revelation. His face was highly charged, singularly resolute. They crossed two roads, Biko marching and gesticulating all the way. 'We are meeting in a park. Some comrades, some students, some lumpens, a couple of workers – the African masses, comrade.' Biko laughed at himself again. 'You will speak for fifteen minutes.'

Viktor spoke in the parched grandeur of the city's central park, ringed by a corroded iron fence. The groups were all supporters or members of the Bulawayo chapter of the Society of Liberated Minds. Most were activists, like Benson, a student and a contributor to the Independent Media Centre. Viktor's conclusion, after several weeks in Harare, was that his white, authorial voice needed to be dispatched, unloaded. So he had to be removed from his toehold as independent critic of the regime's violence to allow other voices to penetrate.

Viktor stood on the second step of the garden gazebo that offered the group broken shade. At one point this oddly misplaced park ornament would have been painted; the municipality would have maintained the facade so that white Rhodesians could have danced and played music on the sprung flooring. Instead the group Viktor addressed was threadbare, wearing jeans torn at the knees, T-shirts with slogans and the faces of their inspiration: Guevara, Sankara, Biko. The students were all gaunt, earnest, hungry to eat and listen, to fill themselves, if they could, on Viktor's words, his confirmation that the struggle in Zimbabwe would be heard in the UK. They needed, somehow, to allow his words to keep them upright until the tide turned in Zimbabwe.

Biko nodded effusively through the long, distraught minutes of Viktor's presentation, as though his head operated a mechanism which kept Viktor's tongue moving and enunciating clearly to the right pitch and volume. Viktor kept his gaze solidly fixed on Biko's shaking head. If only he could speak like Moreblessing, Nelson, even Lenin – each of them so terse in their explanations, so clear, always so much to say, so much to do, always listening, analysing, synthesising.

The sun shone through the bandstand's torn roof and burnt Viktor's freckled arm. After the talk the group crowded round him. Viktor came off the step to meet them. One student who was almost Viktor's height, his arms pressed tightly inside a checked shirt, let out a rush of questions and assertions, smiling as he spoke. 'You are the sort of man who must know the answers! I have been asking my comrades' – he gave a shrug of his shoulders, indicating the group – 'but none of them can answer. What do you think about Cuba? I support Cuba. Cuba's a model for socialism in a country like Zimbabwe. Yes? Would you agree that the type of pragmatism that Castro showed shortly after the 1959 revolution is appropriate for us today? What would you say to that?'

The effect of this short outpouring was to break the reticence of the others. Fresh questions and declarations burst from the crowd that packed closer to Viktor. 'What about Guevara? What do you have to say about him? Sankara, Lumumba, the others – Hani, Biko, Fanon? What do you say about them? Comrade, comrade, what do you say?' shouted voices from thick inside the scrum.

Once the statements and questions were out, the bandstand fell silent and for a moment no other noise rose in its place. The whole city was quiet. Then the park, with its dried brown grass and lost racist majesty, began to click with the sound of distant cicadas, and over the cracked earth small lizards stirred.

*

Hitler was in charge. He poked his glasses up his nose again and stood. 'This won't do, Mr Englander.' He hit play on the heavy old recorder that Viktor carried with him, purchased from a street seller hawking retro nineties technology with a stack of cheap cassettes. The machine slurred into life and two faint voices were heard. 'Where's the volume control, Mr Englander?' Hitler asked, fumbling around with the machine. Viktor leant forward, brushing the hard skin of the officer's hand, and turned the small dial. His own voice jumped into the room.

'Looking back at the protests in 2003,' he was asking Biko, 'why did the movement, the Final Push, fail?'

Biko groaned and slid his head further into his hands.

317

'Comrade, we failed because we weren't prepared.' Biko's voice was loud, strident. 'The MDC were happy to sacrifice the students, to forfeit a few cadre. They stirred up the colleges and universities and did nothing to build the Final Push in the industrial areas or townships. We were beaten by the dictatorship, by Mugabe and his cronies, by the dogs, but set up by our own party. They wanted a Sharpeville – a few dead students, international uproar – but instead we were just beaten.' There was a pause as Biko adjusted his position and finished his coffee. 'But we will break the regime by relying on our own forces. The regime is a hollowed-out gerontocracy, hated by the people of Bulawayo. The police thugs don't even dare to step onto the campus any more. They have been beaten.'

Biko let out another groan.

Hitler laughed again. His two colleagues moved to the door. Viktor turned to them. *Do they think we will try to escape?*

Now Hitler spoke to Biko, hitting the heavy stop button on the recorder before the next incriminating question could be asked, the next declaration of one-man regime change uttered in Biko's glittering, imprudent tongue. The thickset policeman by the door moved to the back of Biko's chair.

*

The group waited for Viktor to respond. A student held his pen over his notebook and looked up. At that moment Viktor had two almost simultaneous thoughts. To start with, he wondered if even these enlightened activists were infected by a belief in the wizardry and wisdom of white men. And then he pondered for an instance how this country's militants could still call themselves 'comrade'. How had they managed to seize the language of socialism against a dictatorship that used the same prefix: 'Right Honourable Comrade, President Robert Mugabe. In the interest of our struggle against Western imperialism … our Third *Chimurenga*, we celebrate the sacrifice of an oppressed people.' The language of social transformation had been put to the service of the lying, murderous state and still these groups, these pavement speakers, these paupers, spoke of *revolution* and *comrades*. Viktor did not know if it was courageous or stupid. He made a mental note to ask Biko, to speak to Nelson and Anne-Marie.

Viktor was thinking hard on these questions; the silence persisted. Slowly the expectations of the group gave way to resignation: their speaker, this oracle, could not help them. There was a further round of queries. 'What are the UK's interests in Zimbabwe?' asked someone. 'Do you think a real, anti-neoliberal alternative can be built here, opposed to both the MDC and ZANU?' A woman whose hair was swept back into a bun asked, 'Was Mugabe right to seize the land?'

In place of Viktor, Biko spoke. 'First, comrades, I don't support Cuba. There are no independent trade unions. What sort of socialism is that? A socialism where workers can't organise? They don't even have what we have in Zimbabwe. Guevara believed in guerrilla struggle, it was his prescription for everything. Armed struggle. Liberation delivered by war. Sankara was an army captain, a good man, but his revolution was a coup. Hani was a brutal ANC hack. For each of them, a revolution from above. Biko and Fanon have much to teach us. UK interests in Zimbabwe? Extensive. Donor funding; political interference; pressure to obey the dogs who have consumed us. Only by directly taking on these dogs, the imperialists, in X- and Y-Party, the fakers, can we build an alternative.'

Then, without pausing, Biko added, 'I think Viktor is tired and needs to rest. Remember,' he said laughing, speaking loudly, effortlessly, 'these comrades are not as tough as us. They haven't been tested by the African sun or the armed struggle.'

He grabbed Viktor's shoulder, pulled him through the small group and started to move to the gate and the exit. The movement, the blinding light, unlocked at last an opinion and Viktor spoke to the group: 'How can Cuba be socialist when it oppresses its gay community?'

The small crowd exploded into speech. A pack of storks flew into the air from the surrounding trees.

'Exactly!' Biko exclaimed. Relieved, he slapped Viktor hard on the back.

Viktor didn't do much better than this one statement, but his hesitancy, his resolute indecision on all meta-questions, on the historical epic, the total narrative posed by the group, drew them nearer to him. *Perhaps*, he thought, *they need my doubt to articulate and fix their certainty, my infernal alternatives to assert their own faith.* Maybe they needed to see the slight, puny reasoning of an Englander.

*

'Stand up.'

Hitler spoke quietly. Biko was still holding his head. Hitler signalled to his colleague who grabbed the chair and tipped it back. The legs skidded on the tiled floor and the chair fell. Biko crashed to the floor, writhed on the ground and struggled to get up. The policemen kicked him expertly. The thud of the boot into Biko's ribs jolted Viktor, who jumped and stood. Hitler moved quickly to him and held him back with an outstretched hand.

Biko stood, holding his side. He shouted in Shona, '*Ibvai pano, imbwa dzavanhu!*'

The heavy officer reached for him. Biko jerked back. The two officers moved towards Biko.

The policeman who had pulled the chair and kicked him was now screaming, '*Tinoda kukudzidzisa chidzidzo, ndiwe uchataurira vamwe kuti hazviitwe!*'

Viktor tried to get to Biko, just to reach him and help. 'What are you doing? He hasn't done anything. It's me you want, it's fucking me!' he shouted.

Hitler lunged at Viktor, missed him, stumbled, tripped. His glasses fell on the floor. 'Mr Englander, this is what we do in Zimbabwe.' He remained calm, picked up his glasses and approached Viktor. 'This is our way. Now you watch.'

Viktor cried, 'Get off him. Do you know who I am? What I'll do? You fucking thugs. Don't you know your fucking messiah is going to fall? He is hated. You are all hated.'

Biko's back was to the wall. The three men were kicking him. He tried pathetically to dodge their blows and, with inchoate jabs of his feet and fists, to fight back.

Viktor thought of a fox hunt, of a cornered, cowering fox, his burrow dug up, dogs surrounding him, as he snarled and snapped at the impossible odds, the inevitable end.

Hitler, beads of sweat on his forehead, came quickly to Viktor, who tried to stand between the dogs and the fox, to stave the first blood.

'Now, just watch, Mr Englander,' Hitler continued. 'Just watch and then tell your British queen that we don't want her interfering here.'

Hitler dragged Viktor by the collar. His shirt slid up his throat and choked him. He heard the pop of buttons as the material gave way. Viktor flailed and pulled until the shirt was entirely open. He now felt a hand to his throat and heard Hitler grunt as he was thrown against the wall. He tried to push the hand away but couldn't. Viktor thought he was going to vomit and faint. The force against his throat slowed his movements. When he was still, the hand loosened slightly so he could breathe again, focus on the scene.

The dogs, tired of goading and coaxing the fox, had drawn their batons – the same long sticks that Viktor had seen outlined against the sky days ago, like swords, he thought. Biko was silent. His efforts at self-defence, the principles of counter-attack, had exhausted him. He bent over so that his back, legs and buttocks faced the torrent of blows. The police hit, their arms moving in great arching strokes, drawing down on Biko's back in chaotic, hammering unison, the only sound in the room their grunts.

With Hitler Viktor stared, the two of them, it seemed to him afterwards, like twin accomplices, watching the spectacle together.

Chapter Twenty-Seven

In a dishevelled street, dirty and potholed, with the stink of a broken sewer, they ate from a pavement stall. A woman served *sadza* from a large aluminium pot over a makeshift campfire burning confidently on the tarmac. Viktor's suggestion that they eat in a high street café was dismissed with a roar of disapproval by the group.

'You must eat like we do,' replied a slight, hollow-chested student, his bamboo frame confirmation of what this would mean.

Viktor paid and they feasted together, shaded in the squalid, narrow alley. The group hunched, bent, eating with their hands from their plastic plates, mopping the sauce and the thin strips of chicken with the *sadza*. Viktor felt for the second time since his arrival that morning that he was pleased he'd come. He was standing, his plastic plate in his hand, feeling the *sadza* press gently against his stomach, the joy of being full and wanting, he realised for the first time in years, to be nowhere but where he was. Most of the group finished eating and lay on the pavement, their plates beside them.

When the police appeared it was as though they had been transported from another city and era. What surprised Viktor about what happened next was that they fought. He had seen arrests and police violence in London, on the demonstrations he had supported from a safe ideological distance, then written about – as Tendai had observed: 'A fucking armchair revolutionary, not even a revolutionary, just an armchair. You are just an armchair, Viktor, a blogger pontificating from your cushioned throne.' But this was different. When the police attacked, all he could think was, *They are trying to kill us*. No one thrashes three-foot batons with such force who does not have death, somewhere, on the agenda.

There were twenty policemen, a few more sealing the road with rifles. To Viktor's mind they had been sent to kill this group of students and this white, long-limbed primate hatching revolt, Cuban-style.

In London, Viktor thought, as the shaded alley was suddenly occupied by police, the sound of sirens rebounding off the buildings, *we throw bottles from a distance and accept when we are outnumbered – yet here, here where the stakes are higher, they fight*. What else could explain the way the group, almost as if to plan, organised themselves in his defence?

'Quick, Biko, Tapera!' The young woman, Eleanor, was the first to her feet. 'Get rid of Viktor.'

Biko tumbled, losing his footing, and moved towards Viktor. The others, acting together, stood quickly, plates scattering on the ground, and stood in front of Biko and Viktor. At the end of the street, in the light, the police shouted something Viktor couldn't understand. As they rushed forward out of the sunlight and into the darkened street, they seemed to disappear into the shadows until they could be seen a moment later running in broken formation with their batons drawn. The *sadza* seller grabbed the oversized pot, kicked out the fire and tried to run holding the enormous scalding pan, panicked not for her own safety but for her income, her plastic plates, the wood, the fire.

Biko seized Viktor and pulled him in the direction of the scattering crowd, the other customers. 'Why don't we all run?' Viktor shouted. 'Or why don't we just stand our ground and explain that we haven't done anything?'

'That's not how it works, comrade,' Biko said, breathless, yanking Viktor harder.

Now only metres separated the two groups: the policemen holding their weapons aloft, his friends waiting, unarmed, their fists clenched.

Tapera turned sideward to a policeman, his right leg forward, his arm out and hand closed into a fist. The others did the same. The student who had insisted Viktor eat with them held his ground and shouted, '*Qina Msebenzi Qina!*' and then, ridiculously, unbelievably, charged the police. He was the first down, struck on the head and then beaten over and over again.

The last thing Viktor saw, as Biko part-dragged, part-carried him in his arms, was Tapera snatching the baton as it came down, pulling hard until he was next to the policeman and then, still gripping the baton, kicking the man in the stomach. The policeman, winded, released his cudgel. Before Viktor was finally wrenched away, from the corner of his eye he saw Tapera wield the stick over his head, shout something and try to make his way to a fallen comrade.

*

Hitler had taken a book from Viktor's bag and, still holding his captive with one hand, the diminutive, thickset policeman held up the book and read: 'The native cures himself of colonial

325

neurosis by thrusting out the settler through force of arms. When his rage boils over, he rediscovers his lost innocence and he comes to know himself in that he himself creates his self.' Staring Viktor directly in the eyes, Hitler smiled.

The blows sliced the air, cut the room into photographic stills; the violence a movie in slow motion, each image a minor distinguishing frame. Within a few seconds one policeman gave up and rested on his bent knees, panting. Biko was still crouched over, clenching his arms, tensing his muscles. The second officer continued to rain blows. The sound echoed through the room.

Even this man, fitter than his colleague, was tiring. *Is this all?* Viktor thought. *Is this all they're going to do?*

Viktor gripped Hitler's wrist with his two arms, struggled to move it from his throat. Hitler dropped his arm and moved away.

'You fucking cowards. You idiots. You know you will regret this!' Viktor rushed towards Biko, leant down to his friend, still shouting. 'You fucking thugs, you know I'm a writer and I'm going to expose you!' Then quietly, in a whisper, 'Are you okay?' Viktor muttered into Biko's ear. The smell of sweat and fear made him recoil slightly. He put his hand gently on his friend's back. Biko gasped. 'Get a fucking doctor, you monsters. Now!' Viktor shouted, turning his head to the policemen.

'Be quiet,' Biko hissed, breathless, 'just keep calm. They have been looking for me.'

Biko's voice was so faint Viktor had to move closer. His cheek touched Biko's. 'What, what did you say?' All he could hear was Biko's pained breathing. Each time his chest heaved and he inhaled more air, he let out a thin, suppressed sigh.

'Get a fucking doctor. You have broken his ribs. He can't breathe.'

*

'Why did they fight against these odds?'

'Because you can't show you are afraid. If you do it will be worse when they arrest you. They will beat you harder. We have to fight, men and women, no difference. Fight,' Biko had replied to Viktor as they ran.

When they were out of the knotted alleyways, back into the bleached, white sunshine, the sprint gave way to a gentle amble.

'Surely we should have all run,' Viktor persisted.

'Then we would all have been arrested, comrade, and you would have been sent back to the UK.'

Viktor, the park-wizard, had been seen preaching under the old Rhodesian bandstand where white couples had once danced, asserting their superiority. The police had been alerted because of him, his hooked frame, his pale face, taller even than Biko – taller than anyone else, a human lighthouse that drew people near so they could be torn to pieces at the rocks of his feet.

Biko and Viktor were now walking, moving between hawkers selling batteries and cheap radios on pavement stalls of flattened cardboard. Viktor's chest heaved and he fought to hold back tears. They had kept the police away, he knew, for him.

*

Viktor felt himself being pulled away from Biko's side by the two policemen. He was dragged and lifted from the ground to the back of the room. The movement was sudden; he didn't react. When he was pinned against the wall Hitler came up to him, put an arm up to his shoulder, leant forward and said in a soft, deep voice that almost sounded comforting, 'Mr Englander, I don't like you. You have no right to interfere in our country. Here no one cares about you.'

Viktor struggled once more, lifted a leg, tried to knee Hitler.

'Leave him. He's done nothing.' Biko spoke, raised himself, his face creased in agony, his voice shrill and taut. 'Viktor, comrade!' he cried.

Viktor continued to move his legs, pushing, trying to make contact. Hitler pressed against him so that Viktor could feel his large, firm stomach and smell his acrid, piercing breath. Then he felt Hitler's hand grip his penis and testicles and hold them hard.

For a second Viktor stopped thinking. The interrogation, the violence, the hand to his throat, Biko's beating, had a fantastical logic that could be incorporated into his conceptual vocabulary, but not this grip that felt simultaneously comforting and violent. Hitler tightened his grip, massaging his fingers around Viktor's groin.

Quietly this time, Viktor said, 'Get off.' Then, a little louder, he repeated, 'Get off me.'

'Leave him!' Biko screamed through his pain.

*

Two mornings later the papers reported the events and included a peculiar, opaque quote from the president. Nothing for Viktor symbolised the breakdown of Zimbabwe more profoundly than Mugabe's comment on the 'Protests and Arrests in Bulawayo'. Why would this mighty statesman, this man of the anti-imperialist *chimurenga* fighting in the last great battle of the continent, bother to comment on these arrests? Weren't these inconsequential students in an inconsequential provincial city? The president expressed his regret at having to 'teach these students a lesson'. The paper reported that 'President Mugabe castigated the so-called radicals now emerging in Bulawayo, who, he said, called themselves revolutionaries but fought for nothing more than *sadza* and more allowances.'

All the students had been arrested.

Biko and Viktor shared a bed and a single blanket in a city squat. Viktor laid the few clothes he had brought with him on the sheetless mattress and tucked his trousers into his socks. Biko fell into an instant and deep sleep, but not before he had spoken about their struggles at the university. His comrades were being tortured, bludgeoned, on Mugabe's orders, and Biko spoke merrily about their campus commune.

'It is not quite the Paris commune, com, but it is not too far away either. That's why ZANU hate us. We are actually showing what poor, hungry students can do in a few square kilometres. It was around, I guess, February. That was the time of price controls. So we had a general meeting and we simply decided that these guys providing us with food were profiteering and students could not afford lunch. So what's the way out of this? The following day everyone wakes up to find posters all over the university that say "Presidential Declaration on Price Controls" – I was the president. And the staple food for students is buns, so naturally buns were our main target; we said no one is going to sell a bun for more than a certain amount. No one is going to sell a plate of *sadza* for more than this much and a number of other things, Freezits, which is the cheapest drink, but that's what students get for their lunch, so we put controls on Freezits.

'And the beautiful part, the really beautiful part of it, was that the language was quite threatening. If anyone fails to abide by this, we said, they are not going to be able to exist here. We are simply not going to tolerate them and they cannot do their business here. So a number of guys, because they knew us, knew our record, knew that we were not playing, a number of them put down their prices a bit. And I tell you, students were appreciative.' Biko's animation as he spoke belied his exhaustion.

'However. One old man, who was the main supplier of buns, adopted our controlled prices, but because initially he had shown some resistance, on the next demonstration he was punished. His shop was looted. People broke in and they looted. But later on he came to me after the looting and said, "I adopted the prices that you gave me but still you are looting my shop. I thought we were now coexisting well." And so on.

'In some cases like that you have to be a little bit diplomatic. You can only say that you will look into this. This was part of the strategy that we have, you solve day-to-day problems this way. We are even working out a transport facility for students. We are demanding that the university gives students a university bus. This is very close to happening because we are demanding that since the university has got buses and cars, students should use the bus as a shuttle for commuting. Because university workers are paying something like a tenth of what students are. Do you see? Viktor, Viktor, comrade, like the commune, like Paris. We were actually inspired by the Paris Commune.'

'So these price controls could be rolled out across Zimbabwe, is that what you are saying?' Viktor asked.

'No, no, not exactly, but they are a start. We can humiliate the market that's come to privatise our services *and* challenge the regime and provide an example. You know, there are good cadre in ZANU who believe in land redistribution, nationalisation, indigenisation. We can take them on.'

Biko was sitting cross-legged on the bed. Night had fallen and Viktor could only see the outline of his face, his arms moving in wide, bountiful arches, the still air disturbed, his hands casting his words across the room to his solitary, worn-out auditor.

Viktor replied, 'Okay, what I think is this. You operated a macho posse, imposing presidential decrees that might be impressive but satisfy your desire for a personality cult. You say the students cry "Biko, Biko, Biko" when you enter the campus. You might be part of the problem. We need movements without leaders – without leaders like you, at least. Too much charisma, Biko, that's your problem.'

Biko laughed loudly. 'Wrong. But there is a danger, I see that. I just pushed, and we need organisations and individuals in them to push.'

Soon they were lying down. Biko slept, as if sleep could be simply willed. He had none of Viktor's discomfort. He had brazenly stripped and now lay pressed against his companion.

Before Biko fell asleep, he thought, *Strange, this comrade sent from* – he had forgotten now – *Harare, from London?* He enjoyed Viktor's insistence and intensity, like his own, he thought, but without laughter – *how serious, these ... these men from Europe, they really mean business.*

'Shouldn't we be parked outside the police station? Picketing? We're sleeping while they languish,' Viktor had said, enjoying the warmth and comfort of Biko beside him.

'We need our rest and sleep to better campaign, comrade. They will be released. It's me they want.'

Biko woke in the night, pleased that his companion was asleep, impressed that he could sleep in this damn heat. He knew he wouldn't be able to beat his way back to sleep, so he got up and moved silently round the bed to the hall and the small, rubbish-strewn front lawn. A cat was scratching at a black plastic bag; he kicked it out of the way. '*Ibva pano!*'

He pissed, leaning against the side of the house. The moon lit the street with an uneven glare. *I should move to Johannesburg,* he thought again. The idea was on a loop he was powerless to unhook; round and round it went. *Mongezi can get me work in the garage. I can send back medicine and food for the family.* Onward to the conclusion: *But the struggle at the university, in Bulawayo, would collapse.*

Biko snapped up his boxer shorts and remained leaning against the house, the cat mewing loudly in complaint at this interloper who had snatched its spot. He saw his sister before him, her sick, thin body on his last visit home, thankful for the scraps he had hustled from the city. A bag of biltong, already broken into; face cream, the lid broken; a small sack of mealie. Scraps all. He had wanted to hold her, to cry, rest his head on her lap – talk, like they used to, about their mother. Instead he had hurried back to Bulawayo, speaking to her with the bombast he used at university. He withdrew to the politics he knew in town, as his father had.

Now, in the familiar routine, he remembered his father visiting him on business two years before, in his only suit, looking too smart, but with an arrogance and pride that made it impossible for Biko to pity him when he got out of the bus. How he had brushed away his son's offer to carry his bags, already too heavy for him, with a dismissive wave: '*Asi unofunga kuti handina kugwinya zvekuti ndinga takura nhava dzangu ndega here nhai mwanangu.*' Then the beers they had shared in the evening with his friends, how his chest had inflated in pride as his father entertained them with stories about the seventies, before you born-frees ...

'Your problem,' he said, pointing his beer at the group, 'is you think my generation is only Grade Four and you are very educated, you think you are now so learned and there is nothing that we, those who freed Zimbabwe, can teach you. I want to show you that we can still outthink you, outfight you.' He got up and started to sway and dance on his feet, swinging his leathery fists at his hosts, the boys. Biko's friends laughed and hooted. 'You see, when I was your age I was already fighting the whites, and you think you are special, so today I want to reduce you to size.'

How he had loved the chiding, the reprimands from these children about the failures of 1980, the failure of the Second *Chimurenga*. Of course there was no business in Bulawayo; of course the city was on the way to nowhere. Biko knew that his father had planned the visit for months because he wanted to see his son, because he missed him. He thought suddenly of his mother, her image forming before him clearly.

Biko started to cry, tears rolling down his face in large, salty drops. The cat edged back to the bag, the rubbish and food. Biko dropped to his knees, the cat curled around his outstretched arm.

The vision of his mother – seventeen years ago – was so clear to him, the blemishes on her face, her worn eyes vivid. If only he could reach out to her like this, as he was doing now with the cat, and pull his mother back, grab her up in his strong grip through the years that separated them, the irrelevant, unnecessary events that had dragged on, since his mother's death, and pull them in, make them nothing.

Biko stood straight, rubbed his nose and eyes with the back of his arm and stumbled dizzily into the house.

Wasn't his father here, right in front of him, not lost, his breath heavy with beer, hot against his son's neck as they staggered, all of them, back from the bar, to the same house, to the same bed?

Biko lay next to Viktor, whose breathing was soft and steady.

*

Hitler closed his hand tightly on Viktor's balls, crushing and twisting them in his hand. Viktor felt a sharp, jarring agony and

333

passed out. Hitler released him from the wall and moved away. Viktor's body crumpled to the floor.

Biko too slid to the floor, repeating in his head, *I mustn't make a noise. Mustn't give them what they want.* The floor felt comforting, the cold tiles steady and reliable against his face. His back pulsed numb. He knew that the pain was about to swallow him, and that then, only then, he would want to scream. He saw the police bent over, panting, their batons lying on the floor.

Moments later, Viktor was conscious. 'I will report you, you sadistic bastards,' he cried, his voice quivering.

Shut up, you white man, shut up, comrade, Biko thought. His nose and mouth were running, a small pool of saliva and blood forming on the tiles. *Stupid, crazy, brilliant white man.* Biko struggled to remember the man's name again, the *murungu*. *What's the bloody* murungu *called? What's he called?* He heard Viktor gasp in pain and tried to move, to get to him. Suddenly he felt the rush of his own pain, a thick, long ripple across his back and up his neck. The gasp was his own.

'Let's give him the hose. Let's give Mr Englander a lesson, show him how we deflower our youth. The Bulawayo Treatment.' Hitler was in the centre of the room, pointing and ordering his men again. 'Are you looking, Mr Englander?'

The policeman kicked Biko into place and forced him to straighten his legs, lie with his arms and legs spread out on the floor, on his stomach. He felt his trousers being pulled down, the floor cold and threatening against his penis and his bare stomach.

'Get it in!' Hitler shouted, his voice breaking.

Biko tried to move again, his chest widened to breathe, and he shuddered as the pain sent the air tumbling out of his lungs. He tried again to catch his breath, only to lose it to the suffocating, stabbing agony in his chest.

'Make it wet and push it in!' Hitler screamed.

Biko heard the sound of throats clearing, spitting, and felt the spittle against his naked back and buttocks.

The thickset policeman squatted and with his hands parted Biko's buttocks. For an instant it felt pleasant; then Biko heard a grunt as the stick was rammed inside his anus. He tried to twist, turn over, dislodge the force, but he couldn't move. The rippling, reeling pain left him pinned to the ground.

*

'I am a journalist and blogger based in Zimbabwe … Where? … In Bulawayo. Two days ago I witnessed seven students being attacked and arrested by the police. They are still being held. I would like your help to get them out.'

'I will see what I can do. We are busy in Harare.' Jonathan Goodmore was a Y-Party minister in the government, now in coalition with ZANU, and his voice was stiff.

'I am told you were a student leader yourself, here in Bulawayo. I am sure it would only take a few calls. We have good reason to think they are being beaten,' Viktor said.

'Of course they are, this is Zimbabwe,' Goodmore replied.

'Then please do something, sir,' Viktor added.

'I said I would try. Phone me back later.' He then hung up and refused to answer the phone, each of the fifteen times Viktor called that day.

Viktor started his calls from the list sent by Rajeev, incautiously, as though he had learnt nothing, thinking as he announced himself that it was important to forget the lessons, the refusal, the failures, and become naive again. In Zimbabwe, to believe he needed to forget the nightmares of the past, the impossibility of change.

Viktor made these calls fluently; he enjoyed the feeling that he was right, without any distractions. Biko sat next to him, mouthing the script, hand-signing what words to emphasise, describing who were the scoundrels and sell-outs, warning him, immunising him against the entire caste of profiteers.

Biko scoffed loudly: 'Jonathan is a coward.' Viktor shielded the mouthpiece as Biko continued, 'We get in the way of their business, we disturb their bonuses. Their deals with X-Party.'

Still covering the receiver, Viktor replied, 'I have to try. The man is in the bloody opposition – on your side.'

'Pah,' Biko snarled, his face spreading out in a smile. 'He is not on our side. He is like them, a fallen giant. He is lining his pockets, getting fat in government. He is on his own side, comrade. That, that' – he tried to find the word in his mouth – 'fool, idiot, capitalist, dog. That dog.'

Viktor, sweating in the sun, returned to the call.

Biko reassured him, his arms flapping, that they could run their pavement campaign like this, in a high street café. *Why do we need to be so needlessly cocksure?* Viktor thought. 'We can't concede the city to them or they'll come after us,' Biko said, smiling, hitting the table with his hand, spilling their coffees. 'They've already got so many of us, com, that's the point.'

Biko had woken Viktor early, when the morning was only beginning to break over the horizon, the eastern skyline tilting to the sun, the sky slowly lighting, the pale, full moon turning translucent, losing consistency. They walked through the overgrown suburb, along the clogged stream that ran into the city.

Viktor awoke resolute. Sleep had washed him clean.

It had been Viktor's idea to lobby the police station. The station could fool you, with its ordered facade and neat red bricks and signposts: Reception, Assistance, Report Any Theft or Criminal Behaviour to Your Local Police. These things lulled Viktor, told him he could make a proper complaint; though broken, the legal edifice of the state still stood.

Viktor announced himself. 'I want to speak to the chief asshole. Not you, the sergeant, the officer in charge, the inspector who runs your station. Innocent people were arrested. And I want to know where they are. I want to see them now.'

Once more Biko had to half-drag, half-carry Viktor from the police.

The sergeant, bemused, stared at Viktor, who stared back until the sergeant asked the two men to stay where they were. His round face and glasses and swept, neat uniform made the policeman, like the station, look ordered and reasonable. 'Don't move, this is very important. Interesting. A complaint,' the officer said. The sergeant left the desk.

*

'Are you watching, Mr Englander?' Hitler bent over Viktor, whose foggy, clouded vision had started to clear. He rolled Viktor onto his side and cupped his head in his hands. 'Look at this show, Mr Englander. This is what we do to our naughty children; we learnt it from you people, from Her Royal Highness.'

At first Viktor could only see the feet of the desk, the white tiles on the floor, and the shoes and trouser hems of the two men, but slowly his focus sharpened and narrowed on Biko's naked thighs and buttocks beyond the feet of the desk, head turned towards the wall.

'Again, man, you missed it,' Hitler repeated softly like an uncle.

Viktor saw a single baton lowered slowly to Biko's back, then firmly dragged along the spine so the skin gathered along the rounded head of the stick, rippling the flesh like water. The baton was raised suddenly; then Viktor saw it plunge violently between Biko's buttocks. Biko's body shuddered and convulsed.

'Once more. Harder!' Hitler shouted, still on his haunches, cradling Viktor's head.

Before Biko passed out he saw his mother. He felt ashamed and didn't want her to see his naked legs and buttocks, his failure. Biko thought of his university study and the money that he'd managed to send to his sister. He'd done this for his mother, to return, somehow, to her the love he felt so keenly, with such abundance. *But now she is watching me and I have failed her.* The pain and humiliation came together loudly, buzzed hysterically in his ears, and then it was over and Biko's whirlwind of sensations shut down.

Hitler dropped Viktor's face to the floor and exhausted, exhilarated, stood.

*

'Nicely done, com, but if we don't leave now we'll be arrested.' Biko tried the door, which was locked. Quickly he jumped over the counter, ran his hand under the desk, searching for the button.

Voices could be heard along the corridor behind Biko, a clutter of movement as policemen moved towards them.

'Get to the door,' Biko ordered. 'Hold it open for me.'

Biko found the button. A light thud sounded as the magnetic plate released. Viktor pushed the door open. Biko sprang over the counter again, levering himself with his arm on the desktop in one clean leap, as though he had practised the manoeuvre.

The door to the back offices and corridor swung open and two policemen in green uniforms came through. Biko landed on the right side of the counter, his legs bent, for a second invisible below the reception desk. The men stood silent. Viktor held the door, ready to run, waiting for Biko. Biko scooped Viktor around the waist with one arm, pulled him away from the station and forced Viktor to move at his speed.

There was shouting behind them.

Now they ran, hand in hand, Biko in front, leading Viktor as they jumped clear of the cardboard pavement stalls, past hawkers selling juice cards, then across two streets, over bodies slumped in the gutters, the shouting behind them, the sound of the street. When they arrived at the café they laughed, sucking in the air, falling on the chairs around a table arranged on the pavement.

I can trust him, Biko thought, *he is serious. What stupid, brilliant audacity. He doesn't hold anything back. Like me.* 'Like me,' he repeated aloud. 'You called the dog an asshole!' Biko laughed, slapping Viktor's back. Viktor heaved breathlessly. 'Totally reckless, comrade, insane, but brilliant in its way.'

The café was shaded by a broken canopy; the sun beat down on them through the torn awnings. Viktor needed the heat. He raised his face to the sky, to feel the sun on him, the large, forgiving expanse of sky. He was comforted. He thought that if he stared hard enough beyond the loose clouds he could see where the night lay watching over the day, its own vastness, its huge frontiers, even greater, more forgiving and ignorant of them than this temporary, fleeting day.

Viktor felt proud.

The tables, similarly half-shaded, were occupied with small groups of men huddled over coffees and beers. Viktor and Biko continued to plan and make phone calls with more stupid, brazen bravado. Hadn't they challenged the universe enough? By late in the afternoon their pavement table, now a campaign headquarters, was strewn with two phones, papers, a notepad.

An old man, his face creased, his clothes loose on him, leant on the edge of the table, beckoned to Biko and muttered in a rasping, deep voice, '*Tora mari iyi chikomana, ndoda kuti uwumbe bato rino bvisa kamudhara ako pachigaro*.' He then removed a note from his pocket and gave it to Biko. Still leaning heavily on the table, he stood, straightened himself and walked away.

'What did he say?' Viktor asked.

Biko hesitated. 'Well,' he said, searching for the words in English, 'I think he said, "Put this in your funds, comrade, and build a fucking riot to bring down the government." I am not sure he said fucking.' Biko smiled with his mouth open, showing his fleshy, pink gums and missing teeth.

'I think that is a good sign. How much did he give you?' Viktor asked.

'More than he could afford,' Biko answered.

Viktor turned his head back to the lists of numbers and contacts they had written. Biko wiped his eyes.

Two hours later the night elbowed out the day. The couple still campaigned on the pavement, the last table occupied in the café. And when they were ready to shuffle their papers, pack away the recorder Viktor used to interview Biko and withdraw, like the day, to the squat – the table was surrounded by plainclothes policemen. They were arrested.

Part Five:

The Campaign

Chapter Twenty-Eight

Viktor felt chastened, ashamed. He put off thinking, refused to do it on the train back to Harare, in the empty compartment. He had bought each of the beds so he wouldn't have to share. Nor did he think as he walked from the station, knowing the route, along the broad avenues, past Harare Gardens. He lifted his gaze so he didn't see the hawkers and potholes, only the distance, the buildings reflecting the late-morning sunlight. Like this, he could pretend the city worked.

Only after he had showered, changed and washed out the dirt would he think about what had happened in Bulawayo. He longed for Anne-Marie, to be held, but she was at another of her conferences. The flat felt too large without her presence and he left quickly.

He crossed Herbert Chitepo Avenue and turned into Mazowe Street, the small road that headed north to the university and the suburbs, where the rich had lived with their swimming pools and gravel driveways, houses now occupied by expatriates with their generators and boreholes, their private enclaves free of society's crisis.

There was a crowd of people standing on the street corner, hailing lifts; Viktor weaved in and out of the stationary bodies. He would visit Louis.

'How was it, friend?' Louis leapt up from the counter, throwing down his paper and embracing Viktor. Viktor gripped Louis's shoulder.

'We've missed you. Haven't we, boys?' Louis shouted, looking up to his staff, his boys, ordering them to agree.

Viktor confessed, sitting at the counter, drinking Louis's free coffee. He told him what happened in a series of short, sensational sentences. He won, at least, Louis's silence when he was finished.

Louis let out only a solitary 'Fuck.'

'I know.'

'I mean, what the fuck are you doing here? You got almost fucked and you fucked your stupid friends. What do you want to achieve? They don't need you. You can't help them.' Louis was disappointed, disagreeable; he had his faults, he knew, but he was not, he believed, incompetent. When Louis worried for other men, it made him angry.

Viktor turned towards his coffee, stared at it, lifted the teaspoon and started to rub the metal with his thumb and forefinger until it was warm and clammy in his grip.

'I mean, what the fuck did you think you were going to do? You are white. Their struggles are not yours, this is not your place, and you don't understand. They will kill you.' He got up and through his clenched teeth emitted another single, taut 'Fuck.'

Louis lifted two rough sacks of coffee beans stamped *Kappas Beans*. The loosely stuffed bags fell heavily on both sides of his shoulders. He grunted and pushed his way through the open kitchen to the back door of the café.

Viktor put down the spoon and lifted a hand to his face. Regret and shame. Shame for leaving Bulawayo, regret for having gone. Everything he had done, each time he had engaged his will, he had brought destruction. In that second he could feel all of his comrades in his body so it hurt him and his breath drained suddenly: Tendai, Biko, Nelson, Moreblessing, even the soft imprint of Rosa's head nestling into his chest, his woman-child who wanted to feel close to him, smell her father's scent before they would be parted for another week, another year. Viktor rubbed his forehead, shielded his eyes from Louis's staff.

Everything is broken, he thought, a trail of loss and heartbreak. *What an expert at leaving and destruction I am*. Having your heart broken is a well-documented pain, but it is nothing compared to breaking hearts – of all sizes, white, black, the hearts of children, his parents, his lovers, his comrades. *Daddy, she called me*, Viktor thought, *and I broke her heart for it. I punished her for loving me*. He heard the kitchen door swing open and kept a hand on the empty coffee cup, the other supporting his head.

Viktor thought back to the train journey, how he had bought all the tickets for his compartment so he could be alone. Each bunk was his, four in total, all for the impossible, long trundle north. Two women both in their sixties had slid the door open and asked him if there was room, cheap canvas bags holding their blankets and clothes. They had smiled at him and called him sir. 'No, they're taken,' Viktor had said, indicating his clothes and bag carefully draped over the carriage. Surely Louis could see he was already a real white man and that he did belong here. The women nodded their heads in silence, slid the door closed again and dragged their bags along the corridor. Viktor tried to pin his eyes closed with his first finger and thumb, to dam his tears by force.

Louis came up to him and pushed a plate of fried eggs and bacon and another coffee under his face.

'We're all fucked, Vik. Eat this and stop feeling sorry for yourself.'

*

In the corner of the cell was a moulded concrete bed next to a toilet. The walls were chipped; prisoners had scratched their names, dates, in English, Shona and Ndebele. Biko shared the small, narrow rectangle with two other men – Samuel Mutambara and Hopewell Guseni. Samuel had assaulted a policeman who had cleared his pavement stall in the city, stabbing him on the street. Hopewell had been in a drunken fight that he no longer clearly remembered.

Blankets were thrown into the cell with each new prisoner. They shared the single, sunken foam mattress, slept together on their sides, one coarse blanket spread under them, the other two covering them. The deep-set cell window that could be reached from the fixed bed caught the northern wind that even in the early spring worked up the blankets and ricocheted in the cell. With the wind thrashing through the room, Biko imagined that the seven-foot concrete room had been cast out to sea, the three men perched in a strange embrace on their bed raft bobbing on the waves. Biko liked to think that they were riding the surf away from Zimbabwe and the prison, on the warm Indian Ocean, a current carrying them along the whole undivided African coast.

When the morning came, their intimate, necessary night-time embrace came apart. The arguments started, the enforced discipline planned like a war, the minutes – so they imagined, unable to record time – to each task, the turn on the cell toilet, each shitting according to the order of bowel movements, the blankets folded, the songs, the same time each late morning, some political, mostly not, and the post-*sadza* lecture. Biko was always charming, bullying his recalcitrant cellmates by force of character, as if he'd been planning for the arrest, the prison, survival in this locked room, all his life.

Biko sat on the toilet, resting on the seatless bowl as his buttocks relaxed, the cheeks pulled wide over the rim. The shit would splutter out, always loose, painful, six weeks later still speckled with blood.

'Those bastards really fucked me good,' Biko said, grimacing.

'Because you're an uppity, disrespectful bastard. *Bharanzi*. Didn't your father teach you not to answer your elders back?' Hopewell was forty, though his face was badly lined and tired; he looked like an old man. Only his body, incongruous, unlined, showed his true age. He started the day positive, jovial even, then spun down in the afternoon when the reflected horizon on the iron door fell below the hatch where their water and food was shoved.

'Respect, comrade,' Biko announced, leaning on one cheek, pouring a cup of water into his prised, parted buttocks, 'is something I have for my parents, not for dictators, their quislings and thugs. The dogs.' Clean, he stood and shook off the drops.

'You're a daft Ndebele – what do you know? You lot have always been defeated,' Hopewell joked.

Biko pulled up his trousers. The pungent, foul odour of decay that had overwhelmed each of them, made them retch when they were first allocated the cell, no longer irritated them.

Samuel spent the first hour of the morning with his head in his hands, talking to the floor, adjusting his gaze, adjusting his expectations for another day. For days after Biko was pushed

347

into the cell, they'd fought. When he first came in, his feet caked in dried blood, he had collapsed on the floor, raving and cursing the police, the president, the entire system, promising retribution that he would personally execute and that he'd lead the charge of the poor and hungry. In his delirium and agony he'd shouted in Shona and Ndebele, '*Shinga Mushandi Shinga. Qina Sisebenzi Qina.* You swines, lackeys, dogs! I'm coming for you!' Then he'd stayed groaning in the same position on the floor, shivering and shaking, clenching and unclenching in pain, calling out between breaths. Hopewell threw a blanket over him, but cursed the noise and wondered how he'd ever get out with this troublemaker causing such mayhem. He tried again to decipher the night of beer, the fight, the knife he remembered holding, but then the memory broke down and he was left with words, the story he had been told about what had happened. He was convinced now that the police had lied.

*

Louis and Viktor were a strange match, the thin, cerebral, frustrated, awkward internet activist and the gruff, squat, thick, loud racist. In the months that Viktor stayed in Zimbabwe, Louis and Viktor saw or spoke to each other almost every day. There was a craving in both of them, a need or hunger for company and belonging. Viktor spiralled, unmoored, in his hopeless search from London to Harare. Louis, for his part, was too outspoken even for his golf-club friends – unsettled, angry at himself, dissatisfied with the pain around him, the pain he knew that he lived off, the pain in him. They knew who they were to each other, what they could give, what they received.

Louis was a fixer. For a man of such broken parts, this was strange. The family could have left Zimbabwe many times.

It had been a topic of conversation for years. The imminent packing – packing for Perth, for Johannesburg, for London – had become a condition of his family life with Vicki. As a young man, after his service in the Rhodesian Army, when the Lancaster House negotiations had signalled the end of Rhodesian history, of white supremacy in Salisbury, his comrades in the army – the last guard – were told to continue the struggle in South Africa. Continue the struggle for white minority rule in Pretoria! The last, most important battle for white culture, for civilisation, was being fought by the apartheid regime at the tip of the continent.

Louis scoffed, even then, not at the racism but at the surrender – the idea that this piffling truce in Rhodesia, this 'sort of independence', could dislodge him and his family. Greek his father might have been, but Louis felt Africa in his soul, with all of its rot, its failures, its stench, its blacks. He was staying – though even this had never actually crystallised into an articulated decision. As friends – skinheads from the demobilised army with their revolvers, their Rhodesian flag badges sewn onto kitbags – abandoned their families to struggle for whiteness, Louis stayed. For a time he declaimed, shouted as loud as he wanted about 'the blacks', 'these dogs' and the mess they had made of his country.

The unholy alliance of unreconstructed racists, with Louis as their exultant representative, and the new black middle class lasted from independence in 1980 to the nineties. When they were not doing business they hated each other – ZANU forcing minor contracts and partnerships on the class of wealthy whites and entitled Rhodesian businessmen.

After a few years the language of socialism and independence had become just empty rhetoric; the white-owned plantations still stretched over the hills of Mutare, the plains of Mashonaland, the fields of crops and cattle and the white families who owned them smug, in control, unruffled. They were like Gainsborough's Mr and Mrs Andrews, the painting of the eighteenth-century English countryside, but with Mr and Mrs Kappas now standing over their plantations, behind them the extent of their estate, agriculture, livestock in the distance, arable land, crops harvested far into the distance. 'Everything you see we own.'

The rolling, undisturbed estates, the private landing strips created, in sovereign Zimbabwe, multiple mini-states, states within states, capitalist bubbles. This was the settlement ZANU had negotiated in 1980. Despite his ravings, Louis Kappas had been one of its main beneficiaries.

When the crisis had unravelled the pact of silence and accommodation in the late nineties, Louis had remained implacable. Two years after dinner with the Queen, Mugabe had turned on white interests, the farms, the businesses, the monopolies. Louis bristled, set his jaw, beat his chest and dug in. The talk of leaving Zimbabwe spilled over to the teeming white shopping centres in the cities, the holiday resorts, the clubs and estates. Louis scoffed again. 'Let the black bastard try – we are not going anywhere.' To his wife's despair, his children's adolescent shrugs, his friends who declared, 'Louis, you have to see what's happening. The game is up,' he only stood wider, more sure.

As Mugabe's intransigence hardened – the long, painful, blustering speeches – Louis stood surer, let his own anger grow. Intransigence was matched by intransigence, gibe by gibe, insult by insult, racist slur to racist slur. When Mugabe or Moyo or Mnangagwa derided the white community, the entire white planet, Blair and Bush in the North, the monopoly capitalists in the South, Louis would leave his house, walk into the middle of his large Harare lawn and under the sun or moon he would slander out loud and call up the racist gods. Inch for inch, abuse for abuse, Louis took on the president. He would not leave Zimbabwe, 'this jungle of monkeys', this Promised Land, because it belonged to him and he was staying.

There was another aspect to Louis's diatribe of resistance to black tyranny, his one-man war, which he barely acknowledged even to himself: he could not survive away from Zimbabwe. Beneath this recognition there was something else that he never spoke about but that Viktor had seen on their first day together: he had a secret, despairing love for Zimbabwe. Towards those most twisted by the world he served, Louis trembled, felt his soul shudder; his stomach, which held his rage, turned over and over. Unable to find real expression it came out of him as anger; these barriers to feeling masked Louis's humanity.

To all of the human agony that woke him in the night, forced him to pace the house, he had become a fixer. Louis had his own tragic projects of patronage and development to match ZANU's. When Vicki asked him about the business, the money from the trucking, the minerals, the coffee, he lied. With the funds he siphoned from his café, from the export of raw materials that were impoverishing the Congo, he supported his staff, paid their children's school fees, bought bags of mealie-meal and paid hospital bills. He fabricated jobs, created positions, drove past the junction at the bottom of Fourth Avenue in the morning where the unemployed touted for work, hoping to be hired, men of all ages, some still carrying cloth workbags with tools from trades they'd had years before, children who had never worked. In the winter the cold would bite hard at the hands and the crowd would swell, a demonstration of labourers. Men could be seen on the pavements in the scrambled grey of the morning light, washing from buckets, sharing rags to dry themselves, patting away the cold.

Louis would drive past the corner in the early morning, swing his large *bakkie* into the pavement and slam on his brakes, then elbow open the door of his cab and raise himself on the tailboard to shout, '*Mangwanani*, I need fifteen men.' Then, in case there was any doubt as to who he was and what he really thought, he swore, 'Get a fucking move on. I need workers. Real workers.' He would then drive badly, the *bakkie* swerving on the road, to let the crowd of men know that he was a white man from the old school.

Once deposited at his warehouse in Willowdale, he would shout again at the men that the sacks of coffee needed to be piled into a pyramid in another corner of the storeroom. The men would look at him, then set to work as Louis paced the floor. Sometimes he would take a few of the hired hands to the café and here there'd be a ridiculous bustle of activity – rearranging the stockroom, cleaning the cleaned floor, sweeping the swept yard.

Setting the men to work on make-believe tasks, Louis fought to keep the scowl on his face. When the work was done the men never entirely left; instead they learnt his system and made requests for loans, for help with their families. And the system? Viktor saw men he recognised coming into the café, staff, temporary workers, even the occasional customer, passing Louis folded notes. Louis would never acknowledge the person but take the note, unfold it, read it, deepen his scowl and nod.

To live in this city, in early-twenty-first-century Zimbabwe, to be white, to have been born Rhodesian, what other options were there? Louis had devised a system.

Even though he shouted at Viktor for implicating himself in the affairs of others, imposing himself when he should not have, fighting fights that were not his, he recognised in himself the same need. He saw in Viktor the same spark of want and knew that here was a man who could no more step away from misery than stop breathing – a man like him.

*

Comrade!

Ridiculous though it may seem to email you so often, to distract you in your important activism, it can't be helped. Indeed it is an ABSOLUTE necessity. I have been telling everyone about Biko, the arrest and what you are doing. We are already having collections at the university. Jason has printed Free Biko stickers.

Thanks to the African and North African workers' revolutions I've stamped Africa (and Biko) all over every discussion in the university for three months, and now the Africans – the Botswanans, Zimbabweans, South Africans, Ugandans, Nigerians – are very much fortified in confidence coming forward. And – a nice little bonus for you – I have printed off some of your articles from *Refutations* and they are being passed hand-to-hand.

Did you hear? We had a meeting last night, and I made the piece on the arrests in Bulawayo you wrote background reading. One cleaner said he was 'unable to put it down'! He lives in a house of South Africans. He has even heard of Nelson. And now everyone – not just you – knows about Biko.

At this stage, many are just starting to get to grips with the fact that in most of the world a young man can lead the charge against a brutal state by doing what we are all doing, discussing and organising. Africa is teaching the West some necessary truths and helping the West to finally grow up and become a political adult in both positive senses: revolutions, and the necessary downside, the horror of what Whitehall, Washington, Brussels have done in Africa for centuries. This is LONG overdue.

I have never been anywhere else but HERE, comrade. I am with you. In the STRUGGLE. THEY tried to silence ME! The fools, the fools! Three states tried to silence, torture and deport me and failed! Though Mugabe came close. And I'm still organising, laughing, loving it. I love Biko without having seen him for several years, because he is Lenin, Luxemburg, Spartacus, Lumumba, Cabral, he is all of them and more! We will free him.

'I am Biko.' I teach everyone here to say it. It's still a bit new to them – I tell them to watch the quite excellent *Spartacus* film, but to replace the name Spartacus with Biko. 'I'm Biko!' 'No, I'm Biko!' Arrests are nothing new to us, beatings were our bread and butter, so know you are not alone. We are fighting here to support the campaign that you are leading.

Take care my friend. I'M BIKO. WE WANT CAIRO IN HARARE! CAIRO IN HARARE! CAIRO TO HARARE! HARARE WILL BE CAIRO! MU-GABE-MU-BARAK, MU-GABE-MU-BARAK! BIKO WILL START IT ALL.

Once we have let Anne-Marie loose on X-Party, the prisons will open.

Sala kakuhle!

Tendai

*

Every time Biko, in his steady student English, tried to take hold of the cell, Hopewell fought with the same refrain: 'You

354

are a boy. What d'you know about life? What's more, you're Ndebele. *Uri kundinzwa here? Takakukundai. Takauraya vana mukoma venyu nana tete.* We defeated you. Killed your brothers and sisters.'

'Tribalism,' Biko spat back. 'None of your thoughts, brother, are yours. Your brain is a sodden, alcoholic mess. You speak as you've been taught. You are ZANU shit, ZANU meat. You have nothing to say. You should be on the other side of this door with our jailors, the police, the dictators. You are a dog.'

When his strength returned, Biko tried to shepherd the cell into self-activity: action to keep their souls together and raise Hopewell's lumpen peasant consciousness. If it meant the war would have to be defended with force when persuasion failed, then Biko would hammer their ignorant heads against the cell walls. Hopewell blustered on for a week, sat stubborn and dejected on his folded blanket trying not to listen to Biko's sermons, hour after goddamn hour, until he saw it was easier to follow Samuel and Biko as they crafted the day into a coherent, bearable whole.

Biko became their teacher. He had a constant euphoria and energy, a pounding, ceaseless rage at everything: the Marange diamond fields, ZANU and MDC corruption, business, the position of women and gays. An answer for everything. No matter the subject, he could readily link it back to the system, the whole.

'Try me,' Biko boasted, standing in the middle of the cell, his arms akimbo.

'Okay,' Hopewell said, twenty-one days in. He was beginning to accept Biko's benign dictatorship, his leadership by hope. 'The gays. I am against the gays. It's unnatural, against God. A Western import. They don't belong in Zimbabwe.'

'Easy!' Biko cried, leaping onto the concrete bed, his eyes glistening. 'There has been homosexuality in Zimbabwe for as long as we have been fucking and loving. As long as we've been human. Which is many thousands of millennia longer than Europe. The Inanke caves of the Matobo Hills have illustrations, drawings of men on men, hand in hand, lovers, chiefs, elders. Our early societies – before even Great Zimbabwe existed – were run by homosexuals. We exported homosexuality to Europe. Mugabe is anti-gay because he has been influenced by European Catholicism, by modern, imported Christianity. Jesus was a working-class Jewish homosexual. Get it?'

'Shameful,' Hopewell replied meekly, more a dying heckle than a challenge. He let out a sigh of resignation: another brick prised from his foothold on life and meaning.

Biko continued, breathless. 'Mugabe is terrified we'll see the charade. The divisions between us are the only thing holding him in place, holding ZANU together. Poor against poor. Ndebele against Shona. Landless war veteran against landless street seller. Gay against straight. Don't be Mugabe's fool any more, comrade.'

The cell filled with Biko's circling, swirling arms, his booming oration and exuberance. His final words were thrown into the air, hitting the walls, crashing against the iron door like lead weights. But the prison was never forgotten. No fields of clover grew over the walls. The prison did not fall away with Biko's explanations – though, slowly, Biko's strange reasoning did begin to illuminate for Hopewell and Samuel why the prison was here, how their arrests and beatings – these seemingly irrelevant and arbitrary acts, the operations of a violent force in a Southern African police station – were at the centre of the world, connected to everything else.

'What has happened to us, comrades?' Biko spoke more calmly, more patiently than normal. 'The insignificant brawls and illegal hawking, my beatings and arrest, are at the centre of things. Linked. Samuel sold vegetables in the high street because two years ago he lost his printing job. Hopewell has always drunk too much – Hopewell *chidhakwa* – but now he does nothing else. He's been jobless for ten years. Ten *years*, comrade. There is not enough to eat because someone is eating our share. We have to seize our brief life before we are thrown back into darkness. This, comrades, is our one chance to live, and we must turn our bodies to the blinding light and make our own destiny. *Ita zvinokupa upenyu kwete zvana Mugabe izvi.*'

Biko's captive audience only vaguely understood.

'Light!' Hopewell screamed when Biko had finished. 'Life!' The lecture, audible outside their cell, sounded familiar to him, like the preachers he had heard before, the church services he'd attended when he had tried to sober up.

Sanguine, uncertain, Samuel shook his head. 'You've lost me, brother.'

'No, together,' Biko ordered, 'we need to take back our light; we have nothing else, no other choice. We must pull our lives, our land, our wealth into the light. This will require a struggle, a grip of iron, like this.' Biko leant forward to the men, grabbed the blankets under them and pulled. Then, holding up the dirt-stained covers in both hands, he shouted, 'Our wealth, our life, into the light, before the night, before the power goes and we are thrown again into darkness!'

Samuel shook his head. The boy was possessed; he would be killed if he carried on like this, even if he had a point. Who did he mean? Them? The light before night, when the bulb shone above them in the cell? Did he mean the power cuts since 2000? The load-shedding?

'After me, brothers,' Biko continued, 'comrades, into the light.'

Hopewell joined Biko, stood next to him; he shouted, his two fists in the air and his heart racing, 'Into the light!' Then they all shouted, Samuel slowly raising himself, rolling his eyes, 'Into the light!' Finally, Biko shouted 'Life!' and the others copied him in a chorus. 'Light, light, light! Life, life, life!' Eventually they were all shouting, creating a great rhythm, hammering with their flat hands on the walls, the door: 'Light! Light! Light!'

Chapter Twenty-Nine

Since his return from Bulawayo Viktor thought that he could simply do nothing for anyone, for his daughter in Bristol, for these new comrades in Zimbabwe. He carried in him some sort of curse. At last the equation was straightforward: he was simply no good. *Good for nothing*, in his father's rough judgement about people. In Isaac's precise dictionary he was simply a schmuck, a putz, a yutz.

Anne-Marie had reacted not with the fury he'd expected, but with disappointment. 'Are you really so stupid, Viktor? Did you think the police would say, yes, of course, white man, here are your friends? That all you had to do was ask to see the station chief? This is a dictatorship, not a restaurant, *mudiwa*. The old man does not care about your white skin.' Her anger she reserved for Biko, for his carelessness. 'Biko is a bloody fool! A bloody pavement café, *mon Dieu* ...'

'I should have insisted we go home, or sat inside. I shouldn't have tried to—'

She dismissed him with a wave of her hand. 'No. Not your fault. You don't know Zimbabwe. No, no, this is Biko, Biko,

Biko!' She shouted the last *Biko* and stamped her foot. 'Biko might be the heart of the Society, but Nelson is its brains.'

'That's not true. Biko has a brilliant theoretical mind, a formidable intellect.'

'That's not what I mean. He doesn't *think*, he just leaps into action. No wonder you like him. You think and never act, he acts and never thinks. You're a perfect fucking pair, *mudiwa*.'

She had paced the room, a difficult feat amid the clutter, then ignored Viktor as she called Nelson to strategise, to find out who could go out to the village and talk to Biko's family. Viktor sat near the window, miserable, tweeting.

@viktorisaacs International solidarity for #Zimbabwe student activist arrested, beaten for dissent. Petition: bit. ly/325235 ... #FreeBiko #Bulawayo6

Now these thoughts came to him in the early morning when the day was not yet in colour, only beginning to break; the long hours of waking life confronting him, opening out before him. *I am a schmuck*, he would think. *Maybe my assemblage of character traits is just no damn good. I am not a nice person. I am a calculating, scheming, hesitant meshugener.*

One week later he heard that Biko was still being held and there was no date for his case, but that the others, the Bulawayo Six, had been released. When Y-Party refused all pleading he organised, phoned, raised funds on the internet – the one thing, even in his despair, he knew he could do. *The armchair and the internet*, he muttered, over another coffee at Louis's, bent over his splattered and finger-worn laptop. He felt he had caused it all: Biko's arrest, his daughter's missing, all caused by his blundering.

Somehow Anne-Marie managed to chase these chattering, corrosive thoughts from his early mornings. Perhaps it was her hot, soft body next to his, how she clung on in the night, called to him, her voice stripped of all straining, when he paced the flat at night, sat on the balcony and listened to distant TVs and crickets chirping loudly for partners. 'Viktor, darling, come back to bed.' But now he burrowed and questioned in broad daylight. Somehow the sun could no longer burn the thoughts away after they had formed.

*

As Viktor fought to free Biko, imperceptibly Louis became the campaign's accountant. He allowed his UK bank account to be used for donations, made the transfers, secreted resources in US dollars through Zambia. He transported money on his trucks across the border, then ran payments to Biko's family. He worked on connections he had in the police, bribing officials, pressuring Bulawayo politicians and paying lawyers' fees into foreign accounts. Louis maintained the whole underground effort, the complex tributary of connections and contacts that was essential to make Zimbabwe move.

Occasionally he would pull up a chair next to Viktor, who was usually working, campaigning on his laptop, and confer. 'Vik, there is a contact who thinks he can get some money to the guards in Chikurubi – I have worked with him before, he is reliable. We have also got your man into his own cell with only two other prisoners.' Breaking momentarily, he shouted an order at an old man who had taken his place by the coffee machine. 'Goodwill, for God's sake, how often do I need to tell you? Do not lean on the bloody machine!' Muttering 'fool', he turned back to Viktor. 'They also tell me that your man is okay.'

Viktor was unresponsive. The effort of criticism – the constant, necessary challenge to everything in Louis's world – was too much. 'What is it, Vik?' Louis probed.

'I just don't know if any of this will make a difference,' Viktor answered. 'What difference does it make if he is in his own cell or not? If you can bribe an official here and there? How do we know if your contact even knows what's happening? The truth is, we know nothing.'

Louis bunched forward, leant on the table, tilting it towards him. 'Vik, listen, if he was crowded in one of the main holding cells with three hundred other men and he was injured, he would already be dead. Dead. He wouldn't last a week.'

Viktor appreciated the exaggeration, the statement made to jolt him out of himself, break the decay of his thinking – he needed these extremes of pronouncement.

Towards Viktor, Louis was sincere; he could let his love flow without holding back or filtering in some prejudice. Viktor wished he did not feel the weight of gratitude or have to extend himself emotionally, to reach back in appreciation and enter into a complicated friendship of uneven exchange.

Viktor saw a ruthless honesty in Louis's relationship with Zimbabweans. There was no untruth, no farce of shared experience or connection. In daily conversations with security guards, taxi drivers and hawkers, Viktor engaged in a complicated game. His effort to see (and be seen) by the poor always descended into a travesty of smiles, fake bonhomie and mutual incomprehension – interests and desires that could never be shared. Louis, on the other hand, had realised that he could never be a friend to the hungry, so he did not try.

Louis gave Viktor the same services he rendered to the campaign: he sourced US dollars at a UK exchange rate and provided water filters and food from his own home. Vicki and Louis packaged moussaka and souvlaki, tzatziki and taramasalata in Tupperware tubs. Every few weeks Viktor received packages, bundled up behind the counter and passed to him like contraband after a morning in the café: jams, pickles, clothes, imported cereals, foreign newspapers. And to Viktor's surprise, Vicki and Louis accepted Anne-Marie without hesitation and treated her with the same generosity they bestowed on Viktor.

*

Nina sent Viktor emails, text messages, news posts. Anger that seemed to him pitiless, unending. He stood up to the fury, puffed out his chest and took it, absorbed the gusts of rage. But each time he received a message or an email, like a dart aimed for his heart, he was diminished. Weakened. His life shortened – how much can our soft, permeable bodies take? How much could he give?

At Anne-Marie's flat, or in Louis's café, a cup of strong coffee next to his laptop, the saucer a lid sealing in the heat. His fingers spread across the base of the cup, stroking, petting the coffee as he waited for the screen to load, the icons to flicker into life. Viktor would open his email, sucking on the air, looking around the café at Louis to see if he was being watched – worried that the people near him would peer into his screen and see the chaos, the tragic mess of his desktop, and see that he was a man of failure, a farce.

He told stories to strangers, taxi drivers, other customers, that he was married and had children – he doubled his failure with Rosa and created an entirely fresh fiction, that he had two girls. Two children. 'It is so hard being away from them.

My little girls. My wife is long-suffering, but I am working in Zimbabwe for several months – what can I do?'

Hurried lies about the man he was, that he would never be. 'I am a father of two. They are the apple of my eye. My wife is in London. I send money home.' He would then show photos, if he was really going for it, even pass photos around – two images of Rosa, at two and six, his two girls – and receive a sweet charade. 'She looks like you. The female version, of course. It must be hard, so hard, to be away.' Viktor was showered in sympathy and in the clatter of compliments, the noisy nothings, he became, he imagined, more human. Even in the decay and mayhem of Zimbabwe, stripped of aberration and absurdity, he felt the need to be accepted.

'Ladies and gentlemen,' Viktor imagined himself announcing, bowing, 'allow me to introduce you to my two daughters, Rosa and Carla. I pick them up from school. I work tirelessly to provide. I would do anything for them. Such is my love – the love of a father for his family. I am a proud, simple man. An ox. A donkey. My wife cooks our meals. I provide. You see, all of you, I am a father, I am you. I have learnt my lessons well. I obey. I bow down. I marry. I reproduce. I suffer. I love.'

Sliding the makeshift lid off the coffee, Viktor lifted the cup, still steaming, to his lips, his glasses fogged, and he sipped, pulling the froth through his teeth. The coffee slipped down his throat and worked quickly on him. His mouse hovered over the email from Nina; his heart hammered, beat to be let out of his chest so it could have its say. The email was headed *Lies*. Viktor closed his eyes briefly, tipped more coffee into his mouth, then opened his eyes and read:

Viktor, you have taught Rosa how to make excuses – or to lie. I am trying to teach her to be scrupulously honest and open. You have corrupted our daughter and started to turn her into a dishonest and deceitful girl, in a word like you, like her father. I will not allow this to happen. I wish you peace, balance and harmony. N

On other days the messages were even more truncated, cryptic, mythical – prophesying doom, promising alignment with the planets, cosmic synchronisation, a route through life's celestial ley lines. Contradictory, competing, ridiculous, the messages kept coming – vindictive, at peace, furious, in perfect balance, offering love, reconciliation, everything, nothing:

Viktor, your photo is on my altar, forming part of the Circle of Perpetual Life. I am proud of our five years together, with all of its challenges, and I will be proud, I am sure, once more, of our friendship. I burn incense every night to cleanse our energy, to free you, to be free. N

Two days later:

Viktor, you are emotionally unavailable. I see from Facebook what you have been doing in Zimbabwe. Everywhere you go you ruin everything you touch, or come close to. And now you are giving yourself to the campaign to save someone, who, from what I can gather, you were responsible for putting in prison in the first place. Your life is a disaster. You do not deserve the love of your daughter. I have removed your photo from the altar. N

A week afterwards peace and balance had returned, cosmic equilibrium – though the natural state of the universe was violent, unequal and indifferent. Nina sent Viktor his weekly horoscope:

This week gets you back down to earth and into balance. Libra, you must slow down to allow for more cultivation of beauty and peace of mind. You have five planets in retrograde and this undeniable energy demands you slow down. The extreme energy of this alignment is confusing. Your ability to think clearly, with certainty, to the people near you, is impaired. In terms of making radical changes and releasing stubborn attachment you must exercise extreme caution. You must be honest about your feelings without resorting to passive aggression. Move forward cautiously, with prudence.

Lucky Days: Tuesday and Thursday
Unlucky Days: Friday and Saturday
Colour of Affirmation: Amber

Tired, worn, his temples aching, his stomach unsettled, Viktor stared at the email, read and reread the message, searched for the meaning. Why must the truth always be hidden, why must it require such a ceaseless struggle, why did life only yield to blood and sweat? He felt his stomach turn. He wanted to settle, find peace, a steady, non-fatiguing climb. Most of all, he wanted a place to stand that didn't tilt and give way. He wanted to feel the comfort of the ground and be sure of his own foundation. Nina's claim on him, on his life, seemed to threaten each foothold he found in the present. But the present seemed to be determined by the ruin and heartbreak of the past.

*

Anne-Marie had invited Viktor to attend a ceremony and drinks at Meikles Hotel on Nelson Mandela Avenue and they had argued – briefly, concisely. 'You want to know Zimbabwe, then come with me. Meet the NGO community, see what we do, meet my colleagues. Viktor, I need you to see what I do.' They were having the conversation in the morning, six weeks after Viktor had returned from Bulawayo, six weeks since the start of the campaign for Biko's release. Anne-Marie sat on the edge of the bed, blindly pulling on her shoes, then standing over her skirt, squatting, finding the hem and pulling it up over her calves and thighs, twisting and turning in her morning dance.

'It's only a question of time. I have limited time and at the end of the day I feel the dread of what I haven't done. The calls, the emails. I need every waking minute for the campaign – without distraction.' Viktor propped himself up on two pillows and let the sheet fall from his torso. His answer was not honest; he did not want to go. He did not want to see Anne-Marie in her industry. He had already seen too much. The large estates in the north of the city vacated by Zimbabwe's white community, the opulent lawns, the sounds of children splashing in private swimming pools, the fleet of new vehicles – the obscenity of privilege in this city of the walking dead. Whole neighbourhoods filled with the foreign staff of international NGOs. He couldn't go, he wouldn't be able to hold the contradiction.

'Rubbish. You can spare an evening.' Anne-Marie hooked her bra over her arms, fastened it, then slid it into place. She pulled the curtains open. The room broke into light and she squinted.

'You are not being honest. You don't want to come because you feel embarrassed about the work I do. True?' She kicked a pile of her clothes on the floor, trying to find her shirt.

Viktor shielded his eyes from the light – somehow the sun was never tiresome, never an irritation, it always lifted him. He felt a second's wonderment when everything seemed newly foreign and unknown to him. He revelled in these moments

– this sense of playing a part and not having to be himself. 'True,' he answered.

'I am insulted. First, you don't see my own criticism of the NGOs – which, you will admit, is a little more empirical than yours. Second, you are refusing an invitation into my world. That's crap, Viktor.'

Viktor didn't respond. It was difficult to make a decision in the bright starkness of the room. His head was crowded with noises: Anne-Marie as she pulled her pale blue shirt over her shoulders and then bent to reach her shoes, the distant sound of traffic, the scraping of feet on the concrete floors in the communal corridors. He knew the question but couldn't formulate an answer.

'Okay,' he said finally, 'you're right. Let's go.' *Of course I should go*, he thought instantly after he had spoken. *How fucking stubborn of me to resist.*

*

The hotel was an aberration. Meikles shone in the night that fell early in Harare. Lights were cast over every surface of the hotel – the great arch, the huge doorway, the driveway that led up from the main road, the trees wrapped in coils of tiny illuminations, the lawns glittering with white fairy lights. The hotel had been rebuilt in the great wave of foreign investment in the nineties, with the execution of the first austerity and adjustment programme. ZANU-PF – the party of the African renaissance and land reform – had pushed through the structural reforms with breathless impatience. The new commandments had come out easily: 'Comrades, in the next stage of the liberation struggle it is our duty to create the best circumstances for direct foreign investment. Brothers and sisters, fellow Zimbabweans, President-Comrade-the-Right-Honourable-Robert-Gabriel-Mugabe has said we all need to make sacrifices.' So, in the name of the people, the second wave of liberation saw an inundation of suffering as hospitals and health centres were closed, universities and colleges were starved of funding and food subsidies were scrapped. The people did not suffer; they died. But Harare *did* experience a building boom of hotels, shopping malls, multiplex cinemas and takeaway outlets, and, after 1994, freed from the burden of apartheid, South African businesses hurried north.

Anne-Marie drove, her mood positive. She played the one failing cassette on her car stereo over and over again – the words came out loudly: *Ngaï na bugui nzéla, Po' bo tikaki ngaï mosika,Yango na komaki sé mitélengano, Koko lakisa ngaï nzéla.* I lost my way, Because you left me behind, That's why I wandered aimlessly, Grandfather show me the way. The voice crackled out of the speakers, high and unbearably sad. Viktor, who had asked for a translation, didn't understand why it was the only song she sang along to or why it made her so cheerful. Anne-Marie turned carefully into Nelson Mandela Avenue, which ran along the high walls of the hotel. Cars swerved round her; drivers shouted for her to speed up and sounded their horns.

Viktor saw on the wall the faded words of the government's old commitment to austerity and adjustment – *You must work, work again, work more, always work.* Involuntarily he shouted, hit the dashboard, fumbled to find the volume on the cassette player. 'Look, Anne-Marie!' He turned to the window, then back to her as the car passed the faded words: 'I have read about ZANU's campaign to sell structural adjustment. Can you see it? Those words. The party of African socialism telling the poor to work harder, to do nothing but work. This, this was the gospel of economic adjustment across the continent, sacrifice and hard work. Disgusting.'

They had pulled up behind a queue of vehicles turning into the hotel. Anne-Marie breathed in, felt the air inflate her lungs. 'Viktor,' she said, her voice tight and controlled, 'when I am listening to Papa Wemba, do not touch the volume. *D'accord?*' She wanted the evening to be normal and their conversation to be straightforward for once, without incident. *Why is he explaining this to me?* she thought. *I know the history better than he does.* She needed them to just dwell in the ridiculous festivities, the food, the absurdity of her work, and for one night suspend the critique. Just one evening free of commentary – that's what she wanted. To live in this world, occasionally we need to suspend it.

'Indulge me tonight, Viktor – just suck it in, take mental notes and tomorrow we will digest together. Do you think I am happy with all of this?' She raised her hands momentarily from the steering wheel. 'No. But I need to take a break sometimes. It's a comedy show. Treat the evening like a comedy show. Try to enjoy it. Enjoyment is the project for this evening.' The car passed the gates of the hotel, the wheels spat up the gravel drive – she handled the car in irritation. She saw a bay ahead and drove quickly, accelerating past a low-hung Land Cruiser full of suited white men. She swung the Golf quickly and veered in fast, right across their path and into the space.

The evening gala was a celebration of Zimbabwe's teeming NGO sector and a minor challenge to the government. ZANU had been claiming that the huge funds pouring into the country's NGOs – US$850 million had been the last stated figure – were meant for anti-government activities. The United States Agency for International Development played the leading role in this plot: Western aid workers, country heads, were stooges in a nefarious plot to unseat the radical reforms of the government. Just that morning, a party intellectual from the University of Zimbabwe had stated bombastically in the government paper, 'The international community of thieves and criminals will receive a cruel awakening to the futility of their attempts to destabilise our radical government. The regime change agenda has collapsed a long time ago and its failure is the result of the choices the people of Zimbabwe made to have Mugabe, the God-given leader, elected. No other leader in the Southern Hemisphere is so universally accepted and applauded by his people.'

Viktor had read the article to Anne-Marie that morning as she crashed through the kitchen, grabbing a plate from the sink, pouring herself juice. He had laughed at the article, jeering at its coarseness, the hyperbole and overstatement. 'They are right,' Anne-Marie had replied. She elbowed the bedroom door open, leant on the frame, plate in hand, eating a piece of bread layered thickly with peanut butter. 'ZANU is right. NGOs were using funds to effect regime change, or trying to. From the moment of George Bush and Tony Blair, the West wanted to get rid of the government, and the NGOs were one way they could siphon funds to projects aimed at destabilising the regime. I have seen the money *and* the documents.'

'So you are basically a stooge, as X-Party claims, for regime change,' Viktor had said, smiling.

Chewing slowly on her crust, Anne-Marie had nodded. 'Basically.' Then, laughing, 'One microloan at a time. My rural women couldn't give a fuck about Mugabe or regime change.' Then, swallowing, clearing her mouth, she had said, 'It was never an effective strategy, and the West was never consistent. They used some of the money to train activists in the early days, but soon the money did what money does – enriched a class of local and international NGO bosses. Zimbabwe is not important enough. We don't sit on oil or occupy land in the Middle East. Casting Zimbabwe into the lunatic periphery of the solar system has helped save the regime.'

Viktor came round the car and took Anne-Marie's hand, and the couple walked slowly together towards the shimmering entrance. Officially, the evening was a celebration of the years of cooperation and partnerships between local and international NGOs. Appropriately, therefore, the banner pegged to two giant stakes in the garden read, 'Zimbabwe's Voluntary Forum: Twenty-Five Years of Cooperation and Development'. Viktor held his tongue, fighting the urge to mock, laugh, analyse.

The gardens that stretched around the hotel came to life at night. There was a cacophony of frogs, lizards, crickets – each struggling for survival against the other, courting, fucking, killing (Viktor wondered if it was in that order). There seemed to be a thousand voices screaming for attention.

Anne-Marie handed the card invitation to the porter, who nodded and lowered his head. They moved into the hotel, a sweep of halls, a mahogany reception desk, polished tiles and a crystal chandelier blossoming high in the vaulted ceiling. Even here, the city beyond the perimeter wall and gardens could not be silenced – there was the sound of the streets, screeching tyres, motorbikes.

Viktor couldn't help it: he basked in the might and opulence of the room, turned his face up to the chandelier and felt its heat on his face. *It is drying me like the sun*, he thought. Anne-Marie pulled him to, jerked him back. The room was packed, the partygoers young, evenly white and black. Behind the crowds were waiters, some holding champagne bottles, others with silver trays and food. Through the lobby was a large terrace,

372

the swimming pool and more guests, men in suits, women in evening gowns.

Anne-Marie wore her own strapless gown in a metallic silver charmeuse, the bodice hugging her curves to just above her knee, then giving way to a flared skirt with a bouquet of silver roses at one side – a glamorous retro-Hollywood look which she'd finished with a simple rhinestone necklace and red lipstick. When she'd hauled it out of a closet and tried it on in the bedroom the night before the gala, Viktor had closed the zipper for her – it was a little too tight and Anne-Marie had to hold her arms up, cursing quietly. Once it was secured, she had sashayed a little, enjoying her effect on Viktor, who was too flustered and aroused to come up with a proper compliment. In a panic, Viktor had asked Louis in the morning what he should do; miraculously, after a call, a shouted order, a tuxedo was summoned up, arriving, laundered, on a wire hanger in a see-through plastic wrapper. Together they looked different, unusual, and in this lavish setting entirely appropriate.

Competing with the faint, distant sounds of traffic, the low drone of insects and amphibians, was a group of musicians sitting in a semicircle, playing Mozart's Haydn Quartets. Viktor wanted to rush into the garden and speak to the musicians – ask them, tell them, *Did you know what Haydn said to Mozart's father? 'Before God, and as an honest man, I tell you that your son is the greatest composer known to me.'* And from Mozart's father, Viktor's mind ran to his daughter – with the frenzy of conversation around him, he remembered all of a sudden the summer he had bought a bicycle and fastened on a child's seat so they could ride around in the morning, singing songs about eating baddies and playing in the swimming pool. Viktor held on tightly to Anne-Marie, the sweat breaking, puckering up on his skin. *Why did I ever stop doing that?* He remembered how Rosa smelt, her sweet, sticky skin next to him, her clutching, adamant embraces. How he had slipped seamlessly into her private monologues. 'Daddy,' she would say, 'can carry two persons. So can Mummy. Daddy loves Rosa.'

Anne-Marie tugged hard at his hand. In the distance, by the doors to the terrace, there was a white couple waving at them. There were American accents; Anne-Marie could hear French. The air whirred and spun with satisfaction. Anne-Marie drew Viktor towards her. 'Look around you,' she snorted. 'These Westerners, the kids, come in dumb and at the end of their tour leave even dumber. Care, Century Agriculture, Hands On – if their missions are less than three months, their foreign staff stay here – look around – they stay *here*.' Her hot breath on his cheek felt comforting.

As they moved slowly through the cocktails, the reception, there were nods and smiles thrown at them; a sort of mocking admiration, Anne-Marie imagined, at the sight of this mixed-race couple. Quietly, she continued to brief Viktor. 'This is Tim and Andy, that is Andrea, from Australia. They work for the competition, Century Agriculture. They are good, better than the others. Now you have to understand the big discrepancies between NGO expats and local workers – it's key.' Anne-Marie was talking quickly, expertly acknowledging her colleagues. They passed a large table of food, plates of red meats, cheeses, crackers, olives. 'The expats earn tax-free salaries in US dollars and live in free accommodation – you have seen the places. They have two accounts, two salaries, one they don't touch in the States or the UK or France and another paid locally for all of their in-country expenses. Now, the locals' – she looked up at Viktor, winked, and pointed a finger to her chest – 'do the grunt work in the rural areas and clear a fraction of the salary.' Viktor was listening attentively. They were now only a few paces from the terrace. 'Mugabe's diatribes against NGOs have given certain protection for local African workers against excessive abuses.'

'My god, *mudiwa*, you sound like an X-Party hack again.' Viktor laughed and put his arm around her shoulder. Tim, an oversized Australian, almost Viktor's height but broad and heavy, smiled and leant down to kiss Anne-Marie. Andy, his partner, put her arms out and touched Viktor's side, her high forehead rising with her smile.

'Rock forward, kids. Isn't this wild?' Tim spoke loudly, his voice bouncing. Anne-Marie made the introductions and turned to present Viktor.

'I'm going to come right over there and give that lovely tall guy on your arm a hug.' Tim passed his glass to Andy, stepped forward and put his arms around Viktor.

'Tim and Andy,' Anne-Marie spoke, amused at Tim's ebullience, 'work shooting short documentaries for Century Agriculture. Since the late nineties they haven't been able to return to Australia. Am I right? They prefer our poverty and misery.'

Viktor looked at Anne-Marie, shocked, pleased – he liked her directness. Andy continued the narrative, speaking quietly. 'It's true. We have never been able to settle in Oz.' Her forehead creased as she spoke. 'After a stint in Thailand and now Southern Africa, we can never go back.'

The couples chatted. Tim and Andy had been together for ten years. Tim shot films in rural schools transformed by the good offices of Century Agriculture, then Andy edited them. On the side – *to deepen their impact* – they sold photographic stills and artwork of poor rural children in Melbourne studios and art galleries. 'Then, once we are back in-country, we have ceremonies – this is nothing to do with any of this.' Tim spoke conspiratorially, waving his hand, rubbing out the gathering. 'At these ceremonies we present the children with an envelope of money for the art we sold in Oz. So the kids get an idea of art as fun,' he paused, letting the words infiltrate his listeners, 'and also a potential income. A way out of their poverty. These people' – another wave of the hand – 'wouldn't get it. But I know you two radicals do.'

Viktor nodded his head and spoke calmly. 'So you sell poverty porn to wealthy Australians to hang next to their Aboriginal art, and give lessons in free enterprise to Zimbabwe's rural children. That sounds like Mugabe's entrepreneurship and business acumen. Congratulations. Don't you think it's exploitative?'

He delivered the line straight, poker-faced. Tim, Andy and Anne-Marie paused for an instant, then burst into laughter. Anne-Marie's was loud – she shook her head slowly. 'Yes,' she said, pleased. 'Exploitative and paternalistic.'

'Excellent,' Andy said. 'Like Mugabe! Very funny.' They all laughed again.

The quartet had stopped playing and a stocky, thick man in a suit had come up to the microphone and started to speak. His tone was warm, familiar. There was movement around the two couples as other guests made their way onto the terrace.

Andy took Anne-Marie's arm, pulling her aside. 'I need to speak to you alone, can we have a quick chat?'

The women moved a few paces to the side, Viktor emptied the rest of his glass and looked around for a refill. Tim waved manically to a waiter moving between the guests with a bottle and indicated Viktor's empty glass. 'A refill for this pisshead!' He laughed loudly.

Tim stepped closer to Viktor. He had a lot of thinning black hair, tightly curled and oily. He wanted to speak, to let it out, make Viktor understand the tension. 'You have to understand us – we think this is all a joke. We've saved thirty-eight thousand dollars, which we won't even touch, but it allows us to do what we want, to say what we want. We could live comfortably on it for five years here. If we decide to settle here we'll probably choose Mutare. Ideally we are looking at a place in Melbourne *and* one in Zimbabwe, eventually even Chiang Mai. This, these parties, the NGO jungle, it's not our game.'

Viktor found it hard to concentrate. Through the terrace doors he saw the man gesticulating in front of the microphone, the crowd nodding, agreeing. The man raised his glass and his black jacket sleeves rose high on his arms. 'A toast, then, friends,' he was saying, 'to the tireless and thankless work we do.'

Tim continued: 'The bottom line is this: we've got some investments, some capital from our families and lots of doors are beginning to open. We need freedom, the ability to do what we want.' Innocently, confused, Viktor asked, 'But why, Tim, do you want investments? Are you going into business?'

Tim straightened, tilted his head back and let out a single loud laugh. The guests around them turned and looked. 'You've got it. You're a real Englishman. The accent, the expressions. The English manners, the direct way of speaking.' He looked furtively around him, saw Anne-Marie and Andy speaking a few metres away from them. 'The bottom line is, you could go far here, we could do a lot together.' Viktor's head started to swim again. He felt himself slipping – his glass had been filled again. He looked towards Anne-Marie. She saw him, rolled her eyes, blew a kiss.

Tim had taken his arm. Viktor saw his forearm tense, the muscles ripple. 'You can't always see it, but we are lucky men. Look at them, they both have a really nice feminine quality.'

377

He pointed his head to their partners. In case Viktor had not understood, was still adrift, he clarified loudly, 'Our women, Anne-Marie and Andy. We are lucky, Viktor. Look at the attention they are getting.'

Viktor was both flattered and disgusted. What was this man saying? What did he mean? Yet he felt a strange connection – this was a man, strong, proper, undoubting, who was seeking an alliance and a belonging with him. Viktor thought about what had just been said. *What is it about this environment?* He pulled back his shoulder, sipped his champagne, took in the crowd. *The heat, the power, corrupts the mind and heart of the expat in Africa. Even if they weren't before, they become idiots. This get-rich-quick class incapable of original ideas and inventiveness. They stew and canker in the Third World – their flesh turns in the heat and poverty and they become avid, insatiable, lost.*

'God damn this place,' Viktor said suddenly, aloud.

Tim had put an arm around Viktor's shoulder and held him in place. Anne-Marie and Andy returned to the men. 'We need to go outside for the pantomime,' Anne-Marie said. She took Viktor's hand and squeezed. The two couples tottered onto the terrace, apologising as they pushed through the crowd circling the pool until they could hear the speaker. The clarity of the night, the slight breeze, felt good, like a release.

'Brandon Joseph runs Hands On,' Anne-Marie explained. 'This evening was his initiative. He's a joke.' She spoke roughly, confidently, and Tim and Andy nodded knowingly. There was something unstable and frayed about Anne-Marie's energy. She was impatient – she knew what this evening would be, but had thought that she could introduce Viktor to a few liberal political players who could provide some assistance to Biko and the campaign. Instead, almost as soon as they stepped out of the car, she had become intolerably frustrated with the place:

the platitudes, the lack of any commitment from the people she knew. She had even imagined that Tim and Andy could help, the couple who existed on the fringes of the NGO world, who drank, smoked locally sourced marijuana and listened to African music – but, she realised, even this had been an illusion. And now she was drunk and pissed off. Andy's private conversation with her had been to fucking gossip and complain about Tim's womanising. She had felt herself beginning to regret everything: the evening, the calamity, her work. These friends.

Their anger moved in different directions. Viktor tended to fall in, to become entangled in his neuroses, while Anne-Marie's drew her out of herself and became clear and sharp. Both couples were drunk; their glasses had been refilled too often. Anne-Marie was beginning to burst – outside she breathed in deeply.

She looked around her and saw faces she recognised. Automatically she smiled and mouthed hellos. She saw a man and a woman she had seen in her offices several times, always impeccably dressed, clean and untouched. The woman's porcelain-cream face, her delicate nose, were in profile; the man, carefully unshaven and mannered. They were talking quietly to themselves and didn't want to be heard, but Anne-Marie could just make out the conversation. 'Even these meetings,' the man was saying, his head slightly bowed, leaning into his partner, 'are run by illiterate fools just out of the bush and into office jobs.' His accent was a broad South African drawl, the consonants long and drawn out. 'Gumbo is tolerable, but the rest of them are ignorant alcoholics.' The woman's mouth curled up as she laughed quietly.

Anne-Marie turned back to her group, shook her head slightly and tried to focus on the man at the microphone, who raised his voice at odd, inappropriate moments. He was congratulating the crowd, the guests, for being there, for helping Zimbabwe – the word he had used was *saving*. Every few sentences he would stop to sip from his glass, and the audience tittered. 'My first mission in Zimbabwe was in the early eighties, when Hands On was a small organisation of ten run from our Chicago office. The problems we dealt with then are in many ways the same we confront today, only the depth of rural poverty is much greater. But now, my friends, as a consequence, my missions are much longer in Zimbabwe.' A few of the guests turned to each other and nodded knowingly. Brandon joined in, smiled, sipped once more at his champagne. 'I am thinking of asking the president for Zimbabwean nationality, I certainly deserve it.' There was further chuckling.

Anne-Marie suddenly regretted the argument with Viktor in the morning. There had to be some sort of political response to the situation, to this absurdity. She almost had to suppress the desire to shout, to pull Viktor away and run from the hotel and these people. Viktor held her hand tightly. She could see him grinding his teeth, his face pulled tight.

Tim had commandeered an entire bottle of wine and leant noisily across Andy to Viktor and Anne-Marie, refilling their glasses. There were a few sideward glances at the four. Some guests moved slowly away from them.

Brandon put his glass down and held onto the microphone stand. 'Hands On wants to welcome a small dance troupe from a village near Chinhoyi who we have worked with since the early eighties - the School of the Born-Frees, as we used to call it. When I first arrived in the country I worked in the school, which was made up of two old shipping containers and whatever I could scrape and beg from colleagues in the States – a blackboard, chalk, even chairs. Now, I am pleased to say, it is a brick building with classrooms and a playing field.' There was a spontaneous round of applause. As he spoke, the crowd started to part and a line of children, of different heights and ages, hunched in their sky-blue uniforms, moved in single file towards the stage.

'Oh, god,' Anne-Marie said loudly, involuntarily.

Concerned only with guarding the bottle of wine, Tim heard her seconds after she'd spoken, and then said, even more loudly, 'Terrible. What is this, a circus?'

Andy nudged him angrily. 'Respect the children, this is for them. This is their moment.' She stared at Anne-Marie.

Brandon announced that they would now dance, a performance they had prepared entirely by themselves. 'Amazing they can actually teach themselves how to dance,' Viktor whispered to Anne-Marie.

People shuffled away from the makeshift stage and stepped onto the lawn to make room for the children.

Divided into two lines, the children in the first row started to dance while the others stood behind, beating a heavy rhythm on upturned ice-cream cartons and rattling bottles filled with gravel. Brandon stood with them, beaming impossibly, his face broad and ridiculous. Gradually the rhythm sped up, the gyrations of the children became more rigorous, their pelvic thrusts completely unavoidable, impossible not to watch. There could be no mistaking the song. A few children, the older ones, their arms horribly gaunt, mouthed the words as they moved: 'Like a virgin, touched for the very first time ...'

There was complete silence – except from Tim, who in genuine enthusiasm yelled, 'Yeah!' and started to move, running his hand down his chest and stomach.

His face puckered, confused, Viktor looked at Anne-Marie. For a moment he didn't recognise her: her nostrils were swollen, her mouth open, eyes ablaze. Viktor then looked up. The hotel was not just wide, spread out from below, it towered up – he tried to count the floors. The light was faint but he could see lit windows and faces looking out of the floors soaring above him. The building was in poor condition. A few floors above the party there was cracked, crumbling concrete, window frames exposed, shattered panes.

He lowered his head and surveyed the party. Viktor had never seen Anne-Marie like this. He leant in, tried to get her attention. 'Are you okay?'

'No, I am not. Can you believe this? These people.'

'Can you believe this hotel?' Viktor enjoined. 'Look up, it's falling down.'

Anne-Marie swivelled round so she stood with her back to Viktor and followed his finger up the building, to the lit windows. Tilting her head back so it rested on his chest, she said, 'You don't know the story of the *bâtiment*? It was a fully operational hotel a few years ago – Harare's finest. But now it's followed the rest of the neighbourhood. It is populated from the third floor to the twenty-second by elderly whites who used to live in the Avenues and have now moved into the hotel to die. It's cheap and they have no family – none that want them, anyway. *Triste, non?* It is more of a retirement home for *ancien* whites who have nowhere else to go. *Ils sont tous perdus.* They are not allowed on the lower floors or by the pool. They have their own entrance and a private garden.'

'So those are their faces.' Viktor indicated the bodies standing in the windows on distant floors.

'I guess so, watching this ridiculous spectacle for free.'

When they turned back, the song was ending. There was embarrassed applause. The group, with the musicians stepping forward, bowed slowly. Brandon was visibly nervous, his forehead wet. 'From a former pupil, Class of 2011, thank you.'

He brought his hands together, one hand on the microphone; there was more applause.

Anne-Marie was consumed again, her hands on her hips – she had moved closer to the children and away from the group. Holding the wine bottle in one hand, Tim followed her, still moving to the finished song. 'Can you hear what the kids are saying? Can you?' Anne-Marie said when Tim was next to her. 'No, I don't speak Shona,' Tim replied.

Anne-Marie turned quickly to him. 'They are not speaking Shona.' Then she added, 'They are complaining that they haven't eaten.'

The crowd resumed their loquacious insouciance, turned away from the stage. Brandon seemed aware that something needed to be done with the children. There was now another man next to him, a Zimbabwean in an expensive suit, his chest raised, his face clean and bright. They were speaking.

Viktor and Andy walked to Anne-Marie. Tim was drinking directly from the bottle. He explained, 'Anne-Marie has just told me that the hotel manager' – he indicated with his bottle the man speaking to Brandon – 'is a ZANU supporter who runs this hotel and a score of others. He also funds Hands On and is providing the food for this event, this,' correcting himself he added, 'this junket.' Viktor looked around the garden. The crowd on the terrace had thinned a little as guests strolled into the gardens or returned to the lobby for food. The children were looking around, still talking nervously among themselves. There was a small child, about eight, with large, dark eyes. *Rosa*, Viktor thought to himself without hesitation. *That could be Rosa*. His stomach turned. His head was unfocused, muddled.

Viktor recognised Anne-Marie's words in Tim's mouth. 'This is a nasty little NGO carnival.' Then Tim shouted, cupping the sides of his mouth, 'We need to feed those kids.'

The children looked up. It happened quickly. Anne-Marie rushed forward and spoke in Korekore, and in a couple of seconds all of the children were around her.

The commotion was total. Guests in the garden and others inside the hotel looked up and started to shuffle back to the pool, curious to see if there was further entertainment. Brandon and the hotel owner had been trying to funnel the children away from the pool to an entrance at the side of the hotel, where they would be driven away in waiting combis.

Anne-Marie turned and the children followed her, through the open terrace doors. They shouted, 'We want food! We want food!' their confidence growing with each repetition.

When they had finished, Anne-Marie spoke directly to the guests. 'These children tell me that they are hungry and have not been given anything to eat all day. They say they are staying on the floor of a community centre in Highfield, without bedding. They say their school has not been open for six months. These children want food, and I propose we let them have ours.' There was total silence as she spoke. Then she instructed the group around her – speaking to them quickly and fluently – to follow her inside the hotel to eat.

There was now a pageant of cheering and dancing as the children moved towards the hotel, the guests mutely moving aside. Tim grabbed Andy and pulled her with him. Viktor felt his stomach and heart lurch. He skipped after the group. The children, who seemed to have multiplied in number, suddenly had the place. They ran round the pool in flip-flops and bare feet, one child splashing the water with her foot, another jumping on a sun lounger.

Even with the mayhem, several guests thought it was another performance for them; some even started to clap. The hotel owner rushed ahead of them into the hotel, his composure lost, his face flushed and panicked.

Anne-Marie waved to Viktor and shouted for him to hurry. Tim staggered and swayed into the hotel, holding the empty wine bottle. 'Fucking brilliant,' he said. 'We should do this with our kids, Andy!'

The children had circled the tables inside the lobby, grabbing what they wanted: tearing the chicken with their teeth, spitting out the bones, swigging wildly from the carafes of juice, the bottles of water, grabbing handfuls of peanuts, stuffing olives and cheese into their mouths. Between mouthfuls there were more cheers.

Anne-Marie put her arm around Viktor's waist. 'Now follow me,' she ordered, breathlessly, to the children. Half-singing, half-shouting, she began, 'I'm a socialist, I'm a socialist, I'm a socialist. My mother was a kitchen girl, my father was a garden boy and that's why I'm a socialist.' Andy and Tim joined the couple. The song was repeated three times, the children stumbling, struggling to keep up – the whole inharmonious choir of children and adults, shouting, trying to find the tune. When they finally stopped, the smallest child, wearing a torn blue school shirt and no shoes, shouted, 'We are free!'

Andy nudged Anne-Marie. 'We need to get out of here, mate, and get the kids out as well. Come on.' She moved around the food tables and walked quickly in the direction of the reception and exit. The others followed. Tim grabbed two fresh bottles of wine from a box stored under one of the tables. 'Here, Vik, take one of these.'

Filling pockets, emptying plates, packing their mouths again, the children followed them out.

Completely calm again, Anne-Marie turned to Viktor and said, 'Haven't I been telling you, *mudiwa*, that we need action and that liberation must happen now – or not at all?'

Viktor's eyes filled. His long strides propelled the couple forward. There were children running alongside them, two dozen Rosas, he imagined. All his children. *No*, he thought finally, *ours, mine and Anne-Marie's*. He answered her, breathless, 'Is this your idea of the Grand Soirée, comrade?'

There were no ramifications, no aftershocks – however Brandon played it, the evening had to be written off. Hard-nosed and pragmatic, the hotel manager was pleased when the rabble of slum kids and their cheerleaders left the building of their own accord. The other guests dispersed noisily, twittering knowingly to each other that this was typical of the Zimbabwe they all knew so well. Only Anne-Marie felt as if she had broken something that could not be fixed – that she could take no more of these evenings.

Chapter Thirty

Samuel brushed down his trousers, crushing in pincer fingers the lice in his clothes and blanket. 'I can't even smell the cell any more.'

'Habit,' Biko stated.

'I mean, when I first came in I couldn't breathe, the smell of shit was so thick, but I don't notice it any more.' Samuel continued his work, his head bent.

'We're adaptable as a species – we adapt to rapid changes in conditions,' Biko commented.

Hopewell was now on his knees cleaning, according to the schedule scratched onto the wall with a chipped stone. It was his democratic turn to kneel and sweep the floor with his hand, shake and fold the blankets. The other men rested, delousing their clothes.

'If we couldn't adapt, how would we live together in this toilet?' Samuel said.

'Because you and Biko are fucking Ndebele peasants, used to shitting in pit latrines in the open – while I come from a family of city workers. In the township we had separate toilets and concrete floors.'

Biko ignored him. 'We have to be careful. We adjust too quickly to barbarity. Soon a concentration camp can seem normal, hunger, killing your neighbour, dying like these lice.' Biko held up his fingers to illustrate his point, snapping them noisily together. The insect in his fingers split in two and its parts divided and flew into the cell. 'Dying of HIV that no one needs to die of. The cell even seems normal. We are already being snuffed out, in the open prison outside this cell, and we think it's normal, God's will. We accept at our peril, comrades.'

Biko knew Hopewell was dying, quicker than Samuel and him. HIV was a topic they'd tried to avoid – until Biko, with his giant shoes, had crushed this taboo too. Hopewell was sick and the prison guards had taken the pills his wife delivered and sold them. Hopewell's face was pale and hollow, his fatless body meant he couldn't find a comfortable position on the mattress they shared.

Hopewell started to cough – a dry, hacking cough that shook his entire body, as though he was trying to exhume his lungs, regurgitate each of his organs, clear his being of the clogged and diseased furnace. He inhaled deeply between coughs. His chest ached unbearably as the air travelled into his lungs.

Nothing silenced Biko except Hopewell's life rattling precariously in these fits. Biko jumped up from the bed and stepped over Hopewell. The coughing subsided. Hopewell wiped his bloodied lips on his sleeve and fell back on the wall, focused only on recovering his breath, keeping upright. Biko hammered the doors with his fists, his arms working all their strength against the iron door. The metal plate on the door echoed like a kettledrum. The sound filled the corridor, waking the other prisoners, who shouted and cursed.

'You bastards!' Biko howled. 'You are killing him. Give back his pills or contend with me, feel my wrath. Listen to him, he's fucking dying.' Even with the medicine Biko knew it was useless. Unless he was eating properly he wouldn't keep the pills down and he'd continue to lose weight. He'd still die.

'Leave it, Biko,' Hopewell said softly. 'I'm okay.'

'Come on, Biko.' Samuel took one of Hopewell's arms and indicated Biko to the other. Together they hauled him across the few steps to the bed, laid him down and covered him. Hopewell tried to resist, to push the blanket off his body and get up, but the coughing had sapped his reserves of strength. The colour drained from him, dragging his features down, turning his eyes lifeless. The skin on his arms sagged.

Biko and Samuel both felt desperate standing over Hopewell. Hopewell looked up at Biko like a child, expecting a formulation of words, a philosophy that would soothe him, but Biko dropped his gaze and turned his head away.

'Goddamn it, I need to shit again.' Samuel undid his trousers, moved to the open bowl, dropped on the toilet and sighed. Hopewell muttered, 'What does "wrath" mean, Prof?' Each man smiled.

*

In the middle of the week, the stream of virtual solidarity, the social media campaign, gushed forth, breaking the banks, flooding the fields in the distance, rushing unstoppable over the great citadels of real power in London and Harare. #FreeBiko was trending all over the world. Viktor felt elated. The walk from the flat to town was pleasing. Viktor strolled with a noticeable spring in his step. It might have been a disaster that had drawn him in, but now he was in his element, his towering, unconquerable best. He swung his arms, felt his lean muscles, tensed his chest, breathed deeply into all of his outstretched limbs. He thought that this must be what it feels like to be a man. A whirlwind of temporary euphoria surged through him and gave him – a man unaccustomed to feelings of confidence – a slightly odd appearance: his loose limbs now tense, his ambling, habitual doubt given direction and focus. He walked Harare's streets like a cowboy, a lunatic on a dangerous high, wanting to be shot. Daring the bullet.

Once the coffee was ordered, his feet planted correctly on the floor, he opened his laptop, fired it up, connected to Louis's fast, password-locked Wi-Fi connection. He opened the browser, sat back, his shoulders opened wide, and looked around, made eye contact with the customers he knew and smiled. His Facebook page, commandeered for the campaign, buzzed pleasingly: 270 notifications. He took a gulp of coffee. His eyes fell immediately on *Nina Thompson commented on your wall*. Viktor slumped forward, his form bracketing the computer. He wetted his mouth and opened the post. Nina had written:

> Trigger Warning: Imposter Alert. Viktor Isaacs is a liar and a fake. He uses people, abuses his daughter and is self-obsessed. His campaign is a front for his damaged ego and spirit. He is abusive, violent and a threat to children.

Then, below this, Nina had posted a picture of Viktor, a grotesque one she'd taken years ago of Viktor emerging from the bathroom, his hair in the air, face flushed, eyes wide and mouth caught in a grimace. They had laughed, he remembered, at how ridiculous he looked. 'A goblin,' Nina had said, 'no, an ogre. My ogre.' Needling him, teasing, tiptoeing up to his face and kissing him, loving him. Under the image Nina had typed, 'Can this man be trusted with your campaign?' Viktor felt the collapse, the truth in her condemnation, as certain as his hope had felt just seconds before. Stumbling, his hand shaking, he hovered the cursor over the corner of the post and hit delete.

He blocked her account from his Facebook page. She posted the same comment and photo to the campaign's public page; he deleted them there. Then in the comments of an article on *Mutations*. The next day she tweeted it at him. A day after that, another tweet from a different account. Sometimes her friends retweeted them. He began to search every aspect of his online presence daily, sometimes twice a day, heart always racing, never knowing where she would turn up next. Once he even found a post about him on LinkedIn.

Each time, with each new-old accusation, his doubt about himself grew and he became more certain of his crimes, his diagnosis: deceitful, abusive, violent and grotesque.

He could taste her loathing in his mouth, the bile rising in his throat, and he would rush to the bathroom as his bowels opened and out he flowed.

Anne-Marie's wisdom appeared clear, certain, like the Zimbabwean skies, her sentences coherent, uncluttered with the chaos of his doubt, the self-hate that clouded his thinking – her uncomplicated radiance that he was destroying with his encumbrances of thought. His hopelessness took with such force everything he was given, each new lesson, every experience, grasping Anne-Marie and throwing her into his sweat and dirt.

Calmly, at night, Nina's messages saved on his desktop, Viktor would show them to Anne-Marie – this complete exposure was new to him, a total release.

Unruffled, unbuttoning her blouse, towelling down her perspiration, splashing water from the kitchen sink onto her face, her shoes kicked off by the front door, Anne-Marie would lie on the bed and look up at Viktor. He was now fraught again, pregnant with his news, pacing with his computer, waiting for Anne-Marie to settle, for this routine of arrival to be completed so she would be rested and he could finally bring his open laptop to her and point to the file.

'Not again. Again and again and again,' she'd say. 'Keep moving, Viktor, keep your eye on the campaign. On Biko.' After unhurried minutes reading the messages, she'd say: 'I hope you haven't responded, *mudiwa*. You must let this come out, all of it, let her *évacuer*, she needs to get this stuff out. The feelings of rejection and pain in every word she writes is unbearable. These words' – she lifted the computer closer to her, squinted, and read – '"Viktor Isaacs has ruined his life and broke his daughter's heart with his absence. He is a hypocrite who cares for no one but himself. He is lost".'

Anne-Marie had already spent some time questioning Viktor about Nina's accusations – were they in any way true? Overwrought, anxious to see himself clearly, she hadn't received a proper answer from him. So Anne-Marie, a feminist accustomed to believing women, had made a balance judgement of this aspect of her lover's recent past.

Lowering the computer, refocusing: 'She is right to be angry. You left. She is the sole carer, bringing up your daughter without a sister, cousin, extended family to help her. But Viktor, listen to me. Viktor, look at me, sit down. Stop pacing around. *Sit*. You must allow this anger to run its course, let the ... *deuil*, the mourning, to pass. It will go. And for your daughter – and for Nina – you must keep moving. Push through the inertia, the paralysis of your questioning, to action. Once you have found that movement you will be strong again for Rosa. Find your way first, Viktor.'

Viktor sat at the foot of the bed, a hand rubbing Anne-Marie's feet, finally looking hard into her eyes for this lesson, this talking-to. She continued, 'Got it? Now, here's what we'll do. Each time you receive these messages, show them to me if you can't see what to do. Even if you think you can. Do you hear me?'

So the routine was now set. Each time he received a message from Nina, an email or a tirade on a campaign platform, Viktor would read them, feel the lacerations, the deep sting of the words as they dug into his flesh, take a screenshot and then delete them from the public forum. Later, he would pace the flat in the hour before Anne-Marie came home, hungry for her reassurances, then follow her around with the computer folded like a Bible and Nina's defamations on his desktop until she was ready to receive him.

Viktor, Rosa cried for three hours last night after Skyping with you. I'm not sure how to help her with her grief, longing, confusion. She misses you and feels like she has to rank her love and doesn't accept that people can love more than one person. And she still really wishes both her parents were together. Please don't talk to her about this. I just wanted to give you an update. N

*

Feverish, uncomfortable, Viktor hadn't been able to concentrate all day. His work had nagged at him. He stared dumbly at the screen, flicked between pages, articles, tweets. Even the dull, ever-present thunder of pain for Biko that normally coursed through him was not present. He tried to write, to think, to commence, but he was in the grip of restlessness. He needed to know what it was, what thing had him, yet he felt only the day's constant, insistent sun, the pestering nothingness. He tried to fight the feeling, got up from his table at Louis's and ordered more coffee, then thought he needed exercise and went outside and walked to the empty parking lot behind the café. He ran, circled the abandoned car park, lifting his knees high, stretched, jumped into a star and felt his heart. He tasted his pulse in his mouth, but still the day would give him nothing.

Viktor's thinking spiralled. He felt lost. The arc of his thoughts spun furiously downward. What was the significance of all this human action, this activity – to what purpose? And what of Viktor's own words? What would become of his projects?

Nothing would last. There would be nothing left of the Isaacses or the Lumumbas, nothing but a few decades of heartbreak and failure. And what of Biko? *He is suffering*, Viktor thought, *but soon enough we will all suffer and then it will be over for us too. Over for everything, everyone – so what is all of this noise for?* The screen flashed intermittently, friend requests, posts, campaign retweets, comments. The whole juggernaut of activity that he had started chirped mechanically at him; the part of modern life where he had sunk himself, sought meaning, bayed and cornered him – a total, complete human loss.

Anne-Marie was working in Gweru. Viktor spent the evening alone. The night cleared some of the misery from the day; the mood of despair lifted. He peeled off the top sheet on Anne-Marie's bed, dropped his clothes to the floor, fell on the mattress and adjusted the pillows behind him. The night was good. He felt embraced by the heat. The curtains billowed and flapped lazily in the breeze and the sounds of the neighbours entered the window and filled the room. He opened his computer and began to play *La Traviata*. He pulled out the headphones and the music jumped into the room, spun into the air, took control.

Opera was part of the sickness that had Viktor in its grip. It enveloped and overwhelmed him, drew over him the comfort of its more beautiful and awful tragedy. Verdi had known that life was concentrated around the great and terrible extremes of existence: radiant, temporary joy and destitution, destruction, death. Viktor thought that the only art that mattered moved quickly between these poles; the life that happened in the space separating joy and death – the ordinary mayhem and the tedium of daily life, the slow agony of existence – was essentially irrelevant.

Verdi understood this heightened, vital sense of life, and his operas moved furiously between these two states. Viktor knew the *passaggio* was not just a philosophical place, but an actual transition, or bridge, in vocal range for opera singers: the movement of the song, the note, from chest to throat and then head – from statement, explanation, to passion and intensity. It was here, in these passages, that love was declared, passion unleashed and life sacrificed. No matter how brilliant the singer, there was always a break and lift, a division between registers rather than full unification. And the *break*, for Viktor, was the point, the transition, the key, for it was here where life could become exultant, could break down, rejoice and die. *You must make a turning point of your life – or it is nothing.*

La Traviata obsessed him, with its quick, tragic movement between love and obsession and tragic finality. His fantasy, that night, as he lay on Anne-Marie's bed feeling the music gradually chase away his own anxieties, was that *he* was singing the title role of Alfredo; that he had become the bourgeois playboy and the beautiful clarity of expression could at last be his. Cleansed, letting the music wash him, the waves of melody, the orchestra subdued by his voice, even his private catastrophes seemed like nothing compared to the drama in the opera. He wagged his feet, moved the computer next to him on the bed, rocked his head in time to the music, comforted himself, then took his place on the stage. *Love is the very breath of the universe itself.*

As Viktor reclined, Alfredo, proud and brave, fell for the frail, beautiful courtesan, Violetta. When Alfredo declared his love for her, she replied that her intention was to live for pleasure alone, untied by love. *From joy to joy, forever free, I must pass madly from joy to joy. My life's course shall be forever in the paths of pleasure.* Alfredo ordered Violetta to love him. He broke her with his declaration of love, given like an order, and from this began the long descent in which her old freedom and independence would be destroyed.

Viktor saw *La Traviata* as a story of resistance – Alfredo creating love where it had not been. In Alfredo's command of Violetta, he saw his own destruction of Rosa – of all the women in his life. Alfredo captures Violetta's heart, beats back her resistance and her will to be free; they live together outside the city and sing the ardour, the prison, of their ebullient spirits. The music filled Anne-Marie's small bedroom, the scene of their life together, their old lives abandoned for each other.

On the bed Viktor started to move his arms, to conduct the music, imagining himself facing the audience. As the music changed, the action moved back to the city, where the couple had to return. The fear mounted as the opera moved gradually, inextricably, towards ruin. The old world gathered itself up, built in the background, the poison of bourgeois society a hypocrisy that pulled Alfredo and Violetta into its old embrace. Viktor felt sleep drain from him, his pulse beating in time to the music.

The couple were together in Paris, but a cruel rumour had spread that they had separated. Obeying a society that refused to accept their love, Violetta believed she must release Alfredo from his ties to her. What was she, anyway, in the nineteenth century – a courtesan, a call girl, a high-class whore? What could she give Alfredo except ruin? The action moved to a party in Paris – gambling tables, rich men in dinner jackets. Viktor felt the music swell, turn, lift, and the terrible inevitability of opera, a feeling he hated as a child, took root.

Alfredo heard the lies and rumours of Violetta's duplicity. He thought the philandering baron was behind it and that this was who Violetta wanted. He confronted her, asking, *Is it him? Is it the baron you love?*

Yes, I do, she whispered. Infected, taken by the music, by the scene, as though it was the first time he had heard it, Viktor felt his heart lift, felt it beat in his mouth. Suddenly, only minutes from consummation, everything was destroyed – *I wish to cleanse myself of such a stain*, Alfredo screamed. He denounced his lover and called in the guests to witness his humiliation of her. He broke her, and himself too.

With the destruction done, Viktor felt comforted – closer, somehow, to a sort of truth. *The proximity of death is in everything we are*, he thought. *This was Verdi's genius. Next to every act of life – love, hope, expectation – is death. Death is the word between each word we speak, the image between each image and only the speed of life hides its presence.* The final act was playing. Viktor let the music crash over him. *Life moves*, he thought, *so quickly that we are not aware of the existence of death in everything we do.* He heard Violetta dying in the background of his thoughts: *Now neither man nor demon, my angel, will ever be able to take you away.* Viktor thought, *I must return to this tomorrow, incorporate it somehow. I will solve this problem tomorrow.*

Finally, satisfied, relieved, he fell asleep.

*

There is nothing strange to Viktor about appearing on stage, preparing in the wings, practising the arias sotto voce. *He knows the words, and* in the infinite possibilities of the dream thinks he might be able to sing. He hears the muffled music, the rustle of activity as the stagehands and cast whisper around him. The audience are silent, but he can sense them, breathless, expectant, the rustle of their presence inches from the stage.

He knows the opera. The music is coming from inside him, as if he is singing each part: Alfredo, Violetta, the Baron, the chorus. He feels his chest vibrate to the music; he moves to the melody. Suddenly Viktor is jolted, pushed by a sea of hands, onto the stage. He looks down at himself and he sees he's dressed in a tailcoat, a stiff white shirt, a bow tie and riding boots. Alfredo. He feels handsome and wants to sing.

Quickly he looks around him. The orchestra has started to play. In the half-room of gambling tables, Persian rugs, carafes of red wine, someone has just spoken. In front of him he sees Violetta and his heart lurches. There is an involuntary uprising of feeling. Something capsizes in him; he can't hold on. He wants to cross the stage and touch her hair, run his hands down her neck, feel the lace of her dress — he wants to reassure her. Viktor realises that he must not ask the question, but he can't stop himself. The order of life is already written. He knows he must sing it. His chest fills and chokes with sadness and he sings, 'Was it the Baron?'

He sees the fear in Violetta's eyes and hears the sigh from the audience. She drops her head and answers, 'Yes.'

Then the terrible second question comes out: 'You love him, then?'

Her head still bent: 'Well — I love him, yes.'

And Viktor knows she is lying, she has never loved the Baron — she loves him, and is trying to protect him, but he can't help himself. Viktor feels the heat from the stage lighting, the eyes of everyone on him, he follows the direction of the words, the feelings, the music, the scene, the tragedy.

Suddenly there is a violence in his heart as intense as his love. He clenches his fists and the echo of his rage sounds across the theatre. He runs to the cardboard door in the false wall. Throwing open the door, he calls, 'Everyone, come here!'

Immediately the room is full of people. The chorus of guests asks, 'You called us? What do you want?'

Viktor feels his arm lift. His finger points to Violetta, who leans exhausted on a table, her shoulders raised, her chest heaving. Viktor looks at the guests, then the audience, and half-sings, half-shouts, 'You know this woman?'

The guests look at Violetta and answer him: 'Who? Rosa?'

Viktor is confused. He loses his way, forgets the words. He turns and, where Violetta had been standing, he sees his daughter. Her head is just above the table. He can see she is trembling, her eyes flinch – there is fear on her face and something else, something worse, incomprehension. Rosa looks around her to the mass of faces in the audience, to the painted set, up to the lights, the theatre rising high into the rafters, to the cast standing with her on this great stage – this fabricated universe of human cruelty with its unnecessary pain, its troupe of fools.

Rosa's face is frozen, her mouth open and dry. Incredulous, unbelieving, his daughter holds out a hand to him. Viktor's finger is still pointed at her. He can see it all: how she is being broken, how they have beaten all sense from her – destroyed her childish instincts of love.

But Viktor can't help fulfilling the role he has been given. He sings, 'You don't know what she has done?' His voice rings with condemnation, with justice and anger.

Rosa whispers, 'Ah, be silent. Daddy, be silent.'

Viktor falters, his vision blurs, the haze of light confuses him. He listens to the music, tries to find himself.

The chorus sings again, 'No. What has she done?'

Viktor answers as Alfredo, his voice rising with confidence. He lets the cruelty take him, he feels it spread through him, possess him. 'This woman was about to lose all she owns for love of me, while I, blinded, vile, wretched, was capable of accepting everything. But there is still time! I wish to cleanse myself of such a stain. I have called you here as *witnesses that I have paid her all I owe.' With violent contempt, Viktor throws a purse down at Rosa's feet.*

Rosa screams — her voice is high, it reaches the circle, the gods. 'Daddy!' she cries, and collapses.

Viktor stares at the body of his daughter on the stage. Two women from the chorus rush to her and fan her small face.

And now the tide of anger has left him and he feels exhausted, lost. The swell of indignation dissolves. His chest heaves and his head drops in humiliation. Finally, with the lucidity of the dream, he knows that Rosa is all of life. Are those the words he hears from the chorus? Is it over? Has the pain really passed? The chorus sings, 'Rosa is everything, not just for him but everyone. He has learnt his lesson; he can still go back to his love and there receive the longed-for prize, wrapped in his sweetheart's arms.'

He wonders, no longer sure who he is — Alfredo or Viktor - if she is also loved by everyone, she can still be saved. Saved from me.

His heart beats loudly in his chest at the thought. Viktor stirs but doesn't wake.

He stands over Rosa, and where the baron stood he now sees Isaac. His father looks at the scene, sees his granddaughter on the floor, his son — 'dressed like this, with those boots, oy vey'. He bows his head in shame and then rushes to Rosa.

The chorus sings, 'Oh, what a terrible thing you have done! You have killed a sensitive heart! Ignoble man, to insult a child so, leave this house at once, you fill us with horror! Go, go, you fill us with horror! Ignoble man, to insult a child.'

Viktor falls back into Alfredo's body, into the riding boots, the black trousers, the dinner jacket and cries, 'Alas, what have I done? I am horrified!'

Isaac looks up, broken, and his voice lifts, growing louder with each word. 'Whoever, even in anger, offends a child exposes himself to the contempt of all.' Then, staring into Viktor's eyes, he declares, 'Where is my son? I cannot find him, for in you I no longer see him.'

400

Involuntarily, without thinking, the words erupt through Viktor's clenched chest to his throat: 'Ah, yes — what have I done? I am horrified. Maddening confusion, disillusioned love tortures my heart — I have lost my reason. She can never forgive me now. I tried to flee from her — I couldn't! I came here, spurred on by anger! Now that I have vented my fury, I am sick with remorse — oh, wretched man!'

The chorus, the other guests, ignore him. Have they even heard his words of remorse, his regret? Do they know that he has sung? Instead they look at Isaac kneeling on the floor, cradling Rosa in his lap, and they sing, 'Ah, how you suffer! But take heart: here, each of us suffers for your sorrow; you are here among dear friends; dry the tears which bathe your face.'

Viktor tries to shake off the dream. He thrashes, beats at the sheets, but remorse fastens him to the bed. He groans. The night breeze thumps dully at the curtain. Outside, in the distance, there is a scream.

He hears Rosa's voice — she has regained consciousness. Her head is raised on Isaac's lap. She doesn't have the strength, but she tries to turn her head to Viktor, to address him directly: 'Alfredo, Alfredo, you cannot understand fully the love I have in my heart; you do not know that even at the risk of your disdain I have put it to the test!'

Rosa's voice is soft. Even if the words are meant for him, they touch everyone, speak to all loss. Sitting up now, Rosa sings more loudly, 'But the day will come when you will know. You will admit how much I loved you. May God save you then from remorse. I shall be dead, but I shall love you still.'

Viktor turns again on the mattress and cries out once more. Through the open window the sadness moves into the street, reaches the trees, climbs onto the branches and neighbouring houses, into other flats, to the distant townships. Soon Viktor's voice is joined by others, the whole weary agony of Harare. Along the silent, potholed roads, splashed by streetlights, the cries of the city ricochet and blur; there are faces and people tumbling, falling over each other.

The chorus has stepped forward and now the whole city is on the stage, their arms out, their chests open, singing. Everyone is awake. The president, alone in his bed, sits up, listens, sees the light outside his window, recognises the pain of the city. He wonders if it is a message to him: 'May God save you from remorse. We may be dead, but still we love. Still we come back for what is ours.' The president is in a fever; he moves in his bed and sings, 'Alas, what have I done? I am horrified!'

Viktor thrashes on the mattress. The sheet sticks to him. He is covered in sweat. Even his own cries cannot properly be heard and he struggles in his sleep to wake, to escape.

Isaac sings, without any of his old reserve, 'I will show you that I am well able to break your pride.'

Finally Viktor wakes panting, breathless, relieved, horrified. He throws the sheet off, swings his legs off the bed, rests his head in his hands. A hollow pain fills his stomach, bloats him – his very blood feels infected. What difference does it make, he asks, that this was a dream? He sees the image of Rosa, slandered in public, terrified, alone. He shakes his head violently; still she won't go. Viktor feels his lungs emptying of air, his chest filling with emotion. He stands, steadies himself on the wall by the bed, tries to reach the light, stumbles.

The curtain flaps like a flag on currents of warm air. Quickly, he looks around the room for Rosa, in case all this time she has been in Zimbabwe with him without him knowing, hiding, scared to come out of the corner of the room he shares with Anne-Marie.

There are shadows, but none of them is his daughter. He hears a noise from somewhere near him. Hope rises briefly, but the only sound in the room is his own tears. He mutters, 'Alas, what have I done?'

Chapter Thirty-One

On the walk to the café there was a large skyscraper, built in the mid-nineties for the Reserve Bank of Zimbabwe, that rose forty floors, narrowing to a sharp summit. On its sides were large plates of reflective glass, so that the rest of the low-rise city was reflected in the mirrored patchwork. The automatic doors slid open and closed for a tide of politicians and bankers, driven to the front door in chauffeured black Mercedes-Benz. The staff cast quick, contemptuous glances around them before being swallowed by the building. As Viktor walked past the door a blast of cool air briefly enveloped him. *If I chained myself to the reception, threw paint on the marble floor, would they listen? Would they release Biko?* On the side of the entrance was a plaque. Viktor read it aloud, his face crumpling in disgust:

THIS BUILDING WAS OPENED ON 8 MAY 1993 BY
HIS EXCELLENCY, COMRADE RIGHT HONOURABLE
PRESIDENT ROBERT GABRIEL MUGABE

He'd spent another night dreaming brief, brutal dreams. A circus of oversized cats, badly tamed, leering at him, demanded to be fed, their worn, patchy fur raised on their arched backs, their teeth snapping at him. Then he woke and grabbed his phone from the corner below the bed. The clock showed that the time had only edged hesitantly forward. He needed to wake Harare so he could resume the campaign, phone his contacts, speak to the embassies, High Commissioners, email, free Biko.

As Viktor approached the internet café where he occasionally worked, where Lenin worked, he felt his phone vibrate in his pocket and answered quickly.

'You tried to get me yesterday. My secretary tells me you've left fifteen messages,' the voice said.

Viktor pressed the phone hard against his ear, kicked open the glass door to the internet café, waved to Lenin, cleaning the tables with a dirty rag, and found a chair. 'Sorry, who is this?'

'It's Kevin Saunders, Deputy High Commissioner.'

Viktor remembered the hurried calls he'd made the previous day, desperate for some leverage, with no news on Biko for a fortnight. In Bulawayo all visits had been refused. Viktor imagined Biko beaten, stubborn in his cell, overturning the bowl of *sadza* and sauce, demanding food fit for human beings, challenging his jailors: 'You dogs. Dogs of a master who wouldn't wipe his feet on you. Dogs. *Muri imbwa dza Mugabe.*'

'Yes, Deputy High Commissioner,' Viktor answered breathlessly, 'it's about Stephan Mutawurwa – he's known as Biko – he was arrested several weeks ago in Bulawayo. He's being held for inciting disorder, but we've heard nothing for two weeks. The police don't respond and we're not allowed to visit.'

'How do you know him?' The voice was clipped, irritated.

'We worked together at the Independent Media Centre. I was with him when he was arrested. I've given a statement and he has a lawyer.'

'What do you think I can do?'

'We hoped you could contact the authorities in Bulawayo. Write to the president, issue a statement.'

'How long have you been in Zimbabwe?'

'A few months.'

'Then how do you think our engagement could possibly make a difference?'

'I think it can. You have better contacts than us, and in the current climate—' Viktor was cut off.

'In the current climate we can do exactly nothing.'

'Mr Mutawurwa could die if you don't, sir.'

'Listen, I have heard about this Stephan Mutawurwa and this so-called Media Centre that you run, illegally. Quite honestly, I find it peculiar – you seem to be purposely stirring up trouble. And this Mutawurwa is involved with Nelson Chitambere's group ... what is it called, the Society for Educated Minds? We know about them. Socialists. Linked to groups in Europe, in the UK, in the US.'

Viktor could feel his blood rising, his face flushed. 'It's the Society of Liberated Minds, though I think that's irrelevant. Stephan is a pro-democracy activist who the British government claim to support.'

'There are many shades of activists, sir—'

'Viktor. My name is Viktor Isaacs.'

'There are all shades of activists, Mr Isaacs, and Stephan and quite frankly your Media Centre—'

'It's a website of opposition voices.'

'Whatever it is, we do not want to be associated with it.'

Viktor was perspiring. He battled the desire to raise his voice and denounce this man, with his heartless coherence, his Oxbridge English and hypocrisy. The sensation was new for Viktor. He felt his stomach burn. To steady himself, he held the phone away from his ear, gripped the table and breathed deeply. 'I see, Deputy High Commissioner,' he said finally, bringing the phone back to his ear. 'Well, if you have a change of mind, we'd really appreciate it if you could help us find out what's happened, why there has been silence for two weeks. You'll understand we're concerned. His family is concerned.'

'There's nothing we can do. If you want to be useful to Zimbabwe, I would suggest you return to the UK and please stop phoning my office.' The call rang off. Viktor threw his phone on the floor. It shattered into three pieces. He leant forward and cradled his head.

What did it mean that Biko was still in prison and that no one could help? His shoddy lawyer had spoken confidently about Biko's imminent release and then fallen silent and couldn't be reached for days. The money the campaign raised flowed healthily into the account that Louis had set up in London. The NGOs that had taken over the terrain now also donated. All of these funds, including the unnamed donations, had not yet managed to buy Biko's freedom. Money had been paid to the absent-minded lawyer who didn't answer his phone. Anne-Marie found someone who would be more attentive. The great, cascading inflow of donor money into Zimbabwe from and to foreign NGOs, Care International, the Rosa Luxemburg Foundation, the Friedrich-Ebert-Stiftung Foundation, the Norwegian Student Federation, had fixed the prices, raised the hourly fee of human rights. Now legal firms brimmed with self-righteousness and defended the Arundel Eight, the Bulawayo Six and now the Biko One.

So Viktor fought harder than before.

He published daily updates, posted articles, appeals, blog posts in a frenzy of action, a barrage of activity and information that he believed would bear down on the Zimbabwe High Commission in London, the prison switchboard in Harare, the ZANU and MDC MPs. This torrent of protest and noise, telephone, email, social media traffic grew to such an intensity that the regime would be forced to its knees, obliged to plead for the crowds, public opinion and the online masses to release their grip. Only then did Viktor envisage that Biko would be freed and the storm, the international frenzy, the social movement crowd that he had stirred into such tumult, would lift. If Viktor kept moving quickly enough between tasks, plugged the holes that opened between emails, online petitions and phone calls, his activism would free Biko.

He wondered if this was how it felt to be totally, completely immersed in practice. Was this the life of a militant, of Tendai, Nelson, Moreblessing? Biko lived by the same principles of involvement, a life given in total measure, no sinew of effort held back for tomorrow, just fanatical loyalty to a single purpose. Viktor felt himself infected by the struggle against X-Party, Y-Party for the new dawn, which caused each of them to be cursed by a throbbing fear and the dull pain of trapped hope.

*

'Brother,' Lenin said, 'You need to rest.'

'I need to get Biko out.'

'But you'll only do that if you're rested.'

'I have no time.'

Lenin picked up Viktor's phone, put the pieces together, turned it on and placed it next to the computer. 'Why are you so stubborn, brother? So, what do you call it? Why are you so anti-rest?'

Viktor sat back in the chair, looked at Lenin and smiled. 'Anti-rest,' he repeated. 'You are right. I am anti-rest. There is too much discord in my head to rest.'

'There is too much discord in Zimbabwe,' Lenin corrected him.

'Yes, too much.'

Viktor was one of two customers in Mandela's Internet Café, which was normally filled with students completing their CVs, sending them to friends, family, contacts outside Zimbabwe, in South Africa, London. All of them Viktor knew by face; some he spoke to. For days students came in and sat blankly at a computer. They could only afford thirty minutes of connection. Through the day, every hour, they'd check their emails – they timed their connections to two minutes an hour, five times a day from eleven. So a single dollar, one tatty greenback, if they were careful, would last them three days of emailing – checking, their backs straight, their hands shaking each hour, their unblinking eyes fixed on the screen. They were waiting for an email with the identification code for a Western Union payment, for the transfer from a brother or sister, or cousin or aunt, in London. As soon as Viktor learnt about this system, this two-minute hourly lottery, he bought internet time for the students who visited the café regularly.

Today Viktor sat next to Ebenezer, a graduate from the University of Zimbabwe, who was drafting and redrafting applications for positions out of Zimbabwe. 'Maybe if I wasn't Zimbabwean, anything but Zimbabwean. Should I pretend to be from England? South Africa? Maybe if I was Haitian? And my degrees? My years at university, to be treated like this – this life is not fit for an intellectual. And I only followed Mugabe's lead. Degrees, hard work, qualifications.'

Viktor left the internet café to buy the men coffee.

Did Viktor feel responsible for Biko's arrest? No one seemed to blame him, not even Anne-Marie. 'They raped him in front of me. *Mudiwa*, this is not a metaphor. He was raped, buggered in front of me. With their truncheons.'

'Don't cry about it, Viktor. Get angry,' she'd said.

Viktor remembered Nelson's words, his easy, unambiguous principles, his uncanny ability to see Viktor's flaws, his neuroses, his soft, spongy liberal's heart, his Jewish morbidity: 'Guilt will drive you to despair, anger to action. Always action, Viktor.'

Viktor counted the words, committed them to memory. *Guilt will drive you to despair, anger to action.* Nine words. The first word guilt, the last word action. *That's right*, Viktor thought as he shouldered the door open to Louis's café, *start with guilt, end with action.*

When he returned, Ebenezer was sitting opposite a dead computer, the loud mechanical beat of the generator and the dull, pulsing light from the overhead bulb throbbing in time to the petrol engine.

'Do you want the good news first or the bad news, brother?' Lenin was sitting behind the desk.

'The bad news,' Viktor answered.

'Typical. The bad news is that we don't have any power.'

Viktor placed three paper cups that he'd carried the two blocks from Louis's café, cutting through side alleys and passageways like a local.

'And the good news?' Viktor asked.

'The good news, Viktor,' Lenin said, savouring the information, 'is that your phone rang and I answered it.' Lenin paused and raised his eyebrows. Ebenezer spun round, turning his back to the computer, and faced the men.

'Come on, please. I'm dying here. The phone rang and …'

'Your man called,' Lenin said calmly, drily.

'My man?'

'The Englander from the High Commission.'

Viktor flinched.

'He wanted to say,' Lenin continued, 'that he'd just found out that Biko was transferred to Harare. To Chikurubi Prison.'

'That fucking creep said that?' Viktor put his coffee down and started to pace the room. 'What did he say, what exactly did he say?'

'He said he didn't do anything, and then hung up.'

'Who did you say you were?'

'You.' Grinning, Lenin repeated, straightening his back, 'Thank you, Deputy High Commissioner, we are very grateful. I am very appreciative, sir. Thank you, Your Excellence, sir. The Queen will be very pleased with you.'

Viktor and Ebenezer looked at each other and laughed together. Viktor hit the front desk with his fist.

'It might not be such good news,' Ebenezer said.

'Of course it is!' Viktor exclaimed. 'One, we know Biko is safe. Two, we can monitor him more closely from Harare. It's very good news.'

Coffee and adrenalin coursed through Viktor's body and he felt his heart race. *Biko's alive*, he thought, *of course it's good news.*

*

The second mission, undertaken several weeks after Viktor had returned from Bulawayo, was to meet an MDC MP. Nelson assured him that this man wouldn't help Biko, but Viktor needed to try, to see for himself.

Viktor would meet Arthur Biti, a prominent Y-Party MP, banker and former member of the Society of Liberated Minds. Nelson explained that Arthur would give him, the campaign,

Biko, nothing. 'At the most, empty promises — that he will speak to Y-Party elders to get Biko transferred or released, and then he won't call, and he'll be too busy to answer. But go and see him, the Great Arthur, the fallen giant. You know, I was at the University of Zimbabwe with him, we led the first protests against the one-party state. Hah, but all of that's in the past now — he is like the rest of Y-Party. Lost. You need to see that for yourself, comrade. But don't think Biko will be helped, don't think that, Viktor.'

Arthur was a giant. Taller than Viktor, wider, strong, his height really meant something; he didn't slump in supplication or apology. Arthur wore his physical presence as an exclamation of confidence. His large head and face were never inert, twitching and moving constantly. He had recently grown a beard, to give his bearing more gravitas, but the effect made him look young and naive.

After a physics degree from Oxford, Arthur had worked as a junior researcher for NASA and, though he had never reached the rank of professor, he was known as Professor Arthur Biti. Or just Professor, or Prof, in the press. To his colleagues he was known as Comrade-Professor-Right-Honourable Arthur Biti Esquire, every permutation of Zimbabwean political development, an appellation for every occasion.

The Prof worked for Standard Bank. He was a minor figure in international banking, moving between Harare and Johannesburg, Y-Party's insider readying himself for government with a real knowledge of the world, of the system he had once denounced. Once he had waved his fist like a conductor's baton, challenging the state, the dictatorship, the imperialist dogs and their agents and representatives in Zimbabwe, as he stood on the steps of the University of Zimbabwe's Health Centre commanding his cadre. His voice had barely been audible at the back of the crowd, but the occasional word had reached the distant ranks – *socialism*, *jackals*, *thieves*, *cockroaches*, *revolution*. His overgrown head and pounding fist had seemed large enough to cloud the sky, cover the sun, order a storm on State House, throw their riches to the street, grind to dust the pathetic forces of army and police. The young Arthur had been more New Testament prophet than Student Representative Council president.

The interview with Viktor – given as a favour to Nelson, to the old times – was held in Standard Bank's ten-storey office block in the city. Viktor held his spiral notebook, turning his biro around his fingers. He explained to the receptionist that, though it was night and the bank was officially closed, his appointment with Prof Biti had been organised for nine p.m. On his second appeal the man, his uniform hanging over his shoulders as loose as if he had fallen into it, phoned the extension, received instructions and then sent Viktor, a label pinned to his T-shirt, to the eighth floor.

Before the lift doors opened fully, Viktor heard the professor's distant greeting. 'Any friend of Nelson's is always welcome by me.'

Instead of a private office the floor was a stadium of desks, each separated by shoulder-height partition walls. 'My office is over here,' the Prof shouted. He stood and beckoned Viktor with his great arms waving in the air, welcoming his guest like he was the proprietor of this universe of screens, carpet squares and sunken spotlights. Only the Professor's desk light was on, shining a yellow reflection against the window, lighting his cheekbones and eyebrows, turning his face into a mask.

Viktor weaved through the cubicle maze and the men shook hands. The Professor sucked on his teeth and sighed. 'A white man in Zimbabwe, come to save the natives!'

'I haven't come to save anyone,' Viktor, said his cheeks reddening.

'A joke, comrade. A joke. So how do you want to do this?'

'Well, it's about a friend – a comrade – Biko, Stephan Mutawurwa, who is in prison. We thought maybe you could help.'

'Of course, of course. We'll get to that. What do you know about me?'

'Nelson has spoken about your time together at the UZ as activists.'

'All of that is true. True.'

On the large desk were papers, three computer screens, a large photo of the Professor in university robes, around it certificates and awards, photocopied and pinned to the half-wall. The Prof sat back, away from the desk on the swivel chair, enjoying a chance to declaim, reminisce, tell the truth about the ABO era – as students had called it – the entire struggle, the first real opposition, the epoch of resistance incarnated by his initials. The Professor addressed Viktor with soaring, plunging sentences, large movements, looking at his pleasing reflection in the glass, the view of Zimbabwe, the great vista over the low-rise city to the hills in the south. The sweep, the view, his reflection gave the Professor a deep sense of satisfaction at what he was, who he'd become, everything he now represented.

Viktor spoke. 'Well, I have always been interested in what the O in ABO stands for.'

'Order. The Arthur Biti Order. ABO era.'

'So it's the Arthur Biti Order era.'

'No, just the ABO era.'

'Wouldn't that be ABOE?'

'No, no. It's not like that. Let me explain. I came from a political family. My father went to Fort Hare, graduated in 1958

413

in Latin and English. My mother was a teacher. Both are late. I have three siblings. The first is a PhD in zoology, the second is a PhD in economics, the third is a PhD in pharmacy. Counting my PhD from Oxford, that's four out of four. Four PhDs. We grew up in the rural areas, so I know the guerrilla struggle. But I was too young to fight. Even up until this day, I have a very soft spot for people who pick up the gun to drive out the oppressor. The principle that the price of freedom is death still inspires me today as a leading politician. As a student I skipped form six and went directly into seven. Four A levels, nine O levels. I read the paper every day.'

'And the ABO era. What was it?' Viktor's head was still lowered.

The Professor angled his chair to the window. Without looking at Viktor, he addressed himself. 'We were the de facto opposition in Zimbabwe. I led the student movement, and the labour movement followed us. We were national. Our agenda and intervention. Against the one-party state. Opposition to corruption, government priorities, everything. This was a sparkling, shining era, unknown before or since. And we were fighting from the left. We said Robert Mugabe had done nothing for workers and that he was a stooge of imperialism. That's what we said, do you hear me? We got no support from white farmers, the Brits or the US. They were in bed with Mugabe.'

'Quite different from today,' Viktor commented.

'Quite different,' Biti repeated.

Viktor leant back on his chair. The Professor was silent. In the reflection Viktor saw his head drop. *How dangerous memory can be in Zimbabwe. How easily erased by the present.*

The Professor looked up, turned his chair, faced Viktor again. 'It was when Mugabe was going from liberator to villain. Now no one notices when you criticise the old man, but I was

414

the first. I was the first person to draw the gun and shoot from the hip. We read – Nelson and I – everyone: Mao, Stalin, Lenin, Trotsky, Malcolm X. I believed in academic excellence and activism. That's why I went to Oxford and Nelson to Columbia. You have a PhD, I hope.'

'I am finishing one.'

'At your age? Hurry up. We didn't stand for indolence. We got it finished.'

Viktor felt his face reddening again. The Professor brought his hands together and the clap echoed around the office.

'I was the first to take on Mugabe. He even remembers it.' The Professor leant forward on his chair, his eyes wide, inflamed. 'Here, take this story for your record.' Viktor straightened himself dutifully towards the page, his notebook. 'A vicious encounter with Robert Mugabe himself. It was the graduation ceremony, 1990. I was still president. He was officiating. The tradition was the procession of graduates was led by the SRC president – that was me – and at the back was the president. We did the ceremony and then came out on the college green to talk and take photos. The vice chancellor came up to me with Mugabe and said, "So, SRC president, this is Robert Mugabe." Mugabe wanted to do small talk and said something like, "Oh, how many graduates are there this year? When I graduated in 1951 there were nine graduates in the country." And I said, "No. I don't want to talk about that. I want to talk about national issues. We are completely against the one-party state by any means necessary." And Mugabe said, "Well, if you are going to take such strong views, we are going to be dismissive." I shot back from the hip, "We have already dismissed you." Have you got that?'

Viktor nodded, wrote, pressing his pen into the pad.

'Now, I don't want you to write down the next thing. Put your pen down.'

Viktor turned his hands up, holding the pen, showing the Professor that it was out of action.

'No, put it down. What I am going to say is very sensitive.'

Viktor obeyed.

'Mugabe is a very arrogant man, proud. He was livid. His sycophants, his circle, remained after he left. "How can you speak to the president like that?" There was nothing they could do because I was already launching into this guy. Mugabe is a petty character. Insecure. He is overrated, not intelligent. He's read Machiavelli's *Prince*, but forgot about the *Discourses*. He is shrewd and understands power. That's it.' The Prof paused, then continued, 'You can write now.' He swivelled his chair back to his reflection. 'Write this: I laughed with the old man about this incident last year. The story illustrates our radical way then. You see, we used every opportunity to fire – and fire from the hip. Back to the story. I work in the bank, developing and operationalising a payment strategy for banks in Southern Africa. Including text payments. I am also a trained lawyer.'

'Why did you return to Zimbabwe?' Viktor felt himself sinking.

'Why? Why? Why do you think? Because I am African and wanted to participate in the African economy. To make a difference for the working class and poor. To the progressive agenda. What are we going to do when we get in? It's not enough to want Mugabe to go. What about macroeconomic fundamentals? I am getting skills. The main point is that I am trying to self-transcend and be part of the African agenda. I want more experience, to be a better cadre.'

'So that's the reason you are working here.'

'You can read sociology, or whatever, know the struggle, but if someone says corporate finance, private equity, you're lost. So I want to demystify this stuff.'

Pulling himself up, surfacing, Viktor asked, 'You never catch yourself, with your past, thinking, Here I am from the ABO era, from the struggle against the one-party state, working in Africa's biggest bank?'

Viktor had his own version of charm. He delivered the question with a shrug, a broad smile to pull the Professor close, flatter him, raise the contradiction innocently. He crossed and uncrossed his legs, shuffled himself into comfort on the chair. His back was wet; the pen slipped in his grip. He circled the only words on the page in front of him: *petty, insecure, overrated, arrogant*.

'A comrade must know how the banks work, how international capital works. I have the science thing — I'm a specialist in robotics. I have the revolutionary stuff. I have the legal training. Now I am acquiring these skills. The bourgeoisie have a monopoly on strategy, business, economics, microeconomic policy. I could have read a book, but I need to see the corporate giant from inside. Basically, I am increasing my value proposition to the struggle.'

'I see,' Viktor said, nodding. *His value proposition to the struggle?* Viktor didn't see, he didn't get any of it.

'When we get the reins of power, we need to know this stuff.' Another spread-eagling of arms, hands, shoulders. 'I do not have any holy cows.'

The Professor reached for a bottle of mineral water, opened the cap, turned it upside down, emptied the contents into his mouth. He threw the empty bottle on the floor and it hit the metal leg of the chair and broke. Viktor started; he stood and looked at the glass. 'Leave it, leave it. Someone will clear it up in the morning.'

Again Viktor nodded and sat down. 'Professor,' he said, 'I was wondering whether you have heard about Biko. We could really use your help – as a lawyer and MDC MP, with your connections, your expertise—'

'Yes, yes. But you need to know the problem with militants today. They need to be *principled*, not populist. My advice to activists – write this down – you are not MDC, you are anti-Mugabe. There is no question about that. Even my grandmother attacks Mugabe. The role for Nelson, for the Liberated Minds Society, is to be the conscience of the people. We had form and substance. You must back up activism with substance. This kid, what's his name? Who's being held?'

'Biko. His name is Biko. And it's the Society of Liberated Minds.'

'Whatever. I have heard stuff. That's he's a bit of a rascal, a bigmouth, a populist. That won't help him. You need academic excellence. I have a degree from Oxford. Books. Substance. You also need to make a little money. An independent source of income. Without money you can be bought. Students today have no independence.'

Viktor could hear his pulse thumping in his ears. He spoke: 'Students are poor. They have nothing. Biko is a principled man, and he is being beaten and detained for his principles.'

'The party can't help every bigmouth. We have to maintain our position. We are involved in very delicate negotiations with ZANU, with the man himself. We can't do anything to jeopardise those discussions.'

The Professor fidgeted, moved on his seat, adjusted the position of the keyboard on his desk, arranged his papers. Viktor breathed in, wiped his forearm across his face. 'Maybe you could make a few enquiries about his situation. We haven't been able to see him for weeks. Just a few enquiries.' Viktor tore a page from his notebook, stood, reached over the desk and placed it in front of the Professor. 'Here's his full name and where he's being held. And that's my number.'

'Of course, of course.' The Professor waved his hand over the note. 'I'll ask around, but the bottom line is we can't jeopardise our position in Parliament at this juncture. Students aren't like they were in our generation. Urinating and defecating in the bush. No discipline.'

Before he had finished, Viktor had already found his way through the labyrinth of desks and office chairs and back to the lifts. The Professor was now a slight, barely visible presence in the distance. The light from his desk was faint, flickering like a candle.

The bell sounded from the lift. As the doors closed Viktor heard the Professor shout, 'Tell Nelson that ABO says hello.'

*

The night was warm and cheerful; it fell on Viktor as he left the building, landing on his shoulders, embracing him. He walked along Samora Machel Avenue. Unlit cars drove past, parting the night with the horn, words shouted from rolled-down windows. An occasional streetlamp shone orange; others stuttered, flashed, failed to catch and light.

Viktor had told Anne-Marie that he'd hail a taxi, that he understood that it wasn't safe for him to walk. *But what does it matter now?* he thought. He started to run, leaping over the broken paving stones, two in each stride. The night blew against his face, filled his nostrils, dried his eyes. He wanted to shout, stand in the middle of the road, stop the kamikaze traffic and point to the light on the eighth-floor window of the bank in the distance, to the Professor-President, the hand of *chinja*, realpolitik, the lawyer-scientist-banker extraordinaire, and scream. He wanted to denounce, expose, bring Biko's wrath on the very building. He wanted to light a fuse with the

419

taxi drivers, the homeless families under the jacaranda trees in Harare Gardens, stand with them and see the building, with the Professor at the window, explode. He imagined the bloody monolith launched to the moon. He wanted to rub out his whiteness, work up his anger in the middle of the street, explain that X-Party *and* Y-Party were playing the same game. With no more supplication, no more excuses for his presence or apologies for his existence, he wanted to show Harare that everything needed to be remade. Erased and started again. Then, on Biko's life, he would get everyone to swear that they would yield nothing. Never again would they give up a sliver of land to the white man or the nationalist, or give up hope to the intellectuals and the PhDs.

Viktor slowed to a trot, then to his normal, haggard, clumsy walk. *Let the city come at me, take my clothes, call me brother.* Desperate, breathless, Viktor dared Zimbabwe to throw its worst at him, heap whatever danger and despair it could muster and see him keep his footing.

Had no one ever told the Professor that he was a rotting, stinking carcass? The decay had been slow, but at some point the odour of his desiccating soul would have been unavoidable. Why didn't anyone – a comrade, a friend, his wife, children – notice that the Prof-president-father-husband-lover-comrade stank? That the family could not finish their mealie-meal when he was in the room with that carrion odour that hung on him? Why had no one told him? When did it start? When he took the bank job to increase his Value Proposition to the Struggle? When he encouraged the students to come out for high principles and not populism? Hoping for a Sharpeville, a small massacre, so the West would bring down its righteousness and give Y-Party the moral prerogative? Had no one said to him, *Comrade, I think you have lost your soul?*

Viktor crossed Samora Machel and started to climb into the Avenues. He took his T-shirt off, walked bare-chested, and didn't hear the catcalls, the whistling from the passing cars. The evening felt good against his chest. Why did someone not shake the Professor, take him by his neck, curl their hands around that thick throat and scare him when he refused to move his great mass, his weight, to save Biko? The hypocrisy! The Professor's. His own. Why had someone not told Viktor that he was wrong? So wrong when he complained about Nina. When he told Isaac and Sonia about Nina's latest denunciation. Why had no one told Nina? Called her off, told her to stop? When Viktor said he had to leave Nina and Rosa – why had no one spoken? *This echo chamber.* The general duplicity, a life sold in daily pieces to a chorus of approval, each voice agreeing, nodding, colluding. No one ever sounds the siren to our lies and self-deception, our selling out.

Viktor brought his ragged T-shirt to his head and mopped his brow. He turned into Tongogara and walked the few paces to the gate. What disturbed Viktor now was not the Professor's refusal to help Biko, but the fear that his own life resembled ABO's. That all lives do, eventually.

Part Six:

The Zimbabwean

Chapter Thirty-Two

Sometimes Viktor hired two computers and worked with Lenin and Stalin, side by side in Mandela's Internet Café, dozens of tabs open on his laptop, each of his email accounts, a Skype call. Nelson was always in the background giving unruffled counsel.

From the MDC Viktor received the telephone number of the Police Commissioner, the British and American ambassadors, the mobile numbers and email addresses of the Chikurubi Prison. Once aroused from their stupor, the MDC quickly sank back into the quagmire of parliamentary privileges, the minor, pathetic concessions that the party had won from the regime it had been charged to unseat. Equipped with this information, Viktor had emailed the three thousand members of the Free Biko Campaign. Dutifully, following Viktor's urgent prose, the prison and police chiefs received a deluge of calls and emails from Australia, South Africa, the UK, the US, Nigeria and South Africa.

Most callers stuck to Viktor's script, written succinctly in his email and his Facebook posts, for the authorities to operate with good sense 'and compassion, to release Biko and allow his friends to see him, for a doctor to give him a medical examination'. Some members of the campaign were more forthright, zealous, issuing threats of their own, warning the director of the prison, an old, weathered veteran of the war against Smith, that he would be held personally responsible if anything happened to Biko. One effusive caller from Maryland promised regime change and targeted bombings of State House and the director's suburban mansion and swimming pool. 'We know where you live and how to get you, man.'

*

Hopewell let out a low, rasping laugh. Biko brought the cup up to his mouth, rested it on Hopewell's lower lip and levered in the water.

On the first night of Hopewell's confinement, the exhaustion that sent him to the concrete bed, Biko and Samuel tried sleeping on the floor, but Hopewell shivered, his body already not completely his own, his legs and arms cramping, and in his half-sleep he'd cried out.

'Com, this isn't working.' Samuel's hushed voice woke Biko.

'What should we do?' Biko asked.

'We need to rub him. It will help the cramping,' Samuel said.

'How do you know?'

'Because I know. Come on.'

They sat at either end of the slab, Biko pressing Hopewell's arms, Samuel kneading the calves. Hopewell sighed, sucked the air over his teeth, his clenched face relaxing. They continued in silence, sliding their hard-skinned hands over Hopewell's legs and arms. The moonlight speckling the cell stretched their bodies onto the walls. Washed by the faint, dancing light, Hopewell's extended limbs danced in the shadows. Biko thought of the heavy, inert arms of a puppet.

'My eldest sister died,' Samuel said. Biko looked up. 'Her husband died three years later. One of her children died last year. My youngest sister in Durban is sick. I look after her children – well, I did. Another brother, Mike, died two years ago.'

'An elder brother?' Biko asked.

'No, the same age.'

'What?'

'My twin.'

Biko was silent. He could do anything but this, these fireside chats about family, always the same – a list of the dead, his aunts and uncles, cousins, friends, comrades. Why didn't Samuel shut up and keep his eyes fixed to the horizon? Mugabe would give them nothing; the waves that broke over the rocks would only concede to their will if they were as relentless and determined as the sea itself. The ocean obeyed the law of gravity, it was impervious to heartbreak and death, to Samuel's storytelling about the dead. *The goddamn useless, traitorous dead. Can't you hear the ocean? Listen, listen, I can hear it roaring just outside our cell, outside the window in Durban, where your sister stays. Don't you know the ocean doesn't care that she's dying and that her muscles tighten and cramp at night and keep her up, as she worries about her children in Bulawayo?*

'What about on your side?' Samuel asked.

'What?' Biko answered dumbly.

'Anyone gone to the three-letter curse?'

'Yes.'

'Aunts and uncles?'

'Yes.'

'Friends?'

'Yes.'

'Parents?'

Biko was silent again.

From that night on they slept on either side of Hopewell, holding him, pressing him together so his body, his legs, arms, hands, head did not come off in the night and the darkness could not claim him. In the morning they uncrossed their entwined limbs and checked that Hopewell was still alive, woke him, showed him the cell, the morning sun, indicated the inappropriate chirping birds outside the prison. Each sign a reason to hold on and to boast to the guards that they'd cheated the night once more through sheer will and comradeship, that they'd denied Mugabe another soul.

*

Anne-Marie had left early in the morning and came in late. She dropped her clothes silently to the floor, her bare feet sticking slightly to the tiles, peeling off quickly as she moved round the bed. Viktor pretended to sleep, pretended that he *could* sleep when she wasn't in the bed. Her only words to Viktor when she left had been, 'Don't feed the bird. You are encouraging it.'

In the morning, Viktor thought, *she will be gone, another Southern African tour for her NGO, another jamboree with donors in a downtown hotel*. Anne-Marie had explained it all to him. The food lavish, the staff supine; only the colourful boubous, sandals, craft jewellery made with cowry shells distinguished their conventions, conferences and workshops from the corporate circuit when they took their turn at the Conference Trough in the Global South.

'It's a farce. I know it, but at least I can subvert some of their budget to real causes,' Anne-Marie argued, her hands circling the air, excusing the excesses.

'Maybe you'll get too comfortable and you won't want to leave,' Viktor replied.

*

Nelson was always the most adamant; his arguments meant something. He didn't speak, he argued. Life as polemic. Viktor heard him speaking to a young organiser for the group. The boy wore a stained, overlarge T-shirt that hung loosely over his skinny build. His alert eyes stared earnestly at Nelson.

'You're a good organiser, comrade, but you need to argue. You have to be hard and you have to go in to win. We're not selling ice cream. *Tinofanira kurwisa uye tinofanira kukunda shamwari yangu.*'

When the boy was gone, rushing out with the gift of renewed energy, Nelson sighed deeply and dropped his face into his cupped hands, letting his dreadlocks fall over his arms. 'Was I too hard on him, Vik?'

'I liked the line about ice cream.'

'So I was too hard?'

'I don't know,' Viktor answered, pleased to be asked. 'Maybe you were. Does it matter that he wins the argument every time?'

Nelson's mouth opened to a smile. 'Of course it does. You know, I don't even think we have to win the argument to stop Mugabe and his thugs. They are puny compared to your lot, the class of murderers you face in the UK. That sophisticated game of hide and seek you play in the Global North. You know what got me? The first war in the Gulf in 1991. The US assembles an army of 250,000 in the Middle East in two weeks to take back their oil, and I thought, They won't hesitate to move against us if it's ever necessary.' Nelson had stood up. Beads of sweat had formed on his forehead. His voice was low. He turned to Viktor, chopping the space in front of him, out of rhythm with his words. *He means it*, Viktor thought. *He always means what he says.* 'We need to win the argument. We need to be stronger,' Nelson concluded.

'Form is important, too, Nelson,' Viktor said. 'It matters how we speak. How we leave people feeling.'

'You're a liberal, an ice-cream seller too. But we need to be a piston box, Viktor, and piston boxes aren't pretty.' He rubbed his face vigorously, fell into the chair again, took out a pen and on a scrap of paper, leaning on his thigh, he started to draw.

'This, comrade,' he said eventually, holding the torn page aloft, 'is what a piston box looks like. It only moves if steam is pushed quickly through it. Then the piston rod moves through the cylinder cover. See? The cylinder cover provides a box to prevent the leakage of steam, to drive the rod. Do you see?' Nelson pointed to his surprisingly detailed diagram, to the arrows on the page. 'The steam is the people, the workers, the poor,' he said, dropping the page. 'They are the movement. But without the cylinder cover, the steam disperses and the piston rod doesn't move. We have to win the argument, Viktor. Build the piston box. Do you see?'

The memory had erupted over him like a party streamer, a gash of colour and chaos.

Viktor rolled onto his back. The morning, in its blind hope, was beginning to squawk. The rooster – Mobutu, Nelson called him – who inhabited the walkway between the flats and each day cleared a path with his feathered chest had begun his morning chorus.

Viktor could picture it all, this city that was no longer really a city, recolonised by the countryside, the rural areas and cockerels. It was Mobutu, not Mugabe, who really held power in Zimbabwe.

'We need to know you are going to stay, that we can rely on you. I'm not saying to burn your passport, never to return, but rather make a decision to stay here with us, with the group. Commit to us, Viktor.' Anne-Marie had delivered this speech as Viktor pulled up his trousers, balancing on the end of the bed. Anne-Marie stood in the doorway, dressed up for meetings, her hair tied back.

'Do you mean us?' he asked.

'No. This. Commit to this.' She opened her hands, unfolded her arms.

'I see.' Though hurt, he knew she was right.

'Okay, yes, us as well. But they are the same thing, the bigger us: Biko, Nelson, the students.'

Mobutu shrieked outside the front door. *Get up, Viktor! Wake up, you lazy white man!* Viktor pulled himself up, the sheet sticking to him, and fumbled in the half-light for his sandals.

There was Rosa's name, he thought, *I argued that we should call her Rosa. I won that argument. I committed to that.*

Viktor walked stiffly to the kitchen, his back painful from the night. The thin, foam mattress, that he had already replaced, his immobile body marked out on the bed, the hard wood boards, pressed against him. He stretched, lifting his arms, his fingers grazing the ceiling.

Mobutu squawked and scratched at the door. Barely conscious, Viktor dropped his hand into the bag, fingered two slices of white bread, closed his hand around them. He walked to the door. Mobutu was tapping now in even, repetitive intervals. The morning feed generated no affection for Viktor; quite the opposite, it seemed. Mobutu had become adamant and expectant – when he saw Viktor in the afternoon he spread

431

his decorative, useless wings and ran towards him screaming. *I feed him and he doesn't like me. If I don't feed him, he'll try to kill me. I can't fucking win.* Viktor opened the door wide enough to push his hand through and he sprinkled the doorstep with the dough and crusts. Mobutu, as usual, thrust his head through the door and rattled his red, spotted jowls.

Viktor showered. It was always the first part of the morning that didn't feel like he was running on automatic.

'We should call her Rosa. After Rosa Luxemburg,' he'd said to Nina.

'No, she needs her own name, not a character from your PhD,' Nina had answered.

'Rosa is not a character in my PhD, she was a Polish-German Jewish revolutionary. She was killed in 1919 by the Freikorps, the forerunners of the Nazis.'

'Great!'

So for ten days Rosa was known as 'the baby' or 'the little one', nameless and bleary-eyed, until Viktor won the Naming Dispute and set his daughter up for a lifetime of political failure and murder. Her fogged and translucent eyes in those first weeks stared through everything, but to Viktor she only seemed to focus when her name was finally agreed upon. At last she could see the world, pin down the flat and her parents. The name Rosa anchored his daughter, declared that she belonged, and could no longer float above them noisily in those early post-birth, maybe days. Rosa had arrived.

Viktor soaped himself, the water turning hot and cold, forcing him to step away from the showerhead to froth the soap, coat his back, chest, penis with the suds, then step back into the water to wash off the lather.

He found his way back to Nina and pictured her in bed, smiling at him, dripping wet from the shower.

'Okay, darling, we'll call her Rosa,' she'd said finally, 'but don't mention the murder until she's grown up.'

Viktor had dropped the towel, thrown himself on the bed and kissed her.

Viktor heard Mobutu again in the corridor, full from his morning meal but still complaining. He felt a pain in his own head from the noise of all his memories; he wanted silence. *My head is a forest of wild birds, living and dead*, he thought.

After the shower he dried himself following the methodical regime his mother had taught him. 'Don't leave any part of your body wet when you leave the bathroom, sweetie, or you'll catch cold.' He dug his fingers into the towel as he rubbed his head dry of water. He pulled the towel back, dragging his hair flat against his forehead, his receding hairline.

He needed to get out of the flat. He'd heard that Biko and his cell-mates were being transfered and he wanted to be there, with the others, to show him that he had witnessed the violence, that he knew the name of the Master of Ceremonies, that he had felt Hitler's hand on his own groin, witnessed his friend experiencing the Bulawayo Treatment. *Make it wet. Make it wet.* Viktor grimaced at the memory.

He chased away the guilt wrapping itself around his guts. He saw himself, his face twisted in the mirror, and he turned away. A biblical sacrifice, all that laconic dialogue, those barked orders and brutality. Viktor had seen the deep state, the abuses that the NGOs spoke about, the impunity of ZANU-PF that the UK government listed as they deported Zimbabweans back to the jails and prisons.

Viktor rushed through the final stages of his ablutions and dropped the towel on the floor, leaving watery footprints on his way to the kitchen.

Mobutu started up again. *Fuck that bird*, he thought, *so goddamn ungrateful. If it wasn't for me you'd be a sickly, scrawny vagrant or dead, bony, meatless addition to someone's* sadza.

*

Viktor swung the door open and the sunlight fell on him. Mobutu was close.

The flat was permanently in the dark; the small windows in the kitchen and bathroom overlooked the walkway that connected the flats. The flat held its temperature, heating up only a little in the day. On good days, when Anne-Marie went in late to work, they would eat porridge in bed under the cheap, rough blankets that rubbed their skin, their exposed arms growing numb in the cold, the curtains open so they could see the unobstructed morning sun that filled the sky with radiant, unquestioned authority. The sun obliterated the night, so the twenty-degree fall in temperature that accompanied the bright, black night seemed impossible.

In Zimbabwe it was easy to forget the night. Too easy.

If Anne-Marie knew I was giving away bread to this animal, she would kick me out. Viktor blinked, shielded his eyes, pulled the door closed and looked around for the bird. This morning duel was a contest of masculinities. Viktor versus Mobutu, man versus bird. Viktor was charged. The bird was half-flying, its blood-red, plumed wings extended, its neck and head forward as it rushed him. Viktor would sidestep the bird, deflect the dictator with his bag.

It seemed that crumbling the slices of bread, handing over the food through a crack in the door, had given the bird the notion that Viktor was stealing the bread; stealing the seeds, the grain, the fields and the land from its indigenous owners.

Mobutu was trained by Mugabe. *The bird is a black nationalist*, Viktor realised. *Mobutu hates me because I am white and he knows I'm an interloper*. Mobutu didn't just want crumbs; he wanted to control the bakery. Mobutu had memorised the party line.

In a couple of seconds he heard nothing from the bird. He hooked the bag, with notebooks, pen, laptop, phone, books, over his shoulder and started his fifteen-minute walk into town.

Viktor waited on the corner of Tongogara. Crowded buses passed, with faces pressed against the windows turning round heads flat and human beings into frescoes. The sun's indiscriminating gaze held Viktor as he waited to cross the road and for a few minutes cast out any possibility of thought. The air was already thick; Viktor revelled in the morning sunshine.

As he moved into the shadows sentences came up quickly, jostling for air. *Maybe I was always going to be a bad father and it was always going to be like this. I was never going to stay with Nina. It was an impossible collusion, an accident that could never have worked.* Viktor thought of the last fight he'd had with Nina.

'I don't trust you with Rosa. She comes back with bruises,' she'd said.

'So now I'm an abuser and a philanderer. Anything else on the list, while you're at it?' He'd slammed the phone down before she answered.

Viktor's thoughts went to Mobutu; he stopped abruptly in the street. *The fucking bird didn't disappear. It's in the flat.* He turned round and raced back.

Mobutu had pecked, scratched and defecated across every surface in the kitchen. He had also found the plastic box on the sideboard containing the bread. When Viktor entered, Mobutu was squatting silently next to the pecked, plastic bread bag, crumbs scattered around him. Slices of the bleached loaf lay hollowed, half-eaten, strewn on the floor like brown-rimmed picture frames. A single crust hung out of the rooster's mouth.

Mobutu turned his head to Viktor and eyeballed his foe. He opened his mouth, dropping the crust, and emitted a solitary squawk.

The dictator had won and he knew it. Mobutu put up only token resistance to being bundled, in a grey blanket, out of the flat. Stuffed and satisfied, he emerged unflustered from the blanket, shook his little body and returned to the roost at the end of the walkway, where he lived like a rat in a hollow in the exposed bricks.

Such unambiguous victory: the flat ransacked, reclaimed in a dirty protest that had calmed the bird's ruffled ego. The following day Mobutu granted Viktor a morning reprieve, free from further assault. But two days later the bird, forgetting its recent victory, screamed at the same hour to be allowed back into the flat.

'I'm coming,' Viktor shouted as he rolled out of bed.

Chapter Thirty-Three

Viktor wondered about his love for Anne-Marie. Everything must have its time; authentic life, he believed, germinated slowly in the tended earth. Love, too, needed a season's sun and rain. Love required careful attention to the emotional harvest. It needed to show itself as a tree, not a sapling, something adamant and large in the middle of the field. Love must look knotted, twisted, old, like Isaac, like Sonia. So this feeling he now recognised, the physical tremble in his stomach, his obsession with Anne-Marie, his worry when she wasn't near him, his attention to her needs, the constant, panicked ruminations – was this love?

He returned to these feelings as he crossed Samora Machel and came out of the shadows along the pavement; on the road a noisy, slow line of taxis rattled towards him. He turned right past Harare Gardens; the warm late-afternoon sun caressed him. A mother walked ahead of him, pulling a small child behind her. The child fell behind her mother, then skipped to catch up; she stared at her own feet and the shadowed patterns they made on the ground. Viktor watched her dance on the street. The girl wore a pair of flip-flops, the foam soles paper thin. The cheap hawker-bought sandals were no protection against the pavement, yet the girl moved skilfully around the street rubble.

Her momentary skipping joy refused Viktor's pity; still his chest lurched at the sight of her loose, naked feet. *No fucking pity, just anger. Let me feel anger*, he muttered aloud to himself. His head sought the facts that he needed. In his head he scanned the newspapers, his recent blogs. The girl was still in sight, trailing behind her mother, then running to draw near. Viktor followed them, turning into Seventh Street. *What was the last article I wrote? The new twin-cabs imported from Taiwan for each MP. The expense accounts, the foreign junkets. No, I need more than that.* He saw the mother and child stop and join a makeshift queue waiting for taxis. The mother's brow was dripping wet; the girl looked up at her. Viktor tried, as Nelson had said, to picture the extraordinary collective wealth of Southern Africa – the gold, coal, diamonds, platinum and the land, the rich, fertile land always in the wrong hands. What would this child look like, what would she be wearing on her feet, if this wealth was redistributed? He was almost beside them. The girl stared intensely at him. *Still too abstract*, Viktor thought. *This collectivised, redistributed wealth is too far away. Too late for this child. Fuck.* When he was finally parallel to her, so that there was nothing between them except the fading light, she opened her mouth and smiled, revealing a gap between her two large front teeth. *Too late for her*, Viktor thought again. Too late even for him to smile back before he had moved past them and she had joined the bustle, barging and elbowing into the open combi.

Just like Rosa, those teeth.

'We're the same now, Dad,' Rosa had said, bouncing on his lap, inspecting his open mouth. 'You've got a gap here,' she put her small finger into the gap where his tooth had been removed years ago, 'and I have one at the front.'

Viktor walked on. Then – he couldn't help it – he put a hand to support himself against the wall. He struggled to breathe; he heaved and sucked in the air. He saw Rosa, felt her on him, his own private dentist, her childish breath against his face. He saw the combi hesitantly move past him on the road, weighed down, sagging with the effort, with the people pushed and squeezed together. Viktor saw the girl's face pressed against the back window.

Rosa, Rosa, Rosa, he said over and over again. *Damn it. Damn you, Rosa. Damn Harare. Damn Zimbabwe. Damn Nina. Damn those fucking flip-flops. Damn them all.*

Viktor thought he was a victim to his feelings for Anne-Marie; sentiments that abounded and stampeded in him, which, he fancied, were not even about her but drawn from his daughter.

Strange, this African revelation. It meant, after all this time, that he still loved his daughter and she had managed, in her adamant, determined way, to burrow quietly to the centre of his being. Rosa was always there, sitting cross-legged on his diaphragm, riding up and down with his breath or lying with her head between his lungs, her face pressed against his throbbing heart. There she was, there she would always be; his first and only born. This child that he had not wanted with a woman he did not know, a woman who now hated him and struggled even to pronounce his name. Nina who couldn't say Viktor, and Viktor who couldn't recognise his role in his daughter's life.

The sun was gone now and the patchy dusk filled the sky. Viktor looked for the moon as he stumbled on, stubbing his foot on a broken paving stone. *Then why am I here?* he thought. Always another question, just when he had finally found the answer. *I need Rosa*, he thought. *I should have given that girl's mother some money, should have emptied my goddamn wallet.*

He felt his phone vibrate in his pocket. He pulled it out and saw Anne-Marie's number flashing brightly; the lit screen flickered against his face like a candle. His stomach spasmed with excitement. 'Darling!' he exclaimed into the phone.

*

Comrade,

Delighted that the students are out on bail! A despot's nerves can make him vacillate! Our comrade students out (even on shit conditions) and an appeal against bail – this is the time to recharge, re-steel, rehearse speeches, yes, from the dock – long ones, VERY long ones – a major emphasis for all supporters now must be to get them to submit any trial to the absolute maximum publicity to try to drag it out for months, not to torment our comrades but to save them from the firing squad. These are Mugabe's tactics – don't be fooled by legalese. He is a murderer. Vicious. Biko is not safe while he remains in jail. Is there any news? He is our Lumumba, there is no Plan B without him. No Zimbabwean revolution.

Now: What to do. This is a list from my experience for you to consider, comrade. Let Nelson and Anne-Marie see it – there is more practical passion and common sense in that woman than in anyone I know. I speak here from my experience in South Africa: I was picked up two years after my release for another invented crime. I had been involved in a township group, a sort of Mugabe fan club, fighting the police on a purely black nationalist programme. When I was released I had shit conditions and an accompanying 24/7

440

constant 'escort' of four of their political police thugs with me the whole time. My lover at the time, Lucia, nevertheless did the right things:

1. Phoned up the entire world press: TV, internet video outfits with helicopters. There was the risk they'd arrange an accident if I tried to get my books, files, records, interviews, photos, videos out of the country – I was on my way to Zimbabwe. Half the national press, three TV channels backed me, because any journalist who told the truth and criticised the state and bosses was also given the treatment I received.

2. Despite the fact that Lucia – a coloured women from Johannesburg – never normally cooked (she was as insanely hyperactive as me), she practically 'force-fed' me to build up strength, to sustain me for when they next locked me up and beat me, which is of course utterly unpredictable until there's a physical and visible solidarity movement.

3. Create intense absolute normality for each comrade while they are out of prison, as this undoes a lot of the trauma effect. This refills your mind, conscious and subconscious, with normal thoughts, feelings and sensations. Lucia gave me incessant ultra-sex. 'Maximum fantasy,' she'd order me, 'tell me now.' This is a fantastic restorative. Obviously we can't help Biko on this front if he's in prison, but when he's out we need to strategise.

4. Hold political meetings for all comrades. Let them relax and rise again politically.

5. BUT also with a large company of comrades from the Society of Liberated Minds, in Bulawayo, in Harare, get them out to a physically naturally therapeutic environment, beautiful countryside or a big park at least,

or any moving water is really good – fountains, streams, even artificial ones will also do. I know a place near Gweru. Take them there with lunches.

6. No obvious pampering – just normal comradely, friendly humour and hugs. People who are overwrought, including family, should be 'diverted' and given tasks. Tell them to cook home-made delicious food, lots of mealie-meal, ready for them to take back inside if they are rearrested. The funds we are collecting at the university can be used for these purposes. Can you get food to Biko, can you deliver daily parcels? Tell me what to do. I am ready for your orders, Viktor, do you hear me?

And this is the really important part: TUNISIA. Egypt. Say it once, say it twice, shout it, sing it, repeat it every day: Tunisia. Egypt. There are lessons for Zimbabwe from North Africa. I have been watching closely.

What has happened in Tunisia and Egypt is also happening, now, in Zimbabwe, in Bulawayo. Biko could be *the* match, the ignition, the dynamite. This point is STRAIGHT, DIRECT from how the Tunisian revolution started. The howling, wailing, hysterical mother was given her son's ashes, went almost loopy with grief and pain (a family member, probably the daughter, uploaded it), lashing, gnashing, screaming deafeningly, pacing up and down their tiny home, with the family unsure what to do. Then suddenly it all turned to fury and she strode out, hands in front, carrying her son's ashes and just walked in a straight line to the local government and ruling party HQ where her son torched himself and where the policewoman was based who slapped his face after stealing his bananas. On the way, 1,000, yes, I repeat, the video shows 1,000 (I counted while it was still online) INDUSTRIAL/FACTORY/CONSTRUCTION

WORKERS, falling in respectfully behind her, like a funeral cortege.

We don't know. It could come to this in Bulawayo. And Harare. There are NO rule books on how a loved one may erupt at even the thought of her little baby being threatened with death or prison. Biko is OUR loved one. It is completely correct to ENCOURAGE those around the framed victims to ACT BRAVELY – obviously with concrete advice – and to get numbers. Don't go screaming to the police station at night, or on a quiet, non-working day. Go during working days, preferably as people go to work, as the hawkers set out their stalls, or just before lunch breaks so maximum numbers see the family. This will make the police more careful. They only want to crush and silence this minority, not turn it into 100 or 200 or more. They've seen the videos of the revolutions as well. Mugabe has prepared them.

NO ONE in our ranks should ever slap down a family member or a comrade who, out of the blue, might say: 'I'm going to demand his release. I'm going to burn down the police station.'

IT'S NOT OUR RIGHT TO STOP THEM! Every human being has the right – it's a human right to grieve in whatever way their deepest feelings dictate. No one else has any right to block that. That parent and comrade has to live with a loss if they did NOT fight hard enough to stop, which is a lifelong death sentence, of guilt, remorse, regret. I know.

The union is still organising COLLECTIONS at the university to send more money. You will lack in nothing – tell Biko that, if you can. NOTHING. *NADA. HAPANA.* We will use our own internationalism to fight with you.

I'm sure the arrests and torture have shaken EVERYONE in their whole circle of course. But Mugabe and X-Party will fall, Viktor.

It's going to happen SOONER or LATER.

Sorry if this smacks of abstract 'preaching' but so few people ever even talk about it let alone write about it. The dictatorship will fall. Have faith, have hope.

As for you, Viktor, you must lean on someone – Anne-Marie, Nelson, Lenin. There's usually one obvious person. Anne-Marie is my guess. She is passionate, fearless, but ruthlessly disciplined, intellectually sharp as a razor but totally – like you and me – emotionally crazy for what we fight for. In the West you can easily separate emotion from political operation. In Zim you cannot. Have courage, which I know you do. You have created something, a movement, a campaign. Now liberally apply more practice.

Tendai

*

In the middle of the week Viktor received another email from Nina. As he read the message he felt life rise in him, then tumble out and drain from him. He was breathless. Guiltily he looked around, as if opening the email had suddenly released Nina's words onto Harare's advertising hoardings, scrawling her insults in red ink on abandoned walls or broadcasting the news in hourly bulletins courtesy of the Zimbabwe Broadcast Corporation: 'In a shocking new development, Viktor Isaacs – who has been in Zimbabwe attempting to usurp our democracy, to undermine the project of black empowerment and redistribution – received a fulsome rebuff from his ex-wife, revealing his past as a child abuser and wife beater. Speaking on behalf of the government, Gideon Gumbo stated: "We want the racist, imperialist government in Whitehall to take back their white detritus and stop sending us their problem children. We say send Isaacs back".'

Viktor, I have learnt so much from your abusive behaviour towards me and Rosa. I have suffered much from your behaviour, which I am only beginning to deal with. We were always misaligned, my Virgo's reliability and intelligence and your Libran hesitation and doubt. I see below the surface and recognise what is right. I discriminate and I am passionate. You are not. Our planets pass on separate orbits; our cycles are not in harmony. I am not angry. I can see that our spiritual paths could never have joined. Do you see this was always going to happen? I have made peace. I have plaited a lock of your hair with Rosa's and placed it on the altar. N

How, Viktor asked himself, *does she have a lock of my hair?* The greater her commitment to their planetary incompatibility, the more Viktor ached for her; a terrible, immense sorrow flooded him. Why did she need to call on the cosmos to testify in some almighty spiritual court of their lowly, desperate, irrelevant heartbreak? No, the universe was too puny to judge their immense loss. What was the universe, he thought, to all of their hurt, to their daughter's unquenchable grief? The universe – didn't she know, how could she not see? – was frail, mute, unable to articulate a single syllable next to the enormity of their calamity. The universe was nothing to the longing he felt for his daughter.

*

Viktor and Anne-Marie decided, in the hot, harsh sun, to swim. Viktor drove down Sam Nujoma onto Central Avenue, followed the traffic curving around the National Art Gallery. He saw the sign for Les Brown. A strange name for a Smith-era Olympic-sized swimming pool with high concrete diving boards. Viktor turned the car to the pavement, slowed, straining with the heavy steering. Anne-Marie opened the boot, dropped her handbag in and removed the towel. They tapped on the clouded glass of the ticket office until an old man appeared and punched the price into the till. Two thin rectangular tickets flew out and skidded across the counter.

The pool was deserted. The sun was retreating across the water in a wavering, uncertain line, the stands on one side of the pool ascending with green-painted benches. Around the pool were palms that jostled noisily in the wind. When Viktor and Anne-Marie entered, the entire complex looked untouched, the clear water unpolluted by bodies, the infrastructure intact. The poolscape was a relic of the whites-only colonial world, bereft of people, life, Zimbabwe. In this ruined city, the pool, the afternoon, was timeless. Only the shower room – a cavernous, subterranean chamber under the stalls, loose pipes without showerheads hanging onto the crumbling walls – placed the watery colosseum into its correct context. On close inspection, the spread of gentle ruin overhung the place.

The couple undressed, draping their clothes over a bench. Anne-Marie wriggled out of her dress, tugging it free of her curves until she stood in her bra and panties. Viktor folded each of his clothes carefully, placing one item on the other as he always did, as Isaac did. Anne-Marie stared at the cloth pyramid resting on the bench, the trousers, the shirt, the vest – he was the only man in Zimbabwe who wore a vest – his clothes organised by size, arranged on top of his shoes. She liked his scrupulous ordering, the lists he wrote in bed in the evening, his towering, leaning frame bent in permanent supplication, in apology for his unusual presence, for his disposition. She loved him for his peculiarities and she wanted him.

Silently Anne-Marie laid a towel on the concrete floor, unhooked her bra, squeezed her two thumbs into the sides of her panties and lowered them. Viktor looked at her, surprised, and she smiled slyly and knelt. Lying on her back on the towel, she licked the tips of her fingers, brought them between her legs and started to move her hand in slow circles. Her feet were flat on the floor, her body open, expectant, as though she was reaching for something above the ground, in the stuffy, heated air. She moaned loudly, opened her eyes, searched for Viktor. He looked around cautiously, worried, then gave in, lowered his shorts, dropped to the hard concrete floor and Anne-Marie's soft body.

Viktor entered her. He inhaled her smell, her sweet, salty sweat that sealed their naked bodies together. The smell of her flat, the bed they shared. Viktor had the sensation, barely formed, that their lives had started to bleed into each other. She whispered instructions. 'Slower. Kiss my neck, kiss me.' Together the defined lines of their individual lives, their separate plans, had started to loosen around them.

Anne-Marie came first, turning her mouth from his to gasp. She raised herself, arching into him, then shuddered slightly. Viktor withdrew and released short, urgent jets of come that stood out on the dark skin of her stomach and breasts. Viktor looked away and tried to lift a corner of the towel they lay on, to clean her. 'No, leave it. Lie on me, *mudiwa*. Don't move away.' Viktor wanted to get up, clean them, wash off their lovemaking with the shower in the corner of the room.

As they lay together Anne-Marie said, 'You always want what you can't have.'

'What do you mean?'

447

She crossed one leg over his. 'And when you have it you don't want it any more, or you want something else. Always unsatisfied, always striving.'

'That's not true. I want you. I want Biko to be freed.'

'I just don't know whether you'll ever be happy with me.'

'That's not true,' Viktor protested.

'Isn't it? If I was to draw a picture of your life, there would be a trail of all the things you've left incomplete. The PhD, your journalism, Rosa, Rosa's mother, your parents, your politics.'

'Anne-Marie, why are you saying this?'

'Next you'll tell me you want to be a novelist, and after you have written your first novel, that you want to be an opera singer. Am I right?'

'No.'

'I don't think I can ever please you. Come on, let's swim.'

*

It seemed to Viktor a pity to break the water. The wind was gently blowing and rippling the surface. The stillness of the pool, of the whole complex of old concrete and ageing grandeur, calmed him. The banks of seats surrounding the pool amplified their voices, turned their whispers into declarations.

Anne-Marie lowered herself into the water from the steel ladder, her straight, long calves and thighs spreading. She had tied her plaits in a knot on top of her head; she kept her head out of the water as she swam.

Viktor walked to the far end of the pool, which was still in the sun's blaze. When Anne-Marie could see him, he dived into the water. He surfaced into the light. Without his glasses he strained to see. His chest hurt; a sharp pain pulsed along his sternum. He breathed deeply, stood on his pointed feet, balanced on his toes. *The awful tragedy is that I am made up of bone and flesh, two large pumping lungs, an intricate, vulnerable system of veins, capillaries, organs. Our entire, fleshy, moist life is a sort of travesty.* He thought of Biko's pathetic flesh, its inadequate defence against police truncheon and gun, his developed consciousness encased inside such a brittle frame. There was something about this that seemed wrong, a failure of evolution to build a more rigorous, determined crust, a surer hold against mortality. Viktor rotated in the water, kept his legs and arms moving, his face raised to the waning sun. *We need a firmer defence against oppression. After all, how long has our species had to evolve a defensive shell, develop an organism immune to torture and inhumanity? How many millennia of oppression have we suffered?*

Anne-Marie swam an Olympic length. Then, shivering, she pulled herself from the water and lay on the side of the pool in the sun, an arm over the edge, her hand immersed in the chilled water. Viktor swam to her, hauled himself out of the water and sat next to her, embracing his bent legs.

'I'm sorry. I didn't mean to say those things,' Anne-Marie said, her eyes closed.

'Maybe you're right.'

'Don't agree with me, Viktor. I don't want to be right. I need you to contradict me.' Anne-Marie turned to her side and supported her head on her bent arm. The imprint of the paving stones marked her back, pressing hieroglyphics into her flesh. 'Sorry I said those things,' she said again.

'Don't be. Don't.'

'Stop telling me I'm wrong to apologise, *mudiwa*.'

'Okay, I won't speak. You speak, sweetie, and I'll listen.'

Anne-Marie was the most certain, clear-headed person he knew. Her life was ordered. The things she set out to do each day were actually completed. In her own way she was sure of herself and her commitments to small acts, saving Zimbabwe, the Congo, one soul at a time. To Viktor she seemed to amplify before him; her worthiness eclipsed him. Her proportions seemed magnified against his weaknesses and deficiencies; to Viktor's moral crisis, his total failure of self-assurance, she hastened and overcame. Anne-Marie broke over the world volubly and mastered herself.

The water turned her impromptu swimwear translucent. The triangle of black hair was visible through her panties. Her nipples, cold and erect, protruded through the bra, the small, alert granules of skin traced through the material. Just minutes ago all of his energy had been directed to her, yet he felt the certainty of desire again and craved the clarity of her body, the self-assurance of their lovemaking.

'I want us to make a trip to Kinshasa when Biko is released, before you leave.'

Viktor was surprised. 'Why didn't you say?'

'I need you to do certain things first. I want you to meet my grandmother.'

'Your grandfather's wife?'

'Yes, Patrice's wife, who else? She's the most determined, stubborn woman I know. She's not political, not in a Zimbabwean way, but she has a keener feeling for people than anyone I know.'

'It sounds like a test. A Lumumba exam.'

'Maybe.'

Maybe? What was this? Anne-Marie never lingered on conditional adverbs or sought what she did not have. Instead she complained about fake prophets and flabby reasoning. Torture would not yield disappointment in Anne-Marie. She sat up, adjusted her position on the towel and hunched, like Viktor, over her knees, the sun on her back.

'I am taking a terrible risk talking to you like this. I don't want what I am going to say to sound like an ultimatum. It's not. I don't even want you to answer now. Not today.' Viktor was silent. They had been so free from introspection and doubt; their relationship had occupied an unusual, unknown place of simple, unequivocal presence. He didn't want this disturbed. '*Chéri*, when I saw you today by the car outside my office, I thought just for a second that there would never be a time when you would be completely here, without some agitated, second thought.'

'Well, that's true,' Viktor replied nervously. 'How can I be anywhere, exactly, when Biko's still in jail? Can't we go home? Talk about this after we've eaten?'

'You need to surrender to something. Not to me, necessarily, but to something. I felt you were beginning to do that, starting at last to give in. But I need to know you're ready.'

'For what?'

'For *life*, Viktor. This. Zimbabwe. Harare. Biko. Us. Me and you. Otherwise you will run away again, on your UK passport, like another expat on an African mission. I need to know that you won't get out and leave all of us hanging. It doesn't have to be here, but once you've decided, you must stay. What good are you to the world, to Biko, to your daughter, otherwise? There are battles to be had. There are people who need you.'

Viktor turned to the pool, lowered his feet into the water and stared into the grainy, descending dusk, the waning sun. He realised then what he had only indistinctly known before: that he had always failed to be what people wanted. Worse even than never entirely pleasing anyone, with his episodic commitment he raised expectations and then dashed them. If he had only been with Rosa, then at least he would be known for his dogged fathering. If he had simply dug in his heels at work and become

451

a trusted comrade to Moreblessing and Tendai and Patience. *I have never quite managed to be a single thing*. Viktor summoned the image of Biko and his one-man war on society, the dictatorship, on Mugabe and his jackals: Biko's great arc of commitment to life.

'Why are you crying?' Anne-Marie asked.

Viktor rubbed his eyes roughly. 'I'm not,' he said.

'I just want you to listen to me, then we'll go home and you can have dinner.'

'I am listening, *mudiwa*.'

Chapter Thirty-Four

Three weeks after Hopewell had collapsed, he lay each day motionless. Biko and Samuel could function in the cell with their eyes closed. Three steps to the bucket by the toilet, the plastic cup bobbing on the water. Two steps to the bed. Biko raised himself from his position against the wall, his large hands cupped round Hopewell's head to pour the water into his mouth. Two steps back; the green plastic cup dropped again into the bucket of water. Three and a half steps to the door to stretch in the early, lightless morning, two fists hammering against the rusted door to wake the prison. From the door, one step to the centre of the cell and to their whole miniature universe, their constellation.

Despite his protests and midday sermons, delivered at the allotted hour one step from the iron prison door, Hopewell's will to death was stronger than Biko's to life.

'So, comrades, to summarise, we must take the war to X-Party like we did in 1996 to 1998: strikes, demonstrations, the war veterans marching with us, not against us. The turmoil across all layers, in the city, towns, the village, each following our lead.' Samuel and Hopewell stared at Biko, his arms fanning the room.

His hands seemed to throw punctuation out of an invisible hat – exclamation points and question marks, hyphens, semicolons marking up his speech, his finger pointed towards his audience – a full stop, a pause, a deep breath, then a statement. 'Leave X-and Y-Party no rest!' His right index finger pointed to the ceiling in exclamation, to harass them, cut off their oxygen. His full hand open, the sentence unfinished, semicolon. 'Let us take the offensive.' One finger, full stop. 'Our mission, brothers,' pause, colon. 'To open a new front. Choke the regime from the south and north.' Another pause, his finger dotting the space in front of him. 'Bring our cadre, our activists from Bulawayo, infiltrate and stir up the population of Mutare, the Eastern Highlands.' Two hands up, his palms facing the men, semicolon. 'We must spread Zimbabwe across Africa, take Africa to Zimbabwe. The mighty Southern African working class will rise again.' Another pause. 'Across the deserts of the North and South, the Great Lakes, across the continent, bring out, infiltrate the north, to Algeria on the Mediterranean and Johannesburg and Durban in the south. Create a great, restless march of the poor, slum dwellers, the workers, shake the whole land without end, beyond the horizon, spread out over each country, across every border.'

Then the staccato finish, two fists hammering the words out like pistons: 'We'll wear out their borders, the nations that divide us, grind our enemies into the earth, bring Africa together, create the continent as one land, one struggle, one people.' Suddenly a pause and a sub-clause. 'Are you listening, brothers?' Open-mouthed, Hopewell and Samuel nodded. 'We will take the absurd, the impossible, strike it in every direction and cast the entire continent into the war.' Then, shouting, 'For life and light against their night!'

Exhausted, Biko finished. He dropped his hands and seemed to break down. Despite his stubborn, repetitive resolve, his prison ideology, he couldn't halt Hopewell's decline. The guillotine fell from a distance high above the prison, the patch of sky over Zimbabwe, over the continent.

At night Samuel and Biko donated their flesh and muscles and the three men lay together, Hopewell cushioned in the odd configuration of limbs pressed around him. The cell vibrated to Samuel's uneven snoring. Biko's head rested on his arm, his face inches from the back of Hopewell's neck. He placed his free hand on Hopewell's back and felt the struggle in his chest, his wet, choked lungs, his ribbed frame slowly surrendering. Biko couldn't sleep. He needed to witness Hopewell, keep him with them by the simple act of observation. He rested his hand on Hopewell's cheek, felt the lolling of his friend's head.

*

Anne-Marie would be pleased with him, with the sleep that came on her instruction and wasn't disturbed by his body constantly trying to find a position, a place, where he might find sleep. Even these drugs were a solution of sorts; she'd understand the concrete steps he'd taken to quiet his mind, to stop the images of the truncheon, the sounds of Biko's pain, the feeling of Hitler's hands cupping his face to make him watch.

Viktor opened the top drawer in the bedroom chest of drawers, where she'd cleared her skirts and shirts that he had ironed and arranged, the only statement of his love Viktor thought she'd really allowed them. In many ways she was so organised, her sense of what was important worked out with no ambiguity. The way she'd declared his presence in her life, matter-of-fact, announcing to her friends that they were together, telling the comrades – and Nelson – that the group could use *their* flat. Viktor had proved himself incapable of

455

clear, decisive action, but it didn't matter, because Anne-Marie could do it for them both, order his life, arrange their lives in Zimbabwe. He would offer his hands for the folding, the scrubbing, the washing-up, a pantomime of action that required no real thought or commitment.

The bedroom was in chaos, the cover on the bed crumpled, the sheets pulled away from the mattress, clothes scattered on the floor. Viktor dropped the box of pills into the drawer; a corner of a photo was visible under a mess of T-shirts. He pulled it out.

He was sitting on a bench with Rosa pressed against his chest. She looked grown-up, as she would look for the rest of her life, her face slightly tense, weary, staring into the distance. His face too, like his daughter's, looked unsettled; he was staring down at her. Nina had taken the photo at the end of the day, after the rides they'd all shared at the fairground, the miniature train they had taken over and over again till they were exhausted and penniless, Rosa riding between them, crying out for more. Their indulgence had been endless that day.

Holding the photo, Viktor sat heavily on the bed. He looked into Rosa's distant eyes. The tears were still there, his words of reassurance to the sudden desperate sadness that had engulfed her, as great as the joy seconds before, on their last circuit of the train. 'You know, sweetheart,' he'd said, 'if we have another go on the train, that'll use up our bus fare and we'll have to walk, and I can't carry you any more. You're too big now. You'll have to walk.'

It had been her choice – as everything was that day – so they rode the train one last time. Then, as they walked away from the fair – for a few seconds they even skipped together, all of them, Rosa holding Viktor and Nina's hands, she suddenly started to cry loudly, looking back to the coloured lights as the rides spun, turned and sparkled in the dusk. Viktor, bending down to her height, held her in his arms, then lifted her up and walked to a bench and sat down with her, whispering into her ear until her tears slowed, her loud, breathless sobs softened. 'Darling, it's okay. There'll be many fairs. When you're bigger we'll ride together on the Big Wheel right up in the sky. I promise. That's what we'll do.' He had repeated these words over and over until her gulping, heaving chest had slowed and she rested against his neck. And then Nina had taken the photo.

Viktor looked again at the photo. Rosa's frozen, sad face was caught, he fancied, in her first hideous realisation that everything comes to an end. The fair, the skipping, the weekend, the loving, the momentary truce between her parents; their joy and her tears, he thought, came from the inevitable, awful conclusion that every pleasure ends just when it has started.

Now Viktor cried too. *We'll ride together on the Big Wheel. I promise. That's what we'll do.* The photo sucked the air out of him, choked him with tears and remorse. He looked at the brown jumper he was wearing in the photo. Tears fell on the photo, wetting Rosa's face again. What he had tried to suppress, clog with his writing, with Zimbabwe, the campaign, was the Rule of Life, his life, of the goddamn universe: not to part from her. Rosa had held him tightly that night, grabbed his hand, her nails pressing into his arm. The day at the fair was over just as it had started. And like the final choice she'd made, to ride once more on the train and walk home in the setting sun, Rosa knew that they could easily, if they wanted, decide not to fight any more and be together. Find a way through and refuse to let go.

Isn't that what it all meant? Viktor now asked himself.

He dropped the photo to the floor and pushed it under the bed with his heel. He stood, straightened the covers, gathered up the scattered clothes and threw the dirty ones to the door for washing. He folded the others, placing them neatly on the bed.

*

Beside the pool, Anne-Marie spoke fluently, as though she had been rehearsing. 'There is the strangest sensation, with you, of always being alone. You are only half present. A part of your mind is constantly absent. I've seen it, Vik: your lips composing your next article, the latest Facebook status. You seem to have given over a portion of existence to the internet. Sometimes it seems that is where you really live and feel and express yourself. Your measures of success, even for Biko, are the numbers of likes you receive or how extensive the comments are on your latest update. That's why you could open up to me the way you did, because it was through that screen. If we'd met in person I doubt you would ever have approached me.' Anne-Marie stumbled, paused. 'You live by a laptop brightness, in a halo of screens. In meetings, in the day, in the toilet, always some message, email, blog post. You have *abandonné, abandonné ta vie*, for' – Anne-Marie faltered – 'some, some *rêve, une rêve*, a dreamworld, a sort of death. A small death.'

A breeze blew across the water, working up small waves; a miniature surf broke and spat against Viktor's legs. His addiction to the world Anne-Marie described was worse than even she knew. He had hidden his longing for even their lovemaking to be over so that he could post another piercing, startling observation, spill more words over some theory. Did he really need to write another word on Sartre? Had the world not already had its say on Jean-Paul? Were there not enough essays and books on Fanon? On the bloody Nazis and Heidegger? The world did not need more books. The stock of answers was already available. *All the solutions to the problems facing us are already present, but the continent and its people are unable to grasp them.* Viktor couldn't stop himself. Each living, breathing segment of the day needed its counter-substantiation online, to justify, to prove, to *be*. Even in Zimbabwe Viktor only felt truly alive when he was illuminated by his screens, the lifeless brightness of his phone and laptop. And now he had dragged Biko into this, his universe.

Viktor had reasoned that the present didn't really exist. Since life moved constantly onward in a complex series of lurches and false starts into the future, there was only the future, with no honeymoon or consummation in the present. Time turned life into dust. In his fevered state he saw life travelling from memories of the past to a future filled by death.

Anne-Marie was right.

Still, Viktor defended himself. 'Yes and no, Anne-Marie. The new media is overused, but it also connects us with each other – London and Harare, Cairo and New York. It gives us a connection to communities that might otherwise be invisible, inaccessible in our neoliberal world, when there is no money for airfares and no time off from labour. This is why I have become passionate about the fight to get us ... us activists to fight for internet freedom. It's why the old man is so intent on monitoring it, checking our emails for insults.' Viktor hunched his shoulders and stared into the dusk. He turned his hands over as if he was offering up this freedom in his open palms. 'These devices of ours,' he continued, 'are proprietary, used to sell things, but darling, they have potential. Imagine how we could use them if we weren't bound by capitalism.' Viktor brought his feet out of the water and adjusted his position towards Anne-Marie.

'We have in Zimbabwe, in London, in our possession the technological ability to access every book ever written, every painting, song, every recording of every opera, every corner of the planet. Imagine – every backstreet revolutionary, shack protester, Egyptian activist, can be in touch with each other. The only thing between us and real access for everyone to total information is capital. The commercialisation of the internet is no less a historical defeat than the enclosures of the commons in Europe and the colonisation of Africa. Do not dismiss the value of these digital commons, that we still control, to change the world if we fight and occupy them.'

Anne-Marie laughed loudly, shook her head aggressively. She enjoyed Viktor's passion, the way his words piled up, falling out of his mouth, his saliva spraying her legs. Yet she didn't know how she had managed to draw Viktor into this debate, when she had planned to make a swift denunciation and move on to the point.

Viktor's passion had been aroused little in the past weeks except his insistence on turning everything, each conscious daytime breath, to Biko. This indulged his craving for distraction and turned every action to high dread. A pervasive obsession drove him on. She had seen it, each day: Viktor digging deeper into the grave. Recently he had not even wanted to raise his expectations. He welcomed each rejection, every refusal by a lawyer, politician or campaigner to help, as evidence of a plot to destroy the single unflawed individual who could have reversed the plunge and torn Mugabe from his throne. Somehow Biko was the only person who had remained untainted by life – no longer a person, a passionate, impulsive, often maddening human being, but a symbol of decisiveness to Viktor's paralysis and confusion.

Anne-Marie worried about what could possibly be left of Viktor if he had already been so taken over by loss: Biko's, Rosa's, his parent's, hers, his own. This impassioned engagement at the pool's edge was a surprise to her. She sat up and let go of her knees.

'*Je ne suis pas d'accord,Viktor. Pas du tout*.The campaign for online freedom is not as great as the struggle against colonialism. In my dreams for a new Zimbabwe, a new Congo and continent, we will spend less time *inhalé*, absorbed, by computers.The use of these, these screens, speak of crisis, *mudiwa*, the reasons why we can't travel, why we remain imprisoned inside our borders. You want to fight for freedom of access so everyone can be turned into the living dead, like you. Slaves to a technology that you say will free us. Hah!' Anne-Marie felt the power of her own reason lift her. 'Skype, Facebook, Twitter, email, they all enslave us, but only once our lives, communities, families have been destroyed. Why do I have to tell you this? I thought *you* were the radical with a ton of theory.'

Anne-Marie was so convinced by her argument, the momentum of her words, that she had become angry thatViktor should be so wrong. She continued, 'Sure, I want an archive of books and music, but if I believed in Nelson's revolution, once we have one, our first liberation, your first act, will be away from our bloody laptops and phones. Then these tools you speak of will be *débarrassé* entirely. Life and work freed from this dependence.Your addiction.' She became calm, then continued. 'I love speaking to my family in Kinshasa, to my mother, but why can't you see that this connection is about our loss and *douleur* ... the, the grief. Our lives are fragmented, broken by separation, whatever you call it.' Talking about her family, she recovered her breath, her tone less insistent. 'You know,Viktor, thirty years ago we could drive across the Congo, from here to Lusaka, Lubumbashi, and then buses, taxis, trains, to Kinshasa. Trains, Viktor, do you hear that? Nineteenth-century technology. But now we have Skype. Text messages,

WhatsApp. Thank the Lord for your phone. Give me back our trains; give me one train, one journey, Lubumbashi to Kinshasa, for all your smartphones. *Mon royaume pour un train*. No, Viktor, *mudiwa*, in my future this technology will find its correct place and serve us, not give us this, this …' Anne-Marie waved her hand over Viktor, his drying, half-wet body, his face, head, his aura, 'this new slavery. More men like you.'

What was Viktor hiding from? How had he turned his life force into the slavery that Anne-Marie spoke of? About this enslavement she was right. His ear was blocked with water; he turned his head to the side and knocked it, pushed his finger into his ear, held his nose and blew. The water bubbled and fizzed against the eardrum.

'What would Lenin make of Facebook and texting?' Viktor asked.

'You mean our Lenin, Nelson's Lenin?' Anne-Marie queried.

'No. Vladimir. Lenin the Bolshevik,' Viktor added.

'Lenin?' Anne-Marie shouted. 'You're not serious! Who cares what he would have made of it? No, sorry, *désolée*, you and Nelson care. I'm wrong.'

Viktor felt his pulse quicken. 'Lenin spent a lot of his time smuggling hand-mimeographed papers into Russia. He created an entire network of clandestine distributors. The point I am making—'

'Yes, please make it before I ask Stalin to shoot you.'

'The point is that this technology has streamlined making papers, books, pamphlets. Sure it's distracting, the instant gratification and validation is addictive, but human beings find a way. We adapt.'

Anne-Marie's laughter was short, ironic, derisive. 'Yes, we adapt to new oppressions. I deal with adaptation every day. I adapt to the old man, to the Third *Chimurenga*, to text-

462

messaging rural households out of poverty. Did you hear that? We give our clients mobile phones so they can *adapt*.'

Viktor ran his tongue across his teeth. 'Every great thinker in the nineteenth century thought the printing press meant the death of language.'

'Facebook is not the printing press. Your blogs are not a great invention, Viktor.'

'No, no, I'm not saying that. But it is the next linguistic shift, a technological turning point. We have to embrace these turning points, otherwise we'll be lost and existence won't mean anything. We won't be able to communicate in the language of the twenty-first century, with the new generation, the young. I know I am right.' As he spoke he genuinely thought he was. There was an easy rhythm to his logic. The plausibility of his argument carried him forward on snaking sentences until he had shed his doubts.

Anne-Marie stood up, the pale creases on her stomach visible; her tall, rounded form, still smelling of moisturiser, flickered into sepia against the darkening day. Viktor craned, his neck strained, he stretched to see her. 'You've spoken to me about Rosa, the Skype calls,' she said. 'The tours she gives you of her room, the apartment. How your relationship with your daughter has become hanging out on a computer screen.' Anne-Marie let out another short, single laugh. 'You can have your technological turning point. Your life in the West. Keep it.' With her hands on her hips, Anne-Marie shook her head. The plaits tumbled to her shoulders as she cast off the remaining drops of water. 'Come on, Vlad,' she said, offering Viktor her hand.

They were silent. The walk to the car, away from the pool, was solemn, their heads ringing with the words of their argument. As they drove back to the flat, Anne-Marie spoke.

'I don't know if I can make you happy, if anyone can. What I want to say is, it would be hard leaving you now, but we would both survive. Better that we do it now, if we need to, than later, when you will be in each step I take and I will be in yours.' Anne-Marie shuddered from head to foot, felt the cold in the air. 'Life needs tenacity, Viktor. Patient blows at the same point, until you really see change. Nelson has that relentlessness. So do the others, in their way: Lenin, Biko. If Nelson has his revolution, his revolt, whatever you want to call it—'

'Sweetheart, that is not what Nelson argues.' Viktor spoke urgently. 'There are these things already, revolts, protests, revolutions. The point is to direct them and lead them. They exist here too, in Zimbabwe, in the Congo. You changed history in 2000. X-Party was almost toppled, only for the movement to be hijacked and stolen. The point is leadership, organisation, how we challenge the NGOs, the middle class, the professionals.'

Anne-Marie thought about her grandmother, Pauline, sitting on the steps to the front door, swaddled in a patterned cloth, a twist of material around her head, peeling vegetables, gutting fish, plucking live chickens, all the time shouting to friends and neighbours walking past the house. Patrice, she said, always wanted her out of the kitchen; he pleaded with her to leave some of the chores to the staff, but she never listened to him. She was unflinching in her impression of her husband as just another noisy man. She saw through the avant-garde city when she arrived in Leopoldville in the 1950s, the gyro-buses, the tall apartment buildings and highways, the intrusion of a foreign power. These riches dazzled her husband but gave the Congolese nothing.

Têtue comme moi, Anne-Marie thought.

This woman had been the one person in her life who drew her out, distracted her, made her heart race and the pulse sound in her ears – who held her, levelled the ground and steadied her grip. And now, now, unaccountably, an entire thought had planted itself in her head: the need, the desire even, for Viktor to meet her grandmother.

For years, when she was studying in Paris, she had made the calls to Kinshasa, to her grandmother, with an interpreter. In language shorn of sentimentality, Pauline spoke to her young granddaughter. 'You are my children. All of you. When you come back to the Congo, I will make a big party for you and dance.'

And the day I arrived I shouted, Je suis là! *Two hours after the plane had landed I was sitting next to her on the porch preparing for the party, sharing a cigarette. It was only the second time I had ever seen her.*

Ignoring Viktor's defence, his interruption, Anne-Marie went on, 'After Nelson's revolution you will need to continue, long afterwards, on the same consistent path. Yes? Understand, this is not what I want or what I am suggesting. If you can become immovable, fixed to one thing, to a single course, then I need to know. Not now, but soon. If you can't, then just let me go to the Congo alone. You see, I need to know if you want this to evolve into something. You have to let me know. If not, then we should tear up the foundations now, or soon, *avant que le travail nécessite machinerie lourde*. You see, *mudiwa*, I have always known what I wanted, and you have already had too much turmoil; this time you need to get away intact – or stay and commit.'

The car windows were open. Though the breeze and the dusk were warm, Anne-Marie shivered all over. She hugged herself and tried to rub her arms free of goose pimples.

'Anne-Marie. I want to go to the Congo with you.'

'I don't want an answer now. I'm tired. Let's just get home.'

Chapter Thirty-Five

Another day, another revelation. Today the thought that gripped Viktor was the question of regret. This tunnelling worm tore into his flesh each day; regret cleared away the past, clarified the future, laid down his character. That morning Viktor had mused, propped up in bed, one leg hanging over the side, his dopey, befuddled thinking beginning to drop away, the hard sinews of thought gradually coming into focus: *I loved Nina, but I can only love her now. When I was with her, my last thought, literally the final thought, the one clear-headed insight that made me feel happy was the unaddled certainty, established from hard, deep reckoning, that I didn't love her. I was relieved that the relationship could come to an end and I wouldn't suffer and I would be free again.*

In his darkened room, the morning heat already making his restful contemplation uncomfortable, Viktor laughed to himself. *Such self-deception. I only know now how I feel now, right now, after I no longer have her. When it is lost.*

Only now could he see Nina, her full beauty, her square shoulders and plump, hard legs and breasts, her wide face.

Fucking hell, we are all lost, Viktor thought as he made his way to the café.

Louis sat pointing and pontificating from his stool behind the counter. The walls were yellow, crudely decorated with ornamental guitars and posters, their corners curled, album sleeves arranged in circles and triangles. Rodriguez next to the Bee Gees next to the Beatles. Viktor objected to this display more than to Louis's racism and abuse, so he sat at the table under the records, debating with himself whether the records were still in the sleeves on the wall, if Louis still played them.

Last week, from the single speaker fastened to the wall, Viktor had heard:

I wonder how many times you've been had sex
And I wonder how many plans have gone bad

He had been shocked to hear these uncensored seventies lyrics in this country of sexual Puritanism and gratuitous violence. He had looked furtively around the café as the record cracked and fizzed on Louis's old turntable, sex perfectly audible from the single speaker:

I wonder about the love you can't find
And I wonder about the loneliness that's mine

Was this Louis's conscience on display? *I was not always this fucking brute who terrorises my black staff, sitting like a demigod at the cash register of life. I too listened to songs of sex and love. I too know that in every hello there is a goodbye. I have also had plans that have gone bad.* Were the record covers proof that Louis had once been moved and disgusted by the world, and that even he understood Viktor's exile, his need for company, his loneliness?

After all, the man seemed to love Viktor. He clapped his hands together in a moment of exuberance every time Viktor

467

pushed the smudged glass door and triggered the little gold bell. These spontaneous gestures, Louis's smile, worried him because of their sincerity – because he knew it was his colour, his London English, his whiteness, that delighted a man whose daily fare of bullying and coffee-grinding had ceased to amuse him.

But the affection Louis held for this shabby, thin-necked traveller he'd adopted made Viktor sad. Despite everything, his freewheeling prejudices nurtured in Africa's fecund soil, he was lost. Viktor had raised Louis's expectations, accepted the offer of his embrace, allowed himself to become 'my boy' and led him along so he could think that they were, somehow, father and son, and that Viktor was a safe place to put his dried-up old man's love.

How many times have I been loved? Viktor thought again, sipping his second coffee. *How often have I allowed love to grow in someone, seen it take hold and rise, and then gone, stopped calling, not walked through the door again? Breaking hearts is killing me.*

Viktor cursed himself as Louis raised his thumb, heralding him, gestured to him from his faraway counter. It had only been two days since he had last visited the café and he could already see the hurt in Louis's eyes.

*

When the power was down, Nelson fired up a small generator, finding his way onto the balcony in the pitch-black night. 'Zimbabweans know what death looks like, comrade, because we enter it every night. Lightless shacks and distant, long-dead stars,' he would say as he groped his way through the flat, his arms in front of him, unsteady from cheap wine, kicking the balcony doors open, finding his path to the generator and then

468

resting his foot on the machine, fingering blindly for the rip cord.

With profits from informal trading, the small import-export business he ran from his stores in the second bedroom and garage, he sank a borehole for fresh water in the communal garden and then decanted the water from grubby plastic bottles into an incongruous glass carafe, presenting the drink as 'mineral water from Harare's mountain spring', accompanied each time by his bass baritone laugh. Always the same joke, each time only his laughter. The crazy paving around the block's swimming pool was crumbling; the pool had been drained of water by residents of the block.

In a recent meeting Nelson had exclaimed, 'Comrades, we've become environmentalists! Eighty-seven per cent of Zimbabweans are food insecure. They go to bed hungry every night, and though we might not be able to eat, we're green. We have simply stopped consuming, and the air above Zimbabwe has never been cleaner. But the problem, comrades, is our lack of consumption. You might,' he said, looking at Viktor, 'have diagnosed that our species is burning too much carbon for the planet to sustain human life in one or two hundred years. But we must see these facts in the context of a global system of unequal states. In Zimbabwe we are dying because we do not burn *enough* carbon. Comrades, don't look at these issues simplistically. We are not African nationalists. *We are not in this together.*'

To the ragged poor, the destitute students and unemployed workers, the landless peasants in the meeting, this was a point of negligible interest. Nelson continued, 'In the Paris siege of 1871, the rich continued to eat well while the poor started to eat cats, dogs and rats. As the siege continued, the rich raided the zoo and served game in the most expensive restaurants.

Except the monkeys. They didn't eat the monkeys because of their resemblance to us.' The audience laughed. 'Our rich have no such scruples. Have you seen the delicatessens? The imported cheeses, fine wines, salamis, meats available at Fife Avenue Shopping Centre? Have you seen the wine bars that have opened across Harare? While the poor collapse and die in the street, starve slowly in the townships, die next to barren fields.'

He paused, opened his arms, questioning, appealing. 'What do they want? *Todya marara here?* Do they really want us to eat dirt?' The group groaned in agreement. 'The Zimbabwean siege has exposed our class cleavages. It has forced the enemy into the open, exposed their drinking holes, their restaurants, their fortified farms and warehouses. Workers, the unemployed, students, hawkers, peasants on one side and black capitalists, bankers, politicians, imperialists on the other. In two words: oppressor and oppressed, now in constant, open, uninterrupted opposition.' Unusually measured, working his way to climax slowly, Nelson rapped the table with his knuckles and spoke loudly, giving up, for once, any effort at control. 'At last, comrades, these groups are in open struggle. How this battle ends – common ruin, global environmental collapse or a revolutionary reconstruction, a classless society – depends on *our* unity, *our* forces, *our* organisations.'

What sense did it make to talk like this? Viktor thought, as Nelson waved his hands over the heads of the small crowd in the room. Like a conjuror in his front room, the TV pushed to the side, the sofas against the wall, broken plastic chairs carried in from the balcony, two long single-plank benches for the exhausted, hungry crowd; Nelson's chosen, his wretched of the earth. *Our puny forces ready to lead the world to revolutionary reconstruction and ruination. Is this the reason Anne-Marie doesn't come to the meetings any more?* He might be right, but the distant, reconstituted planet flickered too faintly in the unreachable starry filament. *Nelson, Africa has had too many revolutions and revolutionaries: Lumumba, Amin, Sankara, Taylor, Kabila.*

When Viktor entered the next day he didn't sit down. Instead he stood at the door. Nelson was lying across his sofa, saw his visitor and raised an arm in greeting, slowly sitting up. He pointed to the TV. 'Do you understand this thing? It's a South African version of *Big Brother*. What are people saying about it? How do you understand it?'

Viktor didn't move or answer Nelson's questions. The TV was always on, when Nelson read, when there were guests and now while Biko festered and rotted in prison. Viktor wanted this man to *move*. Nelson was impatient for the great goal of his life, but calm and deliberate in his refusal to rush anything else.

'Come and sit down, com, drink.' Nelson swung his feet off the sofa and patted the cushion with his open hand, used for the remote control.

'No, Nelson,' Viktor said, still standing, resolute. 'I need to speak to you about Biko. I need the number you promised me. The MDC member, the Y-Party member who will help.'

Nelson's smile was wry and cunning; it irritated Viktor.

'Of course I'll give you the number, but come in first. Do we have any news?' Nelson aimed the control at the TV, found the news, stared at the screen. 'Do you see that? Do you see? Those bastards, do they think their bombs will work? That they will overrun the resistance? Have they learnt nothing from Iraq? From books?'

Viktor inched closer, rested his hands on the back of an armchair. 'Please, Nelson. This is important. It's Biko. We need to move.'

Nelson turned his head again to Viktor, his face broad and open. 'Farai is a bastard. He won't help you, but it will be good

471

for you to see him.' He tucked his loose locks behind his ears, his head turned to the television again, his attention lost once more to the screen.

Viktor felt his face flush, his skin bristle and sweat. 'Nelson, comrade, I need your attention. How can you sit there with the TV? It's Biko! Months in prison and we haven't' – he choked, stumbled on his words – 'we haven't been allowed to see him. I need your help.'

Slowly Nelson stood, walked to the wall and flicked off the power to the TV from the socket. The screen fizzed and a momentary light burst on the set, then the noise, the commentary, the sound of helicopters and explosions, vanished and the room was left to the crickets. Nelson walked, dragging his feet, to Viktor and put an arm on his guest's shoulder. 'Comrade, Biko is strong. All of us are doing everything we can. Lenin with the students. Stalin and Blessing in Bulawayo. You're leading the international campaign. Anne-Marie is onto the lawyers. Tonight we need to breathe, rest, take the long view. Fight when we can, but know when we need to rest. You too must rest. We will be no good to Biko as empty shells, run out, exhausted.'

We grow into stupidity, Viktor thought. *A skin hardens and calcifies around our soft, supple souls until everything we see – our comrades, friends, our lovers and family – becomes like us, hardened, rigid. Then the constantly altering world comes at us, unchanging, and the new ossifies into the old before the day has finished.* Viktor looked into Nelson's soft eyes, the skin loose, his face lined.

'Mugabe will fall,' Nelson said suddenly, 'like countless Mugabes have fallen on this continent. X-Party, national liberation, this false freedom, this curse, will give way to resistance and the edifice will crumble. It has not yet fallen. We are going back into the trenches with no illusions that the regime is on our side.' His hand still on Viktor's shoulder, Nelson swallowed, breathed in and continued, 'In two weeks, comrade, I wanted to tell you, we are spearheading a mass mobilisation to throng the prison. A day of action internationally. I want you to coordinate crowds in London, Washington, South Africa and Australia, on the same day we are outside Chikurubi Prison.'

Nelson went to a small box by the glass balcony door and drew out a leaflet. He handed it to Viktor. 'Marx's favourite historical figure was Spartacus. The slave general. Not Aristotle, not Plato, not a thinker or theoretician, but a man of action, of brutal, raw practice.'

Taking the leaflet, Viktor said, 'Why didn't you tell me?'

'*But I am, Viktor*. Comrade, I'm telling you now.'

*

Even to Viktor, the idea that Biko could be saved online had begun to lose its power. Though the campaign was successful, #FreeBiko was trending, emails and petitions clogged inboxes, Viktor felt increasingly anxious. He spent breathless seconds as he waited for his Facebook page to load, for the pleasing red alerts with numbers – 60, 80, 100 – to appear over his inbox: requests to join the group, to become part of the movement. One enterprising group in Maryland had, on day one of the global picket, printed T-shirts with a grainy image of Biko, his pointing Lenin finger, his other hand hooked into his belt. On day two a comment posted on the campaign wall informed Viktor, 'Sirs, Steve Biko is dead. He died in police custody in 1977 in South Africa. Please inform your members.'

Politicians, UN officials and bureaucrats, minor police officers in Zimbabwe, senior supporters of the regime in

Libya were contacted. Letters were published in two UK newspapers, with a list of signatures: professors, film directors, retired radicals and 'fifty others'. Yet the satisfaction Viktor had expected, the hope of publicity, the vindication of his way of doing things, proof that Anne-Marie was wrong and that his embrace of the internet's restless postmodernity would bring him satisfaction, was not forthcoming.

Instead Biko's silence was compounded by the frenzied activity of the internet. The absorbing, thick prison walls trapped his cries. The machine that Viktor had thought could be wielded for justice, wrestled free from the corporate giants, had left him feeling enslaved, like a piece of human software, an appendage. The stiff concrete perimeter walls of Chikurubi, the soundproofing in State House, the hard, protective skin around the state seemed impenetrable. Only the demonstration in Harare could arouse the regime, force from it a statement.

Each time, Nelson always left Viktor feeling capable of doing what had paralysed him an hour before. Nelson's gaiety, his optimism, raised the ground, filled the chasm. His blind faith in the future, in the coming fall of all dictators and systems, in Spartacus, was its own unbending, irresistible agency. He refused to countenance Viktor's irrefutable belief in humanity's evidently useless passions and cosmic insignificance.

Viktor read the leaflet:

The arrest of Biko (Stephan Mutawurwa) on the charge of public violence and disorder in Bulawayo on 19 March is an example of the dictatorship's desperation. Zimbabweans face renewed attack by the state which strikes at the very heart of their hopes and dreams for democracy. When we express legitimate dissent and criticism, we face vindictive retribution. When the poor defend their rights, we face repression. We are all Biko. Join us for a march on Chikurubi Prison in support of Biko, a fighter for democracy and justice in Zimbabwe.

Convene Harare Gardens at 12 p.m.

In the corner of the A5 leaflet was another grainy photo of Biko addressing an audience, wearing a white T-shirt, his mouth open, his hands out, a single finger pointed towards the camera, instructing the crowd to charge, the photographer to click, the way to the light.

As Viktor read, Nelson took a few steps back and fell onto the sofa. 'We have printed twenty-five thousand of them. We'll distribute them everywhere, in the unions, in a few townships, and send a bundle to Bulawayo with a similar demand for a march to the police station where you were first held. You see, com, Mugabe craves attention and love. An international protest will humiliate him. He longs for the days when he was the blue-eyed child of the West, the Queen's impeccable dinner guest, the English knight – when Grace could shop in Harrods on the arm of her renowned, obedient, respected husband.' Nelson was getting excited. 'He is a spoilt child! The protest will rattle him. He can be a cruel and violent father in Harare, but he wants the tyrant's crown, he wants to be seen as a just anti-imperialist. We'll expose him from the left.'

Viktor thought quickly how the day would look, who he'd email, the Facebook event announcement, the people he could call for support, the words he'd use: BIKO LIVES. #FREEBIKO.

'Excellent, Nelson. I'll spread the word.'

As Viktor folded the flyer, he noticed green print on the back. He turned the sheet over and read:

Dr Rashid Bajja, Healer And Wealth Consultant
1) I Can Bring Back Lost Lovers
2) I Can Do Penis Enlargements
3) I Prevent Bad Luck and Jealousy
4) Making Your Partner To Be Yours Again
5) Getting Rid Of Evil Spirits
6) Financial And Domestic Problems
7) Broken Marriages Solved Quickly
8) Make Your Children Love You

Home Visits On Request. Telephone 04 2927194

Along the side of the advert was a series of clip-art images: a woman in a headscarf grinding maize, a raised palm, a tree plucked from the ground, its roots exposed.

Viktor looked up from the leaflet. 'What's this?' he asked. 'The printer has printed on both sides.' Viktor flapped the paper at Nelson. He pulled back the corners of the pile of leaflets and fanned through the top sheets. 'They're all double-sided, with this, this crazy Dr Rashid Bajja, Healer and Wealth Consultant.'

Nelson stretched out his legs, crossed his feet. 'Yes, I struck a deal with Dr Rashid – his real name is Edmore Nyazamba. He paid for two-thirds of the printing costs.'

For a moment Viktor was silent. 'That's terrible, Nelson. It means that we, Biko, you, the Society of Liberated Minds, will be associated with this, this' – Viktor waved the leaflet – 'quack! A bloody purveyor of fake solutions!'

Nelson laughed, his head tipped back, his mouth wide. Viktor saw lines of grey fillings along both sides of his jaw. He read from the list: 'I Can Do Penis Enlargements. Come to our demonstration and get a bigger cock and find your lost lover. We can't make these kind of promises!'

Viktor read the last point on the leaflet again: Make Your Children Love You. *Children cannot be made to love their parents. Their love is already there, unconditional. Children love their parents even if they have been abandoned by them. Children mourn lost love better than lovers.*

'Listen, Viktor, most Zimbabweans will read both sides of the leaflet and separate the content. If we lose a few to Dr Rashid, then at least we won't be marching with the gullible poor.'

'This is feudal. Peddlers of medieval dreams, preying on the poor and helpless. We can't be associated with him. Dr Rashid would probably advocate stoning Biko to death.'

'Edmore used to be a comrade, he's quite progressive.'

'My god.' Viktor stood, shaking his head. 'I don't know, Nelson, it's a dangerous conflation.'

'Conflation!' Nelson roared. 'I love the way you speak.'

'I'm being serious.'

'Viktor, this is not the bloody sealed train. We need the flyers. The printing industry in Zimbabwe has collapsed. Paper comes from South Africa. The costs are high. I made a deal, and we will have a thousand-strong chorus shouting outside the prison.' Then, after a pause, Nelson spoke quickly. 'And don't you see? If any of our comrades are stopped, they simply say they are distributing publicity for Dr Rashid. It's perfect.'

Viktor smiled. 'Maybe next time we should ask Rashid to include Potions To Help Overturn Entrenched Dictators.'

The two men laughed.

*

Viktor met Anne-Marie outside her office, driving with the front seat of her Golf pushed back so he could operate the pedals. When she came out she was with three colleagues. Anne-Marie waved. Viktor turned off the engine and stood by the car as the group walked slowly towards him.

Feeling himself growing anxious, he rehearsed a greeting: 'I am Viktor, from London. I write on Zimbabwe for an independent website. I'm covering the development of the new government. I'm a socialist. I am an anti-racist. I have a daughter, she's called Rosa, after Rosa Luxemburg, the revolutionary. I listen to opera. I am trying to free Biko. Have you heard?'

The man in the group spoke. He touched Anne-Marie's elbow. His broad chest and strong arms strained and rippled under his work shirt. That easy confidence, delight at life, his freedom from Viktor's interminable preamble – what a contrast to Viktor's chattering, doubting, kvetching, all the noise that clogged his head. The two women laughed loudly. Both were young and beautiful – each of them stood straight, their postures perfect, their presence on earth sure-footed, like God's emissaries. Like gods themselves, Viktor thought.

'*Mudiwa*, come over and say hello!' The group had stopped in the middle of the car park. They stood together, ready to distribute themselves to their parked cars.

Viktor thrust his hands into his pockets and walked across the drive. Biko had spent almost four months in jail. One-hundred and twenty two days. Twelve weeks and two days, in Harare. As Viktor approached the group he fought to push back the day, the layers of images, sounds, colours, that separated him from Biko. If he worked hard enough he could part the heavy pages in his mind, the endless ephemera and find the stout, tall man from Bulawayo, but to do this he needed to look behind the beatings, the police rape, Biko's insolent one-man

478

stand against the regime. Viktor tried to remember when Biko had met him at the train. He tried to focus, to concentrate on the Bulawayo sun setting behind them in the café, the night they'd spent together.

'I've been telling my colleagues about the campaign, about Biko, about the work you've been doing, *mudiwa*,' Anne-Marie said, taking his arm. Viktor smiled and held out his hand. 'This is Major, Taffadzwa and Joyce.'

Viktor fumbled in his pocket, found the folded leaflets and handed them out. 'Ignore the reverse side, it was a printing error.'

Viktor drove. Anne-Marie put her hand on his inner thigh and squeezed. 'I'm proud of you, Vik. Your focus on the campaign, on Biko.'

'We have to get him out,' Viktor replied.

'I know. We will.'

*

On the day of the demonstration the sun, with its furious, angry rays, tried to grind the protesters into dust. Parched, dry, moving slowly, eight hundred people walked more solemnly than usual, three kilometres through the city, their feet kneading the tarmac softened by the heat. Many turned up to watch, holding Dr Rashid's leaflet. When they saw hundreds already standing resolute, gathered to march, they buried the flyer in their pockets and entered the cortege.

Despite the regime's clearance of the informal market and city slums two years before, the streets through the city were still full of children holding up juice cards, hawkers selling footballs, radios and swimming pool inflatables to passing motorists. Men and women in their thirties, forties, and fifties sold mobile phone chargers, the bundles of black wires held like bouquets.

The unusual sight of the protesters neither *toyi-toyi-ing* nor shouting but quietly walking persuaded others to join, even if Biko's imprisonment was unknown to them. Street sellers and the homeless also joined the march, so the group of activists soon swelled to resemble an ambulating procession of early twenty-first-century Harare. A well-made banner – *End Impunity, Release Political Prisoners* – had been printed in South Africa and sent in a diplomatic bag to Care International the previous week – Anne-Marie's doing. Western-dressed members of the NGO swarm marched at the front of the demonstration with their banner, behind them protesters in worn-out flip-flops and loose T-shirts. As the march approached Chikurubi, the crowd began to pulse with a small current of expectation. Stirring slowly, the protesters began to dance, chant, sing.

Nelson couldn't contain himself. Turning to Lenin, he spoke: 'You see, com, this is what Africa looks like now! See the kids, the hawkers, their parents dead, bringing each other up on the street? This is the generation who are going to lead us in the next fight. You see the others?' He raised both hands in a giant sweep of the whole crowd, the entire planet: 'The older ones, they still remember our protests in the nineties, the whiff of working-class power on the streets when we marched like this every week. Together these forces will chase the elites from power. You'll see. The dictatorship hasn't been able to erase the collective memory of our struggles. Do you see?' His eyes sparkled.

'Maybe, comrade, but today the sun is definitely working for the CIO,' Lenin said, mopping his face with his turned-up shirt.

'True, true,' Nelson replied, undeterred, 'but it will be the police who will suffocate in their imported Chinese uniforms, not us.' He laughed loudly, tipping back his head, opening his chest.

When the demonstration arrived at the prison fence, some distance from the actual building, they saw a line of soldiers standing stiffly by the gates behind the portable barrier of barbed wire strung between two giant X-frames. Inside the prison compound were two large trucks, the wheels shoulder height, and under the tan canvas hoods two benches full of reinforcements, men holding rifles, ordered not to drink from their canteens, perspiring into their fastened collars. A few metres behind them a tank was parked inside the prison, its large gun pointed at the protesters. The tank's appearance was incongruous: not a display of strength and the state's confident monopoly of violence but, in the exaggeration and overstatement, a symbol of weakness and vulnerability.

The entire effect of the army, the guns, the tank, the officials speaking into mobile phones, was strangely comical, like a dress rehearsal to a modern production of *Rigoletto*, Viktor fancied. The regime was playing at control, pretending to go into battle.

The poles of the banners were planted in the dry earth. Anne-Marie, who had been holding one side of *End Impunity*, moved away, turned her phone to the side and photographed the crowd. She shielded her hand over the phone's miniature screen as she posted the photo to a group set up by Viktor, who had explained to her how it worked the previous night over a bottle of South African wine stolen from her office.

The initial solemnity of the march had completely disappeared. The crowd now faced the army and police, staring at the reflections of their brothers, sons, lovers, sweating under the same sun, hating the morning, averting their eyes from the demonstrators, desperate not to capture the disapproval and reproach.

Nelson stood on an upturned box he'd brought with him. He wore a pair of horn-rimmed glasses that enlarged his eyes, exposing his face to closer inspection. He waved away the offer of a megaphone; he was an orator and his voice, a rough, gravelly baritone, could easily carry across the car park to the crowd and to the prison.

A group of adolescents, many without shoes, had started to dance and sing with immense vitality, driving dust into the air. A ripple of movement reverberated through the demonstration until others shuffled on bent legs, women lifted their skirts, men their trousers and legs moved to the cries, hoots and long, wavering ululations of the protesters. There was a call and response when a woman shouted, 'Can I get an amen?' The group of dancers, lifting their knees in great stationary steps, replied, 'Give him glory!'

Effortlessly, over the jubilation, Nelson boomed, 'You see? This is how we fight for freedom!'

A cheer exploded across the crowd. From the thick of the group, several women cried out, directing the chant to a shrill 'Jesus is Number One!' The response came almost immediately from the dancers, 'Mugabe is Number Two, Number Two.'

'Did you hear that, old man?' Nelson shouted. 'Number Two! You are Number Two!' Viktor allowed his hood to fall, his hair smeared wet against his head. The dancing stopped and people turned to Nelson. Some sat, spreading out on the ground.

As Nelson spoke again, a policeman who, with a group of his men, had tailed the demonstration from the city tried to interrupt him, coming up to the impromptu podium. He complained that while they had been permitted the march, which he had personally sanctioned, no speeches would be allowed; the officer also explained that they were certainly not allowed to bring God and the president into the proceedings.

Jeers and heckling drove the police officer back to the line of soldiers and police. As the man retreated, Nelson did not join the cheers. For the first time that day he felt worried. Experience had taught him to fear a humiliated police officer; only a stupid man did not know fear.

There was something restless about the day. The bright heat gave way to a breeze that worked up goose pimples on the crowd, forcing Lenin to rub his bare arms. Nelson raised his arms in the air, commanding, trying to silence the demonstration, but it was not the day for speeches. The crowd jostled, pushed forward, lifted on the tide of their subversive good humour, the sense of invulnerability that the catcalls, joking, slogans had given them. Nelson was used to being listened to, but his voice couldn't be distinguished in the voices and laughter.

The chanting and dancing continued. People pushed forward past Nelson, towards the fence, the guarded gate. A woman in a pink skirt and white blouse with a huge girth swung her hips, screamed, rubbed her feet into the gravel. A mist of dust rose around her. The crowd parted, gave her size and movement space. She stepped out suddenly to the gate, in front of Nelson, and seemed to swell in size, enlarge her width and height, eclipse the prison on the near horizon. The lines of police, the empty army trucks, troops in ill-fitting helmets and uniforms, stood in formation, their rifles diagonal across their chests. Suddenly the woman turned her back on the soldiers, raised her skirt and bent, displaying her great buttocks to the lines of uniformed men, their magnificent volume and shape challenging the army, challenging even the clouded sun to come out, show itself, do its best. Everyone laughed. The woman continued to move, skirts raised, shaking her enormous cheeks of flesh. Other women came forward, adding their own witticisms. They too lifted their skirts. In a second there was a row of buttocks, one buttock for each gun. The line of women sent the crowd into a fiercer frenzy of laughter, as if this creaturely demonstration of forbidden, hidden flesh allowed each of them to expel the decade of hunger.

People started to shout again, '*Chinja, chinja!*' '*Jambanja!*' 'The Final Push!' 'Shame on you, let our grandmothers through!' As the skirts were dropped and the women rejoined the crowd, a new cry began: 'Free Biko! Free Biko!' Quickly the mood changed to fury. People surged forward. The first to reach the gate gripped and held on as they were pushed by the lines of protesters behind them.

The sound of shredding and ripping was heard as placards were stripped of cardboard. Instead of a wave of paper slogans, the crowd now carried sticks. Under the great surge of bodies, the troops inside the prison compound moved almost in a single movement, their order broken. If the regime had set itself against the flesh and bones of Zimbabweans, declared war on nature, now their naked buttocks, their arms and muscles, had come for revenge. The heavy sticks that seemed to have appeared out of nowhere were passed to those closest to the police, positioned near the fence and gate. At the back of the crowd several women had started to dig and claw at the hard ground for stones and small rocks, lifting and passing them to a hastily organised chain. Younger hands sent the stones to the front from hand to hand; the tendons on the women's arms strained under the weight of their work.

Viktor was caught inside the group, pushed and pressed by the bodies around him. A woman stood next to him with a baby in her arms, the child's face dirty and passive. She raised the child in her arms, over the heads of those in front of her, tears in her eyes; the child was her banner and slogan, her protest. Others shouted, 'Mealie, mealie, mealie!' Soon the shouting, the different slogans, the demands to eat, to free Biko, layered the air, filled the prison, frightened the soldiers. These men, as young as the men in the crowd, bashful and confused, clutching their guns to their bodies guiltily, could not answer the complaints of the crowd, bring back the needless dead, face them, the world, speak to the old man.

The soldiers saw their chance to reclaim their line and shuffled back into formation.

Over the gate, onto the bent, helmeted heads of the assembled soldiers, the sky darkened as missiles, stones and sticks were thrown. The police were stunned, disorientated by the sudden turn to violence by these ramshackle troublemakers in their rags and flip-flops. The crowd, the entire mass moving against the gate, pushed further into itself, concentrating its weight on the weakest, most penetrable section of the prison fence. Viktor noticed a few better-dressed people, who, minutes before, had held the large plastic banner, squeeze through the crowd, shouting to the crowd to let them through. Viktor searched the crowd for Nelson and Anne-Marie. He saw them together closer to the gate, their faces twisted, their mouths shouting, appealing to the police. Words were shouted in Shona: '*Sunungurai musungwa uyo, Regai tidarike!*' The front of the crowd lunged forward. The gate, gripped in a hundred hands, was wrenched from its hinges; the thin metal chain attached to a post was pulled easily from the ground like a cork from a bottle. The sky continued to hail stones and rocks on the police and the troops. One officer shouted into his cupped hands, ordering his men. Four soldiers strained to drag the coils of razor wire, strung between wooden frames, to block the crowd, slow down the stampede. The troops had now regrouped on either side of the truck, the butts of their rifles nestling into their shoulders. The long barrels quivered and shook.

Once the gate had been cast aside and prison security breached, the mood of the crowd changed again. Nelson shouted, stood in front of the crowd, among the first ranks of young men and women inside the prison compound. The police stood back on either side of the gate, their pistols held in shaking hands, pointed at the crowd, at those who stood inside the prison. The commanding officer, a small man with a pocked face and red eyes, screamed into a radio. Nelson heard the shouted commands, turned quickly to the soldiers, moved towards the officer and with his fingers on each side of his shirt pulled. Buttons flew and spun into the air. With one hand he pointed to his chest and shouted again to the police. There was a murmur of agreement in the crowd. Others stepped forward, men and women, and did the same thing, copied Nelson, ripped open their shirts, exposed their chests and pointed.

The woman next to Viktor pressed her child to him; the small infant clung to his neck as the mother removed her T-shirt, stood with her breasts exposed and shouted so her voice broke. The great compact crowd with their bare hearts challenged the police, the soldiers, to fire – the boys sweating and shaking behind their rifles. Those further back raised their sticks and metal pipes above their heads, addressing the prison and its protectors, bearing witness.

The stand-off lasted for two minutes. The two groups were separated by a few paces, Nelson at the front, the raised arms of the police and soldiers trembling and the stripped bodies of the crowd wet, fleshy, vulnerable. Viktor held the child tightly to him. The boy's soft head sank into the nape of his neck. Instinctively he turned his body so his back faced the lines of police. He bent his head over the child's body and inhaled the deep, hot odour, whispered the few words of Shona he knew: '*Mudiwa, mudiwa ndino kuda.*'

As Viktor embraced the child, his back turned, he saw in the distance, on the crest of the hill, two trucks driving side by side. As they approached, billowing dust and fumes, he could make out the khaki canvas hoods and the large wheels. He started to shout and point, tried to alert those around him, but it was too late. The trucks skidded to a halt and from them police and soldiers streamed out and rushed the crowd. The demonstrators turned, screaming warnings to each other as the soldiers brought the butts of their rifles down. The crowd broke open, dispersed, stumbled, fell. People were hit and bloodied, the single united force wrenched and bludgeoned apart. Viktor ran, leapt over fallen bodies, shielding the boy.

Anne-Marie tried to escape, but a soldier stuck out his foot and she fell. He leant over her body, grabbed the heavy string-and-bead necklace she wore and tore it from her throat, pulling her body back; the string burnt and tore her skin, drawing blood. As Anne-Marie screamed, he drove his fist into her mouth. She choked, collapsed to the ground, turned to her side. He kicked her in the small of the back, then knelt and curled his arm around her neck and tensed, snapping her mouth shut. She gagged.

'You're not so strong now, woman. This is what ZANU does if you disobey. *Munofunga tiri mapenzi. Ndiri kuenda netyava.* You think we are just grade fours and you are very educated, you think you are now so learned and there is nothing that we can do to you. You think we are stupid? ZANU is now going to discipline you. When we meet you on the street, you treat us as uneducated people. So there is no way you can ever love us. You think you are special, so today I will reduce you to size.'

Later she remembered the sensation of the young man's breath on her cheek, the moment before Lenin brought down the rock on the man's head. At once the soldier released and

487

fell back. The gash on his forehead opened for a second – the wound white, the flesh peeled back to the skull – then filled with blood. A red tide flowed over his face and into his eyes, blinding him. Lenin dropped the rock and looped his arm around Anne-Marie's back. He lifted her and half-dragging, half-running, they fled.

*

The next day Nelson's flat was raided, not to seize files or gather intelligence but simply to bludgeon and destroy – not completely, but enough. When the group arrived, Nelson kicking the door ajar, they fell onto their haunches, clutched their heads and moaned. The two makeshift benches were broken; the old computer lay in a bed of shattered glass. The posters, the gallery of photos and placards, were torn down. The photo of the Society of Liberated Minds standing outside in the sun, their arms raised in permanent celebration, was gone. The single desk stood lame beside the windows, two legs kicked away. On the desktop, exactly in the centre, a soldier had defecated. Next to the coiled mound of shit was a skid mark. The policeman, his trousers down, had crouched on the desk and defecated and then, for reasons unknown, he had moved the faeces into the centre of the table.

Viktor entered the room and stood over his folded comrades. He surveyed the damage, made an inventory and began planning how he could appeal for funds to replace the equipment. He looked at the desk, pondered the meaning, the organisation – this element of style and design, feng shui brought to the problems of destruction and bowel movements. Had the soldiers planned which of them was going to defecate? Commanded the man who had drawn the short straw, told him to hold in his morning crap until the allotted time? The confidence, the sheer audacity of the act. Could Viktor, if it came to it, release his bowels and shit in front of his comrades? Could he shit to order? Had the man then used his ungloved hand to move the shit into its ergonomic position? Or had that responsibility fallen to the commanding officer, or maybe a new recruit? If only Viktor could get to the bottom of this mystery, to the real essence, he would be able to understand how the regime worked, the inner logic of Zimbabwe, and the entire fraught and jumbled world of excrement, genitals and sex. What did it all mean?

More perplexing even than the destruction, the deposit on the desk, was the reaction of Nelson, Lenin, Stalin and the others. The human inventory of suffering from the beating yesterday was relatively slight: two broken arms, some bruised and broken ribs and several bloodied noses and heads on the side of the demonstrators; two soldiers had been hospitalised, one from a head injury. No arrests. Violence is not blind; it does know limits. The instructions had been to clear the prison: teach the people a lesson, but don't give them any more martyrs.

Lenin was the first to stand; he walked to Viktor, who stood in a diagonal strip of light. Lenin bent, picked up two pieces of card, scraped the excrement into the cardboard shovel and walked outside. The others stayed hunched on the floor.

'How's Anne-Marie?' Nelson asked, without lifting his head.

'Bruised and angry but fine, thanks to Lenin. We can get this material replaced.'

No one spoke. Viktor tried again. 'We can ask for donations. We'll have the money by the end of the week.'

Still there was no comment.

'At least we got off yesterday. What is this, anyway? Just broken objects. Just stuff. Not people.'

All the heads came up to look at Viktor. 'What?' he exclaimed.

'Spoken like a true Westerner,' Nelson replied curtly.

'Okay, this is not good, but it can be replaced.' Viktor sounded defensive.

'That is not the point.' Nelson stood, steadied himself on the wall. 'As a small organisation we have built our office over years. These things, the desk, the computer, the photos, our archive, are important. We are poor people, Viktor. What we have lost cannot be replaced. We are not an NGO; we're a small, stubborn piston box, built by our efforts. That, that' – Nelson breathed heavily and indicated with his head the broken Gestetner mimeograph machine – 'took us two years to buy, two years of steady fundraising. In the first week we produced the leaflet for the 1998 bread riots. Each paper was printed on that, as you say, object. Objects are important, comrade – our people don't have enough objects.' Nelson couldn't bring himself to turn and address the destroyed machine directly, to look at this inanimate comrade and assess whether it needed to be thrown away, whether anything could be salvaged.

Slowly the others stood and started to gather the fragments of paper, wood, search for bricks that could level the desk, improvise repairs on the benches. Viktor unhooked his laptop bag from his shoulder, rested it against the wall and rolled up his sleeves. Then he lifted the computer from the floor, swept the glass with his foot into an open newspaper, turned the ends over, folded the parcel, left the office. Even though he couldn't see, his eyes blinded by the midday sun, he knew the way, the number of steps, the width of the path, the exact place of the bin.

*

'Samuel, get the fucking guards.'

Samuel woke, stumbled, staggered to the door. He hit it first with a hand, then with both fists. 'Hopewell's dying! Call a doctor,' he screamed. 'Open this bloody door! *Vhurai chigonhi ichi.*'

Hopewell strained and looked up at the cell, then fell back. The bars on the window cast shadows across the small room. Samuel hammered on the door. Other prisoners started to stir and join the shouting over and over again. 'Open the door!' Samuel repeated, tired now, on his knees, panting.

The corridor shook as each cell stirred and the shouts combined with others, turning the whole prison into a metal and flesh orchestra. Voice and iron screamed, sang out. Each of them, every man, every prisoner with his own fury and grief, trying to bring back their dead.

Biko sat over Hopewell, his hand pummelling his comrade's chest, beseeching him with each blow to breathe, to focus on the light, see it filling the cell. Samuel moved from the door and came to the bed. He looked down at Hopewell and put a hand on Biko's shoulder. 'He's gone, Biko. Hopewell has passed over. Let him be now. Let him have his peace.'

Biko covered his face with his hands, jerked his shoulder free of Samuel and sniffed in his tears, extinguished them, clenched his muscles and brought his body and his spinning head under control. He got up and took Samuel's place by the door. In his father's deep voice he shouted, 'Hopewell's gone. We remain resolute. Fight on, comrades! *Shinga Mushandi Shinga! Qina Msebenzi Qina!*'

The corridor, the line of cells, each woken prisoner took up the new chant. '*Hatidzokeri shure, tinonoramba tichirwisa!*' Samuel dropped his hands to Hopewell's face and dragged his fingers across his alert, surprised eyes, whispering a short prayer. With his hand still on his brother's face he thought that they must prepare the body, wash him as best they could with what they had.

Part Seven:

Crocuses

Chapter Thirty-Six

During the early spring months in Harare the heat was relentless, burning away thoughts as soon as they'd formed, sending his daughter, phoenix-like, into the sky in a spiral of vapour. As the weeks and months passed, the clear lines, the colours and smells of Rosa began to fade for Viktor.

He had been keeping a diary for her, describing to her the parrots that are common in Harare.

Like pigeons in London, sweetheart, and boy do they squawk. They gather in the park I walk to every day on my way to the café. They own certain trees and crowd the branches; their bright green bodies decorate the park. They are bad-tempered birds, jostling each other out of position, moving sidewards along the branches, pecking and screaming at each other.

And then, then, sweetheart, on other trees there is the strangest fruit, but you have to watch carefully, stand in the shade – it gets hot here early and in the open if you stand for too long you get the straight blows of the sun. It took me a few days before I realised that this black, heavy fruit hanging off the trees was in fact bats. Giant sleeping bats, hundreds of them, literally, growing out of the tree, blocking the sun. Under these trees it is always dark, an odd, made-up night in the bright, hot day. Isn't that strange? I think they look like Isaac, your grandfather, when he's outside in the winter, holding his coat around him for warmth.

At night the park comes alive. (I never walk through it, though not because of the bats.) You see their shapes crowding the clear night sky like black kites. The parrots and bats keep to separate trees. I've never seen them together. Wouldn't it be lovely if we could see these birds together, even at night? I would hold your hand so you wouldn't get scared.

Like this, in the evening, Viktor would write stories from Zimbabwe in his Rosa book: what he'd seen, who he'd spoken to, what he was doing.

You know that one of my friends isn't very nice? How peculiar people are. Remember the accident I saw when I arrived? Well, this little angry man who has hair growing up his neck and has big muscles on his arms actually tried to save people's lives. I have seen him carry two big children in each arm and not even break a sweat. He has his own coffee shop and he invites your father for meals in his house, which has a swimming pool. But he shouts and says horrible things to the people who work for him. Strange.

Viktor stopped. *I can't write this, it's not appropriate. I don't know how to write any more to my daughter. I never did. I never knew how to speak to her. Nina was right, I was never a good father.*

496

But when he tried to resurrect Rosa in the evening, bring her to life, teleport her into the flat he shared with Anne-Marie, she started to resist, stayed more firmly in London. She held on as he attempted to drag her across the continent, over the deserts of North Africa to the south. The carpet where she stood in London bunched up in cloth waves against her heels, her toes tipped up, her eyes moist – she didn't want to come. Before long Rosa's book, as Viktor's stay lengthened, was opened only three times a week, twice, soon only once, then only when he managed to grip Rosa in his arms, wrap his arms around her waist, pull her quickly into him.

Five months after arriving, one night he opened the book, the scraps, leaves, unsent postcards, photographs he'd printed for her – Louis with his wife Vicki, Viktor between them in his long swimming shorts, his white body like a superimposed figure. There were torn pages, napkins with drawings and stories.

The contents of the scrapbook spilled over the bed and floor of the darkened flat, fragments of the story, the family scattered and humourless. *My girl. My loss. My pathetic jokes. My daughter on a bloody napkin. Did you hear that? My daughter lives on napkins.*

'Daddy, do you love me? Do you love Mummy? Why don't you marry Mummy and come and live with us? Why have you been away for so long? You have been away for ages.'

Viktor started to sweep the pages of the story, the scraps, with his feet.

He knelt and scooped up the loose pages, napkins, cards, and kneaded them together in his palms. All nonsense. These line drawings, in green, blue and black ink to show Rosa and to make her laugh, all now howling at him, piercing his ears with laughter.

Yet when he lifted the ball of papers in his perspiring hands, all he could hear were tears so loud he thought his comrades would hear, that Anne-Marie returning early from work would enter the flat and hear his sobs.

*

Dear Viktor,

We have raised more money, filled buckets for Biko, squeezed the suits and the junior academics to pay out to the struggle you are waging in Zimbabwe, to give if they can't act. The money has been deposited in the campaign account.

Now tonight what I want to say to you is that the individual DOES count. Biko. You. Mohamed Bouazizi's mother in Tunisia. It's teasing those hidden, latent talents and genius out of them, including wild, passionate anger, heroism, courage beyond belief, that can and does change a court case, a community, a town, a country and an epoch. Now tell the comrades this, they must feel the waves rippling across the continent from the North, the seismic struggles breaking up the earth's crust. The old is dying. The new is being born.

Did I tell you before about Bouazizi who set himself on fire after his fruit stall was confiscated by the police in Sidi Bouzid? Well, his mother became half-conscious of her own agency when she'd screamed abuse at the police and party HQ for about a whole half-hour. She was losing her voice and turned on the thousand workers and shouted, 'YOU! CALL YOURSELVES MEN! HUH? JUST STANDING THERE DOING NOTHING!' She held up her son's ashes. 'I WANT JUSTICE FOR HIM, ME, ALL OF US.'

Then a boy worker held up bananas – what Bouazizi had been selling and what the police confiscated, his only income. Then a shaven-headed worker near the front started punching the air and shouted. Others closed up towards him, moving forward. One woman, a boy worker, a man, his workmates and shop-bench mates, maybe twenty, then fifty, then one hundred, closing up around the mother. She's newly emboldened and now faces the cops and thugs again and starts copying the worker who punched his fist in the air. And now she's leading the chants and it's hundreds, then a thousand or so, chanting – then it cuts dead.

This is how it all started and how it can start in Zimbabwe.

Within an hour, the next video shows, a dozen of the same men have gone to the nearby bigger industrial town, low talk, telling the details to a rapt audience, but interrupted by an occasional chant as people who've never dared chant show off. And after all the new guys have heard the story with solemn faces, nervously they all start joining in the chanting! Two towns united. From mother to boy worker to another town, to the country, to the region and continent. From mother to the world.

Think about it, my friend. A powder keg is talking to you: he's called Biko, BIKO. The tyrant Mugabe lit the keg when he arrested our comrades, when he almost killed Biko with his beatings. There in Southern Africa it's public property, everyone knows, and we are making sure people know his name here too. Soon the streets of London and Europe will echo to cries of Biko.

Bouazizi woke up his mother and all of Sidi-Bouzid with her, ensuring every last worker heard her screaming wails of mourning.

Remember this, Viktor: fear is no longer an absolute. A generation of young fighters has made every one of the 500 words for fear in Africa RELATIVE.

I'm so tired this is probably rambling nonsense. I spent the day arguing with the ignorant, deluded, middle management at the university in this City of Darkness, this hell on earth. Sorry, very sorry. I just want to help. I know Biko so well. Tell him, if you see him, that I am with him, that I think about him always. That we are all with him.

Tendai

*

All this willing and wishing of time on and on, beyond the tasks of today, left Viktor reeling. And sure enough, the day would pass and he would stare back, giddy, and feel bereft at the lost time that he had just wished over. If he tried, his eyes shut, he could see everything, his whole near future – the scene outside the crematoria, his sister's night-time call about his mother or father, about the fall, the accident, the death. The blowy, downcast day would be clogged as usual with clouds, heads bowed, his parents dead. There was a brutal, dreadful truth in his relationship with time.

Though Viktor's faith in social media was waning, he still believed Biko could be saved online, that his hashtag campaign would make the difference. This was something that had changed the fate of global action, that the comrades, the old-style fighters Viktor had met, Tendai, Nelson, did not completely understand – the great proletarian massification, the democratisation of the internet. Now, with a bank of phones, a few computer activists in Zimbabwe, in the Congo, in the UK, France, no

500

matter what bloody country, rich or poor, Biko could be saved, crimes exposed, death denied.

Viktor muttered low caffeine curses to himself, his fingers lethargic in the morning, hitting the wrong keys. He would raise the profile of the campaign, lift Biko, hold him aloft on these bent, typing fingers, these clawed hands, punching letters and numbers into phones, keyboards, screens. Biko would be saved by the new revolution. *Don't hide from it, Anne-Marie. Open your eyes, Nelson.*

The days were still short in the early spring the sun intense, the open skies broad; the sun retreated quickly, took its night-time rest in the late afternoon and, recharged, occupied the sky again in the early morning as Viktor laboured on with the campaign.

Viktor sat at the gate. He borrowed a plastic chair that bowed under his weight, the legs widening on the ground. The late-afternoon sun was dying quickly, but its weak, rose-coloured glow reached Viktor and the guard, Lancelot. The two men basked and stretched, craning their faces to the sky, to the crimson, freckled sun holding its position above the tall pines in the distance that ringed Mugabe's palace. The setting daylight cast the trees, lamp-posts and passing cars into languid, long, quivering shadows – the city traffic was quiet, the dog-eared trees marked out on the road. Viktor saw neighbours pass through the gate, people he knew. Further away, people crossed the street calmly, without hurrying, all of them caught in the same sun-bliss, a silent reverence to the gentle light. The whole of Harare in this descending hour, it seemed, was turned red, orange, blood-black.

The universe is huge. Even in the pervasive daily trials of Zimbabwe, everyone knows that there are greater rhythms in life. There is a bigger force that cradles and destroys us, that will destroy this puny dictatorship.

The last faltering light – now struggling to be seen on the horizon, beyond the trees surrounding State House – shimmered for a few seconds and finally died. The dark blue expanse of the sky yielded to the moon. Barely visible, the full, small circle could be traced from the yellowed crescent. Slowly the sky pulsed and glittered with stars.

Viktor felt a kinship with Lancelot sitting next to him, opening and closing the gate. He felt this exultant affinity extend ceaselessly, stretching, embracing Nelson, Anne-Marie, his comrades, all of these strangers – all the same, all like him, all glorious, all insignificant.

Lancelot leant forward in his chair. The newspaper on his lap fell to the ground. He pressed a single finger against one nostril, breathed in loudly and snorted through his nose. A stream of yellow mucus sprayed his trousers and the ground. Lancelot brought his sleeve to his nose, wiped his face clean, then coughed loudly, bringing up a mouthful of phlegm. He spat. When he was done, he looked at Viktor and laughed open-mouthed.

Viktor roused himself, shook his head clear and sat up straight. *All this romance, the sun, the stars, the pointless moon. What does the universe matter when the real arbiter of life is that man ensconced in his palace, admiring the night sky like me? It's the global elite, it's capitalism that orders life and death in London and Harare. Human society is everything,* he thought – suddenly excited, proud of himself. *Until we are done with those arbiters we'll have no time to commune with the universe.*

At these thoughts, Viktor laughed aloud.

*

He wrote the drafts of his articles in longhand, in a supply of lined school exercise books decorated with shiny colour photos of Zimbabwe's historical monuments. One had a photo of Heroes Acre, the burial ground for veterans of ZANU-PF and the struggle against Rhodesia. On the cover was President Mugabe wrapped up in party colours, wearing a baseball cap and punching the air with an arm that he could no longer straighten and a clenched, lopsided fist. On another notebook there was a photo of Great Zimbabwe, the ruins of Zimbabwe's glorious past, a city of stone: the conical, cement-less towers, houses and forts rising out of the ground. In his seat at Louis's café, Viktor traced the photo with his fingers.

He had visited Great Zimbabwe; he had been ordered to by Nelson. 'Just to knock out some of that residual Eurocentrism from your head. Even you, Vik, an enlightened European' – at this Viktor had rolled his eyes – 'will need to shake down that racism and purge it from yourself. I may sound very X-Party, but there is no substitute for experience.'

Nelson had stood over Viktor after a midweek meeting, holding a half-drunk bottle of wine, when his eyes had widened suddenly. 'Do you know Engels said an ounce of practice is worth a ton of theory? You need to travel to Masvingo. Take the bus and visit Great Zimbabwe. You can stay with my parents.' Emptying the bottle, he had leant on Viktor's shoulder. His vocal cords were never enough: Nelson needed to physically connect. Nelson was smaller, the frames of his glasses taped together, his long, neglected locks hung over his back and chest, weighing down his head. He spoke as if his words were emanating through his pressed fingertips. Nelson had pulled out his phone from his pocket and focused with difficulty on the small screen. 'Let's get this done now,' he'd said. He spoke, the phone against his ear, and without a word from Viktor his travel and accommodation were arranged. Viktor had left the next day.

'I wonder what Engels would have made of Great Zimbabwe?' Viktor spoke aloud to himself, staring at the photo. The exercise books with their grainy, dotted brown paper fell apart; the pages would crumble under Viktor's biro and Louis would bring out the sellotape and place it down gently on the table.

On the day Viktor left, the bus set off early, driving into the morning sun. He sat writing when the road allowed it, staring out of the window, wondering how he had been bullied into making the journey. *Next time I will tell Nelson to shut up.* The comfortable old coach was half-full. Adjacent to him sat two women who spoke and laughed. When the bus pulled off the even tarmac onto a grassy verge, the passengers filed out. The sky was now overcast, great dark-grey clouds turning violently overhead, constantly changing shape – even the meteorological situation in Zimbabwe was more harrowing than the grey skies of Britain. Passengers found trees and bushes to urinate behind. The two women bargained for food with roadside hawkers. When the bus shunted into gear again, picked up speed and turned into the road, one of the women sitting on the aisle – her old face uncreased, her hands large and fleshy – reached over the aisle and offered Viktor her brown bag. 'Take one! Mopani worms.'

Viktor had exhausted his notebook and grabbed another one as he was leaving the house from the pile of clothes and books at the bottom of Anne-Marie's wardrobe. It was an older notebook with a few spare pages that he had arrived with; he'd written his valedictory blog post on the flight from Heathrow in it, under the wary eyes of the flight crew. Viktor opened the book and flicked to the last blank pages. He dreaded the beginning, as he did every morning; it took three coffees to pull him fully out of the night, force him to cast a rattled gaze at the world and write. It seemed to Viktor that he only achieved anything when he stood on the edge of a cliff, the frothing white surf hitting the sandy beach, the rocks and shingle littered with bodies. Only then, when his pulse was hammering in his ears, did he feel alive, could he think.

Louis got up from his till stool and stood with his legs apart in front of his coffee machine, a large chrome La Marzocco Linea that was bolted to the work surface. It sat in full view in the middle of the café. Louis made a face for his loved customers, those for whom he changed currency and discussed in gruff, hushed voices business and the racial inferiority of the kaffir government. (The bankers he treated as honourable, exceptional whites.) With methodical precision he operated the machine with his eyes closed, moving his hand over the dials and switches, scooping the coffee grains into the portafilter, packing it down in the tamper, fixing it on the showerhead. Then he was still while the water filtered through to the machine, black liquid trickling slowly into the cup. Louis rested one hand on the black handle of the filter, the other on the cup heater. With his Marzocco Linea his soul was calm.

Viktor, shocked to see Louis for the first time standing in worship before his mechanical god, his eyes sealed, thought, *This is how Louis loves. He can only love machines. With his wife, with Zimbabweans, his anger at life returns.*

Louis frothed the milk, turning up the pressure on the steam until it screamed and his clients were forced to repeat their sentences. He embraced the cup and saucer and weaved his way through the room to Viktor around tables and chairs, bags and crossed legs. His face was calm, the muscles relaxed, his head temporarily impervious to the usual irritants. He stopped in front of Viktor, lowered the cup to the table, bent close to

505

Viktor, put a hand on his shoulder and squeezed. Viktor came to, looked up and smiled. 'Thanks, mate,' he said quietly.

Louis turned away and squared his shoulders, his head cleared. 'Don't leave the bloody dishes piled up like that, goddamn it. The place is a mess!' he screamed.

Viktor brought the cup to his lips, sipped, sighed, closed his eyes and let the hot liquid roll down his throat. The notebook fell to the floor, the pages fanning open. He carefully returned the coffee to its saucer and bent to the book on the floor. It had opened to a page that was blank except for a few sentences written at the top of the page, not in his own hand. He peered at the smudged writing:

May your words flow from your heart to your pen to these pages, so others may share in the truths you see. Nina. May 2008.

Under this, in lopsided, uneven lettering, there was another message.

Daddy, write me a story with pictures and a princess who does magic spells. Never-ending love, Rosa.

Viktor pulled the page closer to his face. The sound of Louis's shouting faded. He stared at the words, tried hard to decipher them. His heart sounded noisily inside his chest. He felt his tongue dry in his mouth. He yanked off his glasses and read the words again: 'from your heart to your pen'. Large tears fell quickly off his nose onto the page. The paper absorbed the water and more tears fell, from his heart, down his nose to the page trying to wash away the words, blur them into something else, tell him that what he had done was right and that he should be in Harare with Louis, in Anne-Marie's bed. Even the page gave in: rivulets formed, water ran along the binding and onto his lap and trousers. 'From my heart to my page to my daughter,' he mumbled.

When he looked up, his sleeve wet from wiping his nose and eyes, Louis was standing over him.

Viktor held the sodden pages open, the inscriptions wet but still legible. Louis grabbed the book, swivelled it round, lifted his glasses onto his head and read. 'For God's sake, Viktor. If you miss her, then go back. Just *do* something. Make a decision. Bloody act, man.'

'It's not that simple. If I go back I might not be able to see her, and when I do, Nina gives me hell. That's why I am here.'

Louis yanked a chair from under the table, turned it round so the backrest faced his chest, his legs astride. He faced Viktor like a cowboy, his muscular arms hairy and tanned. 'You're in Zimbabwe because of your ex? Then you need to be tough, face her down. If she lived here I could help you.'

Louis spent his life fixing problems like an engineer: replacing lost and broken parts, hammering hard to cajole the human machinery into submission. Louis's only lasting love affair, his metaphor for all human relations, was his antique coffee machine, older than Rhodesia and Zimbabwe combined.

'Thanks, Louis. I'm just being silly. Nina thinks I'm the devil, and she has said it so often I now believe her. Maybe it's better for Rosa if I am not in her life.'

'Rubbish. You should have brought her with you. She would live like a princess here,' Louis said. He pointed at her writing. 'Swimming in our pool, a nanny, sun, open spaces. Vicki would love to look after her. God knows, she must be dying in that overcrowded island. All those people.'

'You mean I should have kidnapped her?'

'No, Vik, she's your daughter. How can you kidnap your own daughter? You have a responsibility to her. You should have brought her here.'

Viktor stared into Louis's dark eyes. *He's right*, he thought, his head spinning. *I should have just taken Rosa. We could have gone on the run together – father and daughter.* Images and ideas collided, ran together, jostled, twisted in his head, freezing his speech. Isaac and Sonia, their last words to him: 'Darling, are you eating? How are your bowel movements?' Rosa, freeze-framed in her bunches and her fancy-dress costume, a green sequined ballgown and cape, impractical for their excursions in the rain, to the zoo. 'I want to show the animals. The monkeys, Dad.' Rosa dissolved as quickly as she'd formed; her face melted, giving way to the dark, bristled line of Louis's face. Cars backed up, bodies on the grass verge, the brilliant, hopeful glare of the morning sun and Louis's hard, scuffed hands slamming down on the man's chest. When the images of Biko on the floor came again, he shook himself back to reality.

'Listen, Viktor, come over tonight. I'll cook. No, Vicki will cook; she is amazing in the kitchen. You need to keep busy. You have too much time on your hands with your internet and your politics. Come and stay with us.' Viktor saw Louis's eyes soften; the lines and marks on his face yielded. 'What do you say, boy?'

*

Each evening Viktor came down from the flat so he was ready, cleansed for Anne-Marie. How he jumped up when her car swung into the block. She would slow, lower the window and kiss him.

Today a boy Rosa's age came out too, commanded by his aunt not to leave the block, to play inside the walls. His name was Edwin. He was a pale, orphaned child ordered around by a distant aunt and uncle in a neighbouring flat. Viktor told him stories as he sat waiting for Anne-Marie. Edwin curled up, the gravel marking and sticking to his skin. Each day he edged closer and closer until he now sat, then lay, on Viktor's lap in his dirty school uniform, the blue shirt and torn grey trousers that he wore on the weekends as well as during the week. Viktor spoke in hushed tones, told him the adventures of Lawrence and his dog growing up in London. The fairground where Lawrence lived and worked, the night-time rides on the ferris wheel, his dog, a mongrel with sad eyes and loose jowls who was called Benji. How they'd steal secret entry to the ferris wheel that would lift them into the sky high enough to see everything, even the bend in the river, all the way to Africa and the boy and his tall friend telling stories in Harare. As the ferris wheel spun, Benji and Lawrence were brought together tightly; they would sit entwined, cheek to dog jowl, so that when, finally, at the end of every night, they got off the giant wheel, they would not know for sure who was the dog and who was the boy. The dog was humanised by the boy and the boy animalised by the dog.

Without a word Edwin would slowly lever himself up from Viktor's lap, climb down and run back to his weary, hollering uncle. Then each night he would skid on the backs of his shoes just before the stairwell, sending the gravel and sand billowing around his ankles and trousers and turn. It was his game, Viktor realised. Edwin was pleased with his new, strange friend. He waited for Viktor to come home in the afternoon the way Viktor waited for Anne-Marie.

'He likes you, Vik,' Anne-Marie said. 'His uncle is brutal – he drinks in the day and hawks petrol at night. The aunt travels to Johannesburg every fortnight, loads their twin-cab and bribes her way across the border. They get by, but that boy, that boy,' she said, shaking her head, 'he's suffering.'

'Where are his parents? His mum?'

'Where do you think? You've been here long enough not to ask such stupid questions.'

Viktor wasn't offended. 'Dead. They're dead,' he stated.

'Which doesn't make that boy ...' Anne-Marie left the sentence unfinished.

'Edwin,' Viktor corrected her.

'Which makes Edwin part of the average.'

'We should take him in.'

'You're too soft, Vik. You rub up Edwin's emotions and make him need you. He already expects too much. Take him in? Come on. Like a dog? Only do it if it's for the long haul.'

'Maybe you're being too hard,' Viktor protested.

'Why do you want him to love you, Vik? Don't you think he's been let down enough by life already?' Viktor was silent. 'Don't give unless you can carry on giving.'

Anne-Marie saw them together night after night, waiting, enveloped, their thin, plaited limbs in the shade by the gate – *he feeds the cockerel and seduces the orphan, this ridiculous man who falls in love with animals and children*, Anne-Marie thought. *What is wrong with him? His heart beats on the outside of his shirt.* Pourquoi t'es dans la lune? Pourquoi t'as salé ta vie?

Viktor sat up again on the chair. The boy reminded him of Rosa, his melancholy like hers, like his. *If I leave Anne-Marie, I will hurt her*, he thought. Viktor calculated as Anne-Marie parked the car at the back of the block. *Rosa needs me; Anne-Marie is tough, she'll be fine. She's wise and practical, each day dragging someone back from the brink without fanfare or street fighting.* Viktor pulled the key to the front door out of his pocket. *I love her, her theories, her sayings.* Viktor inserted the key into the lock, turned it, felt the bolt snap open. *Edwin. I could bring the boy with me to the UK.* Nina came into focus: crying alone on the sofa, Rosa in bed, beneath the rage her tears, the panic and loss – like his. He wanted to wrap his arms around her, curl her up too, with Edwin and Rosa, each of them, on his lap.

That night Viktor gave up waiting and made his way back to the flat.

He didn't hear Anne-Marie come in. He stood trying to think, his fingers pulling at the knot, pinching the rope, his nails splitting against the rough cord – he couldn't find a fingerhold, a way in, a way out.

Anne-Marie came behind him, put her arms around him, pressed her head against his back, between his shoulder blades. 'Maybe, Vik, *mudiwa*, you just need to realise that you can't fix up Zimbabwe, or all of us, or even all the people in your life. Be careful with yourself. Take care with your love. Ration it.'

Viktor brought his hands to Anne-Marie's. The deep, warm fragrance of her day jolted him back to the room, to their life.

*

Two days later, to clear their heads of the incessant, necessary noise and activity of the campaign, the couple walked together by the dam. They stopped walking and stood over a rough, broken lawn of flowers.

'What do you suppose they're called, Anne-Marie?'

'I don't know. I am a city girl.'

'I think they must be crocuses. They're spring flowers.'

'So we're going to get a change of season after all.'

As they approached the car they slowed down, reluctant to return to their phones.

In the distance there was the sound of thunder, though the sky was clear.

'What's that?' Viktor asked.

'It's the sound of guns, or cannons,' Anne-Marie answered. They'd stopped outside the car as she searched for her keys. Viktor pointed his face to the dying sun, which flickered through the bare branches of the trees.

'They're burying another struggle veteran at Heroes Acre. Soon there'll be no one left. All the heroes will be dead and Zimbabwe will have only born-frees and traitors,' Anne-Marie said, looking up at Viktor. They leant against the car, felt the breeze; the metal of the car warmed their backs. 'Then we can stop talking about the struggle. Everything has to be a struggle. The only history that has any value is struggle history, the only people who have any worth, struggle veterans.'

Viktor reached for Anne-Marie and took her hand in his. 'Yes. The struggle is the marker of citizenship, of humanity. And people are fighting today, but they're denied any value, as you say.'

'I'm not just talking about the struggle, but all of you who talk about the fight, the next revolutionary moment. The failed transition, the compromised independence and the potential in the coming storm for a new dawn, for a proper struggle, for the reckoning.' Anne-Marie spoke sharply. The cannon fired again.

Viktor enjoyed Anne-Marie's teasing, her challenge to him *and* Nelson – that she linked them. Viktor pictured Nelson standing with an arm resting on his hip, his back straight, his locks across his chest. *Nelson and Viktor*, he thought, and it pleased him. 'What we have got is not the only thing that we could have won. In the strikes and revolts, in Zimbabwe, in the Congo's second revolution,' Viktor answered.

Anne-Marie laughed. 'Now you're an expert on the Congo?'

Undeterred, Viktor continued, 'Inside those movements, the broad front that created the MDC, there was a fight for direction, an attempt to win more than the compromise. Y-Party was our victory and defeat at the same time.'

'*Our*? You mean yours as well?' Anne-Marie moved to Viktor, rested her body against his, wrapped her arms around his waist.

'How could an organisation with white landowners, NGOs *and* workers ever overturn poverty? How could it refigure Zimbabwe?' Viktor asked.

'Life has to be lived now, not spent planning for the future struggle. All you see in the past is failure. There are too many ideal types in your politics and Nelson's. History doesn't move like this. It tramples on us, on the poor, on all of us.'

Viktor brought a hand to her breast, felt her nipple harden. Anne-Marie pressed herself into him. 'Exactly, if we don't build now, win the arguments, carry through the revolt to revolution, then we will be trampled, as you say.'

'Not you, whitey. You can always leave before history catches us, before we're trampled.'

'But I won't.'

The cannon fired again, vibrating the ground.

'Life has to be lived now,' Anne-Marie repeated. 'Lives saved today. We'll all be dead by the time you have built your perfect movements and parties. We would need lifetimes to win these things. Your bloody struggle, all this macho talk, has done nothing for us.' Anne-Marie moved her hand and rubbed Viktor's erection. She spoke more softly now. 'We have to live now, right now. Our lives are too short for your revolutions. There is a biological limit, Viktor, to your struggles.'

The cannon discharged, they felt the tremble under them again and were silent for a moment.

'It makes me sad,' Viktor said, quietly, softly. 'The cannons. Like *Tosca*.'

'*Tosca*?' Anne-Marie asked.

'The opera, at the end of Act One, the distant cannon fire, the tolling of the church bells and the sound of the firing squad. *Te Deum laudamus: Te Dominum confitemur!*'

Anne-Marie laughed. '"Thee, O God; we acknowledge Thee to be the Lord". We're a good pair, *mudiwa*.'

*

Viktor gave in to Louis. He took a taxi from the cinema in Glenview, the driver weaving his wreck between the plunging rocky potholes and debris. The city's roads had caved in, like the country's entire infrastructure, railways, highways and utilities sucked into the ground. The car swung into Louis's drive, the rear wheels spitting up gravel.

The house was grotesque. The four-car garage boasted a luminous new Jeep, twin-cab and two Mercedes. A garden hose sat uncoiled on the driveway. The front lawn was manicured with shears, the sides and corners where the lawn bordered the flowerbeds and drive cut with the kitchen scissors. Viktor had seen Godfrey on his first morning, when he had woken in the enormous bed and not known where he was for a second. When he drew the curtains in the spare bedroom light had poured over him. In the joyful sun he saw parrots in the rustling palm trees, flying off, screaming, returning again, their wings open like petals. Viktor had gasped. The circus of gold, yellow, dark, pale, radiant greens settled and formed in his head, registered themselves.

In one corner of this scene, Viktor still standing at the window, there was a figure, camouflaged in patched, khaki dungarees. He was shoeless. His feet dug into the grass. He

514

was stretched on the lawn as if he was spying, waiting, his body not moving. Viktor looked closer and saw that his back was moving rhythmically under his clothes. Viktor scanned the garden: further from the prostrate man, in the distance by the garages, was a washing line and on it a row of green overalls flapping in the morning breeze. On each were the words: *Louis's House Services*. Viktor dropped his eyes to the man. In his right hand was a pair of scissors. He was snapping at overgrown blades of grass at the edge of the flowerbed with a pair of black and chrome household scissors. On his back were the same overalls that waved to Viktor on the distant breeze. A circle of perspiration ringed his collar. The man's hair was receding, his skin old. Viktor felt sick, dizzy. He put his hands on the windowsill and steadied himself.

When he focused again he saw not the stiff, exhausted figure of the servant, his knuckles too swollen to grip the scissors properly, but his own father, who had never travelled further than France, who sheltered in the summer from the mild sun, whose hands were now like this man's, unfit for purpose, too thick to hold a pen or wield his lunchtime cutlery with any elegance. Viktor imagined that it was his father lying on the grass, the sun burning into his back, humiliated. Viktor had wanted to tell Louis what he thought, that if he too looked closely at the man trimming his garden on his stomach he would see his own father as well.

Louis had burst out of the house, releasing his dogs. Their tails hit the side of the decrepit taxi, the hollow metal echoing loudly. Louis pushed his hand into the cab and a pile of creased notes sprang out. Heavy, bare, crude, Louis walked towards the house with his arm resting on Viktor's shoulder. Under the porch, the security lights flashed on. The dogs barked, bouncing around the men, ecstatic and stupid.

Vicki sat on a tall stool in the kitchen swilling white wine around in her glass. 'Vicki has been cooking all afternoon. We are going to have a hearty Greek meal with Rhodesian hospitality,' Louis chuckled to himself. Vicki put her glass down on the counter, stood up, steadied herself and then tottered to Viktor, rocking uneasily on her heels.

'Darling!' she said, reaching up to Viktor's face. She squeezed his cheeks and then dropped her hands to his shoulder and kissed him firmly on the lips, her mouth open, the smell of alcohol on her breath. Viktor winced. 'Garlic king prawns. Salad. Dessert,' she announced.

Louis opened the cupboard, where bottles of wine were stacked in neat rows. With elaborate overstatement he pulled out a bottle, examined the label dramatically, shook his head, put it back aggressively. He repeated this procedure and on the third attempt he exclaimed, with the bottle held to the light, 'I have the perfect bottle, Vik. We've been saving it.' He filled a glass and handed it to the guest.

Vicki took Viktor's hand and led him to the back patio. The garden stretched out wider than the house, reached a steep, rocky, artificial ridge in the distance, then plunged down to the swimming pool. From the patio the night sky filled the horizon, uninterrupted by houses or trees. The mechanical, repetitive chug of the generator from neighbouring houses competed with the loud, dry click of cicadas and the throaty call of the giant bullfrog.

They sat in the padded wicker garden chairs. Viktor knew how to play his part. 'You shouldn't have cooked, Vicki. You and Louis are too kind.' He couldn't say, 'I know, we all know, that you haven't cooked this afternoon – you supervised other people's labour in your kitchen, skidding on the white tiles in your heels with a tall glass of wine. Please, friends, let's give up this farce.' *And yet some people in Zimbabwe call this cooking your own meal*, Viktor thought. *Mugabe has a point.*

Vicki responded, 'Oh, it's nothing. I'm a terrible cook. It's only Louis who believes I actually do any cooking in this house.'

'What did you say, darling?' Louis shouted from the kitchen.

'I was telling Viktor that he should come and stay with us and bring Anne-Marie. He could have Jack's room; he's not going to be back until December.' Vicki eased her shoes off. Her feet dangled off the floor, her misshapen toes moving together. 'Why don't you?' she asked, her tone soft, her head turned back to the guest.

'Thanks, Vicki. That's very kind, but I am okay in town. I'm staying with Anne-Marie.'

Louis joined them, opening the fly door with his shoulder. He put a glass of wine on the table and from a pocket in his shorts removed a phone and gave it to Viktor.

'Now you are going to phone Rosa.'

Viktor obeyed and took the phone.

'Let him do it alone, at least,' Vicki said, levering herself up and walking onto the lawn, indicating to her husband with a nod of her head to come with her. Louis quickly filled his glass again and followed her. 'No fucking excuses, Vik. *Call.*'

The couple zigzagged to the crest of the hill, then fell onto the grass and hung their legs over the edge. Their bodies were sharply traced by the light of the half-moon, the sky throbbing with specks of ancient light. The sound of the garden, of the city and country, the frogs, crickets, even the generator seemed to Viktor, sitting with the plastic receiver in his hand, a discordant song to the earth – man, amphibian, insect, machine singing together inharmoniously. The black speckled desert sky teemed in its own way with life and noise. *Even these crickets understand their place better than me.*

Viktor pressed hard on the illuminated keypad: the international code, Nina's number. He pulled up his sleeve and saw it was seven o'clock, six in the UK. The ring sounded faint in the distance.

'Hello?' Rosa answered, her voice small.

Viktor was silent. He had not expected his daughter to answer – how could she? How did this miniature child, who could only reach the kitchen counters on her toes, answer the phone? He was ready for Nina, the phone slammed down, an accusation, but not this, not the low, distant voice of his daughter.

'Hello, is anyone there?' Rosa asked.

Viktor shook his head, jerked into focus. 'Darling, it's me. It's Daddy. It's Viktor.' The phone hissed and popped with static. There was no answer. 'Are you there, sweetie?'

'When are you coming back, Daddy?' Rosa spoke so softly.

Viktor saw her holding the phone with two hands, in the hall, where the old office phone was kept on top of a pile of telephone books – the phone he had stolen from work, smuggled home in his backpack. Now Rosa knew the way to the phone and was old enough to stand in the draughty corridor, on the stripped floorboards, and answer it.

'How are you, darling?' Viktor forced his voice to speak loudly, to colour the question with excitement, to skin it of doubt and sadness. 'How's school, sweetie?' He saw her alone in the house and worried, in her pink towelling dressing gown with the plastic Disney princesses on the back. Had she been left by Nina as well? Abandoned at seven by both her parents? Left to shuffle around the flat, butter her sandwiches, let herself out, tiptoe with the key to get in when she came back from school, her bed crowded with blankets and toys to keep her company at night in her parentless world?

Rosa rushed over her sentences, packed the phone full of the lost months. 'I've got a best friend! She's called Lara. She comes over most days. She lives opposite. Mum allows me to cross the road to her house. We play Dr Scar. There's Dr Scar and his wife, Mrs Scar, and they have two children, Benjamin Fire Scar and Lily Roselyn Killer Scar. She's my favourite. When you come over I will show you. We can play together. I will set up a bed in my room. Mum won't mind. When are you coming back? I miss you.'

Rosa's voice trailed off; she was silent again.

'I had to go away for a while, sweetheart. I am still away, but I got you something.' Viktor heard Nina's voice behind Rosa's. 'Do you remember how we went from bookshop to bookshop when we were last together? Do you remember what were we looking for?'

'A proper book of spells,' Rosa answered without hesitation.

'Well, guess what I found?'

'What?'

'A book of spells. And I am going to send it to you.'

'Don't send it,' Rosa said matter-of-factly. 'Bring it with you when you come.'

'Okay.' Viktor looked into the garden. Louis was lying with his head in Vicki's lap, her hand stroking his head.

'Read me one. Have you got the book with you? ... It's Daddy. It's Daddy, Mummy. He's a long, long way away but he's coming home.'

The wall under the porch where Viktor sat was covered in insects, all crawling towards the yellow bulb. The cicadas called out repetitively. The sky flickered with light as if the throbbing stars were messaging earth, instructing Viktor what to say, drawing Vicki's hand across Louis's brow, causing Rosa's excited, nervous heart to pound in her chest.

'Read me a spell, Daddy!'

Viktor dug into his pocket and pulled out the small pink paperback printed on cheap paper: *A Book of Spells*. He had found it in the shelves of the shop opposite Louis's café, a new age cure for 'daily sadness and the stresses of modern living' in, of all places, Harare – a city that had already conquered the mere sadness and stress of modern life and plunged headlong into hell.

'Okay, sweetheart, I have it here with me. Let me just find one.' Rosa was silent. The crackle of the phone, the long distance, filled the receiver. 'I've got it,' Viktor finally announced.

'What's it called? If it's a proper spell it should have a name,' Rosa said adamantly.

'It's called ... wait ... Let me see. Okay, darling, the spell is entitled To Strengthen a Long-Distance Friendship.'

'Read it to me,' Rosa ordered abruptly, issuing instructions to her father as a child should do. *As if*, Viktor thought, *I haven't been away and we are together, crouched low in the hallway, the book open.*

'If you have a close and trusted friend who has moved abroad or to a far-flung town, you will find your time together even more precious.' Viktor's voice faltered as he read the spell. He stopped; he could make out the slight sound of Rosa breathing, her mouth touching the phone. A cricket sprang onto the veranda. Its black body reflected the light. Exposed and unprotected, it shouted louder – *Vik, Vik, Vik*. Was this Rosa's Zimbabwean form: had the insect come to hear the incantation too? Brazen, confident, the cricket stood its ground, chirping in time with the spell. The black mass of insects on the wall behind Viktor seemed to swarm closer, gathering to him, to the phone, to the words on the page. The sound of the insects pounded in Viktor's free ear; he pressed a finger to close it, silencing them.

'Go on,' she almost shouted. 'Get on with it, Dad!' *Forever and from now on, you will take your orders from me. For running away, I divest you of all agency. All rights of action.* 'Go on, Dad,' she repeated, more softly.

'Buy an A4 notepad and, when together, light an orange candle over it. Together, say: "Merry meet and merry part, Before I go, my heart I'll show".'

Viktor felt something on his leg. He leant forward and saw a long insect in two segments, each with a set of transparent ribbed wings. The oval body was striped yellow and black. Its forked claw-mouth opened and shut as it waded up Viktor's calf. Behind it Viktor saw the cicada, its hind legs, rubbing visibly, calling to the others to come off the wall and follow the giant, grotesque wasp leading the assent, the assault, on this man, this imposter. Viktor looked around him. The terrace was being overrun by insects – the chair too. Between the heavy weave of the chair, more life came.

He continued to read. 'Now, each makes a dated entry in the book. Decide on a keeper of the journal.'

Viktor watched as the wasp hauled itself over his knee, moved through his thick leg hair, found the hem of his shorts, pulled itself up and continued across the creases of his shorts to the bottom of his shirt.

'Every time you meet, repeat the incantation and then use the pages to explore your progress and thoughts since you last met.'

Nina's voice sounded behind Rosa, clear and loud. 'You have to go to bed, Rosa. Tell your dad to phone back tomorrow.'

'Finish the spell,' Rosa said calmly.

'Continue to fill in the notebook diary and you will find it becomes a fascinating and enlightening Book of Shadows.'

Viktor couldn't make out the garden any more. He tried to scan the horizon for his hosts, but he couldn't focus. The wall and floor now sang in a dry, rough chorus. The wasp reached his chest and rested, its mouth twitching. Around the chair an audience had gathered. Insects that didn't even have names, that had never been seen before, alive for a day then eaten by their offspring, involved in the same scramble to eat and suck and gather. 'Merry meet. Merry part.' An inch-thick centipede, blood red, long enough to take down a lion, a man, approached Viktor. Others, with pinchers, snapped at the latecomers. Cockroaches the size of mice winged into the air, flew blindly, crashed into the wall, fell and crawled back to the circle, pushing their way to the front.

'Darling, that's it,' Viktor said finally.

'What's a Book of Shadows?' Rosa asked.

'I don't know. Witches, I think, keep their spells in a Book of Shadows.'

Nina shouted more roughly, louder. 'That's enough, Rosa! It's bedtime.'

'We will keep a Book of Shadows. We will keep one together,' Rosa said.

'Yes. You can be the "Keeper", sweetie.'

'We will keep it together.'

'Okay.'

'When will you phone again? Tomorrow. Phone tomorrow.'

'I can.'

'Mum, he's going to call tomorrow.'

'I love you, sweetheart,' Viktor said.

'I love you too, Daddy. Another spell tomorrow.'

The phone clicked. The static cleared. Viktor got up and the wasp fell, hit the ground and scurried angrily away, thrashing its wings. The wall cleared and the light widened, throwing back the shadows.

Viktor saw Louis and Vicki walking towards him.

*

A moment after the cannons stopped firing, Viktor and Anne-Marie heard a scream, then the sound of feet on dry gravel. There was shouting in the distance. From the trees a man came out, yelling, behind his two children. Anne-Marie stepped away from Viktor and tried to make out the figures. A small white and ginger animal was zigzagging ahead of the family.

'What is it?' Viktor screamed.

Anne-Marie swivelled on her heels to face Viktor. 'It's a bloody dog. It's gone crazy, *dingue*, because of the guns.'

The man's scream became more urgent. The dog passed Anne-Marie's car, bounded up the steps to the main road and disappeared. The man reached the car, panting, his face wet, his cagoule open, his eyes ablaze. 'I was telling you to stop the dog!' he shouted angrily as he passed them and bounded up the steps, taking three in each stride.

Anne-Marie shouted after him, 'It's your bloody dog, mister!'

Some distance behind him were the two children, the boy howling, tears running down his face, his sister holding his hand and pulling him on. The girl had large eyes, thick lashes, a centre parting and ruffled, sandy hair.

Anne-Marie knelt in front of them and opened her arms. Viktor walked away from the car and joined her.

'There's no point you running as well. Let's wait here for your dad,' Anne-Marie said.

The boy stuttered, 'Toby's going to die.'

Another thunderous boom echoed, shaking the trees and casting the children into Anne-Marie's embrace. Viktor took the keys from Anne-Marie's bag, unlocked the car and found his phone. He took a photo of the children's white, flushed faces hanging over Anne-Marie's shoulder, their bodies crossed.

The children sobbed, the boy repeating, 'Toby's going to die.'

'No, he won't,' Anne-Marie replied. 'Your dad will catch him.'

The scene was repeated. The dog, his coat shimmering red, ran out of the wood. This time a few steps behind him was the man, yanking his arms free from his jacket, then dropping it on the ground.

Viktor snapped another photo of the children, then ran, his great giraffe legs carrying him quickly to the stairs. The pavement and road were a metre away from him. He saw the lights of a car flash through the trees, turn the corner and accelerate up the hill towards him.

Viktor's hand was clammy round his phone. From his position he could see the entire scene under him. The children had left Anne-Marie's embrace and stared as their father chased the dog, stooping, his arms in front of him, trying to scoop up the animal.

Viktor thought, *How tiring it is being a man, to be a father*. He saw in the children's faces so much expectation, so much love for this ridiculous man. It struck him as deeply unfair how Rosa was obliged to love him, how she had no choice in the matter. From her relationship with him her love flowed abundantly – a torrent, a flood. If she had been able to choose her father, surely she would have found a more worthy vessel for her affections. All these children, his daughter and the two now standing next to Anne-Marie on the gravel, would have chosen differently if they could. If they had been given a choice. *Rosa is stuck with me*. Her love came not from anything he did, but his simple presence and title in her life.

The dog turned to the stairs and for a second time propelled itself, its legs working hard on the stone steps, its speed and momentum so great it seemed to hover above the ground. It flew towards him.

As Viktor knelt he saw the man reach the bottom step and throw himself forward, his arms reaching for the dog, his splayed fingers grazing the back of the animal, inches from a proper grip. The man lay for a second cursing, then tried to get up. He shouted, 'Stop him!'

Viktor recalled the next events backwards, as he was driving back with Anne-Marie. The dog was almost upon him. He had clutched his phone, wondered if he should try to photograph the scene, if the animal would bite him. The dog bounded towards him, its tongue hanging out of its mouth, caught in the slipstream of the chase like a scarf blowing in the wind. The dog aimed for Viktor, on its face a sort of joy.

The cannon echoed again. The road behind Viktor was suddenly awash with light. The car had almost reached the crossing, where the steps met the road. Once more the guns fired loudly above them, like the sound of an orchestra, a distant rumble from the sky. *If only we were all received by death like this*, Viktor thought, *after our momentary glimpse of light, our consciousness scratched on the living planet.*

The curious thing was that the dog was playing, it was enjoying the chase. And this stupid, kneeling white man at the bottom of the stairs didn't realise it. The dog's jowls and wet mouth smiled. The dog ruled the moment; it was free. Viktor stretched out his arms for the animal and knelt further down. The dog trailed spit in long strands from its mouth, its front teeth exposed in a grin and, without pause to assess the gap between Viktor's legs, to contemplate, the animal flew under him. Viktor's free hand tried to shovel the dog into his arm, but he only managed to loosely brush its coat, narrowing the noose. With his phone incapacitating one arm, balancing on the tips of his size thirteen trainers, Viktor toppled over.

He fell, his phone skidding and bouncing on the road. He saw the car, the headlights and wheels, a twin-cab high off the road. He thought that the dog would miss the car, make it to the other side, survive.

The dog was caught by the front wheels, turned on its side and flung under the back wheels. There was only the muffled thud of the animal under the car.

The couple left soon after the father removed the dog from the road and laid it on the gravel path whole, still expelling heat. There was no sign of death on the animal, just rest – its ears alert, the mouth and black lips, the teeth visible in a soundless growl.

'I thought it could be resuscitated. I thought the father was going to breathe life into its lungs. Bring it back to life.' Viktor said in the car.

'They care so much for their dogs. I wouldn't have been surprised if he had done mouth-to-mouth. Dogs and white men – a single entity.' Anne-Marie replied.

When Anne-Marie had heard the car, saw the dog disappear into its headlights, she had held the children and stopped them from rushing to the road.

'All I could think was that if I stopped the dog it would bite me. I should have tried harder.' Viktor spoke quietly.

'Rubbish. The dog was on a mission. It was trying to catch the car, to escape its owner. Its time had come. There was nothing we could do.' Anne-Marie knew the road; she swung around potholes, deftly turning the steering wheel to avoid street debris.

'It thought we were playing a game,' Viktor said. 'I was the last person to see it alive. That panting, happy face. It was enjoying itself. I swear it was just bristling with superabundant life. And then it was dead. It's a message to us.' Viktor stared straight ahead, the road lit only by cars, single headlights veering, swinging across the road like drunken Cyclopes.

Anne-Marie laughed and put a hand on Viktor's knee. 'What's the message, *mudiwa*?'

Viktor adjusted his position, pushed back his seat and stretched his legs. 'Okay,' he started, his pulse quickening. 'The dog had reached the pinnacle of existence, the apex of its dog-being. It had evaded capture. It was almost flying. Did you see how fast it was running?'

The traffic lights ahead were red. Anne-Marie slowed, crawled towards the junction ahead, checked to her right and left, then accelerated without stopping.

Viktor continued, 'The dog wanted recognition from us. It wanted us to see it for what it really was.'

'A dog!' Anne-Marie laughed again.

'No, an equal. Better than us. Faster. Awake to our shuffle. Ecstatic to our depression. Free to our unfreedom. The dog demanded that we see its power. Forced us to give it recognition.'

'You're *fou*, Viktor!' Anne-Marie exclaimed. 'The dog was disturbed by the cannon. It went crazy, that's all. You'd be better arguing that it was killed by ZANU-PF and the Third *Chimurenga*. The latest burial of another war veteran.'

'No, listen!' Viktor sounded shrill. 'The dog chose a brief life and then death to explain something to us. The puppy wanted

527

the children to see. Wanted us to know. But I can't find the answer, what the dog was trying to show us.'

'Nothing, *mudiwa*. Nothing. Life is snatched from us violently for no reason. For no purpose, other than the combination of random circumstances. The cannon, the chase, the car, the road, that stupid *murungu*.'

While Anne-Marie spoke, Viktor raised a hand to his face. With his thumb and forefinger he pressed his eyes closed and muttered, '*Tosca*, you make me forget even God.'

'Oh, Viktor darling, don't turn silly, don't be a *benêt*. What has God got to do with it? It was sad – you should have seen the faces of the children. But it was a dog. The only message is that we mustn't concern ourselves with animals.' Anne-Marie pulled up to the gates of the flats and flashed her headlights. From under the umbrella Lancelot stood, nodded a greeting and pulled the gates open.

'We have to bring life and death together. Exuberance and death. Merge them somehow. Hegel had something to say about this.' Viktor spoke excitedly as they drove into the car park. 'The dog was taking a step along the path of self-consciousness.' Agitated, impatient, Viktor expanded, 'Hegel saw human self-consciousness in the process of life and death. The dog's death was an ingredient in the epic drama of life's struggle, of the spirit's birth.' With tears in his eyes, his skin bristling, Viktor concluded, 'You see, *mudiwa*, it's all about death.' Then, suddenly, he shouted, 'The dog can redeem us from our incarceration in itself, Anne-Marie!'

Exhausted by this revelation, Viktor fell back into his seat.

Anne-Marie shook her head. 'Tell that to Biko.'

She drove into her parking space, turned off the ignition, lifted the handbrake. She sighed deeply and rested her head on

Viktor's shoulder. '*Il faut sortir de l'univers du livre pour tomber dans le réel, chéri.* If we have enough water I'm going to run you a bath, Viktor, and tell you that in the duel between life and death, death always wins. Please tell me you've learnt that lesson. There is no merging, you dope. You have to keep them apart for as long as you can. That's all.'

Chapter Thirty-Seven

In the end the cuts could not be healed. The broken arm, wrapped tightly in a torn shirt like a swaddled child, throbbed and pulsed in continual pain. Biko wondered how long he could bear the questioning, the beatings, the blows – always on the broken arm, the back, the same bruised shoulder, his cut eye and cheek. With Hopewell gone, the police amused themselves with Biko.

For the last four days in Chikurubi he had been beaten unconscious. He had not even been able to utter a single taunt, one curse, to tell these dogs that they would soon be buried, beaten by the system they guarded. Instead, his head slightly bent, he gritted his teeth and held on – tried to summon up his mother's face, the sagging, doleful eyes, the feel of the rough hands on his brow, to stop himself from screaming, pleading, begging them to stop. They were breaking his physical body, but if he begged these men to stop he would have conceded something else. The reason he had given to his life, his understanding of their darkness, would be lost. He also knew it would not save him. The names they demanded – Nelson, Anne-Marie, Lenin, the students in Bulawayo – he knew they already had. With the quivering, uncertain memory of his mother, his father and their stubborn, constant love beside him, he did not speak except sometimes to curse, call the men dogs, jackals, tell them who they were. Explain.

Samuel tended to Biko as best he could. When he was dumped into the cell Samuel tried to make him comfortable, find a way of cushioning his body, lifting and relieving the agony. He would wet the corner of the blanket and gently mop Biko's head, his chest, clean him as much as he could on the filthy floor with the stink of faeces, the scratching of the cockroaches who occupied the prison with such confidence, such impunity, unconcerned by the human interlopers.

*

Two weeks after the incident at the dam, Viktor drove, in Anne-Marie's car, along the road where the dog had been killed. The dusk was turning the trees into shadows, the pines crowding the road, the sky fading into dark blue, the moon a white crescent. Just beyond the steps to the car park was a tall woman dressed in white, leaning on her hips, her stomach thrust out, pregnant. She hailed the car, her thumb thrust confidently into the road.

Viktor slowed down and watched the woman approach the car in the rear-view mirror, her hands on her extended stomach, her bony face empty of expression, her nose bent. By the time she had reached the car, opened the door and sat down, Viktor felt he had a firm opinion on who she was.

The woman uttered a small thanks and, without responding, Viktor pulled away.

The road curved up a small hill. The weak headlights sprayed the road, dispersed into the dark and gave back only a dim, hazy impression of the road ahead.

The woman commented, 'The road is very dark.'

'Where are you heading?' Viktor asked.

'Not far from here. I'll give you instructions.'

Instructions? What did she mean, goddamn it? Viktor was annoyed. He wanted gratitude, acknowledgement that he was giving her a lift. He would not take her where she wanted to go. She could be dropped along *his* route into the Avenues. 'I'm heading home. I can drop you on Tongogara.'

The woman was silent. She looked ahead, the dim dashboard lights marking her profile. 'Turn left ahead,' she said.

Viktor indicated and turned. There was a row of houses set back from the road. Viktor's window was ajar; he heard the sound of crickets in the grass verge, the loud call for mates.

Why the hell did I turn? Viktor asked himself. *Anne-Marie told me, Nelson too: 'Don't stop for hitchhikers, comrade. To a hungry, desperate person you are just a wallet – a stupid, wealthy, white foreigner with a guilty heart. Don't stop.'*

Viktor tried to open a conversation. 'How many months pregnant are you?'

The woman ignored the question. When she spoke her voice was rough and deep. 'A faith that cannot be tested cannot be trusted.'

'True,' Viktor replied automatically.

'Turn left again. Here, beyond the trees. It is truly amazing what God has done in my life. If it wasn't for Him I would be dead.'

'Dead?' Viktor queried.

'Dead,' she repeated. 'An amazing transformation takes place when you acknowledge His power.'

Viktor was relieved. She was a believer. Harmless. Then, suddenly, he thought he should listen. He should try to empty his mind of his prejudices and unshakeable opinions and listen to her story.

'God's power?' Viktor asked.

'When you really go back to the beginning, there can only be God. Show me someone who can make something as beautiful as a flower. A crocus.'

'A crocus,' Viktor repeated.

They came to a crossroads.

'Left again,' she said simply. 'In every fibre of your being you are unique. God knows you.' She lifted her blouse and started to remove items of clothing: a bra, underwear, socks.

Viktor tried to keep his eyes on the road. He was lost, he had never driven to this part of the city. The houses looked abandoned. There wasn't the familiar splutter and drone of generators, the pulsing lights like heartbeats from distant windows. Nothing except the crickets.

'Remember, the devil was an angel, so he knows the Word but he doesn't have Life. We have the power to speak Life into any situation. Would you argue with me that you have the power to speak Life?'

'I am not sure I understand,' Viktor answered meekly, confused.

'God breathed life into us.' They approached another turning. 'Left,' she ordered. 'Always left.' The content of her pregnancy was now folded on her lap: old clothes, rags.

Viktor obeyed, turned the car.

'Proverbs 18, verse 21: "Death and life are in the power of the tongue and they that love it shall eat the fruit thereof".'

'I find that problematic,' Viktor stuttered. 'Because behind the tongue, as you say, are interests, social relations, economic power. Some people have larger, louder tongues than others. Take Mugabe——' Viktor felt his temples start to throb.

The woman ignored him, her hands on the bundle of clothes on her lap. 'There is a choice. If you want death, you will have it. If you want life, you have to drop down on your knees and to say thank you for this day. Reset your day.'

Why can't I believe? Viktor thought, his throat tightening. *Isn't there a chink in my heart, a space large enough to fit her God, to answer my questions, my cravings, my longings, my doubts? The devil was an angel. Doesn't she know that the ship of life has crashed against the continent's shoreline? How can she not know this? How can this wise African woman not understand that for five hundred years the continent has taken life and turned it into death?* Viktor adjusted his position on the seat. *Should I tell her?*

'You will go through trials and tribulations, but at the end of the day the choice is yours.' She crossed her legs. The dress rode up her legs. Under it Viktor saw trousers and on her feet, as large as his, trainers.

Her singsong voice, deep like a man's, danced up and down. 'God will put you through some trials. When you arise again you will be much stronger in your mind. God has predestined you for great things.'

Was she talking about him? Was he predestined for greatness? He thought, *I have always believed that I was different, but never great. We're all great. That's what she means. If we let God in, we will be great. Choosing God makes us great.* Viktor thought of Rosa. His love for her always seemed uncomplicated: a compass point, uncluttered by confusions, a place where he could stand and survey the past, look out at the horizon, see the whole of life, not cower from death. *That's it. She's talking about Rosa.*

The road was straight, the night fully descended. Viktor drove slowly on. He thought he recognised the neighbourhood.

'The Bible says, You will be tempted, but I will give you a way out and I will make a way out for you.'

'You?' Viktor asked.

'No, not me. Not man or woman. God,' she snapped.

The woman lifted her dress over her knees. The trousers were now fully visible. The blouse was undone, her legs open. 'Left here,' she said. Viktor turned, saw the road, the bottom of the hill, the route to the dam. 'Isaiah 43, verses 18 and 19. "Remember ye not the former things, neither consider the things of old. Behold, I will do a new thing; now it shall spring forth; shall ye not know it? I will even make a way in the wilderness and rivers in the desert, to give drink to my people, my chosen".'

Viktor thought of the last six months: the trials, the pain, Biko, Anne-Marie, Rosa, Nelson, Tendai, Moreblessing, Mobutu, Lenin. The tangle of the past, the web of former things – the wilderness, the rivers, the hot, urban deserts.

The road climbed round a small hill. In the distance he saw trees: the pines lining the dam, the stairs that led to the car park. *She's led me in a circle.* Viktor's heart pounded, lifted in excitement. *She's a he. A man in women's clothes. Everything is an illusion, a lie. I need to strip away the myths, rid myself of the past, behold the new, let the fruits spring forth.* The thought suddenly seized him that this hitchhiker was the dog, the spirit of the dead animal returned now to exactly the same spot to guide him, to reveal the real essence, tell him that Biko would be saved. *The thing.* Viktor started to cry.

'Pull up just there.' His passenger pointed to the spot where she'd hailed him ten minutes before. She put the clothes on the floor and wiggled out of her dress, pulling the blouse over her head. Underneath she wore a red tracksuit jacket, zipped to her neck. 'When it is impossible for man, it is possible for God,' she said.

Viktor parked the car and rested his hands on the steering wheel. His passenger pulled at the lever, released the lock, opened the door and put a foot on the road. Turning to Viktor for the first time, he said, 'Speak the word of God. Release it in the atmosphere and catch it.'

Their eyes met for the first time and the man winked and bared his front teeth in a strange smile. He then picked up the pile of clothes, got out of the car and slammed the door. For a moment Viktor remained still, paralysed, staring ahead.

'This is what it means,' he uttered suddenly, aloud. 'History compromises nothing, but reveals everything in a new light: our lives are tragic. Hegel said so. And Marx, too, who added that history always progresses by its worst side. Trotsky also said that our lives proceed along the path of least resistance. Yet we insist on progress, forgetting the losses and the dead, for which nothing can compensate, no revolution, no redemption. He is showing us a way through life, through the deserts of existence, without the blind loss of history. Consider not the things of the past, the losses of the past; things will be as we have decided they should be. Biko will live. THAT'S IT!' Viktor announced to the empty car.

In the rear-view mirror he saw the man standing, his thumb out.

By the time Viktor returned to the flat he was confused again. 'What does it mean?' he asked Anne-Marie. She laughed loudly, her head, as usual, thrown back in laughter, her mouth open. '*Mudiwa*, it means nothing, only that you have a soft, gullible heart, that you're a *benêt*. A fool.'

*

Biko woke from a thin, fraught sleep. He was constantly surfacing, then falling down again, his mind lost in a bludgeoned, restless slumber. He called for his father. 'Baba?'

'It's me, comrade. It's Samuel.'

Biko tried to find Samuel's face, to focus, concentrate, bring himself back. 'Is there anything to eat?' he asked.

'Nothing until morning.'

'Comrade, can't you cook some of the roaches?' Biko tried to smile. A large cut that curled from his eye to his cheekbone opened and the crusted blood broke. He breathed in deeply, drawing the air through his teeth.

'Take it easy, com. I'll get you some water.'

'No, don't. Stay here. Why aren't you asleep?'

'I am up waiting for the dawn.' Samuel adjusted his position and cradled Biko's head, lifting it into his lap. 'How are you?'

'I feel as though my head is going to burst.'

'It can't be long now. They'll have to let us out. Your friend, that man from the UK, is making a lot of noise. The guards were talking about him. The demonstration. We heard them.'

Samuel massaged Biko's temples, moving his fingers in small circles. Biko looked at him, the whites of his eyes illuminated by the dull light.

'I'm scared,' Biko whispered.

'I know. I know. *Ndinozviziva ndinozviziva, ivai neushingi mukoma.*'

Samuel had not been singled out for special treatment, though he was regarded as a problem as long as he was with Biko – binding his wounds, treating him with his ration of water. The guards in Harare were crueller than the thugs in Bulawayo.

Months before Biko and Samuel were transported to the capital, they had been shoved into Zimbabwe's dog-catching van, the police transport. The men sat on the floor of the van handcuffed, the chequered sun shining through the barred window.

They arrived eight hours later at Harare's Chikurubi Prison feral, with wispy beards, knotted hair, caged. Still, those first

537

minutes, the removal from the cells in Bulawayo, the sun on their bodies in this shit-free mobile cell, felt like freedom, like hope.

Biko had become talkative again, speaking loudly to the driver and the police guard with the shotgun across his lap. 'So you can kill us, that's the easy part. How many do you think have already died? You'll kill us all and then there'll be no one left to vote for the old man. You can have your elections, your lies, the stolen votes, but you will never have us. Your wives and parents are ashamed of you. Your children won't look you in the eyes. All the people you kill, the hundreds, thousands, will come back. And the people will inhale the dust from our bones and we will be inside them. The corpses you dumped in the Limpopo will be eaten by fish, and the fish will be eaten by your children and then we will be in their stomachs. We will never be gone. You can never crush us.'

Biko had winked at Samuel with a broad, boundless smile. He needed to exercise, send out his words, let them curve around the bars and bend and moisten the policemen in the cab, who shifted uneasily, swore, told Biko to shut up and show respect to his elders, to the Old Man.

'You arrogant boy. Don't you see you have to be taught a lesson? You must learn how to respect your superiors. We have taught all of you university students that you're not better than us. Your college girlfriends with their degrees and certificates, they think we're stupid, they don't go out with us, but now you have to obey us. You should see what we've done with them.'

Now Biko screamed in pain. Samuel, with his friend's head in his hands, wished for silence, for the pain to be gone.

'You are fucking illiterates. You are Mugabe's dogs. His fools. You are as poor as us but he feeds you, he gives you guns and you do his bidding. And he despises you. You are his murderers.

Fuck, what's the point in speaking?' Biko had rattled his handcuffs, made the van resound with the sound. Then he had resumed his lesson.

'Everything is ending. I can only see the dark. I can't find the way back to Baba, Mother, the township, the comrades. I open my eyes and I can only see the dark. Are you there, Samuel?'

Samuel felt his mouth dry. 'I'm here. We only have to wait a few more hours until morning. Let's carry on talking.'

Samuel had not understood: if the guards beat Biko because he teased them, called them Mugabe's dogs, then he should stop, give them what they wanted, apologise and live. But Biko, with every breath, cursed, blasphemed and decried the dictatorship, the lapdogs, the guard dogs, the mongrels, all the dogs barking, hunting, killing on their master's orders.

Whatever the words, the stories, there was always the beating on the floor of the cell with his hand, laid out flat, in time, the percussion to his talking, his constant, permanent pedagogy. Samuel still thought that life, any life, was better than death – yet Biko, his brother, seemed to be calling up the ancestors to carry him off in a hail of invective and lecturing. Biko was mad. The prison, the beatings had snatched away his sanity.

'If they want you to scream, to cry, then they'll soften the beatings.' Samuel continued to turn his fingers in small circles on Biko's temples.

'The darkness is inside me and I can't find the way to the light.' Biko's voice was faint. He wanted to move, but each time he tried he felt a jarring pain that shot through his arm, ran down his face to his back and took his breath.

'All I know, comrade, about the dark is that's when we wait for the morning. Com, just speak, tell them what they want. Let them think you have learnt their lessons. Show them respect. Fucking pretend.'

The appeal seemed to rouse Biko back to consciousness. He rocked his head gently between Samuel's legs. 'It's not for me to show them respect and apologise. I have no right. There can be no respect for them.' He tried to lift his hand, to indicate the place beyond the prison. 'I cannot give them respect from our comrades, my family, for being poor, for being born in Zimbabwe. This is my life. We can never give them what they want, don't you see?' He paused, tried to find his breath. 'You're as stupid as those dogs and illiterates.' Biko smiled; his teeth shone, catching the meagre, coarse light from the cell window.

Then they were silent. Biko relieved the pain in his head by lolling in the cushion Samuel had made of his bent legs. Samuel tensed his hands on either side of Biko's head and pressed. He felt a mass of love between them, but he didn't know what to do with it, how to wield it so he could reason with Biko.

Biko slipped back into unconsciousness, then into the darkness.

*

Even the rain had come, a rare occurrence in the city. Droughts were common, and when they occurred, public announcements were made on national radio and television. Stickers were printed for Harare hotels and the grotesque five-star complexes at Victoria Falls requesting that tourists restrict their use of water, wash off their holiday sweat with a short shower, sleep for two nights in the same sheets. On the day Samuel was released from Chikurubi Prison, four days after Biko had died, the sky filled with clouds and fell. The city's climate was extreme – weeks of reliable and steady weather was broken by explosive storms.

'This fucking prison is even more disgusting in the rain,' Nelson shouted. He sheltered under his umbrella, its pathetic wire arms broken, the plastic batwings hanging loose, water pouring off them in four small waterfalls. Lenin, Stalin and Viktor were with him, a delegation from the Society to receive Samuel, each still stunned by the news they had received two days before. After weeks of silence, it had left their heads pounding with grief. To Viktor's surprise, Nelson took the news worse than the others. Despite his bombast, his irrepressible vitality, his ability to see behind every apparently random event the logic of a system in terminal sickness and decline, he was unable or unwilling to show his grief in public. Instead he retreated for two days into his bedroom, the curtains drawn, lying on the bed or curled up on the floor. He stifled his pain in his pillows, biting his fists to dissipate the hurt, drawing blood; thought, for once, was useless, analysis unable to reach his distress. When he was finally shaken out of his room forty-eight hours later, the pain had somehow been incorporated.

Lenin handled the logistics, ploughing his own incomprehension at Biko's murder into organising the Society, barking orders at Viktor, Anne-Marie, anyone and everyone who needed to be moved into place. Lenin had a keen sense that death is always with us – however deep the daily charade, no true Zimbabwean of any age could take a single step without the presence of death jostling noisily against them.

Lenin began living in the office, issuing orders with a precision that came from shutting down every superfluous emotion in order to survive. In the hours after the news arrived, Lenin said to Viktor, 'We need to think like Biko. That is the only thing we can do. We have nothing left. *Hapana*. We can't answer his death with death. We can't meet him, go to him, reach him. True, com? We only have one thing and that's life, right? We're alive and Biko's dead. We can't respond with death. We have to respond with life. The more they silence us, kill us, the louder we have to shout. The more of us they kill, the more of us have to live. Our voices need to sound with Biko's. Right? Do you see? Viktor, are you listening?'

Viktor was listening, all of his cells bristling, more awake than he could ever remember being.

'You see, the answer – to everything – is simply life itself.' Lenin no longer sounded like Lenin but Nelson or Biko, some hybrid, patchwork comrade assembled from the parts of every Society member.

'Viktor, we need forty-five hundred dollars from the campaign for the funeral. For the six combis to take comrades to the funeral, the plot, the food. The rest goes to Biko's sister. Then the rest – how much is left?'

Standing, his mouth open, dry, Viktor stared at Lenin.

'How much, Viktor?' Lenin repeated.

Looking up over his glasses, making a quick calculation, Viktor said, 'We have eight thousand in the bank, so minus forty-five hundred, that leaves us with thirty-five hundred dollars – but there are other expenses.'

'Eight thousand dollars. Okay then, that leaves plenty. Two thousand to Samuel and fifteen hundred for the Society.' Grinning, pleased at his cunning, Lenin stepped forward and put his arms around Viktor, pressed him hard. 'Remember that everything we're doing, *everything*, is for Biko.'

Nelson continued to shout against the rain, the others sheltering under the overhang of the gutter to the small outbuilding next to the razor-wire fence and boon where they had demonstrated weeks before. Nelson was going for it, taking on the weather, shouting against all earthly odds. Only the occasional word reached the others as the rain thundered down, steam rising from the ground, bellowing around him.

'Every prisoner will be released when we liberate Zimbabwe. The worst elements, those who are broken and rotten, will have to be given therapy in a secure place until they can be reached by psychiatry, psychoanalysis, medicine. The others will need nothing other than the freedom that we will secure for them. Each one reprieved.' Nelson moved in front of the men lining the narrow wall. 'There are eight thousand souls in here. These brothers and sisters are our natural allies, with a hatred of society we can only imagine. Cellblocks A through C can be immediately emptied – these are just the poor, petty traders, shoplifters. We will need to be more cautious with cellblock D. Here the prisoners are violent, brothers and sisters suffering extreme mental distress. We will need to get our facilities for the reform of prisoners operational immediately.'

Suddenly the rain stopped so abruptly that, simultaneously, the three men against the wall looked up, stepped forward and scanned the heavens. The clouds opened and the sun spilled quickly onto their upturned faces. Nelson didn't notice. He was still shouting, his umbrella hanging over his face: 'Good food, clean, nourishing *sadza* and fresh stew – we'll have great vats of it here,' he indicated to his left and right, 'and here, for when the prisoners are released. And a bonfire of lice-infested blankets.'

Nelson dropped the umbrella to the ground and a few drops of water fell on his face. He blinked them away and continued his wild, utopian frenzy on post-penal Zimbabwe. 'They will see they are not in an open prison – not the place they left – but free, a freedom they can taste. We will give them complete, total love. Gut the prison, remove all remnants of the old and make this building' – he pointed towards the building in the distance – 'a school or hospital. Once we have thoroughly deloused it and ripped off the iron doors, cleared the rooms of torture and death. Lenin will take charge of it.'

They were silent. Disbelieving the details of Nelson's dream of institutional overhaul, confused by the precision of his imaginings, the three men stared blankly at him.

'After we have won, I don't want to run Chikurubi. I will take a holiday,' Lenin declared. 'I will go on a tour of Africa, from South to North. A big holiday. I am not running bloody Chikurubi, comrade.'

Viktor got caught up in the conversation. 'There will be too much to do once we have got rid of X- and Y-Party. There will be no time for holidays, Lenin.'

'You will be exhausted from everything we have to do day and night, but a holiday! A holiday? Pah. Who do you think we are? Grace Mugabe? Holidays? It isn't the fucking *bourgeois* revolution we're planning!' There was real anger in Stalin's voice.

Nelson scanned the wire fencing, the hut the group were standing next to – planning, surveying the material, deciding what could be saved, what would have to be thrown away. From the prison in the distance, its long, sandy, thick walls sealing everything in, there was movement.

A door within two giant doors opened and a single man came slowly out, pausing when he was finally standing outside the prison to shield his eyes from the sun and look slowly around. There was shouting from the gatehouse that sheltered the Society members, instructions to the man to walk to them. Samuel was holding a plastic bag, his clothes too large, trousers too wide, tied round his waist with a scrap of rope. A large striped office shirt hung off his shoulders. His boots also looked too big, the trousers rolled over them. As he walked unsteadily across the dirt moat, skirting the puddles, coming into clearer focus, he gave the impression of a clown. There was no painted smile, no teardrop, but his face was unreal, drained and gaunt, deep hollow half-crescents under his eyes, the skin stretched tight, his expression vacant. His trousers filled out in the wind and his arms hung limp in the shirt.

Samuel was greeted by two uniformed men outside the guardhouse on the inside of the perimeter fence. He was quickly, aggressively patted down, then led by an arm through the building to the door at the other side of the small building.

When Samuel emerged, Lenin and Nelson went to either side of him and spoke quickly in Shona, identifying themselves, then led him to the car and put him in the back seat. They all climbed in. Lenin opened the glove box and removed a cold drink, opened it and handed it to Samuel. Samuel held the bottle in both hands, brought it to his mouth and drank, the liquid spilling out of his mouth and down his shirt. He dropped the bottle and looked at the faces around him, breathing deeply. Viktor and Stalin sat either side of Samuel, with Nelson and Lenin in the front.

Samuel's voice was a whisper. The sun that he had longed for, that Biko had referenced every waking minute, was now an irritant. He was battered by it, they could see; he was blinded. Lenin, still issuing orders, snapped to Nelson, 'Com, drive over there to the tree, so we are out of the sun.' Nelson complied, crunched the Toyota into gear and spluttered fifty metres to park alongside the large trunk of the gumtree. The car instantly cooled down. Samuel's face relaxed.

There was talk in Shona. Samuel spoke first, so softly the others craned towards him to hear, then Lenin answered. Viktor picked out words he knew: 'the Society', 'Biko', '*kurohwa*', '*mhuri*'. He knew what was being said from what they had decided on the journey to the prison – Lenin would describe the campaign, the money they'd collected, what the Society was, and then offer Samuel anything he needed: a bed in Harare, transport to his family in the rural areas. He would explain that money collected for Biko was now Samuel's.

Lenin spoke quickly and pulled out the envelope with the dollars that Viktor had given him – that Louis had given him. Samuel took the envelope, then put his hands together, bowed his head and muttered something. Then Nelson spoke, repeating what he'd said in English so Viktor would understand: 'No, comrade, you owe us nothing. You are our guest now.'

When this was done, Samuel turned his head slightly and addressed Viktor in English. 'All the prisoners used to have a word for Biko: *kumedza*.' He looked to the other faces in the car and Nelson translated, 'Bird, a swallow.'

'Yes. We would say, the *kumedza* is making noise today. The *kumedza* is pecking at the walls. The *kumedza* is eating outside, looking in.' Samuel paused. His pulse seemed to have quickened. He sucked in a breath and continued in Shona, speaking quickly. When he finished, he looked to Nelson and nodded for him to translate.

Nelson started slowly. 'It's a story we were told as children, that the first man and woman lived in darkness because the sun had not been found. Yet the sun had to be found so that people could live properly. The strength of the sun is that its light reaches even in the darkest places, as a swallow can fly across the earth before anyone can trap it. He says Biko was a sunbird, a swallow, who could fly higher than any other bird and not be caught.'

Samuel now spoke directly to Viktor. 'He knew what you were doing. We all did. Biko knew what you were doing.' With effort, he moved his left arm, put his hand on Viktor's, took

546

his fingers and tried to squeeze. He left his hand resting on Viktor's. His skin felt hard and dry. 'He knew what all of you were doing. He kept me alive, he never gave them anything. He was a type of madman – *munhu uyu ibenzi*. A mad, clever man. When he went, when he left …' Even the soft, almost inaudible words took more from him, more than he had. 'I told the others. Got the news out on the door, and the prisoners started to sing.' Pausing, recovering his breath, he started to sing with surprising gusto and skill, '*Ngatirege huvengana, Tibate pamwe, Tese vanhu veAfrica, Tiri rudzi rum we, Tisazviparadzanisa, Tiri rudzi rum we*.' The other men in the car nodded their heads. Breaking off, Samuel continued, 'Then they protested. They sang and then protested. Some in the large cells below set the main hall on fire and burnt their blankets, shouting, "*Mukoma wedu akafa. Shinga Mushandi Shinga! Qina Msebenzi Qina*".' Nelson quickly translated: 'Our brother is dead.'

Samuel continued, 'Some prison guards were hurt. The dogs were scared.' The men laughed, recognising Biko in the story, in the words Samuel used. 'Biko organised the protest. And when they took his body, the other prisoners shouted louder. A guard came to the door and unlocked it and left it unlocked all night. I walked around the floor, greeting the other prisoners. All of them knew Biko. They had heard the stories about his *jambanja*, his fighting the guards. They told me that. When I went back to the cell, I had new blankets and there was a bowl of stew. Proper stew. I fell asleep and woke in the night and the cell had the light of the sky. I could feel Biko there with me, by the window, looking out. To see the moon.' Tiring again, he stopped. Then, remembering, he said quickly, 'He never spoke. I told him to give them what they wanted' – again he paused, overwhelmed – 'but he never did. He never gave them anything. He kept me *amupenyu*.'

Stalin said, 'Alive.'

'Alive,' Samuel repeated. 'I owe him.' He looked round at the attentive faces. 'Everything.' He smiled again. 'He knew everything. He had answers to all suffering. How to end it, you know. Are you the same?'

'We try, we try,' Lenin muttered, doubtfully, modestly. There was a moment of silence in the car that no one tried to fill.

Finally, Viktor spoke. 'Let's get out of here before they arrest us.' The two men in the front swivelled round. Nelson turned the key, leant his weight into the gear stick and eased the car away.

*

Society members came, visiting the Calder Gardens flat like New Testament witnesses to the birth of Christ. Amused, touched, thankful, Samuel dutifully repeated the story of their comrade's last days, recalling his last stand. For a few days Samuel seemed to be the only person who really knew Biko, and his presence allowed them to feel Biko, however fleeting and uncertain, once more.

The group held onto Samuel with a fervour, to appease their grief; when he wanted to leave they tried to persuade him to stay. 'Just another day, com. One more night.' He stayed for five days, then travelled south to Shangani to see his family. Slightly fattened, his eyes still hollowed out, Samuel left. They were reluctant to let him go and when he did the group felt raw with loss – deepened by Samuel's departure, taking with him the final secret of Biko's life and reminding them of his perpetual absence.

Chapter Thirty-Eight

It was a short distance along the undulating, low summits and shallow valleys to the marked grave already dug in a crowded cemetery where Biko's mother was buried, where his grandparents also lay, slowly giving themselves back to the continent. Above each grassy mound was a small wooden cross.

Biko's comrades in the Society of Liberated Minds had nailed a further diagonal plank to the standard-issue cross and painted the wood red, managing to turn Jesus's crucifixion into a communist star. The star, roughly nailed together, was carried at the front of the cortege by two of Biko's student comrades from Bulawayo. Etched on the star, chiselled into the wood, were the words:

Shinga Mushandi Shinga! Qina Msebenzi Qina!
Stephan 'Biko' Mutawurwa
1978–2012
Revolutionary, Intellectual, Student, Brother

Then:

RIP

But this had been crudely scratched out, and the words written with a black marker:

Let There Be No Rest Until We Have Peace and Socialism

Lenin fell back until he was walking alongside Viktor and Nelson. The two older men, drops of perspiration on their foreheads, were both silent with the effort of the walk. Nelson draped an arm over Viktor's shoulder. 'You see, Viktor, this is how we bury our dead in Zim. We march with Biko to say that he is not alone and that we will soon be with him. Look at our numbers.'

It was true: This was the strangest funeral. Maybe a hundred and fifty people were walking and dancing to the grave, each having left the cities, their rural areas, begged, hitched and borrowed to attend the ceremony.

'He was a popular comrade. His brothers and sisters loved him.' Lenin slackened his pace, slowing for the men to catch him, keep apace. Viktor had not known a funeral to be so voluble. The occasion made Lenin want to speak. 'You know, comrade, I have a question for you.'

Viktor nodded, indicating to him to go on.

'Comrade Marx was a brilliant man, the world leader of communism. No one his equal. Pro-poor and for the working class.'

'You mean Karl Marx?' Viktor asked, wishing that Nelson would drop his damn arm, stop leaning on him, and carry his own weight.

'Yes, yes, Comrade Marx.'

'Well, yes, you are right. He was a brilliant man,' Viktor replied.

Nelson was panting, interrupted, excitable. 'Nothing gave him more pleasure than to know that the working class read and studied his books. Remember what he said? "This is a consideration that outweighs everything else".' Nelson coughed and leant harder on Viktor's shoulders, slowing them. Lenin, impatient, moved in front of the two men, bouncing on his feet. He walked backwards, his energy like a child's.

Nelson continued, 'Marx wanted to make *Capital* more accessible to workers and the poor, but he refused to dilute his ideas. He knew that to understand capitalism would require a great effort. He raged against impatience and zealous seekers of the truth.'

'Yes, yes, I know, comrade.' Lenin again walked alongside the men.

Unperturbed, Nelson resumed his lecture breathlessly. 'There is no royal road to science; only those who do not dread the fatiguing climb of its steep paths will reach the dizzying summits.'

Behind them the large group of mourners was led by a line of students, shouting, 'Down with Mugabe! *Pasi naMugabe! Biko ndiye wekutanga!* Biko is Number One, Number One!' The students – many faces Viktor recognised – stopped. The crowd bunched up behind them. They kicked their feet in the air, sang louder, bent low to the ground, twisted their torsos and then, on a signal, rushed forward, screaming in mock battle.

From the small summit on the crest of the hill, Viktor and Nelson could see into the valley the muddied, packed cemetery, row upon row of crosses. Ahead of them mourners prepared to lower the coffin into the narrow, dug-out rectangle, a mound of rust-brown earth heaped beside the hole.

Lenin now had his chance. He seized it. 'Exactly, so if comrade Marx was a giant, for the workers, the poor, all of us—'

'Yes?' Viktor answered.

Lenin smiled, triumphant. 'If he was this great fighter for the poor, why were there only seventeen people at his funeral?'

Lenin let the question fall.

Viktor and Nelson were silent. Lenin pressed his point. 'While Biko, hardly known in the world, has attracted this rally, a great crowd.'

Nelson turned to Lenin, this young puppy of a comrade bouncing beside him. 'I have never thought of it like that, comrade,' he answered honestly.

'A good question,' Viktor agreed.

The funeral procession reached the small, flat cemetery. The sun squeezed through the heavy cloud, shone beams of light on the divided plots. Biko's coffin and the thick crowd were hit by a ray of light. The circle around the dug-out plot opened to allow more mourners to see the grave, the coffin, Biko's last moments above ground next to the carefully marked hole, the spades stuck in the earth, the two cemetery diggers in stained overalls. Lenin arranged the assembly, running, pointing, indicating space, shouting orders, commanding life. Viktor stood back and looked over the heads of the crowd. Anne-Marie stepped beside him.

Viktor inhaled sharply. Even from this distance the geometry was clear: the coffin was a full head larger than the grave.

'They've made a mistake,' Viktor said softly to Anne-Marie.

'What mistake?' she asked.

'Biko is not going to fit into that hole.'

'Yes, he will.'

'No. I can see from here – the hole is about half a metre too short.'

The crowd stood between the packed graves, the small mounds of ploughed earth, crosses, dried flowers, dog-eared photos peeling away from their frames, bleached in the sun.

Mourners stood awkwardly astride the graves, anxious not to step on the dead, straddling the plots.

'That's normal practice these days,' Anne-Marie replied.

'Normal practice?'

'It costs. There are already too many graves in the cemetery. Look.' Anne-Marie spread her arms out. 'So they dig the graves deeper and narrower.'

'To save money?' Viktor asked.

'To save money,' Anne-Marie repeated.

Slow to awareness, his brow stitched, his face tightening. 'So they are going put his coffin in diagonally? Upright?'

'Not completely upright. Diagonal, as you say.'

Viktor was confused, disappointed that Anne-Marie seemed undisturbed by this fact. 'Fuck!' he said.

'Considering the circumstances, does it really matter?'

Viktor didn't answer immediately. The full assembly had descended the hill and jostled noisily in the cemetery. People laughed. The singing and slogans heard on the procession started to fade. There was hope, expectation, resolution as obvious and evident as life, as Biko's blind, subversive determination to dominate death.

'Of course it matters. Biko is entitled to lie flat, to rest on his back! It's madness.'

'There is too much competition for space. Too many people are dying. There is a premium on length.'

Viktor's voice rose. 'Biko needs to lie flat. He needs rest.'

'This is Zimbabwe, *mudiwa*.'

'Are we not allowed a proper bed even in death? So we can yawn, reach out, be ourselves? He is going to be there for eternity!'

Anne-Marie laughed. 'Eternity? Isn't it more appropriate that Biko is partly upright? He was a man who lived on his feet, Viktor.'

Viktor pondered the argument. 'But he's not even going to be upright. He'll forever be at a forty-five-degree angle. Neither on his feet nor his back. Permanently in between.'

Nelson came out of the circle; he nodded to Lenin, who shouted in Shona for the crowd to be quiet. The grassy amphitheatre carried his voice and threw his words over the hills.

'Biko was a revolutionary before anything else. Before he joined us, he was one. As a boy, maybe as a suckling child. You see, he had always said, "Take me. Take what I have. What skills I have. What money I have. What strength I have. What energy I have." As a revolutionary, that's what Biko said. "Take all of me." Every fibre of his life was directed at destroying the world of oppression, not only in Zimbabwe but everywhere. Biko knew what no one else did: that not an inch could be conceded in that struggle against oppression. As soon as the body bends in apology, it can be broken.'

Nelson raised himself to his full height, speaking freely, openly. 'Biko knew that in Zimbabwe in the last fifteen years, life was not the flowering of spring blossoms on our jacaranda trees but an endless struggle against death. Our lives are spent avoiding hunger and violence. Life as despair. Existence' – with a wide sweep of his arms he enveloped the entire crowd, the valley and hills – 'has become simply this slide into death.' He paused, rested.

Viktor felt his life lift into his mouth, his cheeks filling, his mind driven to a single point. The crowd, his friends and comrades, stood still, the sun covering them. Each of Nelson's words seemed to have been spoken directly by the crowd. Their speaking hearts were opening and closing, telling the story of their lovers, brothers, sisters, mothers and fathers swept aside.

And now Nelson spoke again, his words pressing on the rags they wore, conquering their fears to overcome the defeat and loss entangling their minds and bodies. The old fear that despair would simply endure forever was now replaced by this strange communal voice.

'Our enemy has become fatalism; the hope that we can turn around our lives, our society, bring real *chinja*, a new government to power, and build something from these ruins. Often we feel that the only arbiter, the only saviour to a life of suffering, is death. Death will have us all, even the old man and ZANU, and there is no mystery in that.' The crowd groaned in agreement. 'But remember: once our *chinja* determined the world. Now we say: Let God cut down ZANU.'

The crowd sighed again in agreement.

Nelson's face glistened; his head ran with perspiration. He breathed in deeply and then, indicating with an open hand the coffin behind him, said, 'Biko stood against this fatalism. He took away from God responsibility for our mistakes and our tasks, comrades. The struggle to end our suffering is our responsibility. No matter the temptations of individual advancement, quick fixes, the perils of ZANU and MDC, the rich pickings of the NGOs, any of these things. Biko could have chosen, if he wanted, to be a well-paid leader of his generation. Maybe then he would still be alive today.

'Our age of instant and twenty-four-hour internet-based communication, individualism, is the curse that bedevils us. A refusal, an inability to see beyond the screen, the computer, to what has been accomplished before, to a time of collective interests over the individual; to the internet generation it is only their efforts, their interests – a desire for immediate gratification.

555

'It is against this world in the name of collective humanity that we go into battle. Socialism and original Christianity are the two great traditions. Christ, not as the activist of first resort, but the representative of the credo, "Do unto others as you would like them to do unto you".

'And Biko knew that from Marx and Jesus arose Stalin, Judas Iscariot, the Scribes, the Pharisees, who claimed their identity to humanity's project. To these false prophets Biko rose and spoke. With practice, practice, practice we test our lives and the ideas we hold.'

Stopping briefly, wiping his forearm across his face, Nelson continued, 'Biko committed himself to the struggle, to his allotment of life. He gave us an ounce of practice and when one gives, makes the gift of practice for the common good, we do not need to be sad when they leave us. Biko is still with us – in our bellies, in our minds, in our souls, comrades.'

There were louder exclamations, shouting.

'We are the in-between era, trying to fulfil the next steps, to build movements for socialism. We are like the twentieth-century founders who sought to carve out the first parties. From Biko we can learn much.'

Nelson now turned directly to the coffin. Everyone was still, half-expecting Nelson to announce that Biko had avoided death, had somehow remained intransigent even to the call of his own morality and that, with a wave of Nelson's hand, the flimsy chipboard coffin lid would burst open. After all, such a box was an insult to Biko's unbound spirit. To Nelson's instructions he would emerge from the coffin and without pause condemn fatalism and death, lead a march to State House, a human snake growing as they weaved through Gweru and Mashonaland to Harare in a line of humanity longer even than life.

Viktor was not the only one in the crowd to imagine that Biko would appear to them. He saw Biko roll aside the rock sealing the cave, letting air flood in before he sang, like Radamès in Verdi's *Aida*:

Oh heaven, farewell, farewell.
Earth is opening for us.
Dream of joy which in sorrow fades.
For us earth opens and our traveling souls
Fly to the light of eternal day.

But Nelson continued softly addressing the coffin. 'You have fought a good fight, comrade, and we give you a revolutionary salute.' Then he spoke even more quietly: 'Tomorrow, before we are dead, people may decide to establish socialism, and others may be cowardly and helpless enough to try and defeat them. But in this event, socialism will be human truth, and so much the better for us. In reality things will be, as they have always been, as we have decided they should be.'

Nelson raised his fist, trying and failing to stop his arm from shaking. Unevenly, quietly, other fists and hands were raised until the salute, a mixture of open hands and clenched fists, were lifted into the sky, holding up the blue, dispelling the clouds.

Lenin shouted, 'Fists, fists, comrades, not those Y-Party hands of surrender – the fist for Biko, a revolutionary salute!'

Nelson finished. 'Take your rest well, comrade. You have lit the fire burning inside of us.' His voice broke. 'Without you the going will be tough, but we have no choice until some of our comrades form part of the next wave.'

Chapter Thirty-Nine

Viktor organised all of his emails carefully. He had set up a system of labels and tags, filters to apply tags automatically. Every inconsequential reminder to pay a fine, every message to confirm a meeting, each two-line email from his father were labelled precisely and archived for safekeeping: *Your mother and I are worried about you and want to see you. We have decided that you have the same tendency to ruminate as Uncle Max. I need your help to fix the leak in the bathroom.* Isaac&Sonia. Bills. Rosa. Nina. Writings. *Mutations.* The organisation of his virtual universe, his electronic housekeeping, belied a world in disorder.

Since news of Biko's death had reached them Viktor had struggled to sleep. The nights had been hot; the room, even with the windows open, was stagnant. He hadn't slept – aware each time he fought his way to unconsciousness, for momentary escape, rest, that he would soon need to wake. The days came early, so goddamn eager to start, to forbid any escape. The insistence in Harare to act, to lay bare, to present yourself, confronted Viktor each morning.

The morning blew a cooling breeze.

'Now the city chooses to breathe, after suffocating us in the night,' Viktor muttered in the morning.

'Always a complaint, Viktor. The problem is in your head, not in the night.' Anne-Marie rushed to pull on her clothes. she sorted through the pile of cast-offs on the floor with her feet, kicking aside the pieces she didn't want, hooking the others up with her toes, swinging a blouse over her shoulders, tugging her trousers over her hips.

Viktor needed coffee to burrow to the light. As he walked into town he repeated his to-do list for the day, drunk on exhaustion, zigzagging around potholes, pedestrians, swaying, tottering on street corners, staring at the oncoming cars, straining to focus, searching for comprehension. The campaign was over, but he couldn't stop. He wanted to email the supporters, those who had helped Biko. He practised the wording, tried to get the tone right. He needed to send information – a complete dossier – to Amnesty about the arrests, the imprisonment, the death, as the representative had told him the previous day: 'As many details as possible, everything – the school he went to, his family, his interests. The circumstances of his death.' Then he needed to phone the prison and demand to speak to the prison governor. To make his final threats, to tell him it didn't end here. He was exhausted just contemplating it.

Viktor's shoe hit an upturned paving stone. He swore and stumbled forward, his balance lost. He hobbled out of kilter and his torso folded, feet out, arms akimbo. He staggered along for a few steps like a great albatross with its huge wings out, paddling frantically at the air to pick up speed and fly.

There was a counter at Louis's café where customers could stand, rest their coffee, read their papers and then go. Today Viktor decided he would stand, let his entire system hang upright, correctly – to give his tasks urgency and importance.

He felt the drag of the day on his heart, the dread of everything he needed to do. He paused, scrolled down the list of folders, saw the file 'Nina' recording, like all of them, lost time, preserving examples: low, profound, significant and irrelevant events. Viktor looked up at two well-dressed women sitting near him. One was bent over the table, pleading to her friend, it seemed. The other seemed distracted, distant, scanning the café for something.

Viktor opened the folder and scrolled down the emails. He felt his stomach lurch as he remembered the messages – his, hers, their fights, the record of each here, the causes, the courting, the longing. The love in the first messages, the decay in the later ones. In fact, the whole litany of their life together was here, from its festive, impatient beginnings to the slow agony of separation at the end.

'Too much, too much,' Viktor muttered, his head starting to spin, his brow moistening. He searched around the café for relief, stared out of the window to the street, the activity outside, the lack of any commemoration of life in the daily crusade of the city. *Have they not heard that Biko is dead?*

Viktor dropped his head back to the screen. He decided he would find the emails where Nina had slandered him, where, once more, she had used Rosa to hurt him. He searched.

Viktor opened email after email, searching for Nina's crimes. Soon he had dozens of windows open, different browsers' windows, old Word files – each stored as evidence of their life together. Sweat dripping from him, Viktor opened a new email, a message sent years ago, with Nina's delight, her love, on each line. He closed it and opened another, this time a message sent to him a year ago, after he had taken Rosa for the weekend:

Viktor, you seem to have lost Rosa's new cardigan. My mother spent weeks making it for her. I am upset. Are you still planning to take Rosa next weekend? Please let me know. Nina.

Digging deeper, another message – just after he had left her.

Viktor, come home. We miss you. Your place is here. Nina.

Pushing this one aside, he found other notes, files he had kept – he imagined – to show Rosa one day what her mother had done to him. Viktor swallowed, wiped his sleeve over his mouth, pinched his eyes – maybe he was not seeing right. He found the store of her emails, those messages, everything that had been said to him. The hate she had heaped on him, the reason he left – but what did it matter now? he asked himself.

He paused and gripped the table with both hands, letting it ground him. Something solid, real, outside of himself, not this traitorous, unreliable past. Suddenly the foundation for all of his indignation – the bile he had built up, the persecution he had kneaded and baked with his anger and brought to life, collapsed.

Clear, honest, facing the facts, Viktor wetted his throat and realised, with a terrible sadness which tightened his chest, that although he now had these emails open in front of him, they didn't really matter. The ones he read were sad, desperate, lost, her anger translucent and pathetic. They were evidence of Nina's pain, her loneliness – nothing else. When her anger surfaced, he saw it now only as a bid to be heard, to show him her pain.

Viktor leant harder on the counter and it creaked. *We let time go, release it, because the truth of the past is unbearable – the reality of our folly is too crushing.*

A collage of his life with Nina flashed suddenly before him – the whole storyboard of their relationship, its beginning and end. The order was muddled. Rosa's small body, between them on the bench after the trip to the fair. Nina crying to him on the phone. Viktor tried to mop his face with his hand. *What else have I told myself? What other stories have I lived by?*

Then he thought of Biko. He felt the old sickness, loss, the defeat.

Biko's life had presented him with something. He looked up and saw the road, the rage of taxis and cars, the horns, people trying to cross, shouting at each other. Then in the distance he saw two men, one affectionately tapping his friend with a rolled-up paper as he spoke, then placing a hand on his shoulder, laughing. *What are they saying to each other? What's making them so happy? So alive?* The clouds parted and the street suddenly disappeared, washed with sunlight. Viktor squinted. Everything had vanished – slowly he could make out the road again, the men still talking. He felt the heat of the sun through the glass and let the force of the sensation surge through him.

Viktor felt a flow of inexplicable happiness, but no obvious explanation came to him – just the sun, the heat, the day. Was there something in this – a clarity in the darkness? A secret that had finally been revealed to him, turning the darkness in Zimbabwe, in him, in all conditions, into clear light and joy? Turning everything over to the light, as Biko had proclaimed. Viktor laughed aloud and muttered to himself, 'All this time I have been searching in myself for a reason and I have found nothing.'

Viktor remembered Samuel's words: that Biko had always seen beauty, that there was something insane, euphoric about his visions. Beauty from the darkness. Beauty all around us.

Viktor shut his computer, sucked in deeply, filled his lungs, dropped his things into his bag and left the café.

*

For some reason the decision was easy after Biko had been buried and his dead feet, calves, thighs took the strain for eternity, or until he could be buried properly after X-Party had been overthrown.

There was always a chill in the morning, even in the summer before the sun came up. Anne-Marie had taken the morning off to walk with Viktor by the dam, then drive him to the airport. When they stepped out of the car, under the pines, Viktor felt as though the wheels constantly spinning in his head had finally stopped. For once Africa's clock was kind to them and let them ponder Harare's wonderful, waking, dewy morning. While they walked under the trees the world could rest from paradox and contradiction – the exhausting, tireless dialectic of existence.

The couple stood outside the car in the empty car park, staring at the tree line, the path they would take in a minute. When they started to walk there was the sound of the gravel under their feet and the hard rustle of the wind in the trees.

'I have signed up to do a course in physics at UNISIA in Pretoria,' Anne-Marie said as they walked into the thick cluster of trees in Cleveland Park. The temperature dropped. The early sun cast a disordered, speckled pattern on the path.

'Physics? Why physics?' Viktor asked.

'Because I have been interested in physics since I was a child. I received the school prize when I was thirteen.'

They walked towards the large green expanse in front of the dam. The morning felt deceptively normal.

'I didn't know. You've never mentioned it before.'

563

'There is much you don't know about me.' Anne-Marie's reply came out more harshly than she'd intended; the sting of it left both of them silent. *More than I can ever know, now that I am leaving.* Viktor's heart heaved.

'As a child I thought I could explain everything with physics – what was really going on. It shrank our lives and activities into a space as infinitesimal as that spider.' Anne-Marie pointed to two small saplings recently planted – *they are still planting trees*, Viktor thought – with solid sticks holding them straight, evidence of the expansion of the wood, of optimism. Between the infant trees was a large web with drops of dew hanging on it, and in one corner was a spider the size of a hand – too large for the web, too significant, with its yellow-and-black legs and body, for Anne-Marie's example.

'Of course I only scratched the surface, but still I had a sense of studying the building blocks of everything. It broke us down into a mass of particles that made the stars and planets. I even thought that we should adapt the Christianity I was learning: from particle to particle – you know the text.'

'No, I don't,' said Viktor quickly, wanting Anne-Marie to know he was still hurt.

'I thought physics could be used to rewrite Genesis. "Particle thou art and unto particle thou shalt return." I wanted to study physics because physics explains everything, and what of our peculiar behaviour and hurt it could not explain was not important.'

'But it is from our peculiar behaviour that we live.'

'There is enough in life, *mudiwa*, that is already difficult to understand without adding our own.' She reached for his hand and held it tightly. They were barely walking, reluctant to reach the far end of the dam, where they would be forced to turn back to the car.

'Amy loved physics.'

'Your sister?'

'Yes.'

'You don't talk about her much.'

'Well, I am now.'

'Good.'

'We are twins.'

'What, *jumeaux*? Identical?'

'No, she's a she. I have a penis.'

'Viktor!' Anne-Marie exclaimed, laughing.

'Identical in a way. We are the same mass of particles, almost the same height.'

'Why have you never spoken of this?'

Viktor ignored the question. 'She is like you, more rational than me. When we were teenagers and our parents went away, she would sleep in their bed and invite her friends over. Afterwards she'd shake the bedding, brush down the sheets and move back to her room. I never understood that.'

'What didn't you understand?'

'That she would sleep in our parents' sheets, in their smells, where they made love.'

'Now I am the one who doesn't understand.' Anne-Marie stated.

'It was her lack of imagination. How could she sleep? I didn't understand how she could do this.'

The sun was completely out now. Viktor felt its heat. The day doesn't wake gradually in Zimbabwe; it rushes into the sky as if it is playing, searching for the night, driving away the moon and stars so there is only day, only light.

The couple walked beside the large spread of still water, the concrete wall and the grass, the playing fields where once the city had taken its Sunday picnics. Now families and children camped and sheltered here. People were folding up cardboard shelters and shaking out their blankets; others stood in the sun, stretched, yawned, urinated.

'Not everyone is as prone to that sort of thinking as you, Viktor. Life might be easier for Amy without your imagination, if that's what you call it.'

Anne-Marie looked at Viktor, pleading, he thought, with her eyes, willing him to free himself from some of that intensity, beseeching him to understand the meaning of their particle mass, to let life fall into its correct place.

'It wouldn't matter so much, these patterns of thought,' she resumed. 'Your, your – *tête dans les nuages*. You could go on a hundred years, but you take each thing so seriously. Each wrong step for you, *mudiwa*, rebounds.'

'I'm not so bad,' Viktor said. 'It's you today who has the strange theories about physics and particles.'

Anne-Marie laughed again, her great, free, unbound laugh. 'I am not joking. I enrolled on a correspondence course. When I see you again I will be Professor of Particle Physics. I will unpick you one atom at a time until I get to your sex.'

The path along the dam wall tapered out. They could either climb and walk back, circling the park on the road, or turn back. They stopped. Anne-Marie, as she often did at this point, climbed the bank, three steps, until she stood above Viktor. She put her arms on his shoulders and pulled him to her, so his head rested on her chest, between her breasts. He placed his hand on her lower back, felt the rise of her buttocks, the soft, firm cushion of her breasts, the deep familiar smell that gathered in her neck.

They had not made love on their last night; there would have been too much longing. But now, standing close to her, he was aroused and the missing was acute. His body surged with excitement, with craving and loss. Was this love? Had he only made another connection that, like all the others, would lead to loss? Was this worth more than his daughter?

As they walked back, their pace brisker, more matter-of-fact, a woman with a neatly folded blanket under her arm and a small child approached them. 'Sir, madam. Money for food? A dollar.' Viktor pulled out his wallet and handed the woman a ten-dollar bill. The woman stared at the note and called out as they walked away, 'Thank you, sir, madam! Thank you, *mambo*!'

'Fucking Zimbabwe,' Viktor muttered.

'Well, now it's your fucking Zimbabwe as well,' Anne-Marie said.

'I was going to give you ten dollars for petrol, for the run to the airport.' Viktor draped his hand around Anne-Marie's shoulder and tensed, pulling her towards him.

'Let her eat for a week,' Anne-Marie replied.

Even though he'd mentioned it to her before, each day in fact since he had booked the ticket, he said it again now. 'Rosa's concert is in a couple of days. I will go along, if Nina allows it. I have a lot of explaining to do.'

'Give yourself enough time with Rosa and your parents. Don't rush.' Anne-Marie repeated her line.

'And then I'll be back. To visit Kinshasa with you.'

He was leaving Zimbabwe just when Lenin and Stalin and the others no longer judged him as a white man, a *murungu*, when he was almost a person who could be trusted. Without Anne-Marie, he thought, he'd make more mistakes; he'd fall again without her, without them. What would stop him? Drawing a line, making a mental pause, he caught himself: *I can't promise not to make more mistakes, but as long as I know my own mind, that's all that matters — as long as I know my own practice.*

Viktor repeated himself; he felt clear at last, decided. 'I need to see Rosa, then I am coming back.'

Along the same path through the trees, the walk looked different. By a tree on the fringe of the famous park there was a cluster of white flowers, a miniature field. From the small, open, cone-shaped petals hung a long green stigma.

'What are those?' Viktor asked.

'You have asked me before. I still don't know. I will find out the names of all the trees and flowers for your return. The whole ecosystem.'

Viktor rested one knee on the ground and his weight raised moisture in the earth, wetting his trousers. He stared at the flowers and placed one on his finger. He looked into the plant's heart, the thin filaments, the thicker ovary. Then, holding the flower, he pinched it gently between his fingers: an entire plant species with its own desire for fertilisation and existence, the will to extend beyond the limits of life, to spread and prolong the community of flowers where it now grew. A form of life not entirely unlike his, though perhaps with fewer false starts, less questioning.

Automatically Viktor's hand reached to his pocket for the notebook where he kept his ideas. He checked himself and noticed an odd feeling: he didn't want to write. Not another sentence, not a single word about these flowers, or anything. Instead he found the flower's stem. Tracing it to the grass, he pulled it free without another thought. He stood and presented it to Anne-Marie. 'This is for us,' he said.

Chapter Forty

For the flights that now arrived and departed daily from Harare International, a new terminal had been built in the heyday of the boom. This had been in the nineties, when there was a veneer of calm over Zimbabwe, when the old man was feted by the Queen and the country lauded by the West. Shopping centres had sprung up in the city, sprawling malls in the suburbs decorated by the giant cockerel of Great Zimbabwe. And a new airport had been built.

The terminal was empty, the sliding doors broken and held ajar with loose bricks. Anne-Marie and Viktor entered the building without speaking and surveyed the sea of granite, the closed boutiques and wilting miniature palms that divided the long concourse, the flight counters at one end and airline offices at the other. Two children ran around the potted trees and their shouts echoed through the airport. Viktor dropped his bag next to a bench, sat down and offered his hand to Anne-Marie. They sat in silence, apart, hand in hand.

A moment later there was a screech of tyres and a clatter of voices and slamming doors. Nelson, Lenin, and Stalin burst into the lobby, each of them wearing the same T-shirt, a solitary red star circled with the words *Shinga Mushandi Shinga!*

Immediately Viktor and Anne-Marie stood, released their hands and faced the group striding towards them. Nelson's arms were spread out. He was already speaking. When they reached the couple, Lenin took over: 'Comrade Viktor, we wanted to give these things to you.'

As Lenin named the gifts, Stalin passed them to Nelson, who in turn passed them to Viktor. And what was conceived as a simple farewell became a solemn rite. The seriousness of the ceremony surprised all of them.

'The T-shirt,' Lenin declared, passing the garment to Stalin.

'The membership card.' Before the card was passed to Viktor, Lenin read the wording printed on it, squinting and straining: *Viktor Isaacs, Member of the Society of Liberated Minds.*

'The CD.' Stalin handed the disc to Nelson. Viktor accepted the gift and held it together with the others.

'The newspapers,' Lenin announced.

From under his arm Nelson brought out a bundle of papers and took a step towards Viktor. 'Comrade—'

Lenin interrupted, holding out his hand for the newspapers. Nelson sighed and surrendered the papers. 'These,' Lenin announced, 'are original copies of our paper, *Liberated Minds*, covering the uprising in the nineties. The general strike in ninety-six, the food riots in ninety-seven, the student protest in ninety-eight. See?' Lenin spoke quickly, pointing to the top copy of the paper tied down with string: '*Jambanja* Now: Remove the Dictatorship.'

'Can I speak?' Nelson asked.

'In a minute,' Lenin responded curtly. Viktor took the papers and put them on his bag. Lenin straightened himself and stood tall. 'The photo.'

Stalin looked at Lenin, then Nelson. 'I don't have it,' he said after a pause.

Nelson pulled out his keys and gave them to Stalin, who turned from the group and ran to the car.

The friends were silent. Nelson looked at his hands. Lenin maintained his stiff, military pose.

'This is ridiculous,' Anne-Marie said finally. 'Can't we speak?'

'In a minute!' Lenin answered. Nelson shrugged his shoulders. They could hear the car door being slammed repeatedly, Stalin swearing and then, as he ran, his trainers wailing on the tiled floor.

'I couldn't close the door,' Stalin said.

'It doesn't close,' Nelson replied.

Everyone sniggered and fought to hold in their smiles. Lenin repeated sternly, 'The photo.' Stalin gave him a large envelope, then Lenin handed it ceremoniously to Nelson and Nelson passed it to Viktor.

'Do you want me to open it?' Viktor asked.

'Of course. Yes,' the men answered together.

Viktor peeled open the seal and removed a folded, padded frame.

'You have to unfold it,' added Lenin.

Viktor dropped the paper envelope and opened the frame. Inside were two photographs. One showed a group of people: Viktor's head at the back, his unsmiling face staring at the camera, looking as though he had been scratched onto the photograph as an afterthought. The other photo was of Biko, standing with his hands on his hips, staring into the distance with a sly, insolent smile.

Lenin came forward and pointed to each photo. 'That's us at the funeral and that's you at the back, see? And this is Biko,' he said, as though introducing Viktor to himself and Biko for the first time. He stepped back into his place beside the other men.

Viktor put his fingers over Biko's photo and dropped his head. His stomach turned. He felt his swollen, digested life lift, his breath rise and move out of him. His mouth opened. His whole existence reached his head and throbbed and ached.

He spoke in a mumbled torrent of words. 'If only I hadn't gone, if I wasn't in Bulawayo. If I hadn't been there, if I hadn't sat with him in that café. If I hadn't come to Zimbabwe.'

Anne-Marie put her hand on his shoulder and whispered to him, '*Mudiwa*, it's not your fault.'

Then each of them spoke, all at once, over each other, so that what they individually had to say couldn't be easily deciphered. Each tried to make their voice, their reassurances, their own grief heard. Viktor's head was still bent, his body obscured and circled by the group. Anne-Marie pressed herself to him, knowing that, better than her words, unheard anyway, would be the warmth of her skin, the heat of her life next to him.

Gradually the clumsy shuffle of words and sentences reached Viktor. 'No, comrade, are you saying that we should never demonstrate? Never protest, set up parties, take on X-Party, in case they kill us? It was the jackals, the dictatorship ... Biko was murdered, com, you know it, and you tried to save him, we all did ... Biko knew what you were doing ... It is Y-Party that tells us we can't fight, that the regime is too strong. Biko never accepted this logic ... Biko never gave an inch. Like you, comrade, he never stopped.'

Viktor wanted to tell *them* to stop; he needed to block his heart, choke off his throat, prevent more life, regret, sadness from falling out of him onto the frame and smearing the photo of Biko, clouding the smile on his frozen face, running down his body, polluting with doubt Biko's doubtless, certain soul.

Finally Lenin spoke. 'Comrade, Biko isn't dead if we remember how he fought. If we don't yield – if we act like him, with his arrogance, his confidence.'

'His bloody cheek,' Anne-Marie added, smiling.

Each of them laughed, relieved that their earnest bid to hold Viktor up, to dam his pain and their own questions, was now over.

None of the men wanted their farewell, this necessary salute to Viktor, who was leaving them, who had come to help and was now returning, to end like this. Nelson had driven his Toyota wreck to the airport. Lenin made no allowances for the car journey, urging, arguing: 'Comrade, doesn't this car, this damn car, go faster?' Arguing and shouting to each other, Nelson continued a point made the day before. 'No, the road to Harare is through Johannesburg. We need the mighty South African working poor to kick out the ANC, and then we can reckon with ZANU. The people will remember how to fight, relearn their history, find the confidence to stand up.'

Stalin joked, 'Yes, Biko was more stubborn than Mugabe.' They laughed harder.

'What bloody audacity! Look at that smile,' Nelson said, pointing at the photo. 'Behind his bravado, more bravado. Remember when he postered Harare Central Police Station with "Stop Police Brutality"? Remember? Remember?'

To Viktor their laughter seemed to scatter the marble, the great iron-framed terminal, the airplanes, the officials, the customs desks, until they stood under the sky, the burning sun low enough for them to feel the day on their skin. Viktor laughed so his stomach hurt and made him want to rest on the floor. He felt all of them together in the colossal, borderless world, the wind blowing sand from the beaches in the south, chafing their ankles, stinging their legs. He wasn't sure any more where he was, where he began, where all of this ended. He knew that his friends – Tendai, Nelson, Anne-Marie, Moreblessing, Biko – were standing somewhere close to him, even those he couldn't see. They were there. All of them together in a world swept free of distance, borders, despair. Their hearts beat and circulated life to a single rhythm.

*

Viktor sniffed in his tears, wiped his nose and eyes on his sleeve, found his footing again and felt his life slip back into his body, his head clear. Something tugged on his hand, insistent, strong. Rosa had answered the door and taken his hand.

'Daddy, you have been away for ages,' she said.

Acknowledgements

I am tempted to claim that all errors in the text are collective, and that responsibility for blunders, contradictions and mistakes must be shared jointly with all editors, readers and friends. After all, isn't work as 'private' as a novel or as 'public' as teaching equally collective? However, as much as I would like to, I cannot incriminate those who have read and commented on earlier drafts of *An Ounce of Practice* – I alone am to blame.

Still this long and arduous project has been immeasurably assisted by friends and comrades. Sarah Grey has been a constant support, reading, prompting, editing earlier versions of the book, insisting on sometimes painful changes. HopeRoad, who have long published vital and important titles from the 'margins', have been indispensable to the book. Rosemarie Hudson was an enthusiastic supporter of the project from the start, encouraging and urging me on. Jenny Page's deft editing has improved the manuscript, cutting away much of the book's excesses. Joan Deitch's excellent and detailed proofread (and our noisy occupation of the British Library) gave the manuscript an indispensable final polish.

The Royal Literary Fund has saved me from total ruin on a couple of occasions; for this, I am enormously grateful. The Fund knows, as do all materialists, that food and shelter is a prerequisite for cultural production.

I also owe thanks to my comrades in Zimbabwe who for years, in incredibly challenging circumstances, have refused to bow to the dictatorship despite terrible repression. As Colline sings at the end of Puccini's *La Bohème*, as he pawns his coat to save Mimi's life, 'you have never bowed your worn back to the rich or powerful. You held in your pockets poets and philosophers ...'